"*Something Borrowed* is the ha[...] of historical fiction, and McD[...] here! A wedding dress, rich in beauty and history, ties these stories together, but it's the breathtaking tales of love—sometimes lost, eventually found, often unexpected, and always worth the wait—that will connect with the reader's heart. Prepare to get blissfully swept away!"

—Bethany Turner, best-selling author of
Brynn and Sebastian Hate Each Other

"What a charming and captivating novella collection! I have long admired the work of Rachel Scott McDaniel, Allison Pittman, and Susie Finkbeiner. To have their writing all together in one book is a pure delight. Each of these stories features unique and lovable characters, the wedding dress they have in common, and above all, their varied journeys to finding love. Romance readers will swoon for *Something Borrowed.*"

—Jocelyn Green, Christy Award–winning author of
The Metropolitan Affair

"Three exceptionally talented novelists bring us a captivating collection of stories bound together by a very special dress. Each author's unique voice shines in this trio of novellas, each story rich in intriguing historical details, vividly drawn characters, and heart-stirring emotional resonance. A reading experience to treasure."

—Amanda Barratt, Christy Award–winning author of
Within These Walls of Sorrow and *The Warsaw Sisters*

"Rachel Scott McDaniel, Allison Pittman, and Susie Finkbeiner have woven a masterpiece of cleverly crafted love stories from three important eras in twentieth-century New York City, all stitched together by the silken thread of one remarkable wedding dress. Ornamented with wonderful historical details, these beautifully worded creations warmed my heart, and the spunky heroines and swoony heroes utterly won me over. This is a unique collection you won't want to borrow; it'll go straight to your keeper shelf!"

—Amanda Wen, author of *The Rhythm of Fractured Grace* and
Carol Award–winning *The Songs That Could Have Been*

"Three stories stitched together with delicate threads of love, hope, and faith. Filled with sweet romances, touches of humor, and the resilience of the human spirit in times of war, this collection is sure to delight readers."

—J'nell Ciesielski, best-selling author of *The Socialite*

"*Something Borrowed* is a collection that had me quickly turning the pages to experience the stories revolving around the same wedding dress across several generations. The opening novella, 'A Heart in Disguise' by Rachel Scott McDaniel, drew me in from the very first line. With equal parts romance, faith, and mystery, I was captivated until the very end."

—Rebekah Millet, award-winning author of
Julia Monroe Begins Again

A
HISTORICAL ROMANCE
COLLECTION

Something Borrowed

RACHEL SCOTT McDANIEL

ALLISON PITTMAN

SUSIE FINKBEINER

KREGEL
PUBLICATIONS

Something Borrowed: A Historical Romance Collection
"A Heart in Disguise" © 2024 by Rachel Scott McDaniel
"A Letter to Eli" © 2024 by Allison Pittman
"A Daffodil in the Dress" © 2024 by Susie Finkbeiner

Published by Kregel Publications, a division of Kregel Inc., 2450 Oak Industrial Dr. NE, Grand Rapids, MI 49505. www.kregel.com.

"A Letter to Eli" published in association with William K. Jensen Literary Agency, 119 Bampton Court, Eugene, Oregon, 97404.

Susie Finkbeiner is represented by the literary agency of Credo Communications, LLC, Grand Rapids, Michigan, www.credocommunications.net.

The persons and events portrayed in this work are the creations of the authors, and any resemblance to persons living or dead is purely coincidental.

Scripture quotations are from the King James Version.

Library of Congress Cataloging-in-Publication Data
Names: McDaniel, Rachel Scott. Heart in disguise. | Pittman, Allison. Letter to Eli. | Finkbeiner, Susie. Daffodil in the dress.
Title: Something borrowed: a historical romance collection / Rachel Scott McDaniel, Allison Pittman, Susie Finkbeiner.
Description: First edition. | Grand Rapids, MI: Kregel Publications, 2024.
Identifiers: LCCN 2024008808 (print) | LCCN 2024008809 (ebook)
Subjects: LCSH: Christian fiction, American. | Romance fiction, American. | LCGFT: Christian fiction. | Romance fiction. | Novellas.
Classification: LCC PS648.C43 S646 2024 (print) | LCC PS648.C43 (ebook) | DDC 813/.01083823—dc23/eng/20240308
LC record available at https://lccn.loc.gov/2024008808
LC ebook record available at https://lccn.loc.gov/2024008809

ISBN 978-0-8254-4842-3, print
ISBN 978-0-8254-7143-8, epub
ISBN 978-0-8254-7142-1, Kindle

Printed in the United States of America
24 25 26 27 28 29 30 31 32 33 / 5 4 3 2 1

A Heart in Disguise

RACHEL SCOTT McDANIEL

CHAPTER 1

New York City
April 1, 1918

FOR THE SAKE of the Allied powers, Clara Westlake pretended to be a rock. Not in a figurative sense, as in an emotional slab of strength. No, she'd been ordered to imitate a stone. Her knee itched, and a rogue curl tickled the edge of her ear, but she focused on keeping still. After all, whoever heard of a fidgety boulder?

At least she'd chosen a breathable fabric, which helped, considering her whole person was swathed in her latest creation: an earth-toned camouflage suit. The morning dew seeped through the burlap, making her entire left side damp. This posed new questions. Would a soldier prefer a loose, airy fabric for comfortable breathing or one that would prevent moisture from leaking in? The sogginess could prove miserable over time. Would cotton panels on the sides help? She mused over the possibilities while remaining crumpled on a stretch of land in Van Cortlandt Park.

Because even though Clara was safely tucked beneath a towering maple tree in the Bronx, New York, the suit she now tested would be shipped overseas to an awaiting sniper. It was her job to make the soldier invisible to the enemy.

Her superiors had been satisfied with her work so far. She took encouragement from that. If the US government deemed her garments worthy, then who was Hollywood to so easily dismiss her? She'd been a lowly seamstress among elite designers, but it hadn't been her pieces that were inferior. Perhaps if that'd been the issue, she'd still have her job at the studio. But she couldn't dwell on that fiasco at the moment. Or the betrayal from the man she'd blindly trusted.

Noise from the nearby walking path broke through her thoughts.

"There you are!" A masculine shout almost made her jolt.

Had she been spotted? She didn't recognize the man's tenor voice. But that didn't mean anything. Her superior, Lieutenant Towle, would often send naval officers through the park to test the efficiency of the suits. A human scavenger hunt. Thankfully, she'd chosen a hiding spot by the rock ledge. There was no risk of her getting stepped on. It had taken only one boot to the gut early on for Clara to wise up and position herself away from the trail.

Though her current angle prevented her from spying anyone along the footpath.

A rushed *click, click* of heels revealed the man hadn't been speaking to Clara but to an approaching lady. Relief swept through her for maintaining her cover, but she didn't exactly relish the idea of being an earwitness to a lovers' rendezvous.

Especially now, when romance had entirely lost its appeal. Which was a sad position for a twenty-six-year-old woman. Most ladies her age were already married with children. What was Clara going home to? An empty apartment. How was she spending her evening? Doing laundry. So, no. She wasn't thrilled to be a forced bystander to this couple's tryst. It would only remind her of how awful she'd been at past relationships.

Maybe she could crawl away. Though Lieutenant Towle had ordered all the camoufleurs to remain in place unless a civilian spotted them. Upon that occurrence, they were to assess their surroundings, select another hiding location, and try again.

From what she could hear, the couple exchanged warm pleasantries and, thankfully, continued on.

They hadn't noticed her.

A smug smile lifted her lips. Clara wasn't slight of frame. No, she was taller and a bit more rounded than most of the other camoufleurs, which made her concealment a triumph. She hadn't always appreciated her height, but it had led her to learn to not only sew but also design her own clothes. A skill that brought her to this place—helping the war effort.

Just then, Clara's stomach decided to abandon its role as a vital organ and assume that of a jungle tiger. At least the couple was far from earshot. When had she last eaten? It didn't matter she couldn't think of it or—

Another ravenous growl.

She'd gained a lot more respect for the snipers who wore these camouflage suits. They camped out in no-man's-land for hours on end; meanwhile, she couldn't keep her stomach mum for forty minutes.

Maybe curling more onto her side would quiet her stomach. Or she could roll over and face the trail. Right now, she aimed at the footbridge, which, through the sheer face covering, afforded a pretty view of the blossoming cherry trees. Before she could shift, movement sounded behind her. Hopefully the two lovebirds weren't returning, deciding this curve in the path was more secluded for . . . amorous activities.

This could get awkward. Perhaps she should make her presence known.

Then again. She closed her eyes as if it helped her hear better. It couldn't be the couple. The footfalls were different. No sharp click of heels. Instead there was a shuffling noise.

Step. Swish. Step. Swish.

Whoever it was walking toward her seemed to be dragging something along the ground. Seconds later, another set of footsteps echoed on the walk. Heavy. Concise.

Deep voices revealed the persons in question were both gentlemen and unfortunately stood only a few yards from Clara. She wasn't one to eavesdrop. Though even if she wanted to, she couldn't. Not fully anyway. Because the men conversed in German. Which shouldn't be alarming except their hushed tones and shifty inflections almost suggested they were conniving something.

Her parents' longtime housekeeper, Liesl, was from Germany. Over the years, Clara had learned the basics of the language, which helped her pick out snippets of the current conversation. She listened closely, able to identify the words *crowd*, *April*, *island*, and *attack*.

She sucked in a breath.

Island and attack!

Her mind spun to the incident at Black Tom Island two years ago. Located in New York Harbor, it'd been the largest munitions depot in the country. Though ruled an accident, it was widely suspected German agents had blown it up. The massive explosion killed a handful of people, destroyed twenty million dollars' worth of military supplies, and rocked the ground like an earthquake, sending tremors as far as Philadelphia. The shrapnel even embedded into the Statue of Liberty, closing it down for a while.

Could these men be planning an attack? On Ellis Island maybe? There were always crowds. Or what about Staten Island? Long Island? Her gut clenched. This was awful. She needed to warn someone. But what would she tell them exactly?

The men finished their conversation, and she forced herself to remain still until their footfalls faded. Maybe they'd go in the direction of the bridge, so she could get a good glimpse of them. But no such luck. They retreated the way they'd come. She kept curled on the damp ground for a few more minutes, ensuring all was clear. Heart racing, she jumped from her tucked position among the rocks.

At the very least, she could attest this camouflage suit had served its purpose. She'd blended into her surroundings. No one paid her any attention. Though right now Clara wished she'd paid attention to Liesl's German lessons. It sounded as if those men were up to no good, but that was all she knew. Thousands of soldiers had taken up arms and sailed to France, her brother included, to protect this nation. Yet it seemed a plan had been formed to bring the destruction here.

Not if she could help it.

She couldn't fight overseas, but maybe she could intervene in this instance. With quick movements, she unbuttoned the hood and the sides of the suit and climbed out, thankful to get a fresh intake of air. She folded the material into a tight square, and with a forced air of casualness, she fluffed her dark hair and walked the direction she suspected the men had gone. If she hustled, she may be able to catch up to them and follow at a distance. Possibly get a description of them for when she gave her account. The more details the better.

The birds seemed particularly loud today. A dog barked beyond the row of trees. She passed a mother pushing a baby buggy.

But after searching for ten minutes on various paths, there was no sighting of could-be saboteurs.

A sigh deflated her chest. She could be mistaken. Her imagination had been known to cause trouble. But something within her told her not to take what happened today lightly.

She had to report it.

⤝ ⤞

"And you think these men plan to obliterate Ellis Island?" The police officer, Detective Jamison, rolled his pencil between his thick fingers, not bothering to jot down anything Clara had told him.

After the incident in the park, she'd located Lieutenant Towle and relayed everything. Her commanding officer had advised Clara to inform the police, since they had full jurisdiction over the city. But as she sat in a colorless room across the desk from a man with dull eyes and a bored expression, it was easy to deduce the detective wasn't taking her seriously.

She notched her chin higher. "I truly feel it's worth checking into."

He glanced at his watch and blew out a breath.

"It may not be Ellis Island but another one," she clarified. "Perhaps I could speak to the chief?"

That comment made his nostrils flare. "I only relay the cases that have merit to Chief Wallace." He tapped his pencil on his notepad as if punctuating his remark. "So tell me, how do you suggest we *check into* your story? Did you get a clear glimpse of what these supposed German agents look like?"

"No."

"Catch their names?"

"No."

"Are you fluent in the German language to the degree you can translate their conversation without error?"

She shook her head, and Detective Jamison tossed his pencil onto the table in an *I rest my case* gesture. Heat forged her spine.

The detective didn't believe her. Why would he? She'd been in this position before. Miles across the country, in California. This current rejection didn't hold as much hurt as the one that had sent her running home to New York, but it still stung.

Nobody enjoyed being the fool.

"I'm sorry to waste your time, sir." She scooted back her chair. "I honestly felt there was something suspicious."

His brows softened a smidge. "This war has set us all on edge, Miss Westlake."

With a parting goodbye, she stood and made her way out of the office. She understood Detective Jamison's reasoning. She'd given him nothing concrete. No clear information to work with. But he'd so quickly dismissed her.

Outside the station, clouds slid along the slate sky. A fresh scent hung in the air with the promise of rain. Thankfully, her apartment—well really, Desmond's apartment—stood closer than her parents' home. While her brother had purchased the flat with the money he'd inherited from their grandfather, Desmond hadn't been a resident too long before he'd enlisted. She sent up a prayer for his safety. She hadn't received a letter from him since his initial one informing her that he'd made it to France, the world's battlefield.

Being only a year younger than him, she treasured how close they'd always been. Which was why she'd taken over the upkeep of his apartment while he was away fighting for freedom. Freedom that felt fragile, like a single thread pulled taut. She only hoped it wouldn't snap. What would the world look like in five years?

Her mind went back to the incident in the park. She may not have understood fully what the men had said, but she could judge by their dark inflections something wasn't right. Even now, recalling their sinister tones raised the hair on her arms. *Crowd, April, island, attack.* Those four words spun through her like a menacing chant.

And once again, no one believed her. But this time, she wouldn't sit idly by.

{⊱—✕—⊰}

Captain Marcus Reeves disembarked from the steamer ship, completely altered from the man he was when he'd left a year ago. Back then he'd been brimming with patriotism, gunning to annihilate the enemy, and determined to make his mark on this war. Now he knew better. His gaze roamed the familiar sights of New York Harbor while he hiked his meager bag further onto his shoulder, grimacing at the awkwardness. His right hand, his dominant one, was permanently flexed, thanks to shrapnel from a German grenade and the blade of a surgeon's scalpel. Learning to acclimate with his left hand for simple tasks like readjusting his bag proved challenging. Maddening.

He inhaled deeply, as if to dislodge the shard of failure, but it seemed stubbornly embedded. This wasn't how he'd pictured his homecoming. He'd always assumed he'd return with his fellow soldiers after winning the war to a roar of celebration from the stateside crowd.

But no. He'd arrived alone on a supply ship; his comrades were still fighting. The only noises were ones a person would expect from a busy harbor. It all hummed through him, collectively yet somehow separately. The clanging anchor chains, caw of seagulls, hollers of stevedores, and occasional steam whistle. He could pick apart each sound. For the past months, he'd lived in a constant state of awareness, his senses on high alert, sifting every noise, categorizing which held danger and which didn't.

Now that he was back in New York, he should focus on toning down his jumpiness. But it seemed part of him now. Another failure he couldn't expel.

He shook his head. No sense standing around in self-pity. His wounds may have forced him home early, but other soldiers had lost much more. On that sobering thought, he picked his way off the pier to the busy street. He probably should hail a cab to his lodgings, but he always preferred walking over being carted around. The horrors he'd witnessed weren't quick to leave a man. It was as if the sharp edges of his emotions needed filing down, and each step relaxed him more. A respite he'd welcome, if only for a short time.

He started toward the Selkirk building—his new home until he decided what course to take. Major Palmer hadn't given him an exact date to give his answer about a job at the recruiting office, but Marcus doubted the position would remain vacant long. If he accepted, Marcus would go from crawling under barbed wire to sitting at a desk. Most would welcome the break from the chaos, but he'd give anything to be back in France picking off German machine gun nests one by one.

A bicycle sped toward him, and he stepped out of the way, his right hand smacking a metal lamppost. His numb fingers felt nothing, which was a loud reminder he wasn't the capable man he'd been only a couple of months ago.

Maybe he'd hail a cab after all.

With the regions surrounding the piers swamped with activity, he quickly located a taxi and climbed in. He rattled off the address to the wiry man behind the wheel and in no time was at his destination at West 82nd Street.

The driver braked to a stop and subtly raised a brow.

The Selkirk wasn't the ritziest apartment complex in New York, but it was pretty close. The twelve-story building operated more like a hotel, and for a man who'd been sleeping in trenches, it might as well be a castle.

After paying the driver, Marcus entered the Selkirk. The polished floor was a jarring contrast to the caked mud Marcus had trudged through mere weeks before. The people around him were dressed in their finest, a fact that made him ache for the scrubby, haunted faces of his battalion. Faces that flicked through Marcus's mind when he closed his eyes. Those who remained and those who didn't.

An attendant approached, snapping Marcus from the waking nightmares.

"May I help you . . ." His gaze flicked to Marcus's uniform, probably to guess his rank, though he settled on "Sir?"

"I'm staying in 5D." Marcus adjusted his bag. "I know the way."

The attendant's narrow face scrunched into a puzzled expression, no doubt wondering how a man like Marcus could afford a suite in the Selkirk. He couldn't. But that wasn't any of this fellow's business. So he shouldered past, opting for the stairs rather than the fancy elevator. Marcus trudged up the five flights and stood just outside the door to his home for the foreseeable future. Fishing out his key, his thoughts traveled to the owner of this apartment, who wasn't his brother by blood but by everything else. Marcus turned the knob and stepped inside.

His head reared back. Clothes were strewn about. Feminine things draped over chairs and hung from the picture rail. Standing amidst it all was a woman dressed only in a man's shirt.

Clara.

She shrieked, then promptly chucked a scrub brush at his head.

CHAPTER 2

A MAN WAS in Clara's apartment.

The scrub brush smacked the door. A complete miss. But she had another shot. Heart pumping, she grabbed the washboard and raised it over her head. She'd bash the intruder's face . . . his . . . face.

Familiar dark eyes met hers.

She blinked. Then again. Soapsuds dripped onto her nose, her cheek, but she didn't swipe them away. She could hardly breathe, let alone move. Because Marcus Reeves stood before her. The first boy to steal her heart. The last man to break it.

She'd known he had joined the military long before the war started. Then Des had written saying Marcus had been sent to France a year ago, which was about five months before her brother left.

So then, why was Marcus here?

Her arms wilted to her sides. She held the washboard in front of her, a flimsy shield between Marcus and her emotions. He always held the ability to scale the walls of her defenses, taking captive her every affection, leaving her unarmed against his charms.

But that luring grin and smooth gait were now noticeably absent, his lips firmly molded into a frown. The cheeks framing said mouth were lean, angling toward a defined jaw. She knew time had a way of chiseling away boyish features only to sculpt firmer, more masculine ones, but this version of Marcus Reeves? Stronger yet wearied, if that were possible.

Before she could pose a question, his eyes swept over her, and he spun around, facing the door.

Her gaze lowered, and she took in the picture she presented him. Desmond was larger than her, so she was covered by one of his old shirts. More or less. With her legs exposed, her state of dress probably leaned more on the *less* side according to society's standards. She'd always worn her brother's old clothes while doing laundry. If she was going to go through the effort, she wanted everything cleaned. The Selkirk had a laundering service, but she was picky when it came to her wardrobe. They were her creations after all, except for her uniform, and she tended to their cleaning.

But at this particular second, she wished she'd postponed her routine washing. Though how was she to predict she'd be standing unsuitably dressed in the same room with a man she'd not seen in over two years?

Marcus cleared his throat, even as a key also dangled from his left pointer finger, signifying he hadn't exactly broken in. "I apologize. There's been a misunderstanding."

There it was. That voice. Six words was all it took for the memories she'd so carefully hidden away to come rushing back.

Clara set down the washboard. "Marcus Reeves." Her tone was surprisingly steady. "What are you doing here?" She grabbed the decorative quilt from the sofa, tied it around her waist, and slowly approached. "Don't tell me you forgot Desmond has a sister." She'd spent a lot of time with him growing up, tagging along on the boys' adventures. Over the years things had developed between them. At least on her side anyway. She'd assumed he'd felt the same, but his silence the last time they'd met screamed the truth: she meant nothing to him.

He shifted. "I never forgot you."

Words that, if taken in a particular way, held the power to melt a woman into a puddle of longing. But he was simply answering her question. No undertones of anything else. She'd made the mistake of reading too much into things before. And had been heartbreakingly wrong.

"I was on the USS *Moccasin*. Came into port this morning."

Oh. So he had returned this very day. That explained the army uniform, but there was a story behind the slight hunch in his shoulders, the hollowness in his voice. She doubted he'd offer any explanation. As far as she knew, America was in continual need of men to ship off to battle, so why had Marcus left the fight? "You can turn around. I'm decent."

Mostly. She quickly fastened the top two buttons, so not even her collar-bone showed.

He slowly pivoted, and their eyes met.

She expected to glimpse the deep, rich brown, almost black, hues of his gaze, but she hadn't prepared for the intensity of them. There was a brokenness about this man, and it called to her. She always had a heart to salvage. To take the worn pieces, the discarded fabric, and stitch them together to make something beautiful. For this reason alone, she retreated a step. She couldn't allow her heart to become invested again.

He appeared to be taking her in, just as she had him. His attention drifted to her hair, and she couldn't begin to imagine what it looked like. When she'd returned home from her awful day, she'd yanked the pins free, loosening her curls, a mass of chaotic locks to match her mood. Even now she couldn't shake the nagging suspicion she'd overheard something important in the park. But what else could she do?

"I'm sorry for the intrusion." He lowered his bag onto the floor and rolled his shoulder. "Des invited me to stay at his place."

Her mouth parted as her mind spun, processing his words. Invitation or no, Marcus couldn't stay here, but she couldn't concentrate on that tidbit, because of the hope inflating her chest. "So you've seen Desmond recently? How is he?" She ached for any news of him.

The lines in his brow softened. "No, not recently. Des gave me an extra key a while back, at the harbor. The day of my leave." He jerked his head as if the docks were right outside her window. "He offered his place in case I returned before him." Marcus's gaze fell to his bag on the floor. "Which I did."

Her gut sank. Still no word from her brother. Even though disappointment cut through her, she wouldn't be insensitive. Despite his stoic expression, defeat had marked Marcus's tone. It appeared his return wasn't by choice. So what had happened?

As if sensing her question, he lifted his arm and gazed down at his hand in disgust. "It's practically useless now, thanks to the Germans."

Oh. He'd been injured. She couldn't imagine all the pain and discouragement he'd suffered. And from the dejected look in his eyes, it seemed his wounds stretched deeper than his hand.

"Marcus." Her tone was breathless. "I'm so sorry."

His chin dipped in a tight nod.

Perhaps hers wasn't the best response, but she didn't know what else to offer. She very well couldn't offer this apartment. Her brother had also welcomed her to stay here during his absence. Though he'd no doubt expected her to remain in Hollywood. So had she. But life had pushed her onto a different route.

"Is your husband here?" Marcus's startling question yanked her back to the moment.

Her head tilted. "My husband?"

"I thought maybe you were married, because of your . . . uh, shirt."

"No, this belongs to Desmond. I always wear his old clothes when doing my laundry. Just like I always do my laundry on Mondays. That's today." *Stop talking, Clara.* Of course he knew today was Monday. He also knew her habit of rambling anytime she got flustered. Proven by his small smile. At least she broke him of the frown.

His gaze strayed to the radiator, only to snap it quickly away. She didn't have to glance over to understand what caused his sudden interest in the rug. Her lacy undergarments decorated the radiator. When would the embarrassment end?

"Anyway, I'm not married." She rushed to clear the awkwardness and divert his attention. "It's just me here."

His gaze lifted to hers. "Last time I heard, you were in California."

"I was." She managed to keep her voice even. "But things didn't work out as I hoped." She'd enjoyed designing and sewing wardrobes for film stars, and had been good at it. Too good. "I work for the government now." Which wasn't technically a job. She'd volunteered and had been asked to pay forty-three dollars to join the Women's Reserve Camouflage Corps and purchase her own uniform. Thankfully, she'd made more than enough in Los Angeles to cover her current expenses.

Not that her parents couldn't afford to help her, and not that she wasn't appreciative of her family. They'd been supportive of her dreams, but her marriage prospects were never far from their minds. Still, she was thankful for her parents and . . . Wait. That was it. She may have solved this little predicament with Marcus. "How long do you plan to remain in the city?"

He lifted his bag with his good hand and worked it onto his shoulder. "I'm not certain."

"I see." She needed to lighten the moment or else she'd choke on the tension. "Unless you plan on marrying me this evening, there isn't a way for us both to live here."

He coughed. "Well . . . that is—"

"I'm teasing." She laughed, and a bolt of victory sluiced through her at his returned smile. "I'm sorry your plans were derailed. But I do have an alternative. Give me a moment." With a tight clamp on the knot holding the blanket to her waist, she hustled toward the bedroom. It took her a mere handful of minutes to make the necessary arrangements.

She rejoined him in the parlor, only to find Marcus studying her prized sewing machine by the window. "That's Nora," she said, moving to stand beside him. "I named her after the vaudeville star Nora Bayes."

His lips twitched. "Because they're both *singers*."

She nodded with a grin. The Singer model was the top of the line. What a typewriter was to an author, a sewing machine was to a seamstress. Together, they created. And lately, for the war, Clara and Nora made suits that hopefully saved lives.

He gave her a quizzical look. "What is this mysterious alternative you talked about?"

"I hope you don't mind, but I arranged for Robert to pick you up." One convenient perk to living in this luxury flat was the accessibility of a telephone.

"Robert?"

"My parents' chauffeur. You can stay at Westlake House as long as you'd like."

His brow lowered. "I don't want to inconvenience them. I'm sure I can figure out something."

Did he have anyone else? Well, there was his father. But after Marcus's mother had passed, his dad quickly remarried a widow. The man had moved in with her and her five children in upstate New York. Whether out of grief or stupidity, he'd abandoned Marcus in favor of his new family.

Clara gave Marcus a warm smile. "You're not an inconvenience. Mother is delighted to see you. If you refuse, you'll disappoint her." Her mother had always adored Marcus. Between Mother's fussing and Liesl's cooking, he'd be properly spoiled. Which would be a good thing, because the shadows weren't only beneath his eyes but over his entire person. "Mother told me she's asked Liesl to make apple strudel." His favorite. Or so it had been several years ago. "At least go visit them and then decide."

He watched her for a long moment, then gave a tight nod. "All right. I'll consider it."

"Wonderful." She beamed at him, but he still appeared hesitant. Staying at Westlake House would be far better than any ritzy hotel. Her parents' home stood in one of the most posh neighborhoods on the edge of the city. Clara lived here at the Selkirk only because it was closer to her work at the Women's Reserve Camouflage Corps, and maybe also to avoid Mother's well-meaning but entirely misplaced matchmaking. "I'll walk down to the lobby with you."

His gaze drifted over her, and something like amusement lit his eyes. "Perhaps I'd better go alone."

"Oh. Right." Probably not a good idea to traipse around wearing a quilt and a man's shirt. "Then, I'll see you in a couple days."

He raised a brow at her words.

"That is, if you decide to stay with my parents, I'll see you. I always go to the house on Wednesdays for dinner." Which gave her another idea. She'd talk to Liesl about what happened in the park today. Perhaps she could help Clara make sense of it.

CHAPTER 3

MARCUS HAD VISITED the Westlakes' house more than a hundred times throughout the years, and the grandeur still overwhelmed him. He glanced around at the swanky furnishings in his suite. Imported rugs. A four-poster bed with silk canopy. An imposing mahogany wardrobe. Everything hinted at luxury. The room even boasted a set of double doors leading out to a manicured garden.

As if he needed yet another reminder of the huge chasm between the world the Westlakes lived in and him.

The Westlakes owned a construction supply enterprise. With industry expansion in New York City, they made a fortune selling materials to builders. Their corporation had expanded, and now the Westlakes had warehouses all over the country. A construction empire Desmond would inherit after he returned from war.

Marcus had taken Clara's advice and visited her parents, only to be swept in by their hospitality. James Westlake and his wife, Eleanor, had received Marcus as if he were some sort of ambassador instead of a wounded soldier uncertain of his future. Sure, he had a good job lined up. Major Palmer had seen to it. But Marcus had never been confined to a desk. Staring at paperwork all day held no appeal. That was, if he could even do the job to begin with. The past two days, he'd practiced writing, but his inky strokes resembled that of a five-year-old's scrawl rather than an adult's handwriting. Being forced to use his left hand meant he had to almost relearn the basics of penmanship.

He let out a groan and collapsed onto the bed. Eight weeks ago he'd never had to face any sort of weakness. He'd always been strong, capable, and clever enough to get out of any situation. But his injury stretched further than his hand. His confidence had taken a lethal hit. Just this morning, a maid had dropped a tray in the hallway, and he nearly jumped out of his skin. The edginess. The relentless vigilance. It seemed his surroundings pressed into him, increasing his agitation.

A fact he must not have hidden well, since upon his arrival here two days ago, the Westlakes had insisted he take dinner in his room so he could rest as much as possible. He could force his body to be still, a skill he'd mastered from being a sniper, but his mind was chaos, a smattering of images ranging from billows of smoke to the open night beneath webbings of barbed wire to, most recently, a beautiful young woman in a man's shirt about to assault him with a washboard.

He'd been trained to be ready for anything, but Marcus hadn't prepared for Clara Westlake. Growing up, she always had a way of stealing the very breath from his chest. Seeing her again proved nothing had changed. With her dark hair cascading over her shoulders, her blue-green eyes narrowing in challenge, and that familiar dent in her chin giving her an air of stubbornness, Clara seemed almost an illusion, a beautiful mirage that hovered in his line of sight yet always out of reach. If Marcus had thought her too good for him all those years ago, he wouldn't deceive himself into thinking he could offer her anything now.

No, she was perfection, and he was not.

Something he needed to remember as he stood and readied for dinner. Clara had said she'd join them this evening. Liesl had washed and pressed his uniform, but Marcus reached into the wardrobe for his suit. Having sold most of his belongings before enlisting in the army, he had need of new things. Shopping had never been his favorite, but he remembered an old friend who'd since become a tailor. Thankfully, the fellow had a few suits that matched Marcus's measurements, which made the transaction more bearable. Clara may love this sort of thing, but Marcus was never one to fuss over what he wore.

Once dressed, he went downstairs, lured by a feminine voice. Clara's. He rounded the corner, and there she was, standing beside her mother in the reception room leading to the dining hall. Dinners were formal affairs at Westlake House. Not even a global war could shake that tradition.

Clara spotted him first, her lips curling into a warm smile. She wore a sparkly gown that did everything for her curvy figure and nothing to help curb his attraction. Those curls that, two days ago, had made his hand itch to run through were now piled upon her head, highlighting the graceful slope of her neck. Looking at the elegant picture she presented, one would never suspect she'd traipsed about her apartment in a man's shirt, her long, toned legs on full display—a tempting image that Marcus had repeatedly shoved from his mind.

He had once maneuvered across a suspected minefield without hesitation, but standing in front of Clara made him want to retreat. She made him feel. And that was a dangerous thing. Years ago he'd adopted a flirty smile to counteract the serious emotions roiling through him. Now, though, he seemed stripped of that cheeky armor.

His jaw locked, barring any words on his lips. He barely managed a nod at her and her mother.

Clara reached out and smoothed her hand along his lapel. This intimate gesture would appear suggestive, but she wasn't gazing at him, only examining his jacket as an art appraiser would inspect a painting. Her eyes roamed his waistcoat as if judging the spacing of the buttons. Her slender fingers tucked back the edge of his collar so she could get a thorough look at the lining. Floral notes of her perfume tangled his senses, while her nearness about did him in.

Finally, she glanced up at him. "You've been to see Joel Davidson." Approval marked her voice. "He always does good work with quality materials."

She knew his friend? There had to be a thousand tailors in New York. How could she identify Davidson's suits? Marcus didn't know. He could hardly think straight, because she presently ran a finger down the seam along his torso.

"Fine stitching too." Her hand stilled. She leaned in and whispered, "Though I doubt this one has any markings on the lining."

His good hand went instinctively to his trousers pocket. The familiar scratch of burlap brushed his thumb. He exhaled. He wasn't sure what Clara referenced, but it wasn't about the scrap of fabric he held on to since the day of his surgery.

"Oh, for goodness' sake, Clara." Mrs. Westlake swatted her daughter's arm. "We know you love a well-tailored suit, but quit pawing the man."

Clara eased back, completely unaware of what her touch did to him. "I see you're faring well here, Marcus."

He needed to remain aloof, especially since his heart seemed on the verge of detonation. Because one second Clara's eyes held warmth but the next, something else entirely. He'd never been good at guessing her thoughts and intentions. Seemed he hadn't improved any. "I'm faring the best I can, Miss Westlake."

Her eyes slightly narrowed at his proper address. "It's Clara," she gently corrected him. "We were discussing matrimony only two days ago, so there's no need to be formal."

He choke-coughed again. Just like he had when she'd casually dropped the topic of marriage at the apartment. Apparently, she'd filled her mother in on the discussion, for the older woman hadn't even flicked an eyelash at Clara's words. Or maybe she was used to her daughter's remarks. As always, he had no idea how to answer, but he was spared a response due to Mr. Westlake entering the room.

Within seconds, the butler announced dinner.

Throughout the course of the meal, the Westlakes were conversational while refraining from any melancholy topics. It was evident they were concerned for Desmond. Marcus caught Mrs. Westlake glancing over at her son's vacant seat.

Marcus fumbled using his fork at least four times. Thankfully, no one had noticed. Or had been gracious not to bring attention to it.

"How's the job going, Clara?" Mr. Westlake, ever the businessman, seemed to always gravitate toward the subject of work. "Are you still marching and stitching?"

Marching? Marcus's gaze drifted to Clara, intrigued by this turn in conversation.

She smiled. "We don't exactly march. But Lieutenant Towle teaches us about formation and maneuvers. He believes if we understand modern warfare, then we can better serve and protect the soldiers."

Now he was confused. "Protect who?"

"The soldiers. I sew uniforms." Her eyes tightened at the edges as if daring him to think less of a high-class lady working at a factory making military fatigues. If anything, it raised her in his esteem.

He wasn't entirely certain why she needed to train in modern warfare to stitch a uniform, but he wasn't about to question anything.

"Speaking of work, I'd almost forgotten. Marcus." Mr. Westlake's attention shifted to him as the older man dabbed his mouth with a napkin. "I spoke with some of my advisers, and we have a position for you, if you're interested."

Marcus nearly dropped his fork again, only this time, not due to his clumsy left hand. "A job, sir?"

"Yes, a solid position that suits your expertise. We'll discuss it later, so we don't bore the ladies." He winked at his wife.

Once the meal finished, they all moved to the parlor. Liesl brought in a tray of coffee, and upon Clara's insistence, the housekeeper remained for the conversation. It wasn't much longer before the older Westlakes claimed they were ready to retire for the evening.

Clara's father said good night and exited the room.

Mrs. Westlake lingered behind to hug her daughter. "You're welcome to stay." Her tone was resigned as though anticipating Clara's refusal. Yet it didn't stop her from adding, "It's getting late."

"Thank you, Mother. But I prearranged for a taxi to come at nine. That way, Robert wouldn't have to drive me."

"Always so independent." Mrs. Westlake patted Clara's shoulder as if self-reliance were a condition she'd yet to recover from. "That is, until you find a man who can take care of you. Speaking of which, I saw Matthew Hanes the other day. Remember you met him at the yacht race—"

"I remember him, Mother." Clara leaned in and kissed her cheek. "Good night. I'll see you at church this Sunday."

"Good night, dear," Mrs. Westlake said, then gave a parting smile to Marcus.

Once her mother was out of the room, Clara spun toward Liesl, who was collecting the empty coffee cups. "Liesl, I hope you don't mind, but I need to speak with you."

That was Marcus's cue to retire as well, but Clara placed a hand on his wrist as he rose. She quickly realized she held his injured hand, then yanked her fingers back as if his scars burned her.

Her eyes widened. "Did I hurt you?"

"No." He hadn't felt a thing. He wouldn't have known she'd touched him if not for watching her. Though her reaction wasn't a bolster for his pride. Her tentative movements were as if she were handling a fragile bird instead of a hand that once gripped weapons.

"Oh good." Relief lowered her spiked shoulders. "Would you mind staying, Marcus? I think you might be able to help too."

He stilled at her request. What did she need help with? He nodded and lowered beside her on the sofa.

Liesl spoke next. "Now, what's all this fuss about?"

Clara lifted her chin. "I think I overheard a plan from German saboteurs."

CHAPTER 4

THE AIR SEEMED to leave the room at Clara's remark, or maybe all the oxygen had collected in Liesl's lungs after her enormous gasp. Her housekeeper's slacked jaw and rounded eyes were predictable. Liesl had always been easily startled. But Marcus? He'd never been this unreadable. His countenance barely changed. No surprise or . . . any emotion. Only a barely perceptible lift of his brow on his otherwise stoic face.

His daunting expression presented almost a challenge. Her mind whirled back to their exchange before dinner. Clara should've kept her hands to herself. The first touch had been an innocent impulse. Having always been fascinated by fashion, she'd truly been drawn by the impressive cut of his jacket. But after *that* intrigue had worn off, another had taken over, and she'd reached out again.

It was childish, foolish to touch him like she had.

She'd come tonight prepared to keep her heart under tight command, but it'd broken orders and run amok. Then her mouth joined the mutiny and blurted about markings in the lining. She'd referenced another jacket. One he'd clearly forgotten about, given his vacant look. She should've never sewn those words into his coat years ago. Just as she shouldn't have brought it up again tonight. She had no one to blame but herself for reopening the wound in her heart.

She shook her head, hoping to loosen the tangled thoughts, and returned to the matter at hand. "I just can't shake this uneasiness in my gut. I feel certain an attack is coming."

Liesl claimed the nearby armchair, her salt-and-pepper hair escaping her mobcap. "What makes you think this, dear?"

Clara's longtime friend had been speaking with less of an accent recently. She suspected it had something to do with the recent wave of anti-German sentiment since America had declared war. There had been open hostility toward immigrants and their families. It had seemed the popular consensus was to rid America of any Germanic influence. Sauerkraut was now called "liberty cabbage." If Clara wanted a hamburger, she'd have to order a "liberty steak." Some groups had gone as far as pushing for the removal of Beethoven, Bach, and Mozart pieces from orchestra performances.

So Clara had to tread carefully with Liesl. Clara wanted her help, but not at the expense of being insensitive. Truth was, she had the utmost respect for those who desired a better life and came to this country. She was only wary of those who attempted to harm it. "I was in the park the other day. Two men approached and started speaking. I didn't want to move and risk being noticed. They were talking in German, and I was able to catch a few words. I know I missed a lot of what was spoken, but overall there was just something dark and menacing about their entire exchange."

Liesl's forehead creased. "What words did you catch?"

"*Insel.*"

"Island?"

"Yes." Clara nodded. "And then the word for 'attack' and 'crowd.' I also heard them say *April*." Her spine stiffened as something new struck her. "I remember another word. *Vier*." Her gaze snapped to Liesl. "Could that mean . . . ?"

"Four." Liesl's head tipped to the side. "Are you thinking April fourth? That's tomorrow."

Unable to sit any longer, Clara jumped to her feet. Piecing that all together—an attack on an island tomorrow. She paced the plush carpet, her head spinning with this new revelation. What could happen in less than a day? What could she possibly do about it? Her feet froze almost directly in front of Marcus, who'd remained pensive and quiet during this conversation. "I tried to tell the police but was dismissed. The detective said I had nothing, really, to go by. I should've pressed more."

"Those men you overheard . . ." Marcus finally spoke up. His voice, surprisingly, held a protective edge. "Are you certain they didn't see you?"

She lowered beside him on the sofa. "I'm sure."

He studied her for a heart-pounding second. "You're not exactly easy to overlook."

What did that mean? The old Marcus would've flavored that remark with a flirty undertone, but this version of him only watched her with a piercing stare.

"They didn't see me." He still didn't look convinced, and she let out a sigh. "I was dressed like a rock."

"A rock?"

"I was in a . . . rock suit. We test our designs at the park. My job with the military is to sew camouflage suits for snipers. I've been enjoying the work. It's good to be able to help the war effort." Why she rambled, she didn't know. Well, yes, she did, because the moment she said she'd worn a rock suit, Marcus adopted the strangest look. The more she'd spoken, the more his expression slacked. She'd finally elicited a reaction from him but had no idea what it meant.

She knew it wasn't a glamorous job. Only months before, she'd designed gowns for film star Anita Stewart, among others. But Clara's work with the military was more satisfying. She helped the war effort. Never mind she'd been snubbed by some in her social sphere. Most upper-class families chose to donate toward the cause rather than participate in menial work. Though whether a person wrote a large check or knitted a pair of wool socks for a soldier, everyone worked toward a common goal— ending this war.

Clara was also aware that some men didn't approve of women getting involved in the war effort. But if she could contribute, she would. And she refused to be intimidated by anyone who thought otherwise, Marcus Reeves included.

"There could always be another explanation." Liesl rubbed her arm like she always did when deep in thought. "Did you pick up any other words they said?"

"No." Her shoulders slumped with her exhale. "I've been thinking about it the past few days. Maybe some words will come back, but I would hate for it to be too late."

"Maybe"—Liesl's blue eyes met Clara's—"it's not as sinister as you imagine."

Clara began to protest, but Liesl lifted a hand and continued.

"I'm not saying you're wrong. It's just . . ." Her voice quieted, and her gaze lowered, as if she debated her next words. "There's a German diner several blocks south called *Kleines Sylt*, meaning Small Sylt. Sylt is an island in the North Sea. The diner's owned by a German couple from there, and they serve traditional island food."

Clara's brows scrunched. "You think these men were talking about a restaurant named after an island?"

Liesl shrugged. "It's possible."

"What about the attack part?"

Her expression turned sad. "Two weeks ago, someone threw a brick through the front window. A few people were injured, though nothing serious. It's getting harder and harder for German businesses to survive."

Clara hadn't known about that particular incident, but she'd read about communities withdrawing their support from German establishments. Now, sadly, it seemed they'd also turned violent.

"Perhaps these men were only speaking of the attack on the restaurant." Liesl flicked her gaze to Marcus, then back to Clara. "I'm not surprised they kept their voices lowered. It's dangerous anymore to speak German in public."

Liesl's theory made sense. Heartbreakingly so. It saddened Clara that the general attitude toward immigrants was heavily prejudiced. She'd heard of mobs targeting German Americans, dragging them from their houses at night and making them kiss the American flag or sing the national anthem. She was thankful Liesl had a safe place here. While the Westlake name wasn't as influential as others in this city, such as the Ashcrofts or Astors, her family still held considerable clout.

Could Clara have misinterpreted everything? What if she'd unconsciously allowed her own perspective to be tainted by the widespread bias? Shame sliced through her.

Marcus shifted, his thigh brushing hers. "What about April fourth? That accident at the diner happened a couple of weeks back, so why did those men mention tomorrow?"

Clara's gaze snapped up at his question. She'd been so focused on her shortcomings that she'd forgotten that tidbit of their conversation.

"Perhaps they're planning on meeting for dinner at the Sylt tomorrow," Liesl offered. "Even if these men were saboteurs, I can't imagine they'd harm a fellow German's business."

Unless they'd agreed to meet up at the restaurant to further discuss their scheme. Clara was torn. Had she heard correctly? It wasn't as if her grasp of the German language was all that wonderful. But she specifically remembered how her gut had twisted while she listened to the gentlemen converse. Had her heart been convicting her of underlying prejudice or warning her about something awful?

Clara shoved down the rising confusion and gave a quick nod. "Thank you, Liesl." She turned to Marcus and mustered a smile. "Thank you as well. I didn't mean to waste either of your time." She needed to go back to the apartment, spend a whole lot of time in prayer, and contemplate her next move. She rose to her feet. "I should be going if I want to be coherent for work tomorrow." Thankfully, she had only a half day in the classroom; the remaining time would be dedicated to finishing their projects, but she'd already completed hers. That left the rest of her day open to—

"I'll see you to the door." Marcus stood.

It was strange, as if their roles had been reversed. This was her family home, but he intended to walk her out as if she were the guest. She knew she was bristly because of the outcome of this evening. She'd thought she'd get more answers, but in the end, she'd been left questioning her own motives.

She said good night to Liesl and moved in silence with Marcus toward the foyer. He must no doubt be grateful to finally be rid of her paranoid chatter. She opened her mouth to say goodbye, but his hand went to her arm.

His face softened. "Please don't go tomorrow."

"To work?" Surprise lifted her brows. Why would he ask her such a thing? "I have an obligation."

"No." He gave a small shake of his head. "To the restaurant. I saw it on your face when Liesl suggested the two men might've arranged to meet there. You're planning on visiting the restaurant, aren't you?"

Her pulse jumped. Yes, the idea had popped into her head, but how could he have known that? Was her expression that transparent? If that were the case, what else could he perceive just by looking at her? Oh well. Nothing she could do about it now. She lifted her chin. "There's no harm in checking it out."

His jaw tightened. "What if those men are dangerous?"

"Liesl doesn't think they are."

"I think you might be right."

That simple sentence pulsed a bolt of warmth, along with a heavy dose of shock, through her. Marcus believed her. Believed her! She wanted to throw her arms around his neck. Such awareness made her mouth part in surprise. She hadn't been in a man's arms since Ben. That bit of knowledge made her retreat a step. She'd learned two crucial lessons with Ben—never assume and always ask questions. "Why?" The breathlessness in her tone wasn't helpful, for it drew him closer so he could hear. "Why do you think I'm right? Judging by the lack of solid facts, it all sounds foolish."

"It's not."

"What if I'm seeing things through a slanted lens? I could be prejudiced."

"You aren't prejudiced." His nearness made her dizzy. "I've seen a lot of hate. Dark things, almost unimaginable, done by the hands of others." He swallowed, his penetrating gaze on her. "No, Clara. You're not anything like that. Like them."

A surge of emotion flooded her chest, but no words came.

Marcus continued. "Maybe you don't have everything right, but you know in your gut something is wrong."

"Yes."

"One thing I learned over there"—he jerked his head as if France were only across the street rather than an ocean away—"is that your heart knows things your head doesn't. Which is why you should always follow it."

This was not the playful Marcus she'd grown up with. This was a more serious version, a more contemplative one. And while she may have once swooned over his carefree smile, she rather appreciated this side of him. Preferred it, even. "Thank you."

"I still don't believe it's a good idea to go to the restaurant."

Her smile crested. First, he'd become her ally, and now, her defender. In California, she'd been forced to read a lot of film scripts to determine the scope of wardrobe. It was while poring over those screenplays that she'd discovered she was a goner when it came to protective heroes. Marcus Reeves fit the role. "I thought you just told me to go with my gut."

"I did."

She lowered her voice and leaned in as if relaying a secret, though, truly, she didn't want anyone else overhearing. "And what if my gut tells me to go to the restaurant?"

His gaze swept her face slowly, causing warmth to stretch through her. Finally, he exhaled. "Then I suppose I should come along with you."

CHAPTER 5

Kleines Sylt had been expertly hidden among the hundreds of store-fronts lining the New York City blocks. Instinct and his ingrained military training had Marcus rising early for the sole purpose of reconnaissance. From the basic information Liesl had shared, he'd understood the general direction of the restaurant, but the exact location had been discovered thanks to the assistance of a newsie. Paper peddlers knew the streets better than anyone and happily surrendered information for a nickel or two.

So now Marcus escorted Clara down the crowded walk, only to stop in front of a nondescript building wedged between a hat boutique and a shoe repair shop.

Clara gave him a questioning glance.

He nodded. "This is it." No overhead sign. No lettering on the window. The place hadn't any identifier, which Marcus suspected had been a strategic move.

His gaze scanned the area. Even though he'd scouted the perimeter this morning, he was determined to remain guarded. Nothing seemed suspicious. But he was more concerned about what they'd discover inside. Would they encounter any hostility?

Clara reached for the door, but he gently set a hand upon her arm. They'd been doing that—arm touches—often since he'd returned. She'd done so last evening when she'd asked him to stay and hear about the events at the park. He'd learned a lot from that conversation. For one, her life could potentially be in danger. Then he'd discovered she sewed camouflage suits for snipers. Uniforms that had outfitted his men. Him. And what had he done upon hearing that revelation? Just stared at her blankly. Like he was doing now.

He removed his fingers from her arm, ignoring the softness of her skin, and gestured toward the door. "Please let me go before you."

"Do you think there's going to be trouble?"

He doubted any German agent would attack a business managed by one of their own. Unless there was an issue of loyalty. "I'm not certain. I just want to be sure it's safe."

She leaned close and dropped her voice. "Those men were scheming something big. I may not have understood all of what they said, but I caught their tone, and it raised the hair on my skin." She lifted her hand as if the goose bumps were still present. "I doubt they'd waste their efforts on a small restaurant no one really knows about."

He couldn't deny the soundness of her logic. He also grasped exactly what she meant. One could determine if someone was up to no good by the inflections and nuances in their tones. "I understand what you're saying, but I'd feel better going in first."

She moved aside with a smile, moving her hand in a sweeping gesture. "After you."

Her voice held a tease in it, but he couldn't match her playfulness. She'd never gone to battle. She didn't know how things could go from quiet to chaos in the span of a heartbeat.

He tugged the door open and stepped inside. The tangy aroma of kraut and sausage hung in the air. The walls were faded green, the ceiling dotted with water spots, and the flooring webbed with cracks. Booths lined the back and right side of the area and tables the center. A kitchen stood to the left of the room.

Low murmurs of German conversation filled the space. A family of five took residence in the corner, and beside Marcus was a group of elderly women huddled around a table cluttered with coffee cups, empty plates, and lots of yarn. Unless these gray-haired ladies were knitting codes into their baby blankets, this place seemed more of a family environment and less of a spy-ring hub.

He waved Clara inside just as a man approached, coming from the kitchen. Deep lines rippling his forehead and bracketing his mouth indicated his mature age, but the creases framing his eyes revealed his wariness. Marcus expected as much. He and Clara were outsiders.

If he'd learned anything during his years in the service, it was that the element of surprise always proved the best strategy. So Marcus greeted him in German. The older man's taut expression slacked, then gave way to a friendly smile. Marcus could feel Clara's stare on him. She hadn't known he was fluent in the language.

The man introduced himself as the owner, and Marcus offered a few general compliments, relaying he'd heard about the restaurant from a family friend. The man seemed satisfied, for he quickly gathered two menus and led them to a booth near the back corner. All the while, Marcus's gaze searched for anything that could be a potential threat.

Nothing.

Clara moved to take the bench opposite him, but Marcus laced his fingers with hers and gently tugged her to sit beside him. Her eyes filled with questions, but she said nothing. He'd explain once the owner was out of earshot. Though he couldn't explain why his heart lurched in his chest by the simple press of her palm against his or the surge of protectiveness pulsing through him with her nearness.

From his current assessment, the area seemed clear of any danger, but he hated that there stood even the slightest risk. He couldn't glimpse the entire kitchen. He had no idea if any threat hid somewhere out of sight. Frustration gnawed at the edges of his mind.

When crawling through no-man's-land with limited vision, the twisting shadows and darkness tricking his mind, he'd often relied on his skill, his quick reflexes, and his impeccable aim. Now his dominant hand, his trigger finger, remained lame. He couldn't even make a fist to throw a punch. Marcus could rely on his wit, yes, but he still didn't have control of the situation. Which meant he needed to trust God. A twinge of shame cut through him. It had taken an injury, his own talent becoming void, for him to realize how much he needed the Almighty. How much he needed God's grace even for the simplest of tasks.

The owner set the menus on the table, then moved toward the door to greet an older couple just entering.

With reluctance, Marcus released Clara's hand. "This side of the booth is a better vantage point. It's always best to face the room rather than having your back to it," he explained. "It's also better not having to speak across a table where others can overhear."

She moved closer and lowered her tone. The intimacy of it all nearly undid him. "Is there a reason we would need to whisper? Do you see anything suspicious?"

"No. What about you?" He tilted his head toward her. "Do you recognize any of the voices as the mystery men from the park?" Besides the owner, the only other gentlemen in the room were the father of three at the booth adjacent to theirs and the older man who'd recently walked in.

"Not yet." She shook her head. "It doesn't seem like there's any danger here."

He had to agree. "We'll still keep our eyes open, but for now, let's enjoy a nice meal."

The line of her shoulders relaxed, and she picked up the menu. "I'd like that." Her gaze skimmed the options, her lower lip pushing into a pout. "I recognize most of the dishes, but some I don't. I might need you to translate." She met his gaze. "And maybe order for me."

"Happy to." He savored her answering smile.

For the next few moments, they went over the menu. By the time the owner returned with glasses of water in hand, Clara decided on *Reibekuchen*, a potato pancake, while he chose *Maultaschen*, a spiced, minced meat stuffed in a pocket of dough.

After they placed their orders, the owner retreated to the kitchen, and Clara shook her head with a huff of laughter. "I still can't believe I had no idea you were fluent. If I'd have known, I wouldn't have had to wait two days to talk to Liesl. I could've asked you when you broke into the apartment."

"I didn't break in." And he would very much prefer that image of her in a man's shirt to be erased from his memory. "I never imagined you'd be there. I thought you were in California." Questions rolled to the front of his mind. "Why did you return to New York?"

Her thumb slid along the rim of her water glass. "It's not something I talk about. Honestly, I'm still recovering from it all. It hurt pretty badly."

Understanding dawned, but that only spiked his curiosity. "Did a man hurt you?" When she didn't answer, protectiveness blazed through him. "Were you hurt . . . physically?"

"No, nothing like that." Her gaze snapped to his. "He didn't break my heart as much as crushed my hopes."

Marcus wasn't about to try to interpret that statement. She didn't seem to want to divulge any more, so he didn't press her. "Any man would be lucky to have you."

She flicked him a dry look. "At least I hadn't poured out my heart to him. I tried that once before, only to be ignored."

His mouth flattened as he tried not to think of how many sweethearts she'd had after he'd joined the military. "Whoever it was must've been an idiot."

Something between a laugh and a snort escaped her. "If you say you are, then who am I to contradict?"

Clara hadn't been planning on this sort of conversation, but when Marcus had unintentionally called himself an idiot, she couldn't rein in her response. Now the cool, composed army officer gaped at her, shock evidenced by his wide eyes and stiff posture. It was as if he had no clue what she'd meant. Had he truly forgotten?

Silence stretched between them until the owner had brought them their food. Clara wasn't exactly hungry anymore. She'd wanted to shift the focus of the conversation from her terrible experience in California but had chosen the wrong topic—their history. Granted, there remained a vulnerable part of her that wanted answers, though not at the expense of all this awkwardness. She picked up her fork and dug into her carrots. "Forget I said anything."

He blinked as if in a stupor. "I don't think I can." He angled toward her. "Clara, did I miss something? Because I recall things differently. You never poured your heart out to me. I would remember that."

What? Now it was her turn for surprise. "The week before you told me you're leaving for the army, you asked me to mend a tear in your jacket. I left you a note when I returned it to you."

He shook his head. "You *said* you left a note. Believe me, I searched. But there was nothing in the pockets of that jacket."

She swallowed, the burn in her throat sinking to her chest. When he'd given her that coat, she'd known it was one of her final chances to tell him how she felt. She'd gotten a bit creative, but she'd thought for certain he'd seen it. He'd left for the military without saying goodbye, and days later, she'd found the jacket in her brother's closet, heart pierced by Marcus's rejection. "The note wasn't on paper" was all she could say. "But it hardly matters anymore. Nothing can come of anything."

His head reared back as if she'd slapped him. Then his gaze dropped to his wounded hand. "If that's how you feel."

Her chest squeezed. He'd misunderstood. She pressed her hand to his elbow. "I meant nothing can come from rehashing the past. Not because of your injury."

He met her gaze. "I'm not the same as I was. If anyone understands this, it's me."

"No, you're not the same." She kept her hand on his arm, their food forgotten. "You were carefree then. Always teasing. More easygoing than you are now. But you were restless, as if you wouldn't be satisfied unless you saw everything the world had to offer. You're different now, but that's not a bad thing."

He shook his head, though he didn't say anything. She noticed he kept flicking glances to the door and around the room. Ever vigilant. But this place was . . . docile. She had to have heard wrong. Or maybe she'd guessed correctly on her first hunch, and the main target was actually an island. Though for some reason, the most pressing thing on her mind was Marcus. He'd be the last to admit it, but his soul was more wounded than his body.

"Want to talk about it? The injury and how it happened?" She didn't quite expect him to be open, especially considering she hadn't been very chatty about Los Angeles. But she didn't want to relive California, her failed efforts, and even more failed relationship with America's silver screen hero. Ben hadn't captured her affections like Marcus had those years ago, but the man had been well on his way—until everything had come to light, and she glimpsed his darkness.

Marcus sipped his water. "I went out in the middle of the night to get information on a German camp nearby. I stumbled across a machine gun nest. Shrapnel from grenades lodged in my hand, and a bullet grazed my thigh. I managed to stay well hidden in my suit and the underbrush. Come morning, my comrades found me."

"You're a sniper?"

He nodded.

"Did you wear a camouflage suit?"

"Yes. I believe it saved my life."

She tried not to get misty-eyed but failed. This was why she worked so hard. She had no idea Marcus Reeves, her brother's best friend, the one who'd first stolen her heart, had worn a camouflage suit. There were a number of camoufleurs, so she doubted his had been sewn by her own hands, but still . . .

To know that here in America, so far from the battlefield, her part in the war effort made such a difference, saved lives, flushed her with warmth of renewed purpose. "Thank you for telling me."

"What you're doing matters, Clara."

She laid her head on his shoulder like she'd done many times in her youth. It kept him from spying the tears burning her vision. So much had been stolen from her. Her career in Hollywood. Her dreams. That starry-eyed girl was no longer. Those days, those years of dreaming . . . it almost seemed like that time had belonged to someone else. But now, Marcus's words infused strength. Even with the world being in total chaos, ravaged in war, a spark of hope ignited her heart.

CHAPTER 6

THE FOLLOWING MORNING Clara handed Lieutenant Towle her stack of camouflage suits, saying a quick prayer over them like always. She claimed her seat among the other camoufleurs in the training classroom. The soft hum of chatter floated around her, but her mind remained stuck on yesterday's conversation with Marcus. How easily they'd fallen into discussion. The way he tilted his head toward her, listening intently as if her words were of utmost importance. They'd waited at the restaurant until almost closing, then Marcus walked her home.

Something in his eyes had been different than when she'd first seen him again. Less haunted. Perhaps he found peace in his new circumstances. She wasn't foolish enough to believe he'd renewed any interest in her. Not that he'd been head over heels those years ago.

She shook those thoughts away and straightened on her chair just as Lieutenant Towle rose from behind his desk. Though instead of moving to the front of the class, he strode toward the door, then opened it. Clara exchanged glances with the ladies beside her.

Lieutenant Towle stepped aside, allowing a taller man holding rolled paper—a banner, maybe?—to enter. The newcomer, clearly a naval officer judging by his decorated uniform, shook the lieutenant's hand, then faced the room.

"Ladies, this is Commander W. T. Conn." Their superior made introductions. "He'll be teaching you today. Pay close attention. He'll be giving your next assignment." Lieutenant Towle spoke to the Camouflage Corps as if addressing a legion of soldiers instead of thirty-five women.

"How do you do, ladies?" The commander's deep voice filled the room. "This morning I'm pleased to display the latest in camouflage warfare." He unrolled the large paper as one would a scroll and held it up for all to see. It was indeed a banner covered with smatters of bright paint intermingling with black abstract shapes. "We call it dazzle camouflage."

Murmurs rippled throughout. Clara eyed the paper. How could *that* be identified as camouflage? The pictures were geometric designs in loud colors. Nothing about it blended into anything but rather stood out.

Commander Conn no doubt read all their confused expressions, for he smiled. "This technique isn't to conceal but to mislead the enemy. See these complex patterns of shapes?" He pointed. "When painted on our battleships, this particular design makes it challenging for the enemy to determine our range, speed, and direction. The purpose is to trick the eyes."

Clara instantly understood the merit of this tactic. How often had she tweaked costumes using angles and lines to enhance an actress's figure or give an illusion of height?

"It's our newest campaign," he continued. "And the US Women's Reserve Camouflage Corps will contribute to its success. This morning we'll practice painting designs on a smaller scale. This afternoon you'll begin painting a war bond booth for the Liberty Loan drive next week. We want the general public to be excited about this venture and hopefully purchase Liberty Loans to support it."

Eagerness charged the air, but the commander wasn't finished. "If city officials approve, you will also have the distinct privilege of painting the USS *Recruit*. Our men are going to bring the ship right into Union Square."

Clara's brows jumped. Painting an entire ship? Right in Manhattan's historic and popular thoroughfare? And just why did she have a compelling notion to find Marcus after work and tell him about this fun surprise? She stuffed down the idea and focused on the task at hand.

The Liberty Loan drive would begin next week, but the city had been preparing for over a month. Having been immersed in her work, Clara wasn't certain of all the details, but she'd overheard rumors of parades and potential performances of vaudeville acts.

"One more thing I've yet to mention." Commander Conn stepped forward as if sharing straight from a confidential file, then his face split into a warm smile. "The Liberty Loan booth will be unveiled by a surprise guest." He nodded at the door, and a group of young men filed into the room, all carrying crates of art supplies.

Someone tapped Clara's shoulder, and she shifted on her chair, meeting Constance Andrew's beaming face.

The woman leaned forward, seeming to burst with giddiness. "Did you happen to hear the lineup for the parades and loan drive?" Constance pushed back one of her wavy locks that escaped her chignon. "I'm guessing the governor will be the surprise guest."

"A politician? No, no." Another camoufleur, Helen Kalkman, poked her head over from across the aisle, joining their conversation. "The governor won't excite the crowds half as much as film stars."

Clara tensed.

Helen rubbed her hands together, her green eyes brightening with her full smile. "I heard the Treasury Department enlisted big stars to promote the loan drive! Mary Pickford, Douglas Fairbanks." She counted on her fingers. "Charlie Chaplin. And guess who the last one is. I'm certain that—"

"Clara Westlake." Lieutenant Towle interrupted Helen's gossip session, summoning Clara to retrieve her supplies.

To be honest, she didn't mind leaving the conversation. She personally had nothing against the celebrities her friend mentioned, but Clara had experienced her fill of Hollywood stars.

She made her way down the aisle to the front, where one of the young men handed her a box filled with canvases, paints, and brushes. Hopefully by the time she returned to her seat, her friends would be discussing another subject. None of her fellow camoufleurs knew of her work in California. Only Lieutenant Towle had been aware. The same man who now motioned her toward his desk.

Curiosity rising, she approached him. "Yes, sir?"

"Miss Westlake," he began in his usual, warm tone. "I've been asked to select someone from the Camouflage Corps to help unveil the booth along with the guest of honor. Based on your impeccable credentials and past work experience, I hope you will accept the privilege."

Marcus, dressed in uniform, sat across from Major Palmer in a tight, windowless office. He'd arrived five minutes early for his appointment and took advantage of every second to steel his spine. This meeting could determine the direction of Marcus's career.

"Your squadron leader speaks highly of you, Captain Reeves. Not only your sniping talent but your character, which is important in the position I'm seeking to fill."

Marcus took in a steadying breath. It was now or never. "Sir, I realize what a great opportunity it is to work in the recruiting office, but I was hoping for something in the training field."

"You can't shoot." Major Palmer's tone wasn't clipped or scornful, but the words hit like a punch to the gut. "Your skills have been reduced."

Marcus kept a neutral expression. "I have a lot to offer even without curling my finger around a trigger, sir. I can teach. I can train the mental and emotional side of combat."

Major Palmer's head tipped to the side in consideration, then his lips flattened. "I don't believe that's the best place for you. Your good judgment can be an asset in the recruiting office."

Sitting around all day. Sharpening pencils for stacks of paperwork. Probably in a cramped space like this. The restlessness clawed deep.

"You don't have to decide today. But I'll need an answer within ten days." His superior stood and held out his hand. His right hand. Whether by habit or a clever tactic to remind Marcus of his inadequacies, he didn't know.

Marcus stuck out his lame fingers anyway, refusing to cower.

Major Palmer's eyes filled with what could only be respect, and he executed the handshake.

Marcus felt nothing, numb hand to match his numb heart.

He had to make a choice and soon. He wouldn't take advantage of the Westlakes' hospitality much longer. Though it seemed Desmond's parents enjoyed having Marcus there. Their residence was spacious, but old memories crowded him. He'd seen Clara yesterday at the restaurant, but at the Westlake home, reminders of her cropped up everywhere. That, and the painful absence of Desmond. He was overseas fighting. Exactly where Marcus should be now. For sanity's sake, Marcus needed to find his own place.

He took the longer route to the underground transit, his attention snagging on the commotion at the Sub-Treasury Building. People darted about with purpose. Men stood on scaffolding, endeavoring to attach a large, patriotic banner to the tall columns. Others hung bunting on the railings by the steps. Several worked on constructing a platform. Marcus had read in the paper that New York City was the last stop on the Liberty Loan tour.

But what caught his focus was a group of ladies to the right of the Sub-Treasury Building. More like, one lady in particular—Clara. It seemed as though they were cleaning up for the day. As if sensing his presence, Clara glanced over, and their gazes collided. His heart slammed against his ribs. She raised her hand in a wave, said something to the woman beside her, then moved his direction.

He strode toward her as well, meeting her near a vacant park bench.

"Hello, Marcus." She smiled warmly. "I didn't know you'd be in this part of the city today."

"Are you all finished?" He nodded in the general direction of the Selkirk. "I can escort you home."

"I'd like that. I'm all done until tomorrow." Her eyes drifted to the area she'd just come from.

Marcus followed her squinted gaze, noticing several large partitions had been constructed, shielding whatever the women had been working on.

She took in his jacket. "You're in uniform."

"I had a meeting with my commanding officer."

"Was it about your job?" The late afternoon sunlight caressed her face, making her blue-green eyes sparkle.

"Hmm?" Oh, his appointment. Marcus gave a slight shake of his head. In sniping, distraction was just as much an enemy as the opposing forces. One slipup could be costly, which was why Marcus had disciplined his mind to remain sharp despite bombarding chaos. Clara Westlake robbed him of his best defense. His thoughts strayed to her more often than he'd like to admit. "I'm still undecided."

She eased closer to him. "You know, my father was serious when he mentioned a position. He would love to have you working alongside him."

Marcus had almost forgotten. Mr. Westlake had casually dropped the offer that night at dinner but hadn't brought it up since. Marcus had assumed the position was only a passing thought. "I'll speak to him." Wouldn't hurt to ask. "What were you ladies painting today?" he asked as they leisurely strolled toward the transit station. "Is it something for the loan drive?" Not too hard of a guess, considering the women had all been huddled around the Sub-Treasury Building, the site of the event.

She turned curious eyes on him. "What makes you think we were painting?"

He couldn't help the slow grin from spreading. "You have black paint on your nose."

She gasped and whipped her head away from him. "Why is it I so easily embarrass myself in front of you?" Her hand vigorously swiped her face. So caught up in cleaning the smudge, she almost walked into a lamppost.

Marcus hooked his arm around her waist and hauled her to him.

She jolted but remained tucked against his side. Now she brushed her nose against her raised shoulder, clearly on a mission. And she still wouldn't look at him.

He tugged her closer. His lips skimming her ear, he whispered, "Clara, you never need to hide from me."

She blinked but didn't pull away. "It's all so humiliating. First, I'm wearing men's clothes. That alone—"

"Is something I'm trying to forget as well."

She winced, clearly mistaking his remark, as if he were repulsed by her. He almost laughed at the absurdity. Clara Westlake was everything he wanted yet was always out of reach. Though she was now tucked under his good arm, which probably wasn't a wise idea since they were in the middle of the sidewalk.

He stepped back, scraping his willpower to let her go. "I didn't mean that as an insult." He dipped his chin, peering at her face. "Let's just say, I enjoyed the view a little too much."

"Marcus Reeves!" She feebly swatted his chest. "You shouldn't say such things."

He shrugged. "Shouldn't say the truth?"

"Not if it's . . . inappropriate." Her reprimand wasn't exactly convincing, not with her mouth fighting against a smile. Then, as if remembering the smudge on her face, she resumed wiping her nose but missing the smudge entirely. "Did I get it?"

Still there.

Her determined effort pulled a laugh from him.

Her gaze narrowed. "This isn't funny, Marcus."

It really was. It was also adorable how her lower lip pouted, drawing his full attention, making him think things he probably shouldn't. He led her out of the flow of pedestrian traffic. "Let me help." He'd forgotten his handkerchief in his civilian clothes. Of course, he had the swatch of fabric he'd carried since the battlefield, but he wasn't ready for Clara to see that. She'd ask questions. No, another strategy surfaced. He drew near to her, the floral notes of her perfume surrounding him.

Curiosity filled her eyes as he cupped her jaw and tilted her face toward him. He skimmed his thumb over the black spot. Their bodies were close, but he didn't withdraw. He swiped again, trying to ignore the rise and fall of her chest with her quick intakes of breath. He looked into her eyes, those pools of blue-green that he'd envisioned a thousand times during those unbearable hours in the trenches. Even now, the familiar struggle resurfaced. She deserved better than what he could offer. But here, in this moment, he couldn't resist her pull on his heart. He focused on the smatter of paint on the perfect slope of her nose and could only speak the facts. "I can't get rid of it."

Her breathlessness undid him. "We've both tried."

"We did."

"But it didn't work." She rested her hands on his chest. "No matter what we do."

He stroked her cheek. "The traces remain." They weren't talking anymore about a silly dab of paint on her skin. No, this was about them. His feelings for her, and, he dared hope, her affection for him. What he'd told her just now was the utter truth. He'd tried to forget her over the years. He could never be good enough for her. Yet her name had been etched onto his heart.

She trained her sights on him, her hands sliding to his shoulders. "Things like this are hard to brush away."

All he could manage was a nod. This familiarity had been one they'd shared years ago. But at that time, uncertain of her regard for him, he hadn't made a move for fear he'd lose her, which he ultimately had. What would a woman as amazing as her want with a guy like him? He didn't know what had gone wrong between them. His old jacket had been a clue, but it was inconveniently in the closet of her brother's apartment, where she currently lived. Though maybe the only hints he needed were found in her eyes, no doubt reflecting the longing of his own.

As one, they eased closer, gazes locked.

He shouldn't—wouldn't—kiss her in the middle of the sidewalk, but he would finally tell her the words that had burned in him for so long. "Clara, those times back then. I had—"

"Hey, Clara!" Two young women dressed in the same uniform as Clara waved animatedly, unaware of the moment they'd interrupted.

Blinking rapidly, Clara stepped back from him and greeted them with a small smile.

The shorter of the two young women clasped her hands together and held them under her chin. "Congratulations on being picked for the unveiling." She pointed at their work area. "Lieutenant Towle just told us. Are you over the moon? I'm sure you've seen the papers. I'd give anything to stand next to Casanova."

All the color drained from Clara's face, even as the ladies offered a cheery wave and continued on. Meanwhile, Clara remained stock-still.

He touched her arm. "Are you okay?"

"Excuse me, Marcus." She darted off in a hurried pace, almost a run, toward the corner but paused at the vendor's stand.

He went after her. "What's the matter?"

But Clara didn't seem to register his presence, her gaze so absorbed on the *New York Times*.

Marcus scanned the headline. The articles highlighted the celebrities endorsing the loan drive. "People you know?" With Clara having worked in the film industry, she was bound to become acquainted with actors.

According to the article, the famous stars coming to the city were Mary Pickford, Douglas Fairbanks, Charlie Chaplin, and—

"Ben Winsell." She finally glanced over. "It was him. He's the one who ruined my dreams."

CHAPTER 7

CLARA STOOD FROZEN to the spot. When she'd left California, she'd determined to forget Ben Winsell. About what he'd done. All that he had stolen from her. She'd longed to start afresh with her work for the government, and now her two worlds—past and present—would collide.

"A former sweetheart?" Marcus's voice was low and quiet.

She sighed. "Of sorts." The relationship she had with America's handsome hero was never firmly established. One moment he'd kissed her lips, the next he'd betrayed her heart.

"How about we get you home?" Marcus's left hand took hers, and he coaxed her away from the newsstand. He immediately withdrew his touch, making her mood sink lower. Whatever had been building between them a short time ago had already crumbled.

After a stretch of walking, she risked a glance over. Before Constance and Helen approached them on the street, Clara was certain Marcus was going to say something important. She'd glimpsed it in his eyes. The sincerity. The need to release whatever was making his dark gaze smolder.

Then everything had been interrupted with the news about Ben. Her ridiculous stupor in front of the newspaper probably hadn't helped clear Marcus's confusion. "I'm sure you have questions."

"I'm here if you want to talk. But I understand the need to think things through before speaking."

Yet another facet of his personality the war had molded. Before, he'd always been quick to change the subject whenever deep feelings were involved. The man had a talent for avoiding serious issues. Maybe that was why she'd gone the indirect route when it came to sharing her feelings for him back then. Instead of speaking her heart, she'd stitched it into his jacket. Though he hadn't caught her message.

Either way, she was still getting accustomed to this new version of Marcus. The conversation about the paint on her face—which was, unfortunately, still there—had shifted into something else entirely. She hadn't imagined it. Things had begun to blossom between them again. Only to be ruined by the realization that Ben Winsell would be there for the unveiling. Of all people. Him! Her breath bunched in her chest. "I'm sorry for reacting that way. I was told someone important would help unveil the new war bond booth, but I didn't know it was Ben until I read it just now."

They passed several storefronts before Marcus spoke again. "I'm assuming you have a role in the booth's unveiling, otherwise you could avoid him and not attend the program."

"You assume right. Lieutenant Towle asked me this morning to represent our corps." If the news about the celebrities participating in the tour wasn't exactly a secret, then why hadn't Lieutenant Towle told her? Or even Commander Conn when he'd announced the plan about the booth? Perhaps they'd assumed such news would distract the women from their work. But it would've been nice to know. She would've tactfully suggested another corps member for the task. Unfortunately, she'd given her word. Her heart deflated with her sigh. "I'm not sure if I'm ready to see him yet."

Marcus gave a slow nod. "It can sting. Especially if you still have feelings for him."

She paused at his words. "I don't. I mean, I never allowed myself to invest too much in our relationship. Ben was charming, but there was something about his lifestyle that kept me from committing." He had an addiction. "And we didn't exactly part on the best terms." Her pulse lagged even as her mind raced. Memories of that terrible day flashed. "Remember at the restaurant, you asked why I left California?"

"Yes."

She resumed walking, and he kept a slow pace alongside her. "I got fired." Her gaze fixed on the ground before her. "More like, kicked off the studio lot."

"It can't be because of your talent," he said softly, but she refused to look at him. "You're the best at what you do. Why would anyone think otherwise?"

She rubbed her arm and nodded at an older couple passing. "The costume designer, Allen, allowed me to design Anita Stewart's wardrobe. He told me this could be my breakthrough task. If I excelled there, I could get picked for larger jobs. So I worked day and night sewing her gowns. I believed that was my best work."

"I have no doubt."

She sighed. "But Allen took full credit for everything. Looking back, I think I was doing his job the entire time, that he had no intention of letting anyone else know I designed those pieces. I was fool enough to believe he was helping me with my career, when it was the other way around."

Marcus's jaw tightened. "What did you do?"

"Ben was the lead actor. He'd started showing interest in me a few weeks before filming. He knew how hard I worked on that wardrobe. I'd even sewn a couple of his suits. When I discovered Allen was taking ownership of my work, Ben and I had been together only two months. I thought he'd stick up for me when I confronted Allen, but . . ."

"He didn't." Marcus finished the words she couldn't.

She nodded, the emotions surrounding that memory returning like a tidal wave. She'd requested a meeting with Allen and the film's producer to discuss the situation. Allen had denied it all, claiming Clara was trying to discredit him because she wanted his job. She'd never forget the smirk that lined his face when she accused him of stealing her designs. Then the final hit? The producer had called in Ben to give his account. "Ben told the producer I was making it all up. And that he'd caught me in lies before."

Marcus turned to her with fire in his eyes. "He attacked your character."

"He did. I found out later that Allen is a family friend of the studio owners. Ben must've known and didn't want to involve himself in anything that could jeopardize his career."

"That's no excuse." His voice threaded with steel. "He shouldn't have betrayed you."

She tucked her hand around his arm, grateful for an ally. "No one believed me. Not the producer. The director. Or anyone else on set." Rumors had spread faster than wildfire. Her throat cinched as she remembered the scornful looks of people she'd once thought friends. "So I was told my services weren't needed any longer. I had nothing to stay for. The costume designer stole all my designs, all my pieces." She paused. "Well, except for one." Her favorite.

"What happened to it?"

"The dress was for a pivotal event at the end of the movie." A wedding. "Since it was for an important scene, I worked extra hard on it."

"What kept Allen from taking it?"

"He didn't know it existed. For the shoot, Allen chose a gaudy frock with too many layers. It was so loud. But the mood of the scene was elegant and soft. I didn't want to challenge him, so I decided to create an alternative and show him after I finished it. Then he could decide which to use."

Marcus nodded. "Seems like a good strategy."

"I worked on it during off hours and purchased all the materials with my own money. But by the time it was finished, I was already getting suspicious of him. Allen gloated about the costumes already in the movie— the ones I designed—without giving me any credit. My sketches started disappearing. That was the point I became wise to him. Since I designed and created the last dress with my own resources, I held it back." She loved that wedding gown. It would've looked breathtaking on Anita. Now it hung morosely in Clara's closet, directly beside Marcus's jacket. Two significant pieces of her background now collected dust. "After I got fired, there was nothing left for me in California. I came home."

Marcus slowed to a stop, and his gaze fixed on her with an intensity that stole her breath. "And then you began working for the government."

"Yes. Mother heard about the CC needing seamstresses. My hands were as good as any to stitch camouflage suits."

He caught both her hands with his large one. "These." He brought her fingers to his lips and brushed a kiss across her knuckles. "These hands save lives."

She could barely think, let alone come up with a response. Especially when he looked at her as if she were the only star in his universe. "I hope so." Her words were breathy and quiet compared to the loud and forceful pounding of her pulse.

He released her hands, and she tried not to let disappointment show on her face. Thankfully, he remained close as they resumed walking.

"Thank you, Marcus."

He raised his brows in silent inquiry.

"Now that you know what happened in California, you can understand why it was so important to me that you believed what I said about what I heard in the park." She met his eyes. "It meant a lot. Even Liesl didn't fully trust my story. Right now, I don't even know anymore." She huffed a humorless laugh. "I was so certain something was amiss."

Marcus gave her a curious look. "Do you remember the time Desmond and I climbed that maple on the far edge of your parents' property?"

"Oh goodness, how could I forget? You two were so high up, I was scared you'd both break a bone. Or all of them." She shook her head with a smile. Those two had always been landing in one scrape or another. "What made you think of that?"

He shrugged and cut a look at the passing trolley car. "Desmond climbed down with ease and confidence, but I felt almost paralyzed up there. You must've read my hesitation, because you said something to me. Do you recall it?"

"Hmm." She tilted her head as if it would help rattle the memory free from the depths of her mind. "No, I only remember being scared."

"I've never forgotten." He nudged her arm with a fond smile. "You cupped your hands around your mouth and yelled, 'Don't you dare doubt yourself, Marcus Reeves.'"

She laughed. "I was always a tad bossy."

"You have no idea how much your words stuck with me." His piercing gaze shot a bolt of heat through her. "So if you feel something is amiss, then I say the same to you. Don't you dare doubt yourself, Clara Westlake."

She remained quiet for a long second, letting his words sift and settle within her. He not only believed her but believed *in* her. Though she'd felt there was something terribly wrong with that conversation at the park, it seemed they'd hit a dead end. "But nothing happened on April fourth."

There'd been no catastrophe, which she was thankful for, but it had made her question everything. She'd always been self-assured, but ever since the fiasco in California, she'd been . . . less. Less confident in herself. Less trusting of others. Perhaps this was an opportunity to rely on God more, to embrace that Scripture about God's strength being made perfect in her weakness.

"Maybe we need to go back to the beginning and reevaluate."

She nodded, a surge of renewed hope flowing through her.

"Would you like . . . to discuss it over dinner?" His lowered voice seemed heavy with reluctance. "That is, whenever you're free."

Her smile bloomed under his perusal. For some reason he seemed hesitant to invite her out, but she would not waste this opportunity. "Liesl is dropping off some baked goods for the church bazaar tonight. I'm volunteering." She'd offered to help ages ago and couldn't back out now. "How about tomorrow?"

"Tomorrow sounds good." His soft grin melted everything in her. "That gives me plenty of time."

She had no idea what he meant, but the determination in his gaze told her she'd soon find out.

⊱—✕—⊰

Marcus sat across from Mr. James Westlake in his enormous study.

"So what's the government have to say regarding you?" The older man leaned back on his seat. "Because I intend to match or beat their offer."

Marcus's head reared back slightly. He hadn't expected his best friend's father to be so adamant, but Marcus was thankful. This informal meeting already had an entirely different tone than his appointment with the major. "Well, sir, they want me to join the recruiting team."

"Lots of paperwork," Mr. Westlake observed. "Waste of your talent."

Marcus didn't want to speak against his commanding officer, but he agreed. His enlistment with the army was up, so he could resign with honor. "They believe the position is something that fits me and will be a stable career."

"What do you believe?"

"I just want to do what's best."

"You always do." Mr. Westlake smiled. "I have a position open for security detail. You would oversee the security of my construction warehouses."

"Nationwide?"

He nodded. "Yes, this will include traveling. Looking at the buildings and implementing whatever defense features you think are relevant. You'd check the managers' safes, the locks, and test for accessibility to burglary and how to deter it."

Marcus could only stare. This was a dream job. He didn't have to stay in one place. He could use his knowledge to help Westlake Enterprises.

"Furthermore"—Mr. Westlake straightened on his chair—"I'd like to teach you the ins and outs of how to run the company."

Marcus's excitement plummeted. "Sir?"

"I haven't received any correspondence from Desmond in a long while." Mr. Westlake's face turned pained. "Should the worst happen . . ."

"The troops move around a lot and aren't always near the proper channels for mail service." Mail was almost an afterthought in the heat of battle. It was only in the dead of night—that rare sliver of quiet—that men had a chance to long for and miss their families. "Desmond is a good soldier. He'll come home." Marcus wasn't sure how he'd cope otherwise. "I'll think about the security position you offered. If I accept, I'll learn whatever you teach me, so I can help alongside Des when he's back."

The older man nodded. "That's all I can ask."

Not long after dinner, a knock sounded on Marcus's bedroom door. That could only mean one thing: Liesl had returned from dropping off the baked goods to Clara.

He opened the door, but before he could say a word, the housekeeper leveled a severe look.

"Marcus, if you only knew the hassle I went through for you."

His smile grew. "Did you get it?"

Her exaggerated huff rippled the lace on her collar as she lifted the bag in her clutches. "Clara hardly left me alone for two minutes. When she moved to the balcony to water her plants, I dashed into the bedroom and found it in the closet." Her nose wrinkled. "It went against everything in me to cram this fine jacket into my bag. Must have a thousand wrinkles by now."

He chuckled. "You did great work, Liesl."

Her hardened edges softened a bit. "I don't know why it's so important or why all the hush-hush. It would've been much simpler to ask her for the jacket."

"She wouldn't have given it to you."

Her brow arched in skepticism. "You say it's yours?"

"I promise it's mine."

"Okay then." She opened her overstuffed bag and handed him the jacket he hadn't seen since he joined the army. He wasn't certain it even fit anymore, but that's not what was important.

He thanked Liesl, and the moment she walked away, he closed the door. His gaze fell over the familiar dark-brown coat. He carried it to the bedside lamp for better light.

Now to test his hunch.

He searched the inside lining, skimming the left side, the area—if wearing the jacket—that would be directly over his heart.

And there it was.

A stitched message. Four words. He sank onto the mattress with a heavy exhale.

He was the biggest fool.

CHAPTER 8

THE CHURCH BAZAAR was successful, if not a tad exhausting. Clara had stayed after to help clean up. She returned to the apartment around eleven. Her mind still spun from the events of the day, but her body craved sleep. She should turn in soon, especially since she had a full shift of working on the booth ahead of her.

Ugh. The booth. She should've asked Lieutenant Towle more questions before blindly accepting to participate in the unveiling.

She puffed out her cheeks and exhaled slowly. On Monday, she would come face-to-face with Ben. Maybe she should sneak a rock suit and attend in full camouflage. Though she had nothing to be ashamed of. He'd done her wrong.

Talking to Marcus this afternoon brought back all the emotions from her last days in California. She wandered to the closet and shoved back some of the hangers until her fingers found the silk gown.

The wedding dress.

She gently unhooked the hanger from the bar and withdrew it into the light of her bedroom so she could admire it better.

The rounded neckline featured soft lace which matched the belt and the trim on the sleeves. Everything else was simply the silk. This gown may appear understated compared to the heavily beaded and shoulder-to-shin layers of lace of Anita Stewart's other costumes, but that had been the entire point. Clara eyed the dress again. The sleek lines and subtle accents were intended to complement the woman wearing the gown, not detract. If people pinned their gaze only on the dress, then Clara hadn't done her job right.

This gown had been made to stun with simple elegance.

Fatigue sank into her bones. She needed to get some rest. Tomorrow promised a long day of painting. The muscles in her neck cramped as if in protest. With a sigh, she gave the dress one last, sweeping look. Though a movie star may never wear her creation, perhaps she could find it a good home. Because it accomplished nothing staying in her closet beside Marcus's . . .

She blinked at the vacant space where his jacket should be.

It was gone.

❅

Marcus sat up straight on his bed. Someone was knocking fiercely on the door. He pinched his eyes closed and inhaled deeply in hope of settling his racing heart.

Another pounding.

"I know you're in there, Marcus."

Clara.

"Open the door."

A smile touched his mouth. So much for settling his pulse. The sound of her voice had a direct hit on his vitals. But her tone? The low growl signified anger, and he knew why. He cast a glance at the clock on the bedside table. Nearly one in the morning.

Now he had questions of his own.

He slid on trousers and moved to the door, then flung it open.

A tight-knuckled fist belonging to an angry woman poised in midair, ready to assault the door again. Her eyes, narrowed slits of fire, took him in, then rounded wide.

He didn't mean for his shirtless state to render her speechless, but it made him grin nonetheless.

"Did you need something?" He leaned on the doorframe, adopting a casual stance, which seemed to fluster her more. What she'd written on his jacket had given him confidence in more ways than one.

Her mouth opened, then clamped shut. As if remembering her purpose, she straightened and inclined her chin. "Give it back."

"I'm not entirely sure what you mean." He kept his words on the quiet side, so as not to wake anyone. Not that Clara followed suit. Between her thunderous knocking and loud tone, she probably had stirred the entire household. "I don't have anything of yours."

"Well . . . not exactly. But you took the jacket."

"Which is mine."

"Yes, and I'd like it back." In a flurry of soft vanilla and impassioned woman, she stormed past him into his room.

He abandoned his post by the door and slid in front of the closet, blocking her. "Clara, you can't be in my bedroom."

She crossed her arms. "You were in mine. Fair is fair."

He shouldn't laugh. He really shouldn't, but his chest rumbled, earning a glare. "I wasn't in your bedroom."

"You had to be. You have a key." She held out her palm. "Which I would like you to surrender as well."

He tsked. "You're pretty demanding. Is there something about that jacket you don't want me to know?"

At his words, her haughty mask slipped. "Yes. It's embarrassing, Marcus. I just—" She stopped, her face slacking. "You know, don't you? You wouldn't ask so pointedly about the jacket if you didn't know." She buried her face in her hands.

He couldn't have that. He gently approached. "Clara."

Nothing.

"Clara, please look at me."

Her hands fell to her sides.

"We need to talk but not with me half-dressed in my bedroom."

At this, her cheeks reddened as if it finally dawned on her how this would look should someone happen upon them. "Out there, then?" She gestured toward the terrace doors, which led to the garden.

Clara angled away while he slipped on a shirt and shoes. He reached into his closet and retrieved the jacket, only to drape it around her shoulders. Her eyes darted to him in surprise. With an encouraging smile, he led her outside. Being early April, the spring night air held a chill. The light from inside his room lent a soft glow on the pale, stone walkway leading into the garden.

"About this jacket . . ." She tugged on the lapel. "Can we forget what I sewed into the lining?"

His stomach dropped. Did she honestly think he could just ignore it? "I'd rather go back to that time, then if you still want . . . we can move past it." Which would be a lot harder for him than her, it seemed.

She gave a reluctant nod.

He placed his hand over hers, still on the lapel, and lifted back the side. "You sewed, 'I love you, Marcus.'" His gaze stuck to the words that had nearly shattered him earlier. He'd never experienced such hope and loss at the same time. Hope for the feelings he'd prayed she still had. Loss for all the time that had slipped between them. Though she'd written that message a while ago, could he and Clara build from where they'd left off before the war?

"I did." Her voice turned sad.

"I never saw it." He lowered to look into her eyes, but those beautiful blue-greens were downcast. "Believe me, if I had, things would've been different between us."

Her lashes lifted. "They would've?"

He dropped his touch from hers, giving her space. "I thought it was all one-sided."

"Truly?" The natural pout of her lower lip enticed him, especially as it tugged into a fragile smile. "You never let on. I thought I was taking a huge risk declaring my feelings. And then when I found the jacket back in Desmond's closet, I thought you rejected me."

"No." He shook his head. "I never let on because Desmond said he'd pummel me if I ever messed with your heart. He was serious. He may be my best friend, but he's a protective older brother. As for the jacket, like I said. I didn't know about it. I only had Desmond hold it for me while I went off to the army. I knew I wouldn't need it, since I'd be mostly in uniform, and didn't want it to get ruined." The Westlakes had bought him the coat; it was the finest thing he'd ever owned.

Her brow quirked. "You charmed Liesl into getting it, didn't you?" Then as if realizing the answer, she laughed. "No wonder she acted so strangely. She practically sat on her handbag. Now I realize she was hiding it from me."

"It's for the best, I assure you. Because there was another reason I wanted the jacket. I needed to compare your stitches to this." He withdrew that special scrap of fabric. The one he'd carried since that night he'd almost died. He held it up for her to see in the slice of moonlight. "This was sewn into my rock suit."

Her hand flew to her parted mouth.

She'd sewn, "Psalm 91:11." When she'd mentioned last week about sewing camouflage suits for snipers, he'd wondered if she'd been the one who'd sewn his. It wasn't until she'd spoken about the message left in his jacket that he'd started putting it all together. The letters *a, l, m,* and *s* were a perfect match. The Scripture read: "For he shall give his angels charge over thee, to keep thee in all thy ways." The Lord had kept him.

"You put that promise, that verse, in my camouflage suit." His eyes stung. "Just like the jacket, I didn't realize it was there until after the fact. I was lying on a hospital cot in France, and one of the nurses showed me. Since then, I've held this piece of cloth as a reminder of God's promises, his goodness. And now I get the honor of thanking you for this prayer." He cupped her face with his good hand. "Thank you, Clara."

Tears streamed down her face. He thumbed them away.

"God has given me another chance at life. And this time, I don't want to let it slip away." He put his heart out there. "Clara, I know I'm not the same man you once knew. I'm damaged, and—"

She pressed her lips to his, shocking him into silence.

Her hands twined around his neck as her body pressed close. Her mouth lingered on his for a heart-pounding second, then she broke the kiss, her eyes beautiful and glassy. She took his hand, his injured one. He couldn't feel her tender touch as she traced his scars or the warm press of her lips as she gently kissed his marred flesh. She valued brokenness, and his heart almost detonated.

She pressed his hand to her cheek. "Don't you dare doubt yourself, Marcus Reeves."

All restraint snapped. He kissed her like a soldier returning from war, like a man who'd been given a precious gift. He may not have the use of his right hand, but he could use both arms. And with them, he crushed her to him.

Normally, Clara wasn't impulsive. She wasn't a risk-taker. But this moment, she was both, and she couldn't even apologize for it. Because she was kissing Marcus Reeves. Well, now he was kissing her. What she'd initially started, he'd taken over with delicious fervency. Her hands skimmed the tops of his thick shoulders, then climbed his neck to frame his face. Her palms scraped the stubble, taking in the cut of his strong jawline as he kissed her.

In this moment she'd never felt more whole. He'd worn the camouflage suit she'd sewn. He'd worn her prayer day after day. And God had brought him back to her. She clung to him tighter.

He gently broke away, his gaze on her. "I better get you back to your apartment." He pressed his lips to her forehead. "Your father might retract his job offer if he finds me out here kissing his daughter."

Her father would be elated, but that wasn't what caught her attention. "He offered you a position." She knew he would.

"Helping secure his warehouses."

Not only a position but one in which Marcus would excel. She knew it would be something that would benefit him. Her parents loved Marcus. It seemed it was in Westlake blood to adore him.

"Are you going to take it?" she asked.

"I have a lot to consider." He wrapped his arm around her, lending warmth. "Even more so now."

By his possessive hold and his tender tone, she was involved in the equation.

Her gaze strayed to the starless night. Ebony clouds blocked any heavenly sparkle, but she didn't need romantic skies or dreamy moonlight. She had everything she wanted right here.

Marcus pressed something against her hand. The swatch of fabric from the camouflage suit.

Her gaze met his warm one. "I can't believe you kept this." Not only kept it but carried it with him.

"I want you to hang on to it." He curled her fingers around it and brushed his lips over her closed hand. "I leave it to your keeping. Same with my heart."

Then he kissed her again.

CHAPTER 9

THE HOUR HAD been late by the time they'd finished talking—and kissing—and talking some more. Marcus offered to escort Clara to her apartment, but she decided to stay the night in her old room. He had to admit, he liked having her only down the hall from him rather than across the city.

Mr. and Mrs. Westlake had been surprised to find their daughter at the breakfast table, but Clara had quickly explained she'd needed to retrieve something from the house late the previous night. Not entirely a lie. She had *intended* to confiscate his jacket. She'd taken his heart instead. Though he didn't think her parents bought the story, considering the curious glances they tossed between Clara and him.

Clara had then left to return to her apartment to get ready for work, and he spent the day scouring newspapers, searching for any hint about the words Clara overheard at the park. He'd found nothing.

So here they now were, seated around a small table at a local restaurant. He'd been prepared to tackle the mystery behind the German gentlemen, but her enamoring eyes pulled his mind in other directions. "You can't keep looking like that," he teased, even as he dropped his green beans onto her plate.

Her mouth lifted in surprised pleasure. Growing up, he'd always given her his portion of green beans. Now that he was older, he'd developed a palette for them, but he'd gladly sacrifice all his dinner if only to earn her smile. Besides, it wasn't as if they'd had a lot of options this evening. This restaurant had once offered a variety of meals, but because of rationing, their menu was sparse. However, Marcus would welcome organ meats and vegetables over the gelatin-soaked corned beef and hard biscuits served in the trenches.

"I always look like this." Clara tossed him a saucy smile. She wore a pale-purple dress that made her complexion appear extra soft. The sunshine she'd been forced to work in all day had enhanced a spray of freckles across her nose, tempting him to skim his lips over them.

He shook his head. This wasn't working. "I'm referencing the *way* you're looking at me. It makes me want to kiss you senseless, which would interfere with the purpose of this dinner."

She huffed a laugh. "I suppose there will be time for that later." Her expression turned playful. "Hopefully."

If he had anything to do with it, there would be. But as a military man, he recognized her stall tactic. They'd originally planned this meeting to strategize about what she'd heard in the park. Though now he believed they should ease into the conversation, because she'd been purposefully avoiding the topic. Perhaps she still felt foolish about it, thinking she'd made a big deal out of nothing.

His gut agreed with her original instinct.

There was something off about the exchange she'd overheard, and he'd help her figure it out. Yes, she'd been hesitant to discuss anything this evening, but all this week, she'd been striving to piece together the puzzle involving those men's words. It was significant to her. And if it was important to her, it was for him as well. First, he needed to just get her talking. Before this flirtatious moment between them, she'd been on the quiet side. He could guess why. "How'd the painting go today?"

"We hoped to get it all done so we wouldn't have to paint on Sunday, but it didn't work out that way." Her gaze fell to her plate of liver and onions. "We need to finish tomorrow, because the city is preparing for the parade and . . . other events. It's been nothing short of chaos over there."

"I was surprised at how much is planned." From what he'd read in the papers, the loan drive involved not only parades but vaudeville performances and lots of speeches. General Pershing's retired squadron was to march at the rally as well as a regiment from France known as the "Blue

Devils." Why all these French soldiers were currently on US soil and not overseas, he couldn't understand. Because last time he'd checked, the Allies needed every resource available to fight against the enemy.

But he didn't believe the loan drive was to blame for Clara's subdued mood, rather *who* would be participating. He wasn't one to talk about feelings. That particular topic had always sent him running, but he'd learned a vital lesson from battle: he had to visit the dark spaces of his soul in order to carry the light to it.

"Are you okay about Monday?" Marcus asked. "Meeting that Winsell guy again?"

Her gaze snapped to his, as if surprised he'd brought up the subject. Granted, Marcus wasn't exactly thrilled at the idea of Clara being near America's favorite leading man, but she was strong and capable of handling herself. And if, by any chance, she held feelings for the dirty swine, it was best to know now. Fame and fortune were a challenging duo to beat, but if this dandy thought Marcus would surrender gracefully for the treasure of her heart, the man had another think coming.

She took a sip of her water and carefully set it down, the glass tabletop slightly clinking. Another touch of the war. New linens were hard to come by, and so many restaurants preserved their tablecloths by topping every surface with glass. "I won't pretend I wasn't shocked to see his name in the headlines. That life I lived in California seems so different compared to here."

He nodded his understanding. He'd left France only several weeks ago, which oddly seemed like yesterday and yet a lifetime away.

"I'd rather not see him, but I'm much stronger than I was." She gave a smile. "I also was alone out there. Here in New York, I have support."

"You assuredly have that."

Her eyes sparkled with her smile. "Now back to business. Do you think we can come up with something new? I told you everything I remember about that day in the park."

He took a bite of potatoes, taking an extra second to think. "Maybe let's revisit that conversation between the men. I want you to tell me everything again. It may feel insignificant to you, but say it anyway."

She nodded. "I was lying on the ground, testing the latest camouflage suit. A couple came and were being . . . amorous."

He smiled at her blush.

"Then they moved on. But then I heard something again. I thought perhaps the couple returned, but the footsteps were heavy, manly ones. Come to think of it"—she lowered her fork—"there was a shuffling sound, almost as if the gentleman was dragging something along." She shook her head. "That's strange. I completely forgot about that noise until now."

She was remembering new things. A good sign. "A shuffling sound. That can be significant." He toyed with the edges of his napkin. "Then what?"

"They began speaking in another language. I recognized it as German. It took me a second to catch on, because I was distracted by their tone. It was scheming."

This he understood. How often had he been sent over to catch information by spying on the enemy? Most of the time, he hadn't been able to get close, but on the few occasions he had, he'd been able to understand their conniving words. Though Clara may not have a full grasp of the language, she'd no doubt be able to judge a lot by their inflections. "And the words you caught?"

He grabbed the pen and notepad he'd stashed in his pocket earlier. He'd finally broken the habit of trying to reach things with his right hand. He wasn't adept at using his left, but he'd made a lot of progress. He held the notepad out to her. "If you would, write the words down. I think it helps to see them."

So she did. "I heard *four* and *April*. *Attack* and *island*." Her lips pressed together in a grimace. "That's not much, is it?"

"It's better than nothing." He glanced at the list, trying to mentally sort all the pieces. "Since nothing that we know of occurred on April fourth, maybe the *four* means something else."

Clara fumbled her fork. "There was another word. It sounded like *angry* . . . No, that wasn't it." She fixed her serious gaze on him. "Oh yes, it sounded like *stern*. One of the German fellows said *stern*."

This took things to a different level. "Are you sure?"

She closed her eyes and thought for a moment, as if revisiting every-thing. "Yes. It was right after the word *four.*"

Snippets of newspaper articles rolled to the front of his mind, clink-ing into place with this new information, even as dread built within him. "Clara?"

Her brows lifted. "Hmm?"

"The *four* was never a date at all."

"No?"

He shook his head. "It was their target."

"What do you mean?"

"*Sterne* means 'stars.'" He leaned closer. "The four stars."

{-※-}

Her mouth flopped open. Not her best look, but Marcus's words stunned her. Mary Pickford, Douglas Fairbanks, Charlie Chaplin, and Ben Win-sell. She'd seen the headline this morning while walking to work. They were called the Great Four. Why hadn't she made the connection? Mostly because . . . "The island." She shook her head. "I was so focused on think-ing the attack was on an island, because I'd overheard the word *Insel.*" Her breath caught. "It could very well have been *Winsell.* It all happened so fast."

His forehead creased with a frown. "I think we should consider this seriously."

"The city is preparing for the crowds. They expect thousands will be in the streets."

"Which would make for a horrific attack."

Attack. That was another word she'd known for sure she'd heard. Her stomach knotted. "Those film stars are so widely popular." Douglas Fair-banks and Mary Pickford were household names. And Clara knew first-hand how the public prized Ben Winsell. Add in the famous Charlie Chaplin, and they had the country's biggest icons. "If the Germans suc-ceeded in assassinating these stars, the impact would spread from coast to coast."

He exhaled. "Which is probably the objective."

"But how does targeting movie stars benefit them?" She shook her head. "One would think the enemy would go after political leaders or generals." Those who made crucial decisions regarding the war.

"Snipers aim to take down the most important target. These stars represent the heart of America. The public is more interested in their lives than any politician's." Marcus's eyes narrowed. "Take them down, and it crushes our morale. An attack on our homeland would frighten Americans into believing they aren't safe, not even on their own soil."

"The event is in two days. What can we do?"

Marcus's jaw tightened. "We stop them."

CHAPTER 10

THE FOLLOWING MORNING Marcus sat across from the chief of police at a New York City precinct. His superior had secured this meeting, and Marcus knew that Chief Wallace's time wasn't given too freely. Especially on a Sunday.

Marcus had arrived only seconds ago and had been surprised to be led into a modest conference room rather than an office. Though he'd discovered the reason quick enough, for there were two other men present. These gentlemen weren't in uniform but nicely tailored suits.

Chief Wallace spoke first. "My good friend Major Palmer speaks highly of you, Captain Reeves. I want to thank you for your service to our country." The man had thinning red hair and ice-blue eyes hovering over a crooked nose and boxy jaw.

Marcus acknowledged with a nod. "I appreciate you agreeing to meet with me."

"Before we begin"—Chief Wallace gestured to the other men seated across from him—"I'd like to introduce you to Bennie Zeldman and Carlyle Robinson. They are the publicists for Douglas Fairbanks and Charlie Chaplin."

Ah, they were here on behalf of their famous employers. Though how much the major had shared regarding the imminent threat, Marcus was uncertain.

The chief continued. "They've the privilege of traveling ahead of the actors, making sure all is ready for them once they arrive." His voice tightened on the word *privilege*, as if he considered that sort of job a drudgery.

They all exchanged greetings. No one dared to shake Marcus's hand, which clued him in that Major Palmer must've informed the chief of Marcus's injury.

Marcus couldn't think of a smoother way other than the frank truth to transition the conversation to the more pressing issue. "I thought it important to make you aware there's a possible threat on the four celebrities hosting the Liberty Loan drive. A conversation planning an attack has been overheard."

Everyone was silent for a beat. The publicists exchanged looks. Their fidgety mannerisms didn't hint at overwhelming shock, but their raised brows revealed they hadn't been made privy to this information.

The police chief leaned back on his seat and clasped his hands over his belly. "Is your source reliable?"

Marcus nodded. "I wouldn't be wasting your time otherwise." He watched a myriad of expressions splay across all their faces.

Mr. Robinson tapped the table. "I can't say I'm surprised. The loan drive has gained national attention. We'd been in Chicago and Washington, DC, and the crowds were unprecedented. Which is wonderful for the sale of bonds but a headache to prepare for."

The police chief grunted in assent. "Do you know the celebrities' itinerary?"

Mr. Zeldman cleared his throat. "They arrive by train midmorning. They'll speak at rallies in uptown and midtown, then will spend the rest of the time on Wall Street in front of the Sub-Treasury Building."

Marcus fought against a grimace. With the actors traveling all over the city, it would be almost impossible to secure every area. There were just too many hiding spots.

From his jacket pocket, Chief Wallace withdrew a notepad and flipped it open. "Officers are ready to handle the crowds on Wall Street." He mumbled a number. Probably a head count of police on patrol, but Marcus couldn't quite catch it before the chief spoke again. "I've got men from two stations at my disposal to secure the area where the actors will be."

Marcus grimaced. That wouldn't cut it. "With my experience, sir, it's fair to say it only takes one bullet. Sniper rifles can be accurate up to a thousand yards, meaning an assassin can perch practically anywhere—tops of buildings, high windows, any spot they can get a clear shot."

The chief nodded. "There's no disagreement from me. With crowds of twenty thousand, it's easy to blend in."

Too easy. "And we're only talking about snipers. We can't overlook other means of attack, such as utilizing explosives."

The other two gentlemen paled. No doubt, this was a publicist's nightmare.

The chief closed his notepad with a heavy exhale. "We're going to have our hands full controlling crowds. Before you came, Mr. Zeldman informed me of an incident in Salt Lake City. Apparently, when the actors arrived, a mob overwhelmed the train station and rushed their car. We can only imagine what could happen here." His tired eyes filled with resignation. "We'll do our best, but I can't guarantee complete coverage, since the four celebrities are going to be all over Manhattan."

"What else can be done other than canceling the tour?" Mr. Zeldman's nervous gaze bounced between Chief Wallace and Marcus.

"We're not canceling." The chief's tone was firm. "Or postponing. Too much effort has been put into this. And while we take this threat seriously, we aren't fully certain an attack is planned."

Marcus could understand the chief's reasoning. He was basing this solely on Marcus's word.

"Captain Reeves, what if I pull together some officers from other precincts? Just for this security cover. I can possibly get you forty more men, who will defer to you."

Marcus blinked. Forty men in less than a day's notice? "Is that possible?"

"Son, if they know what's good for them, they'll report to you at 7:00 a.m. tomorrow." Chief Wallace's lips twitched. "Now, as for my secretary, who's in charge of making the calls? I might need to get her flowers."

Marcus had to devise a plan. This wasn't unlike no-man's-land. In France, Marcus had to stay alert, because a machine gun nest could be anywhere. The only differences here were, he didn't know the enemy and there would be thousands of innocent civilians milling about. But something stirred within him, something that had been deadened since he'd almost lost his life. It was the desire to rise to meet a challenge, to move with purpose. And just like back in the field, a strategy surged to the front of his mind. "Let me tell you how I intend to keep those actors safe."

Marcus was up hours before dawn, poring over the route the four movie stars would be traveling. Before he'd left the meeting yesterday, he'd studied the times and directions they'd be moving, then he'd walked it. He'd mapped it out—which had been a challenge to sketch with his left hand—and identified key places an attack could happen.

Restaurants, department stores, a few hotels, and a whole host of boutiques lined the route. He'd ensured with the chief that the officers on patrol in those areas spoke to the proprietors and managers, cautioning them to be diligent and keep an eye out for suspicious activity, and if they happened to see anything unusual, to report it immediately.

The pinch in his gut this morning alerted him that something remained off. So he did what he'd always done when conflicted. He prayed. By the time he said, "Amen," a knock rapped on his bedroom door.

Probably Mr. Westlake.

He was due to leave on a business trip, but Marcus hadn't known the older man had intended to go so early. What if he demanded an answer about the job before he left? Marcus remained uncertain about which position to take. Well, honestly, over the past two days, he'd been focused on the Liberty Loan event, hardly sparing a thought for anything else.

He opened the door, ready to request more time, but it wasn't the father standing before him but the daughter. His lips arced in a growing smile. "If you keep coming to my room when it's dark out, I'll consider it my duty to propose to save your reputation."

She feebly swatted him, then grabbed his wrist and tugged him into the hall. "I couldn't sleep." The faint circles beneath her eyes confirmed her story. "What do you think? Do you feel everything will be okay?"

He'd visited her after the meeting with Chief Wallace and informed her of the plan. "I'm to meet with the extra patrol at seven." Less than an hour. "I think we're as prepared as we can be for such short notice." He shifted closer. "Though I can't say I'm comfortable with you participating in the unveiling, I did inspect the booth last night. Thankfully, everything is clear on that front."

Her head reared back. "How did you check it? It's hidden by boards."

"I moved them." It wasn't difficult to unhinge the temporary wall, but it proved challenging maneuvering the slabs of wood with only one working hand. He'd put extra strain on his left side, which accounted for his soreness. But Clara's safety was paramount. "Maybe you shouldn't go. I'm sure Lieutenant Towle would understand."

Her chin notched higher. "I'm going."

He had a feeling she'd be determined, but he wanted to deter her nonetheless. "Is there any way I can convince you?" He dipped his head, peering into her eyes. "I can be pretty persuasive when I try to be."

She kissed him. "I know you can, but if you're going to be there, I am too." She tucked her head against his shoulder. "Besides, we're not certain something will happen today. We could've gotten it wrong like we did with the restaurant."

Possible. But this lead was much more conclusive. "You're supposed to be at the Sub-Treasury Building at noon, right?"

"No, it got changed to eleven, because we couldn't put the tarp over the booth yesterday." She shrugged. "The paint was still wet."

A familiar tension built behind his eyes. Only this time, he couldn't physically combat it. Like Major Palmer so unhelpfully pointed out, Marcus couldn't pull a trigger. But this was where his faith stepped in. In his weakness, God's strength was made perfect. Feeling more confident, he kissed the top of Clara's head. "Just promise you'll stay alert and aware of your surroundings."

She eased back to look at him. "I promise."

He held her tight, only to let her go a moment later.

It was time to face the day.

CHAPTER 11

THIS WAS CHAOS.

Marcus shook his head to regain clarity. He'd arrived early to prep his men, but the crowds had already started forming. People poured in from every direction for the uptown rally.

He had to think like a sniper. He had to figure out where the best positions would be to make the perfect shot, and at those locations, he stationed officers. With that taken care of, he set up lookout posts around the raised platform. This stage was nowhere near as massive as the one at the Sub-Treasury Building, but it would be heavily guarded all the same. And if the tension roiling in him wasn't great enough, add in several long-suffering conversations with two nervous publicists worrying about their famous clients. Famous clients who were completely oblivious to the potential threat.

He felt it somewhat a disservice not to inform the four celebrities of a possible attack, but he wouldn't overstep his superior's orders. Marcus would do the best he could with what he was given. But as the fans kept flooding in, more and more pressure piled upon his shoulders. On top of that, he couldn't keep his thoughts from straying to Clara. He'd see her after the parade, for the final event in Lower Manhattan, but every minute seemed to triple in length. He was ready for this day to be over and Clara, safe in his arms.

Boisterous cheering yanked him from his thoughts. The four celebrities—Douglas Fairbanks, Charlie Chaplin, Mary Pickford, and Ben Winsell—took the stage. Marcus's senses snapped to full alert. As much as his masculine pride wanted to take in Winsell's measure, he hadn't time for petty jealousy. He had a job to complete. So while the famous quartet smiled and waved to rousing, deafening applause, Marcus's vigilant gaze scanned the surrounding area.

Movement to the front caught his attention. The crowd pressed against the patrolmen, who pushed back, straining to keep the raving fans behind the designated line. A few stragglers broke through, intent on charging the stage. Marcus darted that direction. If he reached the steps first, he could block their advance. He gripped a day stick in his left hand but sincerely hoped the situation wouldn't turn aggressive. Thankfully, other officers caught up to the rogue fans and forced them back into the crowd.

Marcus shook his head, his pulse pounding.

This was going to be a long day.

Clara had eaten breakfast with her parents, then taken the underground transit to Lower Manhattan. Her thoughts spun about what this day would bring. Was Marcus safe? She hated the idea of his being in the thick of everything. By now the parade would've paused at midtown for another rally, only to resume and carry the actors to the last event at the Sub-Treasury Building. What if an attack happened and Marcus got injured? Or worse? Her stomach clenched. It would all be her fault. She'd been the one who'd placed the man she adored in danger.

She paused on the sidewalk, scraping in a steady breath, waiting for her riotous heartbeat to calm.

She couldn't permit herself to get worked up. If she allowed fear's claws to sink into her reasoning, she'd be of no help to Marcus. It was important for her to remain guarded and alert. She'd promised Marcus as much.

Which also meant she couldn't think about coming face-to-face with Ben. The dread climbing her spine would just have to make itself comfortable, because she didn't have time to address that either. She forced her feet faster and didn't slow her pace until her soles hit Wall Street.

Her breath whooshed out at the frenzied sight. The area was bustling with activity. Workers from the event committee—wearing red-white-and-blue sashes—zipped about in every direction. But what made her shoulders lower in relief was all the patrolmen. They threaded the crowd of retired soldiers, camoufleurs, and other volunteers preparing for the event. Surely no one would attempt an attack with all this security. Embracing hope, Clara made her way toward the Sub-Treasury Building.

The crowds would soon make their way here, following the parade. So they'd better make quick work of putting the tarps . . .

Her gaze stalled on the fully covered booth.

The tarps were already in place. Was she late? She glanced at the watch pin attached to her uniform jacket. No, she was five minutes early. Maybe she'd misheard the reporting time.

She spotted several of the camoufleurs gathered around. Her tardiness, even if by mistake, was no excuse for leaving the work to the other women. Clara jogged to meet them, maneuvering around the wooden barriers that separated the booth from the general public.

Constance smiled at her approach. "Everything's all finished."

"I see that. I'm sorry for being late. For some reason, I thought I'd heard to be here by eleven."

"No, you're right. I got here only a few minutes ago with the others." She shrugged. "The tarps were already up. He told us the event committee wanted it all done before the crowds came."

Clara raised a brow. "Who's he?"

"Officer Handsome over there." Constance jerked a thumb at a patrolman standing by the covered booth like a sentinel. "The bonds are already inside. Apparently, the committee thought it best to have everything ready before the tarps went up, so the bonds can be sold right after the unveiling. Which is why he's on guard."

Made sense. It would be awful for someone to steal all the bonds. And having said bonds readily available the second the unveiling happened would only increase efficiency. No waiting around for someone to come and stock the booth.

"Since we're free now, I've got an idea!" Constance grabbed Clara's wrist and tugged her toward the Sub-Treasury Building.

Clara shuffled her feet to keep from toppling at her friend's unexpected pull. "But the parade is that way." Most of the camoufleurs were already heading toward the corner of Broadway and Wall Street. The caravan of festivities was to travel from the midtown rally to here, where the final event would commence.

"Those floats all look the same." Constance glanced over her shoulder and rolled her eyes. "It's a genius plan. While everyone else is watching the end of the parade, we can grab a spot by the Sub-Treasury's steps for the show."

Clara almost stumbled. She was already near enough to the stage for her own comfort. "Can't we watch from here?" The platform stood only about ten feet away. Though with the height of it, Clara had to be on her tiptoes to get a good glimpse, and even then, it was from the side. "We'll be away from the crowd." And Clara could duck behind the booth and hide from her former flame until she absolutely had to face him for the unveiling.

"This angle is terrible. And I doubt the patrolmen would let us linger on the ramp." There was a narrow incline so people could go on and off the stage. "No, I want to be so close that I can count Douglas Fairbanks's eyelashes."

"Isn't there anything else that needs done?" She resorted to pleading.

"Well . . ." Constance flashed a smile. "We could spend time chatting with handsome patrolmen."

That wouldn't do either. Not only did Clara hold zero interest in any man besides Marcus, but Constance couldn't be distracting the officers. They needed to focus on keeping the area safe. Of course, the younger camoufleur hadn't a clue about a possible attack, so it was up to Clara to keep her friend away from the patrolmen. Her sigh leaked out slowly. "Let's go with your first idea and find a spot near the front steps."

Constance bounced on her heels like a child promised candy. They waited for the patrolmen to allow them through the blockaded area and entered the main space, where the masses would soon flood.

Maybe a place by the action was wisest. Clara could keep a better eye on things. Not like she had a choice, with Constance practically yanking Clara's arm out of its socket. Clara watched several members of the event committee adding the final touches. She marveled again at the whole spectacle. The platform was indeed enormous. It made a U-shape around the treasury steps where a giant statue of George Washington stood. A gigantic banner saying "Get into the Fight, Buy Liberty Bonds" hung from the roof, spanning the row of white pillars. And of course, off to the left and slightly below sat their humble booth. The canvas-covered box seemed out of place beside all the grandeur.

Time crawled. Sunshine pressed upon her, making her wish her uniform was breathable cotton rather than suffocating wool. Constance chattered away, even while Clara glanced about. What should she search for? She was uncertain, but she held true to her promise to Marcus.

Finally, the faint hum of marching music reached her ears. A retired infantry band was to lead the procession, which meant the parade was moving closer. Within minutes, people swarmed in like bees. It was dizzying how quickly the space packed full.

Those guiding the floats had been instructed to remain on Broadway, allowing the one carrying the four actors to pass through, en route to the stage. The moving platform, drawn by a team of horses and wrapped in patriotic bunting, came into view. Clara's pulse leaped. The celebrities gathered at the other end of the float, their backs to Clara, waving at the crowd. But what caught Clara's focus was the uniformed man behind them.

Marcus.

His fierce gaze swept over the masses. His jaw locked in determination. He stood only a yard from Ben, and Clara couldn't help but note their differences. Marcus's dark eyes and hair were stark contrasts to Ben's fair looks. Both were handsome, but only one had stolen her heart.

As if hearing her inner thoughts, Marcus peered her direction, spotting her immediately. His eyes roved over her as if ensuring she was okay. She gave an encouraging smile, which he returned. After a nod, he resumed scanning the area.

With a patrolman's help, the actors filed off the float and onto the stage.

"Oh, they look so glamorous!" Constance sighed. "Except Charlie doesn't have his mustache."

Clara couldn't help her smile. Charlie's mustache was all part of his act. Only makeup. It never failed to amuse her how people took the things on the silver screen as facts for real life.

The actors walked toward center stage, but Mary Pickford happened to glance over, her focus snagging on Clara. The young actress switched direction, heading down the stairs. Douglas followed, probably to provide extra protection. Two officers also trailed behind.

"Clara!" Mary reached the steps and leaned across the partition, then pulled Clara into an embrace.

The crowd pressed in, knocking Clara's stomach into the wooden barrier. Several people waved notepads in the air and screamed for an autograph. But Mary just hugged Clara as if they were greeting each other in the foyer of Clara's home rather than the cramped steps.

"Hello, Mary," she replied when the actress finally released her. Clara had worked with the young woman on only one film, but it was nice to be remembered. "It's good to see you." And it was. But it was *not* good that Ben now looked their way . . . and locked eyes with her.

She angled away and almost smacked her face on someone's shoulder. She shifted more toward Constance.

Mary's gaze skimmed Clara's uniform. "I saw your name on the itinerary for the booth unveiling and hoped it was you. I love that you're using your talents for the war effort." It was no wonder why America loved Mary. She had that personality that always made others feel valued, speaking to everyone as if they were her close friends. She had the same effect in front of the camera. And no doubt, she was using that magnetic charm to encourage the masses to purchase Liberty Loans.

"Thank you." Clara smiled, even as a gentleman behind her begged Mary for a kiss. "I'm happy to do my part."

Douglas approached. Though Clara had never worked with him, he nodded at her with a friendly grin. Poor Constance seemed very close to swooning, whether from fright because of pushy fans or headiness from Douglas's nearness, Clara was uncertain. Either way, she linked her arm around her friend's.

As if sensing the surging excitement from the crowd, Douglas gently wrapped his hand around Mary's elbow and led her back up the stairs to rejoin the others. Ben whispered something in Mary's ear, then shot another glance at Clara.

She only notched her chin higher. She had nothing to be ashamed of. Ben offered a small smile, one that appeared suspiciously like regret.

But she didn't have time or the willingness to decode it, because Marcus moved in front of her. His presence was both a comfort and thrilling jolt.

"How's it going?" she asked as he reached across the barrier and took her hand. "There're a lot of people here." More than she'd ever seen. Living in the city, she was accustomed to massive crowds. But this? She'd never glimpsed this many people stuffed onto the streets. It was almost suffocating.

He nodded. "We just need to get through the next two hours." He leaned in, and his lips brushed her temple. "Keep safe."

She pulled back so she could see his eyes. "You too."

Marcus gently squeezed her hand, then he jogged to the other side of the stairway and briefly conversed with the patrolmen stationed there.

"You never said a word!" Constance practically shouted in her ear.

Clara blinked. "About what?" Marcus's caution still nestled in her mind. Even though Constance must've heard it, her friend couldn't have deduced anything about the threat.

"You know famous people!" There was unmerited wonder in her voice.

Clara understood the starry feelings. She'd felt that giddy rush when she'd first landed the job in Hollywood, though she'd been quickly disillusioned.

All she could offer was a friendly nod, because the brass band started playing "Goodbye Broadway, Hello France."

The rally was officially underway.

CHAPTER 12

THE ACTORS INTRODUCED themselves, then welcomed a traveling vaudeville group onto the stage to sing a patriotic medley. The next half hour progressed smoothly, but with each passing minute, Clara's nerves pinched tighter. She lost sight of Marcus but knew he was somewhere close, casing the vicinity for danger. After the four movie stars performed a skit alluding to how the sale of Liberty Loans helped the war, the governor took command of the rally and gave a lengthy speech.

Clara glanced at her watch pin. "We need to get back to the booth."

"Actually"—Constance didn't pull her gaze from the celebrities—"it's only *you* who's needed for the unveiling."

So much for moral support.

With a sigh Clara turned from the stage. It would be quicker to cut through the platform, since the newly painted booth stood adjacent. But of course, she wouldn't take that route. Instead, she worked her way through the crowd. By the time the officers let her through to the booth, her foot had been stepped on twice and her uniform cap knocked askew.

According to the schedule, after the governor's speech, the four celebrities were each supposed to give an inspirational talk, inviting everyone to purchase bonds. Then the unveiling would be last.

Ben strode to the front of the platform, megaphone in hand. He wore a tailored suit, his blond curls tamed into submission. He had that kind of sunny charm that most women wanted to bask in, but Clara had witnessed his darker side. Though she'd tried, she couldn't get him the help he needed. He'd refused to accept he had a problem. His craving for alcohol had blinded him from seeing the destruction his addiction created. It'd ruined any chance of a future between them.

She shook her head. It wasn't worth revisiting. She was free of that lifestyle, free of him. Though presently she wasn't exactly free of him, considering he pivoted on the stage, hustled down the incline, and walked directly toward her booth.

Wait. Had they changed the schedule? Ben was listed first to speak. But instead of his giving a motivational spiel, Douglas Fairbanks took center stage, opening his act by doing gymnastics, prompting thunderous applause.

Clara pretended to be enthralled with Doug's antics and ignored Ben's approach.

"Hello, Clara." His voice, usually bulging with confidence, was hesitant. "It's been a while."

Not long enough. "Hello." She spared him a glance. He was thinner than when she'd last seen him. His pale-green eyes were red-rimmed, noting his exhaustion. Understandable, considering the four of them had been touring the country, traveling from rally to rally. Or perhaps his bloodshot gaze could be blamed on his addiction. It was difficult to tell with him.

He cleared his throat. "It's good to see you."

She wouldn't return the sentiment. Instead, she gave a small dip of her chin to acknowledge him. She wasn't completely ill-mannered.

"When Mary told me you were here for the unveiling, I ... uh ... felt it would be a good time to apologize."

She eyed him skeptically. It wasn't like Ben to admit any wrong.

He tapped a fast rhythm on the edge of the megaphone. "I'm sorry for how I treated you. I should've stood up for you, but instead, I looked after myself."

She opened her mouth to say something, but he continued.

"You see." His lips pressed together, then broke apart on a quiet sigh. "I thought you turned your back on me first."

Ah, there it was. Of course he'd manage to make it all her fault. She shoved down the rising ire. There was no chance she'd let this man have any more control over her emotions. "How?" Her tone held surprisingly even. "I've done nothing to you."

"You confronted me about . . . my drinking."

He no doubt viewed that as a personal attack. "Ben, I had only your health in mind. Your drinking was getting out of hand." A definite understatement. He'd been able to hide his addiction well for a time, but it finally caught up to him. He arrived on set reeking of alcohol. Then he missed lines or slurred them together. Not to mention the time he stumbled and nearly fell through the set wall. "I just wanted to help you."

"I know. I see that now." He ran a hand through his hair. "You're the only one who was brave enough to say anything about it, and I pushed you away."

She didn't know what to say. He was right. He had blocked her out, but she hadn't exactly handed over her heart either. She'd withheld her affection, partly because of her lingering love for Marcus, but also due to her wariness about Ben's addiction. "I'm sorry I made you feel like I was against you. That wasn't my intention."

"After you left, I realized my mistake. I'm sorry for everything." He scratched the back of his neck. "I've been getting help like you suggested."

"I'm glad to hear it." And she was. She'd seen others go down that road and sabotage everything, especially themselves. Ben had a bright future if he kept away from the bottle. "Apology accepted." Now that they'd both said their piece, there wasn't anything else to be addressed. "I won't hold you up since you have a speech to do." Hopefully he'd take the hint and return to the stage.

He adopted a casual stance, as if preparing to remain awhile. "I'm staying here for the unveiling. We . . . uh, switched things up. We're going to feature the loan booth next."

What? "Does Marcus know this?"

His blond brows lowered. "Who's Marcus?"

Surely the actors had been warned about the possible threat, hadn't they? Marcus had even joined them on the parade float. Had no one said a word? From Ben's oblivious expression, perhaps not. "Why is the unveiling now?"

"It was Doug's idea. In Chicago, Mary was speaking and drummed up a lot of sales even during her talk. He thought it'd be a good idea to try that again. She's even decided to auction off a lock of her hair. The place is going to go nuts."

No question. And with the masses in an excited uproar, what better time for the enemy to strike?

Clara frantically searched the crowd for Marcus. He needed to be informed of the change in plans. While she was looking, someone else came into view—an older woman holding a crate filled with . . . Liberty Loans?

"About what I said," Ben continued, but Clara's attention was on the approaching woman. "I feel awful for the way things were left between us."

"It's all in the past now." Clara moved to brush past him, but he stepped in front of her.

"It doesn't have to be."

She glanced over his shoulder, keeping the woman in sight while trying to register what Ben had said. He couldn't mean what she'd thought. "Ben, it's not a—"

"Come back to California with me. I'll tell everyone you were right, that Allen stole your designs, your ideas. You'll be vindicated. You'll get your job back." His voice softened. "And we'll be together."

That was not the life she wanted. *He* was not what she wanted. If he'd been that devastated about betraying her, why hadn't he already spoken up in her defense? It had been several months since the incident; the man had had plenty of time. Again, she couldn't get wrapped up in the past, because the present demanded her full attention. "Ben, we're not right for each other. But I do wish you the best and every happiness."

His expression slacked, abject shock widening his eyes. Obvious signs he wasn't expecting a rejection. But she capitalized on his surprise, stepping around his stunned body and rushing toward the lady clutching the box of loans. "Hi there." She met the older woman's dark eyes. "I see you have the bonds. Are those for replacement in case we sell out?"

She shook her head. "No, these are to go in there." She glanced over at that tarp-covered booth. "I was instructed to hold on to them until the time of the unveiling."

Wait. "Who told you this?" Because according to Constance the loans were already in the booth.

The wrinkles framing the older woman's mouth deepened. "One of the policemen. He said the event committee thought it unwise to leave the bonds unattended."

No, no, no.

The stories didn't match. A patrolman had told Constance he'd been assigned to watch over the booth, because the bonds were inside. Now this woman said an officer cautioned her *not* to put the bonds in the booth until after the unveiling. Which was it?

The hairs on the back of her neck stood. Something wasn't adding up. Her gaze darted. And where was that officer now? "The man you spoke with. The policeman. Can you describe him for me?" Was the patrolman who'd instructed this lady to hold back the bonds the same one who'd spoken with Constance? All Clara could remember was he had light hair. She should've gotten a better glimpse at him. It was foolish of her to blindly trust her friend.

Constance would certainly know what the patrolman looked like. Perhaps it was only a mix-up. Clara lifted onto her toes, waving at her friend, but Constance was too enthralled in whatever Douglas was saying.

"The policeman . . ." The woman reclaimed Clara's attention, her gaze straying to Ben, who'd joined Clara. "Umm . . . he was tall. Had light eyes and blond hair."

The light hair matched what Clara remembered. But that didn't prove anything.

"And now, for the unveiling of the new Liberty Loan booth." Douglas's booming voice made her jolt.

"Oh!" The loan lady perked. "And he had a limp in his left leg. It made his steps shuffle."

Shuffle.

Steps.

Sounds.

Clara gasped. Could that have been the sound she'd heard in the park? The dragging noise. If that patrolman was the man in the park, then that meant—

"Brought to you by the US Women's Reserve Camouflage Corps and the US Treasury," Douglas continued, "this booth features the latest in camouflage warfare."

No! They couldn't unveil now! But what could she do? Before she could think better of it, she snatched the megaphone from Ben's hand. "Thank you so much, Douglas." Her voice squeaked loud, and every head whipped her direction. "We're excited about the big reveal, but first . . ." First what? She needed to stall. She glanced over at a stunned Ben and mouthed, *Sorry.* "Ben Winsell will recite a patriotic poem." A strangled noise came from Ben's direction, but she wasn't done. "And will Captain Marcus Reeves and Miss Constance Andrew report to help with the unveil?" She handed Ben the megaphone with an apologetic smile.

He leaned close. Too close. "What are you doing?"

"Buying time." She tried shooing him away, but if anything, he drew nearer. "It's important, or I wouldn't have done this."

He frowned. "I don't know a patriotic poem."

"You're an actor, make one up." She gave him a light shove, even as Marcus came along, another officer in tow. Thank goodness.

Marcus's gaze shifted between Clara and Ben, before settling on her. "What's wrong?"

She pulled him to the side. "I think I found our sniper."

His frame tensed, eyes serious. "Where?"

"He's in the booth."

CHAPTER 13

EVERY TENDON IN Marcus's body tightened, his muscles poised for action. But first, Clara. He couldn't think straight with her in firing distance. So while Ben Winsell rattled off the strangest poem Marcus ever heard, he wrapped his arm around Clara, intending to lead her away from potential danger.

She gave a fierce shake of her head. The determination filling her eyes clearly communicated her decision, though she whispered anyway. "I'm not leaving you."

Stubborn woman.

There wasn't time to challenge her. He slid his body between the booth and her, then waved over Officer Delaney. The man was really a kid in a patrolman's uniform, barely nineteen. But Marcus couldn't abandon Clara to scrape together more seasoned officers. They needed to act now.

Delaney raised a brow in question.

Marcus pitched his voice low. "Possible sniper in that booth." He gestured to the tarp-covered box, which just last night he'd inspected thoroughly. Time was of the essence, but he needed more details. He turned to Clara. "Why do you believe a gunman's inside?"

Before she could respond, another young woman—dressed in the same uniform as Clara—almost knocked right into them. Her narrow face was flushed pink, and her chest heaved as if she'd just run for miles. "This crowd is ridiculous." Her brows lowered. "I came as quick as I heard. Why did you call me over, Clara? What's wrong?"

His fingers twitched at his side. They couldn't waste any moments chatting. Thankfully, the raised noise of the festivities drowned out their muted voices. If there was indeed someone inside that booth, they couldn't hear this conversation.

Clara bracketed the other woman's shoulders and leaned close to her ear. "Constance, that policeman you spoke to earlier about our booth, did he have a limp?"

Constance nodded. "Yes."

Clara drew near to Marcus, her expression flooding with worry. She quickly clued him in about the situation. A man with a limp told Constance the bonds were inside the booth and must be guarded, yet earlier, he'd told the Liberty Loan woman to bring the bonds after the unveiling so nothing could be stolen. Basically, he contradicted himself. Why? It appeared the patrolman wanted the space both covered and unattended. His hiding spot perhaps?

"Do you see this officer anywhere?" Marcus asked.

Clara, Constance, and another woman he suspected to be the Liberty Loan lady Clara had referred to, all glanced various directions. The three shook their heads almost in unison, confirming the officer was nowhere in sight, increasing the possibility he was inside the booth.

"What are we going to do?" Clara's voice shook.

Marcus raked his gaze over the tarps. "We need to strategize."

He that dwelleth in the secret place of the most High shall abide under the shadow of the Almighty.

The verse was but a whisper in his heart, but Marcus ignored the gentle nudge and focused on the officer.

"If there's a killer in there, we can easily flush him out." Delaney's hand moved to his holster. "You stay here and patrol, while I gather more men. Then we'll surround him."

Not a bad idea. As a military man, Marcus knew the effectiveness of a surprise ambush. Yank down the tarps while training a line of weapons on whoever's within. Then if it turned out the space was empty, no harm done.

But if a gunman was inside . . . "It might work, but with all these civilians, we can't afford to turn Wall Street into a shooting gallery." He wasn't about to let things spiral out of control, especially if it risked the woman he loved. *Under the shadow of the Almighty.* "Let's form a different plan."

Delaney's shoulders slumped, but he squinted at the tarp like he might set it ablaze with concentration. Marcus wished he could, but that wasn't an option. So while the crowd chanted for Mary Pickford to speak, he recalled what he'd learned from his inspection of the booth last night. The structure was made entirely of wood. With a large, open window in the front and an entryway on one side. It wasn't positioned over a manhole or sewage grate, so there was no alternate escape route. Something didn't add up. A trained assassin would always provide himself a way out in case his assignment failed. If the gunman tucked himself inside a booth edged by thousands of people, he couldn't easily slip away. Though it could be a suicide mission.

Marcus had to think. Every second counted. Usually, he'd have a dozen strategies materializing in his brain by now, but nothing came. Unless he counted the Scripture rolling through him like an unending loop. *Under the shadow of the Almighty. Under the shadow. Under the . . .* He stilled, his gaze dropping to the ground. A narrow shadow fell upon the sidewalk from where the two tarps overlapped. There was also a slight gap he could slip beneath.

That would be foolish. He'd have to crawl on his stomach to get under, leaving himself vulnerable to whatever enemy waited inside the booth. Such action went against everything drilled into him.

But it also felt . . . right.

So despite logic, he'd go under the shadow.

He addressed Delaney. "I'm heading inside. Go get more officers. But when you return, don't you, or any of the men, touch the booth until I say so."

Delaney nodded.

Marcus turned to Clara and repeated the warning. "Stall the unveiling the best you can. Keep people away from the tarps."

Her mouth pressed together as if trapping her protest. Her glossy eyes and paled complexion relayed fear, but she straightened her shoulders in a show of bravery. For him. "Be safe," she finally whispered and pressed the prayer cloth he'd given her this morning against his hand. "Bring this back to me."

He kissed her quick, then turned to face an unknown enemy. He dropped to the ground onto his stomach. And before he could talk himself out of it, he pushed on his elbows, crawling beneath the tarp. His uniform caught on the rough sidewalk.

He paused, listening for movement inside.

Nothing.

With a prayer on his heart, he continued crawling until reaching the open entryway. One sweeping look told him the booth wasn't empty. No officer. No assassin. No human at all. But there was something else just as menacing. He pushed on his good arm, bringing himself to his knees.

With brisk but cautious movements, he stood and peered into a crate of grenades. Enough explosives to kill everyone within a fifty-foot radius. Wires were connected to each grenade, one attached to the pin, another rigged the lever. His gaze slowly tracked the line of cords to where they'd been tacked to the tarp's top edge.

Wickedly clever.

The unveiling would've detonated this crate. Because one good tug on the tarps, and the cords would pull the pins from all the grenades and free the levers. Now he understood why he'd been impressed to crawl under the tarps rather than pull them down.

His gaze hitched on a small inscription, barely visible, on the inner edge of the box. Something he'd examine later. Because all his focus remained on eliminating the danger.

Thankfully, this was simple to disarm. Yet no less dangerous. All he had to do was cut the cords, an endeavor far easier if he had use of both hands.

"Who's ready for the big unveil?" A masculine voice boomed through a megaphone, igniting a riot of applause.

Marcus didn't have time to get help. The tarps could be yanked down any second, triggering the explosives. He needed to secure the area, now.

He yanked his knife from his pocket, then flipped it open.

Now for the challenging part.

He had to hold each cord without accidentally pulling it. One wrong move, and the cord would unsheathe the pin, resulting in an explosion. So instead of fingers to clamp the wire, he'd use the next best thing—his teeth. With sweat dotting his forehead, he bit into the cord, holding it still with his teeth. Once taut, he sliced it. He repeated this process until all the wires were cut. After one more check, ensuring he didn't miss anything, he exited the booth.

Patrolmen surrounded the perimeter, their weapons drawn. Chief Wallace's imposing form cut through the line of men.

"Delaney found me," the older man said. "He said a sniper's in the camouflage booth."

"No assassin, sir, but there's a large crate of explosives in there." Marcus nodded at the booth. "They've been disarmed, but we need to remove them."

Chief Wallace ordered men to retrieve the grenades.

"There's a faded marking on the inside lip of that crate. Hard to see," Marcus noted to the chief. "Might be a good idea to trace it. And we have some women who can provide a description of the believed saboteur."

Wallace nodded. "I'll assign men straightaway."

Marcus had done his job. Clara was safe. She'd accomplished what he'd asked and stalled. For, right now, Douglas Fairbanks carted around Charlie Chaplin on his shoulders. The crowd erupted in cheers, completely oblivious to what had transpired. More like, what hadn't transpired.

Clara weaved her way through the swarm of patrolmen, her gaze locking with Marcus's. Tears streaked her face, and he hated that he'd put her through the worry. He opened his arms just as she fell against him.

"You're safe." She cupped his face, her fingers trembling against his jaw.

He nodded. "Can't get rid of me that easily." He kissed the side of her head, breathing in her vanilla scent. "You were right all along. There was an attack planned. But you saved it from happening."

She hugged him tight. "We saved it."

With the threat removed, they proceeded with the unveiling. The four actors remained ignorant of the foiled attack, smiling and laughing with one another and the crowd. For Marcus, on the other hand, it took a long while before his pulse settled. He hung back beside Officer Delaney and watched as Clara, alongside Ben Winsell, pulled down the tarps. Tarps that were now free from trip wires linked to explosives.

Next, a naval commander explained to the masses the purpose of dazzle camouflage—the paint technique featured on the booth—and how effective it is in combat. Mary Pickford concluded the rally by enrapturing the audience with a stirring speech that led to a mass sale of Liberty Loans.

The event ended, and Marcus finally breathed easier. With Clara's arm tucked around his, they began the trek to her apartment, only for Clara to lead him aside. He recognized the spot as the very one they'd paused at late last week, when she'd had paint on her face.

She twined her arms around his neck. "There. That's better." She rested her head on his shoulder. "I need a moment."

He couldn't agree more. Though the danger was all over, his mind kept wandering to what could've happened. The undeniable fact was that he could've lost her had she not listened to her gut about the threat.

Her hands skimmed that patch of skin between his collar and hairline. "You can't imagine how scared I was watching you enter that silly booth."

"I can imagine"—he gazed down at her—"if it was anything like the dread that hit me when I saw those grenades, knowing you were only a couple yards away." He swallowed against rising emotion. "The moment I saw you again, I wanted to wrap you in my arms and never let go."

She lifted onto her toes, placing their mouths luringly close. "Then why don't you?"

One inch—maybe half that—and his lips could claim hers. "You're tempting me, Clara. Do you realize what you're saying?"

"Very much."

"The way I feel right now, I never want to waste another day apart." He was spent, his nerves were shot, and now his words ran in tandem with his heart. He should rein in his thoughts before he said anything else. He released her. "It's been an emotional day, and—"

"Don't you dare backtrack. Or blame our devotion to each other on a stressful day. If anything, what happened only helped me see how delicate life can be." She grasped his face and gently tugged him toward herself. "I know what I want. I know my heart." She inclined her chin as if to show him the truth in her eyes. "I love you, Marcus. I would've married you before you enlisted, had you asked."

His chest tightened. "You love me?"

She nodded, her beautiful grin breaking free.

His left hand gripped her waist, easing her closer, erasing any distance between them. "I've loved you for years, Clara. I always will." He nuzzled her temple. "I got a second chance to have you . . ." He kissed her forehead, her jaw, her lips. "And I never want to lose you again."

"Then don't." She smiled against his cheek. "I'd marry you tomorrow, if you'd ask." She peered up at him and winked. "I even have a dress."

CHAPTER 14

CLARA HAD BEEN correct about the two men she'd heard in the park that day as being the criminals behind the botched attack. The authorities had traced the marking on the grenade crate, which led them to an abandoned warehouse—the German agents' hideout. The saboteurs had been apprehended. One of the agents had confessed to wooing an event committee member in order to procure all the details involving the rally. While the other man, the fellow with the limp, had admitted to weaseling his way into getting hired on as extra patrol for the event. They were presently in custody, awaiting trial.

The citywide manhunt for the masterminds of the attack brought attention from the press until they uncovered the intended attack. Police Chief Wallace released a statement giving Marcus the credit for thwarting the bombing attempt, and the papers were filled with articles highlighting his bravery.

Clara was elated all of New York City and beyond heralded her beloved as the hero he was. Her fiancé, however, wasn't as pleased. Marcus's integrity couldn't allow Clara to be overlooked in the matter. It had taken some persuasion, but she'd finally convinced him she'd rather keep her name out of it. She didn't want attention or accolades. All she wanted was to become Mrs. Reeves.

Two weeks later, her wish was granted.

Before the double doors leading to the church sanctuary, she stood in a wedding gown she'd initially sewn for a movie star. A dress that God had intended for her all along. She ran her hand down the smooth silk, a smile lifting her lips. Because just like the camouflage suits, this dress had a secret. Marcus had requested she sew the prayer cloth, something meaningful between them on their special day, into its hem.

The rich chords of the "Bridal Chorus" floated to Clara's ears as Liesl adjusted her veil one last time. Father, who'd been misty-eyed all morning, held out his arm to Clara, which she affectionately took before Liesl opened the doors.

The guests rose to their feet, but Clara channeled her gaze down the aisle to Marcus, waiting for her at the altar. Her breath hitched at the sight of him.

He wore the jacket. The one with her words of love stitched inside. Tears stung, but she blinked them away. She wanted to have a clear view of her groom, to commit this moment to memory.

They'd once been separated. For years, their hearts had been divided, but somehow, their souls had remained entwined. They'd survived their own personal battles and now stood as a united front.

After the ceremony, they would spend their honeymoon at Niagara Falls, only to return in two weeks so Marcus could start his new position as an investigator for the New York Police Department. After the Liberty Loan booth debacle, the police chief had been so impressed, he'd offered Marcus a position.

Marcus still intended to help Father with security for Westlake Enterprises on the side but without all the traveling. Both Clara and Marcus wished to be home when Desmond returned. They'd finally received his letter, confirming he was well. Clara and her family would continue to pray for him as well as all the other soldiers risking their lives for a better world.

Clara reached the front where Marcus stood, and his gaze drifted over her, her gown. There was something special about this dress. Maybe it was the sheer fact that when she had been sewing it, she'd been utterly oblivious to all God had in store for her. Or maybe it was that each stitch of this garment served as a memory she had with Marcus. A single stitch by itself was nothing consequential, but flowing altogether, many stitches created something beautiful. Something that would last a lifetime.

AUTHOR'S NOTE

THE US WOMEN'S Reserve Camouflage Corps was created during WWI. This group of camouflage artists—or camoufleurs—designed suits that allowed snipers and scouts to blend into their surroundings. These women truly did test their creations by lying in parks, such as Van Cortlandt Park in the Bronx. The entire top floor of 257 Madison Avenue served as the corps' headquarters, with Lieutenant H. Ledyard Towle as the corps' commander. Lieutenant Towle believed the women should be taught modern warfare, which included army formation and maneuvers. The women learned dazzle camouflage. They started small, by painting objects like a war bond booth, then graduated to larger projects. The women dazzle camouflaged an entire ship—the USS *Recruit*—in the middle of Union Square.

On July 30, 1916, German agents sabotaged Black Tom Island, which served as a munitions depot. The blast is considered one of the largest nonnuclear explosions in history.

In April 1918, Mary Pickford, Douglas Fairbanks, and Charlie Chaplin toured the country promoting the Liberty Loan drive. From Los Angeles, they'd gone to Salt Lake City, Chicago, and Washington, DC, and concluded the national tour in New York City, to unprecedented crowds. It was also fun to incorporate Charlie Chaplin's and Douglas Fairbanks's real-life publicists. Some of the antics listed in the novella truly happened. The stars held the main rally on the Sub-Treasury's steps. Mary Pickford did indeed raffle off a lock of her hair, and Douglas Fairbanks hauled Charlie Chaplin on his shoulders.

Another fact that is worth mentioning is the severe anti-German sentiment that increased during WWI. Some signs were mild, such as changing the name of sauerkraut to "liberty cabbage," while other aspects were extreme, such as blacklisting German business owners. My great-grandfather came to America just a few years before WWI and suffered persecution because of his nationality. So I was intentional about highlighting the struggles German immigrants faced during the war. It was a challenging time, to be certain, but we can learn from history and help create a better today.

A Letter to Eli

ALLISON PITTMAN

My heartfelt thanks to the Greatest Generation.

Thank you for your courage.

Thank you for your sacrifice.

Thank you for your stories.

CHAPTER 1

New York City
Spring 1943

NOBODY ELSE ON the street seemed to have any place pressing to be. Bette Barry shouldered past men and women, rarely bothering to mutter, "Excuse me," because, after all, sidewalks were called side*walks* for a reason. Not side strolls, or side meanders, or—for Pete's sake—side *stands*. This thought came as a group of women came to an abrupt halt right in front of a window display featuring summer bathing suits and sandals.

"Hey!" one of the women said when Bette's elbow checked against her shoulder.

"Oops." Bette included no sense of apology in her response. She didn't even look back.

It was a peculiar time to be out walking in New York City. Not quite three o'clock in the afternoon. Meaning, children were still in school, their restless mothers out taking advantage of these last moments of purpose. Businessmen and secretaries and everyone else who spent their days in one of the offices looming overhead wouldn't be flooding the street for another few hours, when they would head to restaurants and bars to shake off the day.

Bette couldn't imagine such a structured life. Same place, same time— every day. At least, not one spent behind a typewriter. She was just now leaving her job at the Garrison Hotel, where she'd spent the morning changing beds and cleaning toilets and wiping ashtrays until a new cigarette's ember would reflect itself in the glass. She clasped a knapsack of treasure under one arm and held it close as she quickened her steps.

Everybody else in New York might be poised to wind down their day, but Bette wasn't even halfway through.

It was late March, and in New York, the legendary lion and lamb remained locked in a monthlong battle, whistling up wind and sunshine and unexpected pockets of cold. She hit one of those pockets now, rounding a corner, and welcomed it. Who could have known that the girl from a small upstate town, one with a population that could easily fit in one of these looming buildings, would feel at home with a life confined to roughly six blocks of concrete and bricks and only occasional patches of fenced-in grass. She'd grown accustomed to looking straight up to see the sky, and when she didn't look up, she assumed it was still there, stretched clear in some shade of blue or gray.

There were times when she might have forgiven the strolling pace of her fellow city dwellers. Summer nights thick with trapped heat of the day, or winter afternoons dotted with fresh flecks of snow. This afternoon, however, she felt driven not only by the wind nipping at her skirt but also by her self-imposed urgency. She did little to slow her stride when she hit her destination—the revolving door of Goode's Department Store. She did, however, take on a more dignified pace the moment it spat her out onto the shining marble floor and perfume-scented air of Women's Cosmetics and Accessories. There she paused to catch the eye of Alice Goode, her best friend, who stood behind the counter, artfully balancing a feathered hat on her hand.

Alice shot Bette a look that was equal parts welcome and warning.

"Dinner, yet?" Bette asked in a theatrical whisper.

Alice handed the hat to the waiting customer and excused herself before stepping away. "Another half hour," she said with an apologetic scrunch to her face.

"Think he'll let you skip out a few minutes early?"

He was Alice's uncle Ray Goode, who owned the store and employed Alice out of a sense of family obligation more so than her dedication to selling perfumes and gloves. His motto was "We'll never beat Macy's if we don't beat the clock." He liked to think of his employees as being well-groomed cogs and wheels and occasional springs, moving the store forever forward.

Thus, Alice gave a quick shake of her head.

Bette heaved an ironic, exaggerated sigh. "Fine. I'll find some way to pass the time."

Alice's perfectly arched eyebrows shot up. "Don't—"

But Bette sent her a wink and a grin and headed to the escalator, taking it to the second floor, Children's Shoes, where she came face-to-face with Ray Goode, his finger already raised in chastisement.

"Bette," he said, his voice tinged with irritation.

"Uncle Ray," she replied, as if this were an ordinary greeting between friends.

"What brings you to Children's Shoes?" He pursed his lips, creating something comical of his thin mustache. "Is there something you've been hiding from us?"

"Just waiting to have dinner with Alice. Killing time."

"And you wouldn't consider *killing time* in a department where you might actually make a purchase?"

"Is there a department where you would consider giving me a family discount?"

"You're not family."

"I'm family's best friend."

"Close, but no cigar."

"You don't sell cigars, and I don't like them anyway."

If Bette thought Alice's uncle harbored any true dislike of her, she wouldn't have enjoyed sparring with him half as much. He'd been an old fusspot since the first time she met him; he'd probably been a young fusspot too. His affection for her might have been begrudgingly predicated on her friendship with Alice, and it might be icy thin, but if that ice ever cracked, the result would be an affectionate hug, for which neither was prepared.

From the corner of her eye, she spotted a fashionably dressed and flawlessly coiffed woman who held the hand of an equally stylish little girl. The child must have been about four years old, and she held her head at an angle identical to her mother's, looking down her nose as she perused the footwear display.

"No," Uncle Ray said, anticipating Bette's next move.

"Come on," she wheedled.

"You don't work here."

Bette gestured broadly. "No one's working here right now."

"The girl's at lunch. I can bring Thea over from Women's Shoes."

"I promise to send her over to Thea to make the sale. I wouldn't have to beg you if you'd just hire me already."

"I'm already paying one family member I can't afford."

"Good thing I'm not family."

Uncle Ray acquiesced. "Fine. I'll let you play shopgirl. These rations will be the death of me. Push the galoshes, will you? We're overrun with them."

Bette reached out and pinched a bit of his jacket sleeve. "Thanks, Ray."

She divested herself of her coat, hat, and satchel, tossing them behind the sales counter, where she picked up a pad of sales tickets and a short pencil. When Bette and Alice first embarked on their New York City adventure, Uncle Ray was quick to employ the girls with a semi-living wage, but while Alice excelled at salesmanship with her buttercream beauty and affable way, Bette's forthrightness and starker appearance often proved off-putting. She lasted little more than a week at Goode's—a parting that was mutually amicable. And while she truly loved her job at the Garrison Hotel, she liked sticking a toe in the Goode family business pool from time to time. Mostly this was because she had a lifetime of invitations to dinners, holidays, and all manner of celebrations. She'd had a toothbrush in the bathroom cabinet for years. It would take more than a pink slip to push her away. Besides, irritating Uncle Ray was a tradition, much like pecan pie on Christmas Eve. There was safety in his scowl.

Bette arranged her face into an expression of cordiality and approached the two, clearing her throat before offering assistance.

"What can I buy that isn't rationed?" The mother said the word *rationed* as if it denoted something vile.

"Here are some lovely patent-leather dress shoes," Bette replied in her best make-do voice. "Shall I measure your little girl's feet and see what size we need?"

"I suppose," the woman said, looking at a pair of red-and-white leather saddle shoes with something akin to hunger.

Bette helped the little girl onto a chair, then gently took off her shoe—a high-quality lace-up that seemed barely worn through. She stood the girl up and then knelt down to place her heel snuggly in the metal measuring apparatus. The size indicated matched the size she was wearing. Bette put a hand on the little girl's shoulder.

"Are your shoes bothering you? Do they pinch or feel too small?"

The child shook her head.

Bette looked up at the mother. "It appears her size is the same."

"Can't a mother buy her daughter a pair of shoes just for the sake of it?"

"You could," Bette said, standing. "But with the rationing down to three pair a year, you might do better to wait—"

"I'll take a pair of the patent dress shoes for church. White, as it's nearly spring. And these." She held up the red-and-white saddle shoes in defiance.

Bette kept her face frozen and polite. "Let me just check that we have them in her size."

She didn't blink until she was safely hidden within the shelves of cardboard boxes. Mr. Goode kept this room half lit, so she used the flashlight stationed at the entrance to scan the size and style printed on each box. How could this woman be so wasteful? Bette would wager that little girl had a dozen pairs of perfectly good shoes at home, lined up neatly in some posh pink closet. Bette would have given anything—not that she *had* anything—for an experience like that. Not so much the shoes. She herself took loving care of the few pairs of shoes she'd had since high school, including her beloved brogans and red ankle-strap pumps, determined to make them last until the war was over. Other than that, she shopped only the ration-free styles—treated cotton and Endura-flex soles. But to have a mother to stroll with, hand in hand, a mother who took interest, loving or not, in what she had or didn't have . . . That was the thought that fed the deep sigh in the darkness of the shoe room.

She could stall no longer. Holding both boxes like treasures to be offered to a queen, Bette emerged from the stockroom. "Shall we try these on and see how they fit?"

The mother scrutinized the boxes. "Are they not the proper size?"

"They are. But sometimes a different style—"

The little girl tugged at her mother's skirt. "I want to—"

"I'm afraid we're in a bit of a rush. I'll return them if they don't fit."

Bette tightened her grip on the boxes. "It would only take a moment, ma'am—"

"I simply do not have a minute."

"Then might I quickly suggest a new pair of galoshes? Spring means lots of rain and splashy puddles"—this she said directly and conspiratorially to the little girl—"and since we all need our shoes to last . . ." Bette stepped over to a display and held up a gingham-patterned boot. "We have the same style in Women's just across the aisle, there. Wouldn't it be cute to match?"

She thought she saw a crack in the woman's façade, accompanied by lifting her perfectly plucked brow.

"Oh, don't worry," Bette pressed on. "Not rationed at all. These aren't made from the same kind of rubber used to make the boots for our boys. Not nearly as high a quality, but they are adorable and will do the job of keeping your shoes"—she gulped, looking at the woman's silk-clad legs—"and stockings dry."

"How lovely," the woman said. "Yes, I'll take those too."

"Lovely," Bette repeated, matching her tone. She looked at the woman's feet. "Size five?"

"Five and a half, actually."

"Then let's go with a six to be safe. Come with me to Women's, and Thea will take care of the rest."

The walk to Women's measured only a few aisles. Bette, following the customer, held up the boxes and galoshes in triumph when met with the quizzical expression of Thea Jergen, manager of the entire Women's department, assistant store manager, and sometimes salesgirl.

"If you wouldn't mind," Bette said, "finalizing this lady's purchase? She would like a pair of galoshes to match her lovely daughter's. Size six."

"Right away," Thea said, ever in on the ruse. While she'd been an enthusiastic supporter of Bette's firing, the two always had an easy friendship. Thea took the items, engaging the little girl with a smile.

Bette took that moment to pounce.

"One more thing," Bette said, stepping in the mother's path. "I'm sorry if our rationing system is an inconvenience to you."

"I beg your pardon?" The mother looked to Thea for vindication, but Thea was staring at Bette, her eyes sparkling with a silent plea meant to stifle Bette's building diatribe.

It's not my pardon you should beg. You should have to look into the eyes of one of our boys slogging through the mud in his worn-out boots and explain why you should have the leather for your daughter's saddle shoes. This is not a time for frivolity. She doesn't need shoes. I don't think she even wants shoes. Stop for a moment and think about what matters.

All of this, though, was what made her a stellar concerned citizen but a lousy shopgirl. She gave Thea a reassuring look and took a deep breath. "I mean, I know rationing is an inconvenience. Let's hope this all is over before your daughter grows out of these."

She avoided using the word *war*, not knowing how much the little girl knew, but she didn't have to. There was no conversation, whether between friends or strangers, that could escape its shadow.

The fourth floor of Goode's Department Store was comprised of office space, employee lockers, and a special room dedicated to the store's Christmas overlay and Santa's throne. Here, too, was a modest cafeteria where every worker, from the department managers to the custodial staff, was entitled to a free meal for every five-hour shift. Goode considered it a compensation for the fact that the wages paid under his employment were significantly lower than those in other stores. A well-fed staff was a loyal staff, and for some, this might be the most reliable meal of their day. While the dinners (or breakfasts or lunches) were free to employees, Bette took it upon herself to extend them to *former* employees as well, though she always dropped a dime in the jar set up to collect tips for those who prepared the food.

The meal offered to the employees was always a simple one; tonight, it was a tomato-and-pea soup, a cheese sandwich, an apple, and a gingerbread cookie. This had been Alice's choice. She had already set herself up at a table. She waved Bette over and commenced to dipping one corner of her sandwich into her soup. Bette, however, opted for her usual bowl of oatmeal, ladled from the seemingly endless pot of the stuff cooking on the stove. Once served, she swirled in a generous portion of maple syrup from the jug at the end of the counter and requested a spoonful of raisins from the kerchiefed attendant behind it.

Alice, as always, wrinkled her nose at Bette's choice. "You know we could make that stuff easily enough at home," she said before taking a dainty sip of her soup. "It would be fresher. I think that's been sitting on that stove since before the war."

Bette dug in. "Maybe that means if we ever reach the bottom of the pot, the war will be over."

"Well then," Alice said, raising her glass of water in salute, "to the Oatmeal of the Duration."

"To the Oatmeal of the Duration," Bette echoed, clinking her glass of milk.

Despite a nearly lifelong friendship, the two young women were more different than they were alike. Alice was small and fair, with pink cheeks that flushed to various shades of rose depending on her level of anger, embarrassment, shyness, or passion. Everything about her was dainty and reserved—her gestures, her words, her laughter, her opinions. Alice could pass through a room undetected, skimming just below the eye level of most adults who might only move to seek out the source of the unique floral scent that seemed to cling naturally to Alice's skin. While Alice was almost cartoonishly curvaceous, Bette was tall and what men called *lanky*, with hip bones that protruded through her dungarees and breasts the size to make any brassiere a useless garment. She had long, thin fingers that prompted new acquaintances to say, "My! You must play piano!" to which she would often reply, "No more than you play the tuba."

Exactly the kind of thing sweet Alice would never say.

"So," Bette said, stirring her oatmeal, "do you want to hear an exciting story about my day?"

"Does it have something to do with that?" Alice pointed her pert nose at the satchel Bette had plopped on the table.

"Today yielded *three* silk stockings just tossed in the trash. And get this." She leaned forward and dropped her voice. "Just after noon, an older man and a very young woman checked in. Now, there's nothing good happening when it's an old guy and a young girl getting a hotel room in the middle of the day."

"Maybe she was his niece? Visiting the city?"

"This was no niece. Anyway, they get a room on the fourth floor, and I'm working in the room right next to them, and all of a sudden, there's this screaming match and a glass hitting the wall, and she's saying things like, 'What do you take me for? Some kind of tramp?'"

"Easy enough to get that impression," Alice said, "what with the hotel room at noon and all."

"Exactly. Anyway, I start to wonder if I should maybe call for security, or at least tell the desk clerk. So, I poke my head out into the hallway, the door flies open, and this woman comes storming out of the room, still wearing her coat, and he's running after her, pleading with her to come back and talk things out. But I'm pretty sure she'd already talked everything out. So I follow her onto the elevator, just to make sure she's safe—"

"Good Samaritan that you are—"

"And she bolts right through the lobby and leaves. The mister comes down in the next car and drops a few bucks on the desk and leaves without a word. Marty, the desk guy, says to me, 'Well, that's one room you won't need to clean.' But I tell him about the broken glass, and he gives me the key, and the room looks pretty much perfect, except there's a box on the bed, a fancy one with a ribbon and tissue. It's been torn open, and guess what's inside?"

Alice held aloft the crust of her sandwich. "Tell me."

"A nightgown. Beautiful, with lace straps and"—Bette sat up straight on her chair to deliver the coup de grâce—"pure silk."

Thea appeared at Bette's elbow, dropping onto a chair with a tray identical to Alice's, with the addition of a cup of tea. "What's pure silk?"

Bette brought her up to speed on the story thus far. "What's more? It was ripped. Completely torn from the bodice to the hem. I figure it's ruined, and that lady didn't seem interested in coming back, so . . ."

"You took it." Alice said.

"I did."

"You took it?" Thea asked, incredulous.

"That's the whole reason she took that job," Alice explained. "Maybe not the whole reason, but a perk, right, Bette? All those silk stockings left behind by all those high-class guests."

"Each one will have a much nobler life as a bunch of ammunition powder bags." Bette took a bite of her oatmeal and licked the back of the spoon.

"I guess we're lucky you weren't swiping the stockings off our shelves," Thea said.

"Only because you didn't have any," Bette said.

"As long as you keep your grubby hands off my wedding dress," Alice said good-naturedly.

Thea leaned across the table. "Wedding dress? Is there something I should know?"

"She got it when she was twelve," Bette said.

Alice sparked to life. "Oh, now *that* dress is classy. Elegant. Beautiful silk, trimmed with lace, rounded neckline. But not flashy, you know? Understated."

"It sounds lovely," Thea said.

"And something else," Alice said, her face going dreamy, "like it's carrying a secret."

Bette picked up the tale. "The woman who designed it used to make costumes for the movies. And then she became a camoufleur, creating camouflage uniforms with maps stitched inside for paratroopers during the Great War. *Real* work."

"Your work is real too, Bette," Alice said. "We're all doing our part."

So like Alice to say such a thing. She was always there to prop Bette up if her spirits seemed to sag. When their sad attempt at Victory Garden tomatoes seemed poised to yield no fruit, it was Alice who swore she'd never eat another tomato again until there was peace in Europe.

Thea propped her elbows on the table and leaned in. "So how is it that our Alice came to acquire this dress at such a tender age?"

"The designer, Clara Westlake, gave a talk at Alice's school," Bette said, remembering the thrill of sneaking away from her own school for a day to blend in for the presentation. The speaker told story after story, the ones about Hollywood nearly as exciting as those about war. "She auctioned off some of her movie gowns for a veterans' charity. This was one of them. Parents were invited to attend, and Alice's father bought it for her."

"And the moment I met my Frank," Alice said, her face still dreamy, "I saw myself in that dress. Fitting perfectly, I might add, walking down the aisle to the sound of a string quartet playing 'Jesu, Joy of Man's Desiring.'"

Only Bette's undying love for her friend kept her from rolling her eyes at Alice's tale. In it lay another gulf between the two: Alice was the eternal optimist, believer in happy endings, champion of romance, and Bette did not have the resources for such hope. Too much of her life had been stripped away to value planning beyond this bowl of oatmeal. She kept her dreams firmly on the ground, her trust in her sturdiest shoes.

"Anyway," Bette said, eager to change the subject, "do you have news about the nylon sale?" She looked back and forth between Alice and Thea and their identical sandwiches.

"Matter of fact, yes," Thea said. "Ray's found an inventory, and we should have it here in about a week. Plenty of time to put an ad in the paper and get some signs up in the store."

"Hooray," Alice said, lifting her spoon aloft. "What a treat for our ladies. Imagine, brand-new nylon stockings for your new spring dress."

Thea clinked her spoon to Alice's. "Here's looking for a boost to morale and sales."

Bette added hers. "Let's have a box for silk donations, to turn this sale into a drive. 'Strip off the old stockings, purchase the new.'"

"'Be Goode to yourself,'" Alice chimed in.

Thea dropped her sandwich and snapped her fingers. "That's it. I'll bring it up to Ray in the morning."

⊢—✄—⊣

Bette had one more stop in her six-block world before heading home to the tiny fourth-floor walk-up she shared with Alice. In her satchel, beneath the ill-gotten negligee, were three library books to be returned. She would peruse the shelves of her neighborhood public library for three more: one novel, one biography, and one work of historical nonfiction. Joining the New York City escapade with Alice derailed Bette's original plans to go to college. But then, she didn't exactly have the money to buy the college ticket. Cleaning hotel rooms didn't exactly require mental stimulation, so reading was her way of keeping her mind sharp, active, and occupied. With the borrowed books, she could read about love, learn about history, and be inspired by men and women who did great things despite their circumstances. Bette didn't know if she would ever do great things, but scrap drives were a place to start.

As evening fell, Bette put on water for tea and searched out their meager offerings for a late supper. Life in the apartment was limited by space more so than budget. They shared the narrow bed in the bedroom rather than forcing either to endure the Murphy bed that unfolded into the kitchen. Not that the kitchen was much use beyond a single-burner stove and oven with barely enough room for a pie plate. Besides, they were city girls, living within steps of every restaurant imaginable, not to mention Automats and street vendors and the occasional thick, greasy hamburger.

The kettle hadn't even begun to hiss when Alice came through the door and hit an abrupt stop, as if seeing Bette for the first time in her life.

"We've got a couple of hard-boiled eggs, unless you want to save them for break—" Bette broke off.

Alice clutched the distinctive, familiar envelope with its red-and-blue stripes around the edges, but her expression held none of the usual glow that heralded every other letter from her beloved Frank.

Bette reached for her friend's other trembling hand. "Golly, Alice. What is it? Is it Frank? Is it bad news?"

"No," Alice said, disengaging. She hung her hat and handbag on the hook by the door and fluffed her hair. "And no. You need to sit down."

Bette's senses prickled. Alice was never one to say who should sit and who should stand. Silently, Bette obeyed, backing up until she felt the chair hit the back of her knees, then sitting. Alice joined her. She set the letter on the table, and only then did Bette notice the name on the front.

Hers.

"It's addressed to me."

"Yes."

"But you opened it."

"Yes."

"Why would you open a letter addressed to me?"

"Because it wasn't written to you. Not really."

"Not *really*?"

Alice wasn't coy. She didn't speak in circles. Neither of them ever did, not to each other anyway. But now Bette sensed her friend being evasive, secretive, and careful to keep her thumb clamped over the return address. She wasn't quite careful enough, however. One word peeked out.

Hospital.

A new churning started. "Who's it from, Alice?"

"Please, Bet. I can explain."

"Just tell me. Who is writing a letter not really to me that you have already read before coming upstairs?"

Alice scooted it across the table and removed her hand.

PFC Eli Landers.

"But how," Bette ventured, running a finger across his name, "how did he find me? How did he know where to write?"

"Like I told you," Alice said, just as the kettle worked itself into a whistle, "he's not exactly writing *to* you. He's writing *back*."

CHAPTER 2

BETTE BARRY AND Alice Goode grew up in a picturesque, small town in upstate New York. They'd been inseparable from the moment they were assigned to be kindergarten "playground pals" and tasked with walking hand in hand to and from recess each morning and afternoon. The girls soon discovered they walked an identical path home from school, one turning to the left and the other to the right for the final block. On Saturdays they met with their dolls safely tucked in carriages for a morning at the park.

There they go, neighbors would say. *Thick as thieves.*

Peas in a pod.

Double trouble.

Though they were never trouble to anyone. They grew up acting as each other's cheerleader and conscience. When Bette was nine years old and her father died in a freak industrial accident, she poured her tears onto Alice's lap, too afraid to enter into the circle of her mother's debilitating grief. And when, seven years later, her mother took to her bed and never got out, it was Alice and her family who took on the role of caretaker, providing a home for Bette without question of recompense.

The twosome became a foursome their junior year of high school, when Alice introduced Bette to Frank's best friend, Eli. They were as inseparable as couples as they had been as friends. The romance of Alice and Frank rolled out like something from a matinee—one of Mickey Rooney and Judy Garland's films—suspended by war but bolstered with a promise to marry the moment Frank returned to American soil. The romance of Bette and Eli? That was better cast with that other Bette—Bette Davis—

and Paul Henreid. She'd seen *Now, Voyager* a dozen times, never knowing she would someday draw on its tragic premise—lovers separated by circumstance, forever circling around each other's lives but never truly connected. In the final scene, Bette Davis says that they should not expect to have the moon. They should be content with the stars—bits and pieces scattered across a lifelong sky. While Alice's world orbited around Frank, Bette worked very hard to keep Eli out of hers. Hence the long hours at the Garrison and empty hours absorbed in books and the welcome distraction of every scrap of silk or metal or rubber she could get her hands on. *For the boys.* Keeping her focus on all those boys fighting in the war kept thoughts of Eli well at bay.

Until that night when Alice busied herself pouring tea while Bette tapped her fingers on the envelope bearing her name.

"How?" Bette asked, forcing all her questions into that single word.

Alice set two cups of tea on the table and opened a tin of crackers. "Do you remember last winter, when we stayed up until dawn reliving our entire senior year?"

Bette did. It was a bitter, cold night with the radiator on the fritz (again), and they'd huddled under every blanket they owned. With Alice's high school yearbook open between them, they tried to recall one story about each face, stringing a chronology of remembered games and dances and dates and carnivals, joking that if they fell asleep, they might just freeze to death.

"I wrote to Frank that morning after you went to sleep and told him all about it," Alice continued. "And when he wrote back, he told me he did the same thing when he was up late on watch. And I thought, 'Of course he does,' but for him, dying's not something to joke about."

A reverent silence fell between them, the way it did sometimes when they had to share a silent prayer.

Alice picked up her cup. "Anyway, he wrote something like the war being this stitch between our past and our future, and if he could hold on to the past, he'd have the strength to believe in the promise of the future."

"Such a poet," Bette said with all respect. Alice was forever sharing lines from Frank's letters.

"Isn't he just? But it made me think about how all those memories included Eli, and as far as I knew, he didn't have anybody writing to him—except, I assume, his mother and sister."

"Ah yes," Bette said. "The sister. Tabitha." The girl was much younger—probably just now a teenager—and never anything more than an annoyance.

"So I found out how to get a letter to him, and . . ." Alice gave a little shrug as if no further explanation were needed.

But Bette needed more. "And . . . ?"

"Honestly, almost exactly the same as what I wrote to Frank. How I sat up all night thinking of all the fun times the four of us had together and how good and warm it felt to laugh about the old days. It was a short note, really, more than a letter. And when I got to the end, I realized I hadn't used either of our names, so I just took a deep breath and signed it. 'B.'"

"And he wrote back?"

"Yes."

Everything in Bette wanted to ask what he said, but there was something cold and hard within her that put forth another question. "My voice? My handwriting?"

"We both learned our penmanship under the watchful eye of Miss Bernadette. I can still feel the smack of that ruler if I didn't hold my pen at the proper angle. I'd say our writing is pretty indistinguishable. And I only signed with your initial. Not 'with love' or anything so personal. That wouldn't have been right."

"Because you love Frank."

For the first time since the conversation began, Alice regarded her with a hint of remorse. "I only wanted Eli to have a friend here. That's all. To know that he was loved and wanted and prayed for—to have someone to come home to."

"But you never bothered to ask me if I wanted to be that person."

"I assumed that, now that he's home safe, or at least *here*. Now that the danger—well, most of it—is over . . ." Alice let her words trail off as if the completion of her sentence was obvious. Bette imagined Alice's vision of a perfectly paved path, neat and tidy.

"What is he expecting from me?"

"I guess we won't know until we read the letter, will we?"

"You haven't read it?"

Alice shook her head. "It's addressed to you."

Bette pressed her fingertips against the envelope until her skin turned white. "You know I'm furious with you right now."

"I know." Alice worked the envelope free and took out a single, small sheet of paper. Her mouth was poised to read when Bette reached across the table and took the note away. These were Eli's words; she wanted to hear them in his voice, even if they were clearly not written in his hand.

"Goodness," she said, showing Alice the scrawl on the page. She looked at it again. "There's a notation at the bottom that says it was dictated to a nurse."

"A nurse who could have benefited from some time under Miss Bernadette's Palmer Method tutelage."

"Look at those lowercase *f*'s. No loop at all."

The bit of nervous banter helped soften the nascent animosity Bette felt toward her friend, but her heart constricted at the thought of an injury so severe that Eli had to dictate such a brief bit of writing.

> *B—*
>
> *Well, what do you know. I'm home. Or close to it, I guess. I'm afraid I won't be up for a night on the town. Not like I promised.*

Bette looked up. "Like he promised?"

Alice looked away.

> *But docs say I'm going to be here for a while. I'm not asking any promises. Or making any new ones.*

Here, there was a hard line drawn, and a PS from "Ginny Muse, Registered Nurse," assuring that this soldier was as handsome as a fella could be, then giving the ward, room, and bed number where he could be found.

Bette stared at the writing until it became an even more convoluted mess. Something between a buzz and a ring filled her head, the sound wrapped in an unfamiliar heat. Anger. Anger itself was nothing new, but anger toward Alice?

"This is a betrayal," Bette said, her jaw clenched. "Of our friendship. If I wanted to write to Eli—"

"He's my friend too, Bet."

"Then sign your name. Not mine. I let him go for a reason."

"Not a good one."

"That's not for you to say." Bette kept her voice controlled only because she did not want it to become lost in a flood of tears. She stood and crossed the room to grab her coat and pocketbook. "I'm going to the hotel."

Alice was on her heels. "What? You can't. It's nearly ten o'clock."

"I cannot be here right now. I hate being angry with you, and I am so, so angry at you."

"But don't you even want to—"

Bette whirled, and her friend had never seemed so small. "I don't want anything right now. I don't want to hear another word." She took a deep breath. "I'm fine. I'll be fine. I'll blow off some steam in the laundry." She allowed half a breath for her joke to land. *Steam. Laundry.* It was enough to restore her heart to a healthier rate. "And we can talk tomorrow. But, honestly, Alice, you've dredged up a lot of pain for me, and if I stay—"

Alice reached for her own pocketbook. "I understand, but let me give you some money. At least take a cab."

Bette opened the door. "No, I need the walk. It might cool me down."

CHAPTER 3

BETTE WIPED THE crystal ashtray until it shone like treasure in a pirate's cave. She smoothed the clean sheets with hatchet-like hands, tucking in the corners with swift precision, and fluffed the pillows until the feathers nearly cried out in protest. The towels were white and folded into perfect squares, the curtains pulled back to let in the afternoon sun, and the stationery neatly centered on the desk. She ran the Bissell along the carpet, humming a note just below its pitch.

The night working in the laundry had served its purpose; the monotony of folding and stacking towels and linens restored her heart to a natural rhythm. Sometime after two in the morning, she caught a quick nap on a cot in a closet dedicated to that purpose, and by seven, she was in uniform, filling her cart, prepared to take on the tasks of the day.

She'd read the letter at least thirty times, until Ginny Muse's penmanship transcended the page and Eli's words traveled in his own voice. Bette read it until she didn't have to anymore, until it was as familiar to her as the lyrics of a favorite song. In all, though, one line stood out from the others.

"Not like I promised."

The phrase filled her mind with the same monotonous repetition of the linens and the towels and the vacuum. What had he promised? They never were ones for making promises to each other—especially not ones out of their power to keep. She would not permit anything like "I'll come home" or "I'll wait for you." Yet here they were, having kept them anyway, even if unconsciously. Bette didn't stay away from other men out of a sense of fidelity to Eli. She simply kept herself too busy to date. Plus, with the country's young men signing up and sailing out, there weren't enough suitable prospects *to* date. All the men in New York City were old, married, or on leave. If she couldn't depend on a guy for a fun evening a few nights in a row, what was the point?

He'd kept an unspoken promise too. He'd come home.

Though not like he promised.

Bette took a clean dusting rag from her apron pocket and ran it along the edges of the furniture, bringing the wood to a gleam. Today was not a day to daub the cloth with the scented oil. That, according to her own mental system, came every other Saturday. She simply reinforced the luster on the surfaces and dragged a corner of the cloth through the decorative crevices.

They'd shared a room once, she and Eli, in the days between his enlistment and when he left on the train. It was nothing like the Garrison. Nothing in their little town came close to this level of elegance. Eli hadn't told her where they were going, but the heaviness in the car gave a clue that this was no ordinary date. After the foursome shared a chow mein dinner, Alice and Frank walked to the theater to be distracted by a Three Stooges movie, but Bette and Eli declined. It had been playing in town for over a month, and they had all seen it three times. The gags had grown predictable and stale.

Silently, Eli drove to the outskirts of town and then out altogether, eventually parking in front of a string of nondescript rooms lined up beneath a neon light. He took an unfamiliar key from his pocket.

Neither spoke—uncharacteristic for the pair who spent most of their time in verbal sparring. Suddenly they stood on the brink of answering a question neither had bothered to ask.

Bette let him hand her out of the car, because she trusted him, then she stood at his elbow as he unlocked the door, and followed him inside. It was late afternoon, nearing dark, and when Eli closed the door behind them, the entire room took on a greenish hue, like they were trapped in some unwavering sea.

"Why are we here?" she asked finally, even though she knew, and even though she should have asked when they passed under the last stoplight in town. She knew, because she could trace every moment leading up to this one. Instead of answering, he kissed her. Instead of pushing him away, she fell against him. She locked her fingers into his curls, and he molded her body to his. Part of her knew she should be nervous, maybe frightened. But this was Eli, who loved her. Eli, whom she had seen every day since she'd met him. Eli, who complemented her in the way Alice never could. Bette shared secrets with Eli, keeping nothing from him. She briefly, in a moment when their mouths parted for air, wondered what her mother would think of her daughter kissing a man in a roadside motel. But then, when a new kiss descended, she remembered she had no mother. No one to tell her where to be or what to do. Only Alice, who need never know, and Eli, who was here.

Bette knew it was the way of the war, but she couldn't let the war take *everything*.

"Wait." She splayed her hands against his chest and stepped back, feeling the bed pressed against the back of her knees, keeping her upright.

"We can't wait," he said, his forehead touched to hers. "I leave in nine days."

"And this will keep you here?"

"No—"

"Because if it will, you can have me. All of me."

"Oh, Bet." He took her in a crushing embrace, void of any kiss or caress. He buried his face in her hair; she, her face against his shoulder; and the two of them clung to each other like there were a shared lifeline between them. "I have to go. You know I have to."

Bette knew no such thing. Everyone else in the country had men to spare—sons, brothers, fathers. She had nothing, no one. The selfishness of Eli's choice to sign up for a war that would take him to the other side of the world was one thing, but to bring her here to send him off? In that, she would have some say.

She loosened her grip and sidestepped away, far enough—and the room now dark enough—that Eli became a featureless shadow. "Why didn't you ask me?"

"Before bringing you here?"

"Before you enlisted. Did it even occur to you to ask me?"

His silhouetted hand reached for hers, she gave it, and they sat on the bed, Bette at the foot, Eli at the side, a corner between them. Safe. She could see the slow shaking of his head.

"No. It didn't. I love you, Bette. Like I've never loved anyone. But I'm not . . . beholden to you."

"Then you know how I feel tonight, don't you? You didn't ask me about this either."

He'd been stroking her pulse with his thumb but ceased. "I thought . . . There've been times . . ."

She took her hand away. "I know. But this is different. You planned this without me and just . . . brought me along. I'm going to be out of school in a few months, and I can't expect Alice's family to take care of me forever. I have to take care of myself, Eli. I have to make decisions for myself. I don't have anybody else."

"You have me."

"Only for a few more days. Then the war has you."

"You'll always have me."

"You can't promise that. War or no war, we can't promise that to each other. And I'm not going to be one of those girls who gets tossed aside once—" Tears choked out the rest of her words, bringing with them everything she feared.

Eli was up like a shot, and when he sat down beside her, his weight caused the mattress to sag, sending her body to crash against his. He draped an arm over her shoulder and pulled her closer, then dropped soft, hushing kisses into her hair.

"I'd never toss you aside, Bette."

"You say that. No surprise you say that now, because you want—"

"To spend every moment I can with you. Wherever, however . . . You decide."

She sniffed, trying not to rub her nose against his shirt. "Do you mean that?"

"I do. But don't ask me to take you home yet. It's not that late, and we're here, and I'd just like to have you to myself for a little while." He stretched away and pulled the switch on the bedside lamp, filling the room with amber light.

"Check in that drawer there," she said, dabbing at tears with the back of her hand. "There might be a Bible. We should read it to clear our thoughts."

Eli opened the drawer and shot a grin over his shoulder. "Here we go."

"A Bible?" Bette's stomach churned. She'd face lecture enough from Alice when she got home.

"Even better." He held up a small box. "Some generous soul left a deck of cards. How about a few hands of rummy? Loser owes the winner a kiss."

Her heart swelled with love in that moment as they kicked off their shoes and settled comfortably across from each other on the bed. Game after game, laying winning hands on the worn bedspread, they leaned over for quick, chaste kisses and sometimes long, lingering ones. They played until both were too tired to focus on the cards, then put them aside to lie beside each other, hands clasped, talking and telling stories until words became scarce and pauses between them invited sleep.

When Bette awoke at some unknown hour, she turned her head to see Eli's handsome face scrunched up against the pillow and indulged herself in the study of him in the gray light. Left to their own devices, his dark curls fell across his forehead, and she mourned the fact that they would soon be shaved away. Her fingers itched to touch the lawn of stubble on his cheek, but she didn't want to wake him. Didn't want to speak or kiss or listen to anything other than the sound of his breathing. In this moment, he belonged to her completely. She rolled over and stared at the slice of dawn trying to work its way around the shade. She closed her eyes and vowed that nothing—no person, no war—would take him away. Instead, she would give him over to whatever God had planned.

"What are we going to tell people?" she asked later, when he was awake, and they worked together to smooth the rumpled bedspread.

"That I'm going to war, and we wanted to spend a final night together," he said in a calm voice that made it all sound so uncomplicated and right.

"But they'll think—"

"They'll think what they want."

She surveyed the room, noting how it looked exactly as it did when they walked in. Bette took Eli's hand and planted a kiss on his shoulder. "Neat as a pin." It was something her mother used to say whenever their house was set straight and clean. Bette had kept up the ritual, saying it every time she looked back on a pristine, clean room, breathing in the scent of the furniture wax and the lingering, distinctive smell of a newly vacuumed carpet. Saying the phrase out loud that morning sent a feeling of warmth and approval through her.

The restored silence in the room after turning off the Bissell brought Bette out of her reverie. "Neat as a pin," she said, rubbing her cleaning cloth over the doorknob, erasing all trace of her presence.

She repeated the ritual ten more times over the course of the morning, recovering no abandoned silk but pocketing nearly five dollars in tips left by the guests. Along with all she did to collect for the various war drives, she considered her hotel work as a devotion to the war effort. Yes, the rooms were infrequently occupied by Wall Street lechers and the occasional tourist, but more often, the guests were American officers on leave, sometimes spending a precious night with a wife before returning to duty abroad.

Ten rooms left *neat as a pin* before she rolled her cart into the service elevator and soon emerged in the basement's laundry room. The overwhelming swoosh and swish of the water and the running of the machines made conversation impossible, so she merely signaled to the laundress that she was dropping off a load of bedding and towels, then left to find the manager of housekeeping. By Bette's calculations, she'd finished her assigned rooms with more than an hour to spare on her shift. Normally, she wouldn't think of asking for an hour off, but she hadn't felt normal since reading Eli's letter last night. Her next block of rooms would be waiting when she got back. For now, she had a promise to track down.

CHAPTER 4

"DIDN'T I ALREADY fire you?" Uncle Ray said with a mock check of his watch. "And if I didn't, you're late."

Bette took his response to her entrance in stride, ever appreciative of his affectionate disdain. She skipped over any polite greeting. "I need to talk to Alice."

"Alice is working."

"I know that." She looked around his shoulder and sent a wiggling wave to her friend behind the counter. "But she's not with a customer. Now's my chance."

She moved around him like she was one of the boys on her high school football team, careful to slow her pace to something more ladylike when she knew she was in the clear. Her throat clenched as she approached, remembering how she used to tease Alice about the sweet scent of the department coming from her own exhalation as much as any perfume. Now, the air was just as sweet but tainted by betrayal.

Alice's eyes were wide and pleading, the only sign that she wasn't a perfectly composed expert on face powder and bath salts. "Have you forgiven me yet?"

"No."

Alice leaned one elbow on the counter and gave the side smile that most often proved irresistible. "Is that because, really, there's nothing to forgive?"

Bette leaned on the counter too. "No."

Alice pouted. "Well, I don't regret what I did for a minute. Not a single word."

"Funny," Bette said, "I want to ask you about a single word."

Alice lifted a questioning eyebrow.

"*Promise.*"

"*Promise?*"

"As in, he writes that he's here but not like he promised. What does that mean?"

"Excuse me," a cultured voice interjected. "Miss? Miss, can you help me choose a new face cream?"

Bette turned to see a well-dressed middle-aged woman in an expensive suit and exquisite hat vying for Alice's attention.

"Give us just a minute," Bette said. "We've a bit of business to finish."

"Actually," Alice said, "this can wait for a bit." She took a side step along the glass-topped counter, planting herself in front of the customer. "How can I help you, ma'am?"

"I need something—"

"I'm sorry," Bette said, moving forward to where her shoulder brushed the woman's, "my friend here and I have something to settle."

"And my *customer* and I have a matter to decide. So perhaps ours can wait until my lunch break?"

"Oh sure. Since our *matter* has been going on for well over a year now. What's another hour, right?" This last question, Bette posed to the customer, then drummed her fingers on the glass, impatient for a response.

"Well, I . . . um . . . ." The woman looked from Alice to Bette. "What exactly is this matter at hand?"

"This one"—Bette gestured with her thumb—"wrote letters to my boyfriend—former, I should say, boyfriend—who is over fighting in the war."

"Oh, how awful." The woman lifted her veil and scowled at Alice.

"A letter I wrote on Bette's behalf," Alice said, "signing her name."

The woman clutched a gloved hand to her heart. "Oh, how *romantique,*" she said with an affected French accent. "*Très* Cyrano."

"No!" Alice and Bette spoke at once.

"Not 'très Cyrano,'" Alice said. "No 'Cyrano' at all. I'm not in love with him. At all. I have a fiancé, also fighting in the war."

"And neither, might I add, am I," Bette said. "In love with him, I mean. I am not."

"Really?" The woman's voice dripped the word with the thick richness of the pearls around her neck. "Don't presume you're fooling anyone, my dear."

Bette reeled back in shock.

"Aha!" Alice bounced on her toes and pointed a triumphant finger. "What have I always said?"

"I don't," Bette said, her resolve quickly depleting.

"She hasn't had a single date with a guy since he shipped out."

"In case you haven't noticed, all the guys in the city are married, old, or not fit for service."

"And she talks about him all the time."

"No I don't."

"Because she doesn't realize. But we'll be making egg-and-cheese sandwiches, and she'll say something like, 'Can you believe Eli would put ketchup on an egg-and-cheese sandwich?'"

"There's your love," the woman said, "knowing how a man likes his sandwiches. And not just knowing but having an opinion."

"Don't you need some kind of face cream?" Bette said, heading off her mortification. "You're in good hands with Alice here. Look at that face. Nothing but peaches and cream."

Instead of responding, the woman asked, "How long have the two of you been friends?"

"Forever," Alice said.

"Since before the boy?"

"Long before," Bette admitted.

"Then take a bit of advice from a woman who has learned a few lessons the hard way. Men come and go, but a good girlfriend is like a patch of gold in dark times. If this war has taught us nothing else, it's that women work best when we work together. Wouldn't you agree?"

Suddenly, Uncle Ray popped up out of nowhere to tower over Alice. "Mayhap *work* is the operative term here. As in, wouldn't it be nice to see my lovely salesgirl work with this equally lovely customer?"

"Okay, okay, I'll go," Bette said, shoring up to do so, "but I have just one question. Alice"—she captured her friend's full attention—"he wrote that he's here but not how he promised. What does that mean? What did he promise?"

Alice looked like she wanted the floor to swallow her whole. "I don't know."

"You don't know?"

Alice shook her head.

Her uncle and the stranger gasped.

"What do you mean, 'you don't know'? What did he say? What did he write?"

"I mean . . . I didn't open any of his letters. I always figured they were written to you, not me. It seemed an invasion of your privacy. I know that sounds crazy now, in light of . . . everything. And I've been wanting to—meaning to—tell you for ages, but the time never seemed right. I was worried you'd be angry."

Bette's mind went from an empty space to a simmering skillet as Alice spoke. If not for the growing audience—Uncle Ray, the woman, and a smattering of other ladies craning their necks as the story unfolded—Bette might have given full volume to the obvious. Of course she'd be angry. Of course that sounded crazy. Of course this was an invasion of privacy. Instead, she took three deep breaths before saying, "I think I'd like to see them."

Alice broke into a smile, and the gathered listeners let out a soft sound of approval. Even Uncle Ray seemed pleased.

"All right then," Alice said. "I'm supposed to get off at six, but maybe . . ." She looked to Uncle Ray.

"No," he said definitively.

"No," Bette echoed. "Tell me where they are. I'll find them."

"You know my square-dancing dress?"

"Yes." Alice and Frank were regular participants for the Saturday Night Squares in the Episcopal church's basement.

"I chose that one, because I knew you'd never borrow it. The letters are in the front pocket. I've kept them all."

Bette nodded and turned to leave but paused with one more question. "You opened the last one. Why?"

"It was different. It was from the hospital, so I was worried. Does this mean you'll go see him?"

"Oh, my darling," said the woman, "you simply must."

Bette patted her hand reassuringly. "Let's see what the letters have to say."

CHAPTER 5

THE "CLOSET" IN Bette and Alice's apartment consisted of a single rod stretched along the shorter of the bedroom walls, and a single four-drawer dresser nestled within the hanging clothes. As always, Bette was immediately drawn to the wedding dress. She and Alice were working girls living on working girls' budgets. The silk stood out from the everyday wools and cottons like a patch of pure-white light on an autumnal forest floor. Almost ritualistically, Bette took a pinch of the silk between her fingers; she could never sweep the dress off its hanger and hold it against her the way Alice did. It wasn't Bette's. It wouldn't fit. And though she knew it was silly to talk to a garment, she rubbed her thumb along the fabric and asked forgiveness for her short temper.

Three dresses down from this elegant gown, the blue-calico dancing frock stood out among its sensible, solid sisters. Alice had agreed to keep the crinoline petticoats stored at her parents' house, as they were so voluminous Bette threatened to charge them rent. Besides, there would be no square dancing until Frank came safely home, if Bette had any say in the matter.

She found the small stack of thin envelopes tucked into the square patch pocket on the front of the skirt. Her breath caught just seeing the handwriting of the address—the blocky, uniform, entirely uppercase way Eli had, which Miss Bernadette would have roundly punished. There were only three letters in all, arranged by the date on the postmark. Bette laid the latest two on the bed beside her and held the first, thinking, *He held this. He touched this*. And for countless minutes, that was enough, just to hold it and know. Eventually, she slid a shaking finger under the seal and brought the single sheet out, unfolded it, and felt the air rush out of the room when she saw the first line:

YOU MUST BE BETTE!

They were the first words he'd ever said to her long ago—well, in the grand scheme of things, not so long ago—when Frank—acting under Alice's orders—all but threw him in front of her at Alice's seventeenth birthday party. Bette knew who *he* was, one of those Most Everything boys in school. Popular, athletic, smart. Student government and district ambassador. Bette, as a new student, transferred in shortly after her mother's funeral and enfolded into Alice's family, had watched him from the shadowy corners of the unfamiliar campus, hearing his voice ring greetings in the hallway or calling plays on the basketball court.

Having noticed him, she'd asked about him in the most casual way she could manage. Alice and Frank had been on five dates already, on their way to becoming an item.

"Oh," Alice said in the offhanded way that comes with privilege, "that's Eli Landers. I can finagle an introduction."

And finagle Alice did, ordering Frank to bring him right over to where Bette stood with a bottle of Coca-Cola in one hand and a Lorna Doone cookie in the other. When Eli said "You must be Bette!" Bette replied, "I must be," wondering—but never asking—what Alice had said to make her so knowable.

There was an immediate seamlessness to that first conversation, like Eli and Bette were picking up an abandoned thread. He knew the band playing on every record, and she knew the moves all the kids were doing on the floor cleared for dancing, but neither made a step to the music. Instead, they danced in words, wrapping sentences around each other, pulling closer with questions and ideas. They broke away to sing "Happy Birthday" and allowed Alice and Frank to square up and join in while they balanced tiny plates of cake.

Now, in the silence of her and Alice's tiny apartment, she heard the ghost of the music and tasted the cake on her tongue.

*I can't tell you what your letter meant to me. I'm afraid
if I do, I'll never get another one. I don't mind telling you
that I live by those memories. I also can't tell you where I
am or what surrounds me, but there's nothing soft. Nothing
sweet-smelling or warm. Nothing that is everything you are.
(I know you don't think of yourself that way—soft and warm
and sweet. But I do.)*

*So I go back, all the time, to those days, when everything
was bright and beautiful. Everything we had. Everything
you wrote about, all that time. I hope you see this letter, Bette,
because I have to ask . . . Do you think we can have it again?*

Love, Eli

She read the letter over and over, fighting back the tears that threatened to blur the lines. What memories had Alice recalled to him? How could she have inspired such a response? Bette took in one final detail. Along the left-hand margin of the page, he'd sketched a series of playing cards, and another along the right. One was clearly a winning hand, the other a worthless jumble. He'd drawn an arrow to the winner and wrote "mine."

Meaning, she owed him a kiss.

She paid up, pressing the paper to her lips, leaving behind the faintest mark of lipstick. Then she folded the letter almost reverently and slid it back into the envelope.

The second letter awaited.

September
Dear B—

*I have not heard back from you, but I know it can take time
for a letter to reach its intended. I forgot to tell you how swell
I think it is that you and Alice are living in the city. That must
be an adventure for a couple of small-town gals. Please ask her
and send along any news you have about Frank. I think about
him all the time and cannot figure out how two jokers like us
could possibly be where we are right now. (Wherever he is . . .)*

Like that merry-go-round. Remember, on the playground? You and Alice would sit in the middle, and Frank and me would run and run, spinning it until you almost flew off, then we'd jump on and hang on for dear life, spinning until we just about got sick and laughing our heads off like a bunch of kids.

The physics there (I can see you rolling your eyes at another one of my science lessons) is that the force of the middle of the spinning merry-go-round works to knock us all off. If we didn't hold on to something, we wouldn't have a chance of riding it until it stopped.

I can still feel it. Me holding on to the bars, then jumping on so you could hold on to me. This world spins too, B. And things like this war want us to fall apart. But I'm holding on to you, even from the other side of this spinning globe. Doesn't really matter if you hold on to me or not.

Hello, Alice, if you happen to be reading over Bette's shoulder. Don't worry. Frank's holding on too.

Was that it? The promise? To hold on? She read it all again, blood rushing in her ears bringing back the feeling he'd described when she and Alice clutched each other in the center of that spinning disc, like all four of them might go flying off into the surrounding sky. How they welcomed that fear. Laughed at it, even. Later, on a slow walk home, Eli explained the physics of the spinning, though she hadn't heard a word. Mind, she loved the sound of his voice when he spoke like the aspiring engineer that he was, how his normal, even cadence turned into piles of excited words and terms meshed together from familiar and unfamiliar realms. Those were moments when the boy that he used to be and the man he hoped to become tangled together too, a fusion of engineering and antics.

On this second note, he'd sketched another winning hand attributed to himself, and Bette actually scowled and said, "Not again," before bringing the letter to her lips. Pulling it back, she looked at the date. Seven months ago. What if she'd read this seven months ago? Seven months of staring into the dark, praying for his safety, wondering if she had done the right thing in walking away, secretly knowing that she hadn't. All this time Bette had been listening to Alice moon about Frank, watching her blush at whatever he had written in his last letter, and listening to her giggle shamelessly as she wrote her reply. All the while her friend knew Eli's words were hidden away in the pocket of that ridiculous skirt.

Anger rose up to such a degree that Bette crushed the letter in her hand. Then, realizing, she smoothed it out on the bed, whispering an apology.

Her hands had been shaking when she opened the first letter, but now, coming to the third, they functioned like obedient deadweight. She tore clumsily at the envelope and took out the letter, having already become accustomed to the fragility of the paper. According to the date he'd written at the top, this one was written a month ago.

> Bette—
>
> *I know you told me you wanted to break it off before I left. And I believed you then. And I believe you now.*
>
> *I'll always be grateful that you wrote to remind me of what we had together, because there are times here when it seems impossible to believe that life was ever sweet or that it made any sense at all to have hope for better days.*
>
> *Because how could days have ever been better than a sunny walk or a dark theater or a late-night drive with your head on my shoulder?*
>
> *I can still feel the weight of it. And every time I get to close my eyes and sleep, I remember what it felt like to wake up that morning and see your face.*
>
> *I didn't bring a picture of you, because my heart was just too bitter to give myself the satisfaction. But I don't need one. I see your face in the morning. I see it across a room full of dancing kids—just like us, only not as still.*
>
> *I'd ask you to send me one, but sometimes they get taken, and it might get lost. Something tells me I should make some sort of promise here.*
>
> *Maybe even one not to write to you again. But that's not something I can say one way or another, because I've got no*

control over any minute of my life here. I've seen men die with unfinished letters in their pocket. So if I don't write again, it's not out of spite. It's because I won't until I hear from you, before I know if you are still holding your end of the lifeline you sent out when you wrote.

But this, I will promise.

As you can see, you've won this hand. I owe you a kiss. One day, if God allows, I'll be at your door. You owe me two. I owe you one.

We can settle up in New York City.

Bette laughed out loud, a harsh, barking sound. That was the promise. To show up *here*, at her tiny apartment. Instead, sometime after writing these lines, he'd suffered an injury catastrophic enough to send him to a hospital bed, unable to write at all. He'd faced some bullet or bomb without hearing a word from her.

The three letters lay on the bed, their one-sided conversation uninterrupted, as his voice changed: joy, nostalgia, sadness, strength. A longing she'd pushed down deep sprang to monstrous life, ripping at her choices.

She could find him, go to his bedside, and confess Alice's sins.

She could find him, go to his bedside, and plead ignorance of his letters. After all, twenty-four hours ago, that was the truth.

She could find him, go to his bedside, and concoct a story of amazed innocence. Of letters that must have gone missing in the overworked post office. Or lost at the hands of irresponsible mailmen.

Or she could wait here, knowing Eli to be a man of his word. If he made a promise to storm her doorstep, he would follow through. They could fall into each other's arms and after three kisses, forget all about the letters. It wouldn't matter what she did or didn't do. What she said or didn't say.

After reaching in her purse, she took out the only token she'd allowed herself to bring to the city: the deck of cards from that long-ago night. She'd stolen them without telling Eli; he would have made her take them back, to possibly rescue the virtues of the next couple who rented the room.

The winning hand sketched in the margin of the first letter came to life on the worn bedspread as Bette laid it out, card by card. Just as she'd set down a nine of diamonds, a knock sounded at the door, and the rest of the deck dropped unchecked to the floor.

CHAPTER 6

"Uncle Ray could tell how distraught I was and cut me loose early." Alice, laden with two bulging grocery sacks, shouldered past Bette into the apartment. "And he gave me a few bucks to get something nice for supper, so I stopped by the market. Tonight we eat like kings!"

Bette closed the door behind her.

"I mean, kings who have to abide by ration books," Alice prattled on, taking an assortment of cans and boxes from the first bag. "I had high hopes to get a chicken, but we'll have to make do with this." She held up two cans of soup. "But I have a good, fresh loaf of sourdough bread and—"

"Stop," Bette said, and Alice obediently set the cans on the counter.

Their little room was rarely silent. The stretch from yesterday evening until this moment might well have been the longest span of time the two were ever in each other's presence without an accompaniment of laughter. Normally the sound surrounded them like soaring violins in a movie's score. Bette recognized Alice's attempt to fill the space with chatter, but Bette would have none of it. The words from Eli's letters still swam before her eyes. She heard *his* voice cutting through the quiet.

"Do you have any idea what you've done?"

"Bette, how many times can I say, 'I'm sorry'? I didn't think—"

"No, you didn't. And that's the problem."

"I only meant for him to feel . . . connected. To someone. To you, like Frank and me—"

"But we *aren't* Frank and you, are we? We didn't follow a fool's path—"

"You think it's foolish that Frank and I got engaged?"

Bette allowed a breath, remembering a night in the bedroom she shared with Alice when they were younger, pink lace coverlets on two narrow beds and pictures of movie stars on the walls. Bette was typing a paper for her senior English class when Alice came bursting in. To be fair, it was the same way she usually burst in, only this time, she shut the bedroom door behind her before running to wave a shaking hand under Bette's nose and announcing, "We're engaged!" She had a thin band with a blue chip of a stone and went on and on about how she would plan the wedding while Frank was away. She pronounced *away* like he was headed out of state to college or to some city to work in a branch of his father's company. Nothing on her face or hand matched the circumstances of a young couple about to be forced apart by circumstances that could very well end in tragedy.

"Yes," Bette said now, making no effort to feign enthusiasm the way she did the night she learned the news. "Yes, I think it's foolish to hold each other to a promise neither of you has any power to fulfill."

Alice's face deflated, much like the empty bag on the table in front of her, a certain light snuffed out—a light that had always worked to sweep Bette into its illumination. "You've never said anything like that about it before."

"Well." Bette wished desperately she could take it back, tell her that she didn't mean it, not really. "Maybe not so much foolish as unreasonably optimistic."

A smile tugged at Alice's lips, and Bette released a breath of relief. "That," Alice said, "is what some people call hope, you know? Or even faith. That belief in a promise you can't see."

Bette glanced at the door. "Do you know what he promised?"

"Hmm?" Alice was preoccupied once again with the grocery haul.

"Eli promised to show up here. If he was able. Meaning, here, at our apartment. I'd just read that in his letter when you knocked on the door, and for a moment, I think maybe I hoped—"

"That it was him!" Alice clutched a sad-looking bunch of radishes to her chest like it was a dozen long-stemmed roses. "Oh, see? Oh, I knew it. I knew you wanted—"

"No, *he* knew what I wanted. And he agreed, or"—Bette remembered his face that night on the bleachers, the last time they looked into each other's eyes—"he didn't try to hold on. But he was hurt, I know he was. And now, when I—you—didn't write back, we hurt him all over again."

"There's only one way to fix this," Alice said, her voice just short of cajoling. "You have to go see him. Explain everything."

"You mean confess your sin?"

"If you insist on seeing it that way, yes. Maybe if he forgives me, you can too?"

Bette wanted nothing more than to feel some swell of affection for her friend, but her heart remained a dull, still mass. She ached thinking what Eli must have felt, waiting for her to respond. Because of that, despite her own wishes, she could not reconcile with her friend. Not in this moment anyway. Still, there Alice was, pleading silently, so Bette sidestepped.

"Do you want to read what he wrote?" Sometimes Alice shared lines of Frank's letters, especially when he reached out to Bette.

"Really? They're not too personal?"

"They are, but I'll get them. I think he assumes you'll be reading over my shoulder."

While Bette read Eli's letters aloud, Alice heated a can of soup and toasted bread, swooning once or twice and exclaiming, "Oh, read that again," which Bette did, relishing the feel of his thoughts mingled with her breath.

Alice sighed. "Didn't I say . . . before you even met, that you two were meant to be? Remember?"

"I remember." Bette was, in fact, reliving that moment, her heart racing at the idea of this boy who seemed both fantasy and consuming.

Alice brought them together once, and now she was poised to do so again.

"I'm free tomorrow. I'll go to him."

Alice briefly grasped Bette's hands in celebration and gratitude, then clapped joyously. "Do you want me to go with you? I will. Uncle Ray will understand."

"No," Bette said. After all, if Alice came along, Bette couldn't change her mind.

CHAPTER 7

THE RETURN ADDRESS on the envelope directed Bette to Halloran General Hospital, but nothing could have prepared Bette for the sight of it. The imposing brick structure sat amidst acres of close-cropped grass. The exact scope of it, she couldn't quite process. After one city transfer, she'd boarded the bus out to Staten Island to be dropped with her fellow passengers under a covered portico. A sign directed visitors with one painted arrow and volunteers with another. Bette fell in with the other visitors, distinct from the volunteers with their strained faces and fidgety discomfort.

Nurse Ginny's scrawled note corresponded to the signs, bringing Bette to the correct building and, ultimately, the right ward. The place was a cloud of noise—efficient, soft footsteps; indistinct conversations; and cutting through it all, intermittent and unmistakable sounds of pain.

As directed, by both the signs and the behavior of her fellow visitors, she stopped at the desk at the ward's entrance. The desk was expansive, gray, and serviceable, much like the woman behind it. When Bette's turn came up, she dutifully (again, in obedience to printed instruction) took up a pen and wrote her name, then Eli's, the date, and the time on a sheet of paper in a four-inch binder.

"And your relationship to the patient?" the volunteer asked. Her hair was iron gray and her teeth a few shades lighter. "Wife?"

"No," Bette said, perhaps too quickly.

"Are you family?"

"Do I need to be?"

"Let me check." The volunteer—Dolly, according to her name tag—pulled another binder from the corner of the desk, licked the solid rect-

142

angle of her thumb, and hummed a Cole Porter tune as she turned page after page. "Some of our boys, well, they're nervous about who comes to see them. Depends on their injury. We don't want to upset them any more than we—Ah. Here he is. Eli Landers." She looked up and smiled. "You're in luck, hon." She proceeded to tell Bette the exact information needed to navigate the halls of this ward of the hospital. And then, all of a sudden . . .

Well, it wasn't sudden at all. Bette had left a thousand steps between the front desk and this doorway to the room number Ginny Muse scrawled on the bottom corner of Eli's last letter.

"Can I help you, miss?" Yet another volunteer—Bette had passed at least a dozen in her journey—stepped from the room and placed a soft hand on her arm. She was a pretty girl, close to Bette's age, who looked like she should be heading to math class.

"Yes. I'm here to see—" Bette's mind went blank. Surely she couldn't say just *Eli*, but his official rank escaped her. What was the protocol? "Eli Landers." Her voice lifted at the end like a question, as if she might be turned away despite what was written in the binder.

"Oh, that one," the girl said with a dreamy smile. Her name tag said *Caroline*, but Bette would make an easy wager that her friends called her Carrie. "Little hint of a cleft in his chin? Looks kinda like Ronald Coleman. If I didn't read his name on the chart, I'd be asking for an autograph." She made a cheeky sound and pointed. "Third row, left."

"Thank you," Bette said, somewhat suspecting that the girl said the same thing about every patient. Eli didn't have a cleft in his chin any more than Ron Coleman did. She clutched her handbag, fingers itching to reach inside and find her handkerchief. The smell of antiseptic here battled the darker, undefinable odors. It would be rude to cover her mouth or nose, so she fought her instinct and took a deep breath instead. She kept her head bowed and her peripheral vision out of focus as her steps led her away from the volunteer.

One row.

Two rows.

Third row, left.

And there he was. Bare-chested, like he'd be if he'd just shucked his shirt to make a running leap off the deck at the lake. He was thinner than she remembered, his skin lacking the golden tones of summer, and one arm—his left—was held aloft in a complicated-looking contraption, while his right rested motionless, his hand splayed on his stomach. A thick bandage was wrapped around his torso.

Bette stared openly, allowing her eyes to take in the shape of his legs under the blanket, the rising and falling of his chest, the beauty of his hand, remembering what it felt like against hers. She used to love the way he moved. She'd watched him from the bleachers, tracking his jersey when he ran a football downfield or in the gym when he leaped to drop a ball through a hoop. She'd shouted at the poolside when he swam, and held her breath when he vaulted from the diving board into the sky. His body, the strength and speed of it, consumed her imagination. Long before they met, she studied it from afar, and once he became her boyfriend, she stole moments to puzzle over how someone so virile could also be so beautiful. She would send him on little errands—retrieving an abandoned book or a forgotten sweater—just so she could watch him walk away and back, straight to her.

Now, the luxury of her gaze came at the expense of his eyes. They, too, were bandaged, and the gauze stretched over some protrusion. Soft curls brushed the top of the bandage, and his nose—narrow and slightly crooked from a childhood fall—appeared swollen beneath it. His lips, though, hadn't changed. Bette touched her own, remembering the feel of his. She realized that she'd been holding her breath since stopping at the foot of his bed, and when she inhaled, a small gasp escaped.

Instantly, Eli's head moved as he inclined his ear. "Is that you, Nurse?"

His voice was soft, timid in a way Bette couldn't place. Needing to bring him back, she searched for an answer that would make the war between them disappear. "You wouldn't think so if you saw my grade in biology."

His reaction was not instant but gradual, starting with a tilt of his head—the same tilt he affected before laying down a winning hand of cards. Then a smile spread wide enough to take down an egg-and-cheese sandwich in a single bite.

"You must be Bette."

CHAPTER 8

THE FIRST TIME Bette fell in love with Eli was on a Tuesday afternoon, in the school library during last-hour study hall. She was strolling the stacks, looking for something romantic to take her mind off her dead mother and failing grades. He was sitting at a table with an open math book, his pencil moving busily and purposefully on a sheet of notebook paper. He looked up and smiled—not at her but at a boy who was passing by with a hand raised in greeting. The distraction was momentary before Eli was back to his studies, but the encounter ignited something in Bette. She wanted more than anything to know that boy, to have a moment of full recognition and welcome pass between them.

Then she fell in love with him in that dark corner of Alice's basement.

Then, again, the first time he put his arm around her and tucked her close as she cried along with Joan Crawford in a darkened movie theater.

Then in the gray dawn of a roadside motel.

Then, when she found him again, his heart scrawled across three pages full of the same careful script with which he solved equations.

Of course, it wasn't a new love each time, any more than each wave on the ocean was a wholly new creation. It receded and gathered more water, more sand, more tiny creatures hidden away in shells. Bette's love lapped and overlapped itself, sometimes playful and flirtatious, other times trapping her in an undertow that dragged her away from her own senses. Yesterday, when she read his letters, hesitant hope flourished. Somehow, today, sitting on a wooden chair beside his sightless, immobile body, that lighthearted love reignited.

She sat there with a head full of questions, wanting to know every detail of how the invincibly strong boy came to be this wounded soldier, but she tucked them away, choosing instead to offer the most innocuous of truths. "I'm so happy to see you, Eli."

Without missing a beat, he said, "I'd give anything to see you."

She took no time debating whether or not to laugh. The sound nearly bubbled out of her before colliding with the mass of unshed tears and bursting out in a most unladylike choking sound.

"Aw, hey. Hey, B . . ." He didn't reach for her. She surmised he couldn't, his bare arm seemingly pinned to his torso.

Now was the time for a handkerchief. Bette retrieved it from her pocketbook and held the thin cloth to her mouth, breathing in the scent of the sachet in her linen drawer.

"Lavender," Eli said softly.

"What?"

"Remember that picnic when I cut my thumb slicing strawberries, and you gave me your handkerchief to stop the bleeding? I remember that smell."

"You should. You kept the handkerchief."

"I did. But I'm sorry to report, it doesn't smell much like lavender anymore."

"Oh?" She gripped the lace-trimmed square tighter, crushing the stain of her lipstick in its folds.

"Dealing with a bit more than a little cut here," he said, engaging the entirety of his body in a gesture that seemed to encompass the scope of his injuries. "So, sorry. Looks like I won't be returning it to you at all."

"Hankie thief."

He grinned. "Add it to my list of charms."

Bette folded the handkerchief into a smaller square, lifted his hand, and placed it against his palm. "Is that okay?" She curled his fingers around it. "Does that hurt?"

He shook his head. "Doc says I have some nerve damage. Whole arm's useless right now, and might always be. Says the other should heal up, but I might have to go on with life as a lefty."

"There are worse fates," she said. *Like not going on with life at all.* "Try to keep this one clean."

"I hate to interrupt"—the cloying tone of the volunteer's voice made Bette question whether she *did* hate to interrupt—"but it's time for this soldier to have some lunch and then an appointment for PT."

Bette glanced over her shoulder to see petite, pretty Caroline balancing a tray with a bowl of soup, a sandwich, and a large glass of milk with a straw. Bette looked back at Eli, surmising that he would only be able to eat with considerable help.

"It's time I go anyway," she said, standing. "I'm due at work in a couple of hours."

Eli grinned. "But not at the store."

She smoothed her skirt. "No, I—" Bette glanced at the volunteer and hated the wave of self-consciousness threatening to overtake her. She'd never considered her cleaning job as anything other than good, honest work. Work she enjoyed, even. But here in front of this fresh-faced girl and Eli, she felt a bit like a charwoman from a Dickens novel, and she hated Dickens. "I wasn't quite up to Uncle Ray's standards. Now, I work at a hotel called the Garrison."

"Doesn't surprise me," Eli said.

Caroline set his lunch on a metal tray beside the bed, then turned a crank, working to raise up the bed to a sitting position.

Eli spoke right over the noise. "You always were one for cleaning."

Bette tried to keep her tone light. "So you assume I'm a maid?"

"Silly," he said, laughter in his voice, "you told me you were."

"Wh—" *When?* But she caught herself. Of course, in her letter. "When I wrote that, I was hoping to have been promoted by now. Front desk or something. Though I do sometimes work as a hostess in the lobby, in the evenings when there's some kind of event. There's a fancy uniform for that. Black dress, lace collar."

Caroline spread a clean white cloth over the expanse of Eli's chest. "No shame in being a maid." She settled onto Bette's abandoned chair and picked up the bowl of soup. "You wouldn't believe the messes I clean up around here."

"I'll try not to dribble," Eli said, giving Bette the clear impression that he and Caroline had a long-established banter.

"I'll just go, then," Bette said, backing away. She held her hand up in a parting wave before realizing the uselessness of the gesture. Eli could neither see nor wave back, and Caroline was completely absorbed in her task.

Eli strained his head above his pillow. "But you'll be back? There's so much I want to say."

"Yes."

"When?"

Caroline touched the spoon to his lips.

"Soon, Eli. As soon as I can."

CHAPTER 9

WHAT BETTE LOVED most about her work at the Garrison was the perfect combination of physical labor, silence, and solitude. It was comfortable, nostalgic work that brought to mind all her after-school afternoons and Saturday mornings spent dusting and cleaning the little apartment, wiping around the edges of the quiet, sad life she shared with her mother. The hotel guests rarely looked Bette in the eye in hallway greetings, let alone engaged her in conversation, and she kept away from locker-room gossip with her fellow maids. The twenty minutes or so she spent in each small space meant a reliable, measurable source of accomplishment and achievement. Messy room coming in, clean room going out. And in between, the daydreams she wove around the detritus of the guests' stays— the scraps of paper and receipts, pillowcases smeared with lipstick, puddles of spilled hair tonic—all spoke of lives filled with either adventure and romance or bureaucratic importance. Bette had none of this but savored the small part she played. She pictured women coming in and exclaiming how very clean the room seemed with its gleaming furniture, sparkling mirror, and tightly tucked sheets. The men would appreciate the anonymity, the lack of fuss and frills, and the clean slate at every visit.

Good, honest work.

But nothing about her seemed honest after her visit with Eli, after her confrontation with the lie Alice roped her into telling. Bette had grown up behind a lie, or at least a deceitful façade. Young Bette baked her own cookies and cupcakes for school parties and bake sales. She'd taken down the hems of her own skirts with every growth spurt and taken herself in to be measured for her first brassiere. She ran to the grocer's with a list written in her own hand and squirreled away the change to buy notebooks and pencils and new hair ribbons when the popular girls switched the acceptable colors.

Only Alice knew the entire truth. She alone was trusted with the knowledge of the gaps in life that Bette could not fill. The friendship was genuine, but the dinner invitations were purposeful. The midweek sleepovers when Mother's wailing crossed into fits of rage were granted without question. Alice—and by necessity, her whole family—knew all about Bette's sad, lonely life and offered on multiple occasions to take her in permanently. Or at least until her mother got "better." But then, Mother never did get better. Bette spent the night at Alice's house the day of the funeral and never left. It seemed natural, given the entire town thought of the two girls as a single, giggling entity. The truth of silent neglect behind Bette's closed door died along with her mother.

Until Bette met Eli.

She'd poured into him every detail, relived every frightening moment. First, to explain why she was new to school and not already enmeshed with the crowd of kids he, Alice, and Frank ran with, then to explain why she sometimes seemed so guarded, so careful with her words.

"I'm kind of a tangle," she told him once. They were lying on the hood of his car on one of the last warm days of October. "Like how a tree can grow straight up, but underneath, it's just a mess of intertwining roots."

"So you're a mess?" His voice was lazy with autumn sunshine.

She concentrated on the feel of the metal along her spine. "Yep."

"But you're *my* mess, right?"

She thought about reaching across to hold his hand, to seal herself to him in that moment, but she was so warm, so settled. Her own hands were clasped to each other on her stomach, her arms melded to the hood of the car. To move would break the spell and dislodge her.

"No." She drew out the word, searching for its meaning. "It's mine. It's always been mine, and I've learned how to carry it."

"Maybe I could help you carry it? I'm pretty strong, you know, if you haven't noticed."

Now, he couldn't lift his hand. Couldn't feed himself a sandwich or shield his eyes against the sun.

She only worked half a shift that Saturday, having called in a favor with one of the girls to work her morning so she could visit Eli. Her final room clean, Bette rolled her cart down the hallway and rang for the service elevator. On the short ride to the basement, she calculated her tips, separating out the nickels. It was a ritual that she and Alice had to meet for dinner at the nearest Automat every Saturday evening after their respective work shifts. Normally, this was the high point of Bette's week, but a part of her heart still burned against her friend, no matter the fragile truce they had declared. Alice turned Bette into a liar. Alice let Eli go into battle thinking Bette didn't care for him. Because of Alice, Bette's final memory of Eli wouldn't be of the strong, determined man with the windblown hair and eyes holding her in place. Instead, she carried the image of those eyes bandaged with blindness and arms that might never hold anything again.

She returned her cart, restocked it, and went to the women's locker room to change out of her uniform. She was buttoning her blouse when Anna, one of the older women working in housekeeping, entered.

"Miss Bette," she said, her worn face creased in a smile. "I am always on the lookout. Here, for you." She held out a crumpled silk stocking. "Left in the trash. I rescued it. For our boys, like you say."

Bette took it and folded it with an attitude of near reverence. Until today, the boys were images in newsreels and strangers on the street. She dropped the stocking into her handbag. "Thank you, Anna. I have several pieces that I'll be taking in on Monday."

"Our God is bigger than Hitler." Anna lifted her fist in the air, then opened it and brought it down to make the sign of the cross over her chest. "But no reason not to give him a little help."

"Amen."

Bette dropped her uniform in the laundry cart and paused at the mirror to run her fingers through her hair and refresh her lipstick. She had time—nearly three hours—before she was due to meet Alice. Any other Saturday, she might while away the time in the library, but she'd left the apartment in such a fogged state that morning that she'd forgotten her books. Instead, she walked with no clear plan other than to fill the time. She made no correction when her feet took her away from the familiar path home or when they bypassed the Automat, where she was meant to go, or when they boarded a bus to Staten Island. This time they moved with familiarity, taking her up the steps and through the door. They waited patiently while she signed the visitor's book, then led her confidently through the hallways, to the room, to the aisle, to the bed where Eli waited, still as a lake on a windless day. She spoke, and he rippled.

"Bette? Two visits in one day?"

"I had time on my hands." She wasn't ready to tell him she couldn't think of a better way to spend it.

"And I've got nothing but. Pull up a chair and tell me about your day."

She detected the faintest twitch of his shoulder, his body creating the invisible gesture. "Oh, the fascinating world of hotel housekeeping. Today I used a drop too much of lemon wax on the desk, so if some poor girl tries to sit on it, she'll slide right off."

His grin was just shy of wicked. "Are you saying you did this on purpose?"

"I'm not saying anything. Another one of the girls found a stocking. There's a dry cleaner around the corner from the apartment that takes donations. I've got quite a haul to take in."

"A true girl for the war effort."

She tried to block out the soft sounds of pain coming from all directions. "You can't imagine how helpless we all feel here, wanting to do something. Anything. And everything seems so small."

"It isn't small. And believe me, I'm developing a true understanding of feeling helpless."

"Forgive me." Would she always have to choose her words so carefully? "That was thoughtless."

"There's nothing to forgive. For the rest of my life, people are going to be looking at me and choosing their words carefully, trying not to hurt or offend. Don't be one of those people, Bette. Always speak your heart with me."

"I will. You know, I didn't plan to come back to see you."

"Today? Or ever?"

She didn't have an answer, so she glossed over the question. "I just . . . followed my—"

"Heart?"

"—feet."

"Well, I don't care if you were following your liver or your elbows. I'm glad you're here."

"I'm supposed to be at an Automat right now, meeting Alice for dinner. It's our Saturday-night routine."

"I know. You told me."

"Of course I did." *Of course she did.*

"But tell me more. What's it like? I'm the only guy in my unit who didn't go to one during my New York leave."

Bette scooted the chair closer, as if preparing to impart a secret or magic charm. Eli inclined his head, and she caught a whiff of shaving soap.

"It's an amazing place. For less than a quarter, you can have any combination of food you want. I like the Salisbury steak with mashed potatoes and a slice of chocolate pie and coffee. Alice gets the chicken pot pie."

"And there's a machine?"

"Not so much a machine. You put your nickel in a slot, turn a handle, and the little door pops open so you can take your food. You get glimpses of people working on the other side, but it's more fun to think of everything just magically appearing on those little plates. And the coffee?" She inhaled deeply, smelling it. "Don't get me started. It's the best; it's the only coffee I'd ever drink outside of home. The spigots look like silver dolphins, and you can imagine some mythical, endless vat of the stuff pouring out from the café of the gods."

"You'll have to take me, then, once I'm sprung from this place."

"I will," she said, caught up in the moment. In the breaths that followed, she realized she'd love nothing more. "It's reason enough to stay in the city forever."

"You don't think you'll want to leave once Alice and Frank settle down? I don't think there's a restaurant in the world that could convince Frank to live in the city."

"And you'll never get Alice to live anywhere without Frank. But I'm hoping to build enough of a life here that I could stay on my own. Goodness knows, our apartment is better suited to one tenant."

Any other conversation would have transitioned to Eli. Questions would be presented about his plans for the future. Where did he see himself settling down? But Bette couldn't bring herself to ask, and he volunteered nothing but a silence that kept them next to each other, wondering.

"Dinnertime!" There must have been a shift change, as the volunteer making the announcement did so with the affection of a mother calling her family to the dinner table. Bette turned to look and felt a sense of comfort at the woman's presence. Pauline was round and soft, her brown hair streaked with gray, twisted and secured in a thick knot. She set down the tray on the metal table and all but nudged Bette off the chair to crank Eli's bed.

"Thus endeth our visiting hours," Eli said. "Feel free to come back tomorrow."

"I can't come back tomorrow." Bette spoke over the woman's broad back, straight to Eli. "Alice and I go back home on Sundays for church and dinner."

"I remember those Sunday dinners."

"They aren't quite as lavish in days of ration books."

Pauline stood and placed her heavy hands on her hips. "Look, I hate to kick the two of you off memory lane, but unless you want to feed this man his supper, I got to get you to go."

Bette craned her neck and looked around the woman, making a face that Eli couldn't see, yet he twisted his mouth in a mirror expression.

"Do you want to?" Eli's question held the hint of a dare, like he was asking her to jump off a cliff or pet a feral cat.

Bette responded in kind, upping the stakes. "Do you want me to?"

"Listen, kids," Pauline said, stepping back, "I'm just going to leave this here and let you do whatever you're going to do. If the food's still here after my rounds, I'll shovel it in myself."

She left, and Bette stifled a laugh behind her hand.

"She didn't sound too happy," Eli deadpanned.

"She didn't look too happy either. Now"—she sat on the chair and scooted it closer—"how do we handle this?"

"I, the hungry one, open my mouth. You, the one with two functioning arms, put food in it. A fairly simple process."

"Unless you've never done it before."

"You aren't in this alone, my darling. I'll be right here with you."

Before proceeding, Bette made a softly sarcastic reply about being thankful and relieved to have his guidance. Remembering what she'd seen at lunch, she unfolded the napkin and let it waft down to cover his chest, then—*unlike* Caroline's method—brought her hand to smooth it in place, holding her breath as his muscles tensed beneath her touch. Battered and bandaged he might be, but he was still the man who sheltered her body from the wind as they gathered with friends around a bonfire at the lake.

He cleared his throat, and she followed suit. "You hungry, big guy?"

"Yeah."

"All right then. Here—it's . . . here." She brought a forkful of mashed potatoes and felt her own mouth opening as if to eat them. Eli opened his, then closed his lips around the fork, muttering an appreciative sound once he'd swallowed.

After the first bite, feeding him became easy, seemed natural. Bette kept her nerves and hand steady, monopolizing the conversation. She told him about her job at the hotel, the colorful guests, the famous and the powerful. "And then there are the couples. An officer in uniform and his wife catching a few hours together . . ." She let the thought slip into silence as she dabbed at the corner of his mouth with the napkin.

"You always did love cleaning," he said.

"I have," she said, and told him about the font of silk the job provided: stockings and negligees and men's shirts stained too severely with red wine to survive the most dedicated laundry. "I think I work better without direct supervision. Without having every minute counted and every move scrutinized. That was my problem working at Goode's. I would never have thought to work there at all if not for Alice, and I wouldn't have lasted as long as I did without her."

"Always one to help," Eli said through a mouthful of pastry.

"Yes."

"Best thing she ever did, bringing us together."

For the first time, Bette was grateful he couldn't see, because she flinched at his words. Did he know about the letter's true author? Confession danced on the tip of her tongue, but she bit it back. "Because I asked her to."

"See? A good friend. More pie please."

Bette complied, and her stomach took that moment to rumble its protest of the lateness of the hour.

Eli laughed, then sobered. "I'm sorry. I didn't think about your missing supper to stay here and take care of me. You can have my piecrust, if you want. I know it's your favorite part."

"I was going to eat it anyway and just tell you the army makes crustless pies." She picked up the remainder of the pastry with her fingers and bit it in half. It had a nice balance of salty and sweet but was nowhere near as good as the pie from an Automat. She spared him the comparison.

Before leaving them, Pauline had pulled the white sheet surrounding the bed to allow them a bit of privacy or maybe to spare Bette the sight of those soldiers who did not have the strength or means to enjoy a fine American supper. Still, she heard them—soft moans and cries, pleas of "Nurse?" and "Doctor!" Mumbled names and whispered prayers and cooing assurances. This was what passed for silence here, and she wondered how it didn't drive Eli mad. True, her little apartment offered little protection from the noise of the city—cars, sirens, voices—but those were the sounds of *life*. The men on these beds may, like Eli, have survived their wounds, but what kind of life waited?

"It won't always be like this," Eli said, reading her thoughts. "I know this isn't what you envisioned."

"I never envisioned anything."

"Right. That's why you sent me away without so much as a kiss goodbye."

"Should I have been more like Alice? With my wedding dress waiting in the closet? Never really knowing if—"

"You're nothing like Alice. I'm not in love with Alice."

"You're not in love with me either, Eli. Or you wouldn't be, if you knew . . ."

"If I knew, what?"

"That I don't know if I love you. Anymore, or if I ever did. That you were this fantasy of a boy, this beautiful . . . *thing*. Something that I wanted and I had and I gave away."

Perhaps she was wrong about the lack of silence in the room, because a wall of it went up between them—one made of truth but mortared with lies, the greatest of all being the one etched in the air. She removed the napkin and now looked down at his chest, the one part of his exposed body that looked as it did in those days of picnics and swimming and clumsy games of tennis. Beneath it, his heart was beating, and she remembered the feel of its rhythm against her cheek. She felt her pulse thrumming in her ears, and before she could stop herself, she leaned forward, bent down, and pressed against him. The heartbeat in her ear matched that of her memory; moreover, it matched her own in this moment. She felt herself rise and fall with each of his breaths. She closed her eyes, blocking every sense that wasn't him, sharing his blindness, salting her eyes with tears.

"I'm sorry." Her lips moved against his skin, almost like a kiss.

"It's all right." His voice rumbled through her.

"It's not. And it isn't true. None of it."

He made a shushing sound, and she wished he could hold her, stroke her hair, touch her cheek. Without a doubt, he wished so too. Slowly, reluctantly, like climbing out of a warm bed on a cold morning, she rose up. Taking his lifeless hand in both of hers, she brought it to her face and wiped her tears with his fingers.

"Can you feel that?" she asked, genuinely curious.

"Some, but I can't—" The almost imperceptible twitch of his fingers explained the rest.

"Does anything hurt?"

"Nothing I can't handle. These other guys . . . I know I got out pretty good."

"Pretty good," she echoed before placing a soft kiss on the back of his hand and laying it on the bed beside him. "I should go, I guess, if I want the slightest chance of Alice forgiving me for ditching our dinner."

"One thing before you go. When you said goodbye to me, I never expected to see you again. At least not until I got home. And then you wrote to me—"

"Eli—"

"But you never wrote *back*, so again, I never expected to see you. And then this morning, you were here. And to tell you the truth, after seeing me, I never thought . . . But you're here, aren't you? What do you want?"

"I don't want anything, Eli. I just had to see—"

"To see what happened to that 'beautiful boy'? Let me tell you, B, he's gone. He's going to walk out of here with one good eye and one good arm. This man is never going to be that boy. And even if"—he took a breath, fighting to control his voice—"even if I were whole, I'd never be that boy again. Everything I did over there, everything I saw—it killed the beauty in me. So if you came back looking for him—"

"I haven't. And you're wrong. You can come back."

"But you can't come back to me. Not here, not again. I don't want to see you until I can really, truly *see* you. And I hate imagining the pity in your eyes when you see me . . . like this."

"I don't feel pity."

"I don't believe you. How could you not?"

"Because I feel—" She stopped and swallowed, making room in her throat for a portion of truth. "I hate that we lost so much."

"I'm sorry. I know I'm not the man—"

"Not that," she rushed in. "Maybe if you thought I was waiting for you—"

"The enemy's fire might have missed me?"

She suppressed a laugh. "I might have prayed . . . more. Differently. And I didn't write back to your first letter." Silence cleared the way for a confession. Or an accusation. But she couldn't tell him, not now. Not while he seemed to be resting in the shadow of self-pity. "We've lost so much, Eli. Not just you, but me too. I lost what I didn't even know I wanted."

"You can't possibly want me like this. I don't want you to want me like this. So I'm telling you, don't come back."

Bette sat up straight. "You can't order me around, Eli. You can't tell me what to do."

He laughed, a good and healthy sound rooted in his chest. "Well, that hasn't changed at least." He managed a twitch of his finger, and she instinctively covered it with hers.

"I'll come back and bring Alice with me. We have an afternoon free together next week. Maybe I'll bring our record player, and we can listen to some music. Like old days."

"Don't come. Don't bring a record player, and don't bring Alice."

"Well now, darling," she said, giving his hand a final squeeze, "I'll give you one out of three."

CHAPTER 10

BETTE CAME HOME to find a note from Alice scrawled on the back of an envelope informing her that, when Bette didn't turn up for dinner at the Automat, she took Uncle Ray up on his offer to drive her home, where she intended to stay for the weekend, with plans to return Monday afternoon.

> *PS I do hope you're not dead in an alley. I'll give you a call tomorrow morning around 8:30 a.m., before church. Please pick up so I don't have to call the police.*

And so, Sunday morning, with a cup of coffee and a cheese Danish from the deli around the corner, Bette waited by the common telephone in the apartment building's lobby. She picked it up on the first ring.

"You're alive!" Alice sounded genuinely relieved. She might not have been so certain if she could see Bette face-to-face. A long, sleepless night had left her pale with bags under her eyes big enough to hold her Danish.

"I am."

"You sound odd." Her friend was never one to miss a detail.

"Haven't had my coffee yet. You sound . . . chipper."

"Do I? Maybe because I might make a guess as to where you were last night and why you didn't show up for our sad Saturday-night date?"

"Yes . . . I saw him."

Alice emitted a shrill so sharp Bette had to hold the phone away from her ear.

"Oh, I knew it. I *knew* it! I want details, but this is long distance, and

Dad set the timer. Sand's running out, and I'll get an earful if I go over. You remember."

She did. She could picture the three-minute timer with its blue sand used every morning to poach the perfect egg.

"So dinner Monday. Automat. My treat. Tell me everything, Bette. Good, bad, happy, sad. Everything. And I have news too, about the nylon sale. But—time's up."

They said a hasty goodbye, and Bette took a sip of her coffee from the waxed cup, pleased to find it drinkably warm. She took her breakfast upstairs and sat at the table, savoring the relative quiet of the city. She should go to church—she *would* go to church—but that was a couple of hours away. She took Eli's letters and laid them out, reading and re-reading, looking for the places where the boy she'd known crossed with the man she left lying in a hospital bed. He would have to learn to write again, using his nondominant hand—something that would have been frowned upon under Miss Bernadette's instruction.

At precisely 10:30 a.m., dressed in her best blue dress and last year's most stylish hat, Bette stepped out for the two-block walk to church. Its bells were clanging by the time she arrived, and she tried to blend in with the families filling the pews. She knew nobody by name; she and Alice attended here only on the Sundays when a trip home proved impossible. Alice was always quick to say, "Good morning," and shake a hand, but Bette welcomed the cloak of anonymity. She'd hated the long, sad looks meant to buoy her up the aisle at her mother's funeral, and the even longer and sadder ones each Sunday after. She remembered every clicking tongue, every *such a shame*, every pitiful sound about *that poor girl*, coming from women who would never profess to being her mother's friend. They spoke as if she couldn't hear them, saying things about her mother that simply weren't true—that she was such a kind woman and a wonderful mother. They wondered aloud how the poor girl would manage, as if Bette hadn't been taking care of herself all these years in the cold shadow of her mother's darkness. The lies spun in every direction, and they were the worst kind of lies too, because they sounded like kindness and caring. They sounded like vows, like the kind of love Jesus talked about, to care for widows and orphans. Her mother had been a widow all those years, and now Bette was an orphan, but the ladies of the church offered nothing but whispers and sandwiches.

Here, though, this morning, the conversation was a single, impenetrable sound, promising nothing. She moved through it with her head high and her eyes purposefully aloof. Her faith always felt strongest when it was wrapped in solitude, even if that solitude came in the midst of a crowd. Maybe especially so, since she'd grown up behind a brave face. She took her preferred seat in the back, near a stained-glass depiction of Jesus washing the apostle Peter's feet. The moment captured in the image drew her in. Of all the big things Jesus did—the crowds, the preaching, the healing—here was a bit of silence. This morning, she thought of Peter in a way she never had before. How, soon after that, he messed up so badly, how he denied loving, following, and even *knowing* Jesus. But there he was, captured in a moment of loyalty and love. And later, after the betrayal, after Jesus—healed, though scarred—took Peter back.

Would Eli ever forgive her? More so, could she find the courage to ask? Or could they take this as a fresh start, forget the yawning emptiness of the past, and build their lives upon each other?

This Sunday Bette wouldn't have the pew to herself. A family of three joined her—mother, father, and a boy she estimated to be about nine years old. Rather than sitting between his parents, he sat between his mother and Bette. He stood and sang solemnly from the hymnbook and bowed his head in prayer when directed to do so. When the congregation sat to listen to the sermon, he dutifully opened his Bible, but with a glance, Bette noticed that he had another book tucked within it. Whatever he had between the pages held his attention, and he became lost in it, feet swinging beneath him. She noticed that he held the Bible at an artful angle to hide its true contents from his mother. To keep herself from laughing, Bette pulled her attention away from him and focused on the words of the pastor at the front of the church. Today's sermon, like too many others, began with the reading of the names of the wounded and dead sons of the congregation. There were blissfully few this morning, but Bette silently added Eli's name to the list. She joined the congregation in saying, "Amen," to the petition that God would restore the bodies of those who were wounded. She inquired, too, that God would bring peace to the families of those whose sons, fathers, and brothers gave the ultimate sacrifice of their lives in order to bring peace to the world.

When the parents went up to receive communion, the little boy was left to himself, and Bette opted to stay behind so he wouldn't be all alone. She had another motive for waiting a turn. She tapped lightly beside him on the pew, calling his attention, and when he looked up at her, she asked in a soft whisper, "What has captured your imagination, there?"

The boy eyed her with suspicion, but Bette's grin must have made him feel welcome to share a secret. He slipped the book out from between the Bible's pages, revealing its title: *The Wreck of the Dumaru.*

"Oh, that's a good one," she said. She remembered Eli speaking of it as being one of his favorite books when he was a kid. It was a story of adventure and survival—something that must have seemed so desirable at the time. She knew she should chastise the boy, or at least take possession of the novel until the service ended, but the idea of being an ally proved too strong. He trusted her, and she would prove worthy of that trust. Moreover, she imagined sharing the encounter with Eli, sharing the boy's subterfuge and a hearkening back to Eli's childhood. Eli, morally upstanding even at a young age, would never have sneaked a book about shipwrecks into church, where, if one wanted to learn about adventures at sea, one could learn about the adventures of Jonah. Still, wasn't there glory to be found in all stories of rescue?

When she got home, she took it upon herself to clean the little apartment top to bottom. Alice often said that Bette shouldn't have to clean since that's what she did for work. By that token, Alice shouldn't always be talking Bette and herself into buying new lotions and perfumes. But the truth of it was, if it were left to Alice to clean the apartment, they'd never be able to take a single step in the squalor. Few people could truly understand the therapeutic nature that cleaning was to Bette. The repetitive motion, the scent of soap, the strength of wringing warm water from a mop—each a means to make a hundred lazy choices made right.

Even so, when she finished, it was barely six o'clock, and she couldn't face this stretch of the evening home alone. So without any summons of any kind, she walked to the Garrison Hotel, found her black dress uniform and lace collar left unused in the women's locker room, and spent the evening roaming from one guest to another and cleaning up tiny messes. She emptied ashtrays, walked empty glasses back to the bar, tidied up abandoned newspapers, and discreetly wiped up spills and sloshes, working with a deeply satisfying invisibility until it was well past midnight and time to go home.

She heard Uncle Ray's car earlier than expected the next morning. Not even 10:00 a.m., which was odd, because the family always reserved the right to come in late on a Monday, leaving the store in Thea's capable hands. Bette had already been up for hours; she never was one for sleeping late at all. She was barely one for sleeping, truth be told. She looked out the window and saw Uncle Ray holding the vehicle door open for Alice, who emerged with the help of his hand. She moved slowly from the car, seemed to refuse Uncle Ray's help any further, and disappeared from Bette's view.

Something was wrong.

Bette opened the door and ran downstairs to meet Alice halfway, but her friend rushed right past her, as if she were as blind as Eli.

"Alice?" Bette said but got no response in return.

She followed Alice upstairs, and though there were mere seconds between them, the front room was empty. She went into the bedroom they shared and found Alice sitting on the bed clutching the wedding dress in one hand and a yellow telegram in the other.

CHAPTER 11

"His parents got it yesterday afternoon." Alice sounded like she was projecting her voice from a deep, dark place. "They came over to the house in the evening, just as Mom was serving pie."

Bette crouched to take her friend in her arms. Alice was stonelike in every manner of being, unbending to the embrace, her cheek cold and dry to the touch. Obviously, the telegram held bad news, but there was such a range of news that could come from the other side of the world.

"Is he"—Bette searched for the right sequence—"is he wounded? Missing?"

"Gone." Such finality saturated the single, small word. "His ship . . . his body, unsalvageable."

"That's what it says?" She gently reached for the telegram, but Alice only gripped it tighter.

"You have to read between the lines a little, but Seaman Frank McGinty was not listed among the survivors."

Bette looked at the telegram and knew it had not left Alice's hand since she first took it in her grip. Dried mascara tracks made it clear she hadn't washed her face, and her hair bore the messiness of a sleepless night. Bette had never seen her friend so devoid of life, and felt a prick and the start of her own slipping away. Since they were children, it was Alice who devised their plans and led their play. Alice who encouraged and chastised. Alice who set the tone, approved the emotion, gave off the energy to make one minute lead to another. If Bette ever exuded a bit of confidence, it was because Alice taught her how to do so. She'd grown strong in the wake of Alice's wave. She didn't know what to do in the midst of all this stillness.

"They shouldn't have left you here alone."

"Uncle Ray dropped me off. I assured him you would be here. He had to get to the store."

"Why didn't you call me last night? I would have come up to you."

"I didn't want to spoil your time with—" Alice's voice broke, and for the first time, her big blue eyes brimmed with tears.

Bette had yet to shed her own, dammed as they were by the shock of the news and the need to be the strong one in the moment. "Let me run you a bath." She stood. "Make you a cup of tea? And some rest. You need to sleep."

"I don't want to sleep. If I sleep, I'll wake up, and it will all be real again."

"It's real now, my darling." Bette helped Alice stand, remaining rigid as her friend fell against her. Alice's small body heaved with sobs, leaving Bette helpless to do anything other than wrap her arms around those soft shoulders and hold her close. She kissed the top of Alice's head and whispered platitudes that she wasn't sure she believed. Things would not look better after a bath and sleep. Alice was not going to be all right—not anytime soon anyway. The only truths Bette spoke was that they would weather this together and they would hold on to each other. The biggest truths of all, the one too unwieldy for words, were Bette's forgiveness for the letter and the guilt that was solely responsible for holding her upright.

She ushered Alice into the tiny bathroom and turned on the tap in the tub. Gingerly, promising to keep it safe and in sight, she pried the telegram from Alice's weakening grip and set the slip of paper on the shelf above the sink, where it lay terrible among the jars of powders and creams. As Alice stepped out of her shoes, Bette held her up, then helped her out of her sweater and skirt and brassiere and slip. By now, the tub was half filled, the room scented with rose oil. Bette held her friend steady as she stepped into the water, not letting go until she was sitting, mostly submerged.

"Shall I brush your hair?"

Alice nodded, then scooped water to her face.

Bette balanced on the edge of the tub and took Alice's hair in her hands. For a while, the room was silent, save for the occasional lapping of the water at the tub's edge and the sound of the bristles against Bette's palm. Alice had always been so strong in the times of Bette's grief, but Bette had no idea what else to do in this moment.

So she asked, "What can I do?"

"Tell me about Eli," Alice said, staring into the water.

"I can't. I mean, it doesn't seem—"

"Tell me everything. I need some happy news."

"Well . . ." Bette plaited Alice's hair into a thick braid, stalling for time. Was Eli the embodiment of happy news? She pictured him, blind and helpless—but alive. "He recognized my voice," she said, coiling and pinning the braid, "because, of course, he couldn't see me."

Alice swiveled her head. "He's blind?"

"Not completely. Or permanently."

"Thank God for that," Alice said, turning aside again.

"Yes." Bette plunged the washrag in the water and lathered it with lavender-scented soap. She trailed it along with rivulets of water across her friend's back, while telling her of Eli's other injuries—the suspended shoulder, the limp and lifeless arm—infusing her descriptions with a lilting hope of healing. "He'll never be exactly who he was." She finished bathing her friend and rinsed her off before Alice finally responded.

"But he's here." Alice's whisper echoed back from the water.

Bette wrung out the washcloth and draped it over the side of the tub. "I'll see what we have for lunch."

She spent the rest of the day watching Alice sleep and keeping toast and tea at the ready for those moments of tearful wakefulness. The next morning, she called in to the hotel to beg off work, explaining in truthful detail how she was needed at home to care for a friend. And that afternoon, Uncle Ray dropped by to say that Alice was welcome to take the week off.

"No," Alice told him resolutely. "I can't just sit around here like a tick on a tail. Frank wouldn't want that. Plus, there's the nylon sale on Thursday. You'll need all hands on deck for that."

"They don't have to be your hands," Bette said, looking for Ray's approval. "I'll switch shifts at the hotel."

"Maybe Alice is right," Uncle Ray said, jumping in a little too quickly. "Sometimes busy hands heal a broken heart."

"This isn't a *broken heart*," Bette said, fighting for civility. "She's in mourning."

"I'll be fine," Alice reassured. "I'm not the only woman to face this. The city—heck, the entire country—is full of women like me. What would happen if all of us just curled up in a ball and died alongside our men? Our country would die too."

"The country will survive with one less countergirl selling perfume and face cream," Bette said.

Alice's wide eyes filled with tears. "Those women who come to me have husbands and sons and brothers fighting over there, just like we do. Or *did*. You don't know how many come and tell me they haven't worn perfume in years, but their sweetheart is coming back . . ."

Bette sat in respectful silence.

Uncle Ray, however, shifted from foot to foot, clutching and unclutching his hat, clearly wishing he'd sent a note instead of paying a visit. The girls had always said the apartment was too small to accommodate a man, and here he was, proving the point.

"I help them feel pretty," Alice said once composed. "I give them hope that someday, this will all be over, and women can just be . . . *women* again."

Under any other circumstances, Bette would have bitten back, *"Who's to say we aren't women now?"* Indeed, this was an argument the two friends had had before—dozens of times. Alice longed only to be a wife. She lived with her wedding dress in her closet and her fiancé appointed before high school graduation. She'd always been far more serious and detailed in playing with her dolls, pretending they were real children with nap times and feeding schedules, whereas Bette was constantly leaving hers in the park under the slide or at home under her bed for weeks at a time. She never had the luxury of building a fantasy world or living in the future. Alice never had to scramble for footing in a given moment. Frank's was the first death she'd ever known, and it had happened so far away—like something in a movie. Nothing in her world—not in this *tangible* world—need change at all. If not for the crumpled telegram, none of them might even know. Not like Bette, growing up in a slowly emptying house, with her mother's slowly emptying mind.

Thankfully, Uncle Ray piped up to spare the need for any reply. "Take the time you need, my dear." He laid an awkward hand on Alice's shoulder.

"Maybe just one more day?" Alice dabbed at her eyes. "I look such a mess right now, nobody would trust me to recommend a bar of soap."

Bette joined her in a self-conscious chuckle.

After a perfunctory hug, Uncle Ray left, as if in escape.

A new silence settled. Bette went to the kettle. "Can I make—"

"No more tea," Alice said with a weak smile. "One more cup, and I'll have to find myself a new home across the pond." She delivered the final words with an attempted British accent that never failed to make Bette laugh.

"Spare me," Bette said in surrender. "I just don't know what to do. I'm no good at this. I don't know what to say. I want to feel, I don't know, useful?"

Alice reached out and took her hand. "Being here and being my friend—that's more than I can ask for."

"Of course. I'm here, and I'm your friend. I love you."

"And forgive me?"

It was a beat before Bette could even conjure what she had to forgive Alice *for*. "All's well, kitten. No harm done."

"So you told him?"

"Told him?"

"That I, not you, wrote the letter?"

Bette gave a final squeeze to Alice's hand, then busied herself at the sink. "Not exactly. And by 'not exactly,' I mean 'no.'"

"Bette! How could you?"

Bette spun around. "Now hold on. You don't get to chastise me for carrying on what you started. I wanted to tell him. I truly did. But the right moment didn't come along. He seemed . . . frail."

"Eli? Frail?"

"You didn't see him. Plus"—a deep breath took Bette to the truth—"it was nice seeing him, spending a few moments together like old times."

"Good for him? Or good for you?"

"Both, I suppose. He told me how much that first letter meant, and if he knows I didn't send it, he'll think that I never cared. Maybe even that I don't care now."

"But you do?"

"I do."

"That's why we should tell him together."

"*We*?"

"Take me to see him."

"I don't think that's a good idea."

"Not today. My head is pounding, and I look a mess. But tomorrow morning? You don't go in to work until the afternoon."

"You know I'd do anything for you, but—"

"Frank was Eli's best friend. The four of us were—Well, you know what we were. He should hear it from us."

Alice, who had at times been barely able to whisper a coherent string of words since Bette found her clutching the telegram, had grown back into her voice. The voice that said, *"Let's move to the city!"* and *"Work a few days a week at my uncle's store! It'll be fun!"* Bette had no doubt it had been Alice who finagled an engagement from Frank before he shipped out.

"Fine," Bette said, as Alice must have known she would. "We'll go first thing."

CHAPTER 12

BETTE WAS STILL running her fingers through her pillow-flattened hair when Alice's face popped up from behind her in the bathroom mirror. Her hair was pinned up in a perfect victory roll, a feat Bette had never been able to accomplish. Beyond Alice's shining curls, her face appeared fresh, accented with a touch of rouge and mascara, her lips pink with a tentative smile.

"Mornin', Alice," Bette said through a yawn. "You look like you slept well."

"I did. Thank you."

"For what?"

Alice gave her a squeeze from behind. "For everything. How long until you're ready?"

Bette met her eyes in the mirror. "You tell me."

Alice laughed. "I brought home a sample lipstick from the store. Berries Delight. I think it'll suit you. Wait right here."

Bette took a deep breath, relieved to see a bit of her Alice returned, but worried, too, that her presentation might be no more than a fragile façade. How would she respond to a room full of wounded men, most—if not all—of whom would return to their wives and sweethearts? Bette splashed her face with cold water and dampened her hair enough to bring it to some sort of style. She was powdering her nose when Alice returned, holding out the lipstick tube.

And something else.

The wedding dress.

"Alice?" Bette reached tentatively for the lipstick, avoiding the merest touch of the dress.

"I don't know what to do with it now," Alice said, her voice so empty it echoed.

"Sweetie," Bette said, softening her tone as the grandeur of the dress diminished in the dim light of the single bathroom bulb, "you don't have to do anything with it right now."

"No, I mean . . . I've ruined it." Alice lifted up the bottom of the dress in display. There was a jagged place where the hem had been ripped asunder. "Didn't I always say that I thought the dress held a secret? I found it." She'd been keeping the hand that held the lipstick closed but now uncurled her fingers to show something that looked like a tightly rolled bit of fabric on her palm.

"What is it?"

"I don't know. I wanted to be with you when I looked."

Bette set the lipstick on the side of the sink and took the bit of fabric from Alice's hand. It was coarse—nothing like the silk of the dress—and brown. Plain. She found the edge and, with instinctive care, began unrolling until it revealed itself to be a trimmed scrap of burlap. There was something stitched across it, which Bette couldn't quite make out.

"Turn it over," Alice said. "This is the back side."

Bette turned the fabric over and laid it across Alice's palm, still open and suspended between them. Their voices spoke in unison, reading aloud: "'For he shall give his angels charge over thee, to keep thee in all thy ways.'"

Alice spoke the chapter and verse—Psalm 91:11—alone, whispered as if a prayer.

"How lovely," Bette said, attempting to roll the scrap up again.

"Not so much a secret as a message," Alice said, stilling Bette's progress. "Why do you think she put it there?"

Bette shrugged. "Who knows? A blessing over her marriage?"

"Or for the next one." Alice gave over the scrap. "I've always known there was something there. Why didn't I look earlier?"

"What difference would it have made if you had?"

"Don't you see? It's a prayer of protection. I could have given it to Frank.

He could have put it in his pocket. I could have stitched it into his uniform."

"Never mind that you can't even sew a button. But, Alice, my dear, you can't believe that a scrap of cloth would have spared that ship." Bette wadded the cloth in her grip. "This is burlap and thread. You prayed for Frank every day. I know, because I prayed *with* you."

"It wasn't enough."

"It was all we could do, and all that Frank would have wanted. Do you know what I think?"

Alice looked up and sniffed. "What?"

"I think this message is for you. Frank is with God right now, but you're here. You're the one left here. You need the angels to surround you, to keep you safe. To maybe steer you toward peaceful moments. I feel like that happened when my mom died. I know it's not the same, but I would always just stumble across things that made me think of her—the good things about her."

"Everything about Frank was good."

"I know, sweetie. I know." Bette pulled Alice in for a hug, heedless of the dress crushed between them. When Alice began crying, Bette pulled away to see too-familiar tears glistening on her friend's cheeks. Without thinking, she brought up the scrap of burlap to wipe them away, not thinking of how the fabric might feel coarse against Alice's skin.

But then Alice offered her a thin, wan smile. "Maybe it's meant for you?"

"The message? Or the dress?"

"Both?"

"First, I don't need angels watching over me. I have you. And as for the dress? You know it would never fit me. Not even close." Bette reached out, tracing a finger along the lace. So many promises were in each stitch. And now, to think of this added bit of beauty hidden within, for though the burlap was rough, the blue thread stood out bright against it, the words stitched with care and precision that would have met with the approval of Miss Bernadette. "The dress is beautiful, though. I've always thought so. But it's not meant for me, Alice. We can share this"—she held the scrap aloft—"but not the dress. It's not for me."

Alice gathered herself, brightening her countenance with a sniffle. "You're right, as usual. You always were the levelheaded one." She folded the dress over her arm. "I'll just put it away, I suppose."

"What about the verse?"

"Keep it," Alice said over her shoulder. "Better yet, give it to Eli. He needs the angels now."

Bette opened the cabinet above the sink, revealing a few narrow shelves lined with pretty little jars of all the creams and lotions that Alice perpetually brought home from her counter at Goode's. Bette loosely folded and laid the scrap of burlap among them. This seemed a fitting home, at least for the moment, because she would not, in fact, bring the fabric to Eli. He couldn't see it, let alone read it. The fingers on one hand were dead to its texture, and the other, suspended in such a way as to disallow a grip. The cloth had been hidden away all these years and would remain so until Alice was a little stronger.

Now, it was time for Bette to take care of herself.

Once dressed in a light wool skirt and blouse with full sleeves and a purple collar and cuffs, Bette touched the Berries Delight color to her lips. It was a deep, warm color, the shade berries took on when baked in a pie. She pressed and popped her lips and practiced a smile to her reflection. She worked her face into one angle and another, silently mouthing, *"Hello, Eli,"* then shaking her head in chastisement. She could visit Eli while wearing pin curls and a face full of cold cream, and he wouldn't know the difference. Unless she kissed him, obviously.

Which she wouldn't, obviously. Not with Alice right there.

They stopped for a quick breakfast at the local Automat, where Bette dropped a nickel in a slot, turned the handle, and brought forth a plate of steaming scrambled eggs, while Alice made her own selection. Alice secured a table near a window and sat with the food while Bette fetched coffee. She grasped the mystical dolphin spout and remembered Eli's simple wish to visit this place. She indulged herself in a moment of imagining a future that included Eli at her side.

Over breakfast, Bette tried to prepare Alice for what she would encounter at the hospital. The sounds, the smells, the desire to look away and the strength it took not to. She again described the details of Eli's injuries, preparing her friend for his frailty and helplessness in an effort to downplay the ever-growing relief that he was alive.

Alice and Bette rode the bus in silence, the packed crowd making it impossible for conversation, and when they were finally deposited on the sidewalk, Alice looped her arm around Bette's and drew her away from the other women. They'd arrived at that perfect hour of midmorning, when chill gave way to warmth as the sun settled in for the day.

Alice inhaled. "It really smells like spring today, doesn't it?"

Bette breathed in. "It does."

"Mom always said that spring was God's way of showing us hope. A gift of new beginnings all wrapped up in green. Do you think, maybe . . ."

It was plain Alice was stalling, gathering strength, and Bette was more than happy to comply. The lawn that rolled and stretched in every direction might still bear patches of the brown of winter dormancy, but obvious pains had been taken to keep it clipped. Alice and Bette silently promised each other a quick stroll, leaving the women's voices, jingling in gossip and laughter, behind. If they hadn't stepped away, perhaps Bette would have missed it. From the breeze-driven silence around them, a sound cut through that made her knees buckle.

"Bette? Alice!"

Eli's voice called to her. The same voice had called her to a picnic spot or from the line where he waited to buy their tickets to the newest Clark Gable film. He called her name with a question, Alice's with confirmation.

Alice tugged her arm. "There he is."

But Bette had already seen him standing next to a wheelchair, while a nurse hovered close by, indulging in a cigarette.

"You said he was—"

"He was," Bette whispered out of the side of her mouth, as if he could possibly hear them across the expanse of once-green lawn.

"Well, he's not anymore."

Alice tugged again, but Bette wanted one more moment to savor the sight of him, standing, robe draped artfully around his suspended shoulder, his other arm sleeved with his hand tucked in the robe's pocket. Locks of his curly hair danced in the same breeze that sent her skirt to tap against her leg. Most of all, he could see her; he was seeing her right now. Gone were the bandages that wrapped around his head just days ago. One eye remained hidden beneath a patch, but over that, he wore a pair of dark sunglasses. His face was shaded with a three-day beard, leaving him to look like some wild, almost-foreign being. All traces of that familiar boy had disappeared, save for his voice. He called to her again, and now she dragged Alice along.

"Look at you," Bette said, hating how her words spluttered. "Standing and . . . everything."

"Trudy, here, has to take me around," he said, motioning his head back to the nurse, who acknowledged his comment with a wave of her ciga-rette. "You'd be surprised how hard it is to keep your balance with one eye and no arms. But I tell you, I don't mind standing right here as long as it comes along with fresh air, sunshine, and two beautiful women."

"Hey," Trudy said, exhaling smoke.

"Sorry. Three." He turned his full attention to Bette. "I told the doc that if a girl was going to come see me, I wanted to see her right back. I still need these"—he squinched his nose, making the sunglasses dance—"so the world's a little shady but sharp as ever. You cut your hair."

Bette brought a self-conscious hand to her curls. "Yes. I could never get the hang of all the styles, like Alice does, so this just seemed . . . easier."

"I like it." Then, ever the gentleman, he turned to her friend but with a distinctly sober tone, he simply said, "Alice."

He knew.

"My family visited yesterday," he said, by way of explanation. "Every-body back home is just—"

Before he could say another word, Alice let out a whimper and charged against him.

"Easy," Trudy warned, but Eli had braced himself for the impact.

He could not, in turn, wrap his arms around her, but Alice had hers firmly locked around him, her face buried against his chest. He bent his body, laying his cheek on the top of Alice's head but looking at Bette.

It's fine. Bette projected the thought with a nod. She allowed herself a single twinge of jealousy, wishing she could be so free, so *obvious* with her feelings. But then, this was Alice's first encounter with loss. The pain of having a future stripped away was still new. After a few heartbeats of pondering envy, Bette stepped forward and inserted herself into the embrace, making them three friends braided together by mourning.

"I still can't believe it," Alice said, her voice muffled. She stepped back, dislodging them all.

At Trudy's insistence, Eli lowered himself onto his chair.

"Take a seat over here." The nurse directed them toward a bench, then guided the wheelchair closer to it. "Just a few more minutes, and he has to go inside. Sun's getting too bright."

Bette and Alice followed, but only Bette sat down.

"I'll give you two some time," Alice said. "I think I'd like to take a walk."

Bette wondered if she should have stopped her, insisted that Alice stay with them to reminisce. But the absence of Frank must have felt so blatant in this moment, destroying the balance of her memories.

Bette sat on the bench facing Eli directly, while the not-so-vigilant Trudy proved it was possible to stand listlessly.

"How is she doing?" Eli asked as soon as Alice seemed a safe enough distance away.

Bette thought back to the dress and its hidden blessing but decided the subject was too complicated for now. "As well as can be expected, I guess. We have a big day planned for Thursday. The store is hosting a huge nylon sale. It's something we've been planning—"

"Hold on. *We*? I thought you were done with the store."

"Done working there, but you can't really be done *with* a thing like that. Anyway, we've had it set up for a while, but I don't know if she's really going to be up to it. She and Frank, they were . . . close."

"We all were, Bet."

"But they were unbroken. Like this whole war was just a blip. They wrote to each other—golly, he must have written every day. Letters arrived almost every week, as if they were around the corner from each other instead of around the world. She never, ever had a moment of doubt about their future. Never questioned it at all. What a rotten thing to have that much love and that much faith and then—"

"It's all taken away."

"It's crazy, because I know what it feels like to lose everything, but I don't know what to say to her, because I've never lost that kind of love."

"Neither have I," Eli said, and she knew they were done talking about Alice.

Almost.

"Eli?" She wished there was some way to take his hand but settled for scooting herself closer to the edge of the bench, so their knees touched.

"Bet?"

"There's something I have to tell you."

She could not see his eyes through the darkness of his lenses, but he faced her with an intensity that assured his complete attention. The words waited just behind her lips—*I didn't write the letter; Alice did*—but she could not bring them forth, give them breath. Instead, she said, "The letters you wrote? You sketched a losing hand. One of us owes the other a kiss."

A slow smile broke within his unshaven scruff. "You owe me two, if I remember correctly."

"Yes, well, that hardly seems fair, does it? You held all the cards."

"Still, I cannot allow you to welch on a bet, can I?" He glanced over his shoulder. "Little help here, Trudy?"

The nurse sighed, stepped to him, and braced against him until he was standing again. "You good, soldier?"

"Almost. Go back over there." Then he said, "Come here, Bette."

It never occurred to Bette not to comply. He could not reach for her, so she reached for him. A lifetime of self-consciousness about being the tallest girl in her class disappeared when she found herself nearly nose to nose with him.

Then she moved even closer.

He'd told her that the night they first met, he wanted to kiss her after inviting her on a stroll around the block so he could feel like he was walking her home. They'd stood hand in hand on the porch, where he asked flat out, "Can I kiss you good night?"

And she'd said no, reciting some kind of line about not wanting him to think she was the type of girl who would kiss a boy she barely knew, but in reality, she had feared that, if she kissed him, she might never be able to do so again. Something about being near him felt like being in the middle of a spell, a wall of magic holding her in place, an invisible force giving them a space to share. Saying no to him that evening was the last time she felt in total control of her mind and body in his presence. Their first kiss was three nights later, in that same spot, when the sky was newly dark, when the days spent apart and the hours spent together frothed between them. Bette had never thought a lot about kissing; she only knew the chaste, closed-lipped ones she'd seen in movies. Nothing had prepared her for this invasion. She had no idea of the power, the strength, the depth, and the helplessness she would experience as she gave her mouth over to Eli, drawing him in with some instinctive lasso.

It was the first kiss of hundreds. Thousands, maybe, if she counted all the little ones—his lips to her temple, her lips to his cheek. Soft, fluttering kisses to stretch out an evening's *good night*. Silly kisses blown through car windows or from school bleachers.

She felt them all in this moment. Her heart raced, and she lifted the corner of her lips. "I don't know, Soldier. There are so many people around . . ."

"Bette," he said, and suddenly there weren't any people anywhere—only his face, eyes shaded, hair wild, cheeks whiskered. She knew they stood on a spring lawn with a building looming behind her, a building filled with men who might never again have a moment like this in their lives. She knew Alice wandered somewhere, mourning with her memories and grieving the future. It seemed cruel to let this opportunity fall to the side, so she briefly touched her lips to his, then drew back.

"One."

A quizzical eyebrow shot up over the rim of his glasses.

"For the first letter." She leaned forward again, leaving her lips on his long enough to feel the prickle of his whiskers (and decide it wasn't an unpleasant feeling) before drawing away. "Two."

"Were those yours or mine?"

"Ours." Bette slid one hand around the back of his neck and snaked the other around his waist, giving him her strength and balance as she kissed him for the worlds that passed between them. He groaned, and she pulled him closer, as she knew he would, were he able.

"Three?" he said, his lips still against hers.

She tilted her head back. "I'd say that, and four, five, and six."

"Shall we go for an even dozen?"

Bette braced a hand against his chest and stepped away. "No. Not now."

"When can I see you next?"

"I—I don't know."

Eli cocked his head, making it impossible to escape his gaze. "Was that a goodbye kiss, Bette?"

Bette caught sight of her friend making slow progress toward them. "Alice needs me right now."

"I need you."

"You have the entire US Army helping you."

"They don't kiss like you do."

Trudy, who had stepped discretely away, now closed in from the opposite direction of Alice, and Bette felt the sense of a closing door, more so when Eli went to his waiting wheelchair and sat down.

"Come closer," he said. "Alice brought us together twice, but I'll be hanged if I let her keep us apart." Then he sent a good-natured, "Let's go, Trudy!" and waved to Alice as he wheeled by.

⊰⋈⊱

Alice and Bette were halfway home on the bus before Eli's words fully registered.

"Alice brought us together twice."

Twice.

The first time, when she'd got Frank to grab him by the elbow and haul him across the room to introduce them. The second time? There was only one answer.

The letter.

Bette grasped Alice's hand. "He knows."

"Knows what?"

"He knows you wrote that letter."

"Did he say so?"

"Not so much." But then, Bette couldn't tell her exactly how she knew, because then Alice would know that Bette was choosing to step away from Eli to take care of her friend, and Alice would have none of that. "It's just a feeling I have."

"Always good to trust your feelings," Alice said. "You know, I've read stories about other women like me, women who have lost . . . and they say they had a feeling before they knew. Like a sense of impending loss or a bolt of sadness or something. But I didn't have that with Frank. No kind of hint at all. Just a regular morning at church and helping Mom with dinner and then—"

Bette squeezed her hand. "You don't have to talk about it."

"I want to. It helps a little, makes it seem real. Imagine, all those days between when it happened and when I learned . . . All those meaningless days."

The bus lurched over a bump, causing the women to drop their grip and brace their hands against the seat in front of them. Light, nervous laughter rippled among the passengers.

The distraction provided enough time for Bette to collect her thoughts. "They weren't meaningless days. You were working and taking care of yourself. You were being my friend and a good daughter. Would you call them meaningless if Frank were still alive?"

Alice drew herself up and away, then pressed against the window. "You don't get to say such things."

"'Such things'?"

"I don't have the luxury of talking about what-if anymore. I had years of, *What if Frank McGinty asked me out on a date? What if he kissed me? What if we get married?* My life is at the bottom of that ocean with him."

Bette turned on her seat. "Are you crazy? Of course it's not. You're young and alive and smart and beautiful. You can—" She'd started to say that Alice could find love again, but even the assumption of such a thing seemed unusually cruel. "You can get through this," she said. "You have your family. And me."

Alice snorted. "I saw you and Eli. You're not going to want this third wheel hanging around."

"'Third wheel'? Alice, you're my best friend. You mean more to me than a thousand Eli Landerses."

Alice offered a weak smile, conveying that she didn't believe a word of what Bette just said but that she was grateful for the sentiment.

They got off the bus and joined the crowd waiting for the transfer.

Bette checked her watch—still more than an hour before she was due for her shift at the hotel. "I think I'll walk. If you feel up to—"

"I'll be fine," Alice said.

"For the rest of the day?"

"I might do some crying. And then, I don't know, listen to the radio."

"I can call in."

Alice laid her hand on Bette's arm. "You've been a real trouper and absolute sweetheart these past few days. But I think I might like a little bit of time to myself."

"If you're sure," Bette said. "I'll be back late."

"I'm sure. But not too late. We have a big day tomorrow. The nylons, remember?"

The days had managed to slip one into another, and the date Bette had seen emblazoned in newspaper ads and on signs in the store's windows flashed itself anew.

"Oh, Alice. Are you sure you're in any shape to . . . Uncle Ray would understand."

"All these things we do," Alice said, "all the rations and collections. Well, it's not just *for the boys* anymore. It's for Frank. And Eli. They're our boys now."

CHAPTER 13

THE FIRST PROJECT Bette and Alice ever took on together was the great pencil drive of 1933. It was the fall after Bette's father's death. Her first day of fifth grade felt like a walk into a different world. Her dress was the cleanest, her shoes the shiniest, and she was the only one with a pencil case, even though it was last year's. The students around her, many with smudged faces and patched clothes, had nothing more than a single, thin Big Chief tablet. Midmorning, the teacher, Mrs. Warner, gave each child a pencil and half of a Pink Pearl eraser, with solemn instructions to be careful not to lose either one, as they would not be given another.

Bette accepted the gifts, quietly locking them away with her own brand-new pink eraser and three fresh pencils (including a coveted red wax one and a thin box of Crayola crayons). At her old school with Alice, the children would spend the first recess showing off the wares their parents purchased at Woolworth's. Here, when the first recess let out, the children left the classroom empty-handed, and Bette followed suit. Girls played hopscotch with smooth rocks rather than rubber disks and lined up for a turn at a single jump rope. Nobody invited Bette to join them.

For the rest of the week, she wore what her mother called her "play clothes," back when her mother paid attention to those kinds of things. (Mrs. Goode had walked Bette through the aisles of the dime store with a crisp dollar bill to purchase her supplies.) By the third day, Bette was begrudgingly allowed a turn at the jump rope.

That Saturday, when Bette and Alice saw each other at a distance from the corner where they would forever meet, the girls ran into each other's arms. Their words tangled between them about their separate experiences.

"A single pencil?" Alice said, hands clasped to her face.

"I guess I'm poor now," Bette said.

"Like the Little Princess," Alice said, referencing their favorite book. "You need a mysterious benefactor."

"*They* need that more than I do." And with that, Bette had the germ of an idea.

At school Alice moved among her schoolmates, pestering them to give her a pencil. Or two. Then Bette claimed a headache and asked to be excused from recess, using the time in the empty classroom to slip pencils into her classmates' desks. They continued this throughout the year, and if any of the children caught on that it was Big Bette (as she was called after growing three inches before Christmas) behind the endless supply of pencils, nobody ever offered either challenge or gratitude. Still, Bette felt warm and full, doing such a small, helpful thing.

It was with that spirit that the two now-grown friends had worn down Uncle Ray's initial reluctance to host a special nylon sale at his store. How could they have known all those weeks ago how their lives would change? That afternoon when they'd sat in Uncle Ray's office, Frank was a promise and Eli a memory. Now, as Bette and Alice hit the sidewalk on their way to the store, neither could summon even a fraction of the enthusiasm they'd had in the beginning.

"It seemed like a good idea at the time," Alice said.

Bette quirked her lips into a wry smile. "Do you mean a *Goode* idea?" She emphasized the word for the pun. "It was, and it still is."

"My heart's not in it, I suppose."

"Your heart is busy with other things, my friend."

They then engaged in lighter conversation, coming close to the breezy banter that had always fueled their friendship. In a separate, deeper part of Bette's mind, she thought about Eli's parting words.

Alice brought us together twice.

Bette hadn't brought the question of the letter to Alice's attention since the bus ride the previous day. Every conversation about her duplicity had thus far led to an unpleasant argument. True, Bette and Alice had reached something of a truce, and Bette liked to think of her forgiveness as complete, but now, with the idea that Eli might have known all along, she felt like the two were unknowingly conspiring against her. She couldn't imagine facing him again with this lie laid bare between them.

Long before she and Alice turned the corner, Bette heard the women—an enthusiastic mix of chitchat and laughter, the vocalization of anticipation. It was just after seven in the morning, nearly three hours before the store was due to open, and Bette estimated more than a hundred women lined up at the door.

"Oh, golly," Alice cooed, clutching Bette's arm.

"Yeah," Bette's voice trailed after hers, though her reaction came more from a place of trepidation. "How much stock do we have?"

"At least a thousand pairs. But I'm pretty sure Uncle Ray was negotiating to get more from the supplier. I don't have a final number. Maybe Thea does?"

Bette calculated. "Are we placing a limit on the number each woman can buy?"

Alice furrowed her brow in thought. "I don't think so. Why?"

"That's a whole lot of women for a Thursday morning, considering we aren't opening until ten."

"I'm sure it will be fine. These are ladies, after all." To emphasize her point, she offered a jubilant wave and sang out, "Good morning, ladies! You're here bright and early for your stockings!"

The crowd responded with an affirming cheer.

"Don't forget," Bette chimed in, "patience is a virtue!"

She was somewhat soothed by the laughter she received in response.

They shouldered through the crowd and rang the bell at the employee entrance in the alley.

Thea came to the door, her usually perfect hair somewhat mussed, tendrils plastered to her temple with sweat. "Oh, thank goodness," she said, holding the door. "I admit, I thought it was overstretching to have you come in this early, but now I'm not so sure. Have you seen those women out there?"

"Yes," Alice said, her zeal unchecked as she sashayed into the store. "Isn't it wonderful? It might end up being the biggest event the store has ever had."

Bette and Thea exchanged a knowing look, and then Thea locked the door and took Alice in an uncharacteristic embrace.

"I'm so, so sorry about your fella," Thea said. "You should have skipped out of this madness."

"This madness was my idea," Alice said against Thea's lapel.

Bette took the moment to study the scene around them. Columns and columns of small, flat, white boxes, each ostensibly holding a pair of folded nylon stockings. They were stacked as high as her shoulder, flush against each other to maintain stability, lining a wide path through the stockroom to the doorway of the store itself. She walked that path, mindful to keep her bag close to her side, and stepped onto the dark floor. Uncle Ray stood behind the cosmetics counter with the poster propped up on an easel beside him.

> *Ladies!*
> *Be Goode to Yourself Today*
> *Nylon Stockings*
> *$1.25 a Pair*

Velvet rope cordoned off a pathway from the door to the counter, behind which nylon boxes were stacked with a small space left open for conducting the sales.

"Morning, Ray."

Uncle Ray looked up, looking less displeased than usual to see her. "Bette. How's our Alice?"

"Doing as well as can be expected, I guess. She's excited about today."

Uncle Ray's expression made it clear that he did not share his niece's feelings. The blinds were drawn over the front window, but the mass of women gathered on the sidewalk outside was clearly visible around the edges. "I don't know what I was thinking, going along with this."

"You were thinking it could be a great morale booster for the women in this city and an even greater way to bring new customers into the store."

He twitched his mustache. "That sounds more along the lines of what you were thinking. *I'm* thinking I just got suckered by Alice's big blue eyes."

"That too," Bette said. "I think we all know that feeling."

Uncle Ray came out from behind the counter when Thea and Alice came to join them. He stood with his finger poised against his chin, turning in a slow circle, humming a radio jingle just under his breath.

Thea jumped in. "So the plan is, the ladies come in through the door, form an orderly line, make their nylon purchases here, then move to the left, where they'll have to walk through at least three departments before exiting through the Men's Apparel department entrance."

Alice had gone to take a peek out of the window and came skipping back. "The line is clear to the corner; isn't this fabulous?"

Uncle Ray, Thea, and Bette made little sounds of agreement.

"As long as everyone obeys the rules," Thea said. "I was at the butcher's yesterday and saw a couple of broads go at each other over the last pound of bacon."

"I'm wondering," Uncle Ray said, "if we shouldn't open early. What do you think, Thea? What time are all the other girls scheduled to come in?"

"Nine. Gives them an hour to get ready when we open the doors at ten."

"I say we open at nine," Uncle Ray said. "This could turn into a restless crowd." He turned to Alice. "Go into my office and call as many of the girls as you can to see if they can get here early. Tell them it's a"—his face twisted in visible pain—"five-dollar bonus to everybody here by quarter past eight."

Bette held out her hand. "What about us, Uncle Ray?"

"First, you're not one of 'the girls.' You're family. Second, this was all your idea. If not for you, I would be at home drinking coffee and listening to the stock report. And third—"

"Never mind 'third,'" Alice said, reaching up to plant a kiss on his cheek. "Just think of all the women who are going to be walking through this store for the first time and seeing what they've been missing."

"Yes, yes," Uncle Ray said, softening. "Now go. The store Rolodex is in my top left-hand drawer."

Bette waited until Alice was out of earshot. "May I suggest one more thing?"

Uncle Ray lit a cigarette. "How could I possibly stop you?"

"I think you should put a limit on how many pairs each woman can buy."

"That's not a bad idea," Thea said.

"And why would I do that?" Uncle Ray said.

"Imagine the first woman in line wants to buy ten pairs. What are you going to do?"

"I'm going to take her"—his mustache twitched, calculating—"twelve dollars and fifty cents and put it with the thousand or so more I hope to get today."

"And what are you going to do if every woman wants ten pairs?"

"I'll pour myself a brandy and count my money and get back to the business of running this store."

"And what about the women who were in line hours before the store opened who will get nothing because we sold out before the store's official opening hour?"

Thea drummed well-manicured nails on the glass countertop. "Do I need to remind you of the bacon battle of Munson's Meats?"

Uncle Ray sighed, exhaling smoke, and looked at Bette with a thin smile that seemed to be holding the last tendril of his patience. "What limit would you suggest?"

Bette thought for a moment, imagining a woman guest in her hotel, dressed to the nines, going out to dinner with her officer husband. She would be wearing a pair of nylons, having washed the pair she wore on the train, which would be draped over the shower bar, drying. "Three," Bette said, decisively. "One to wear, one to wash, and one to save for the next occasion."

As if in chorus Uncle Ray and Thea repeated, "One to wear . . . one to wash . . ."

Thea snapped her fingers. "We'll train them to say just that as the ladies walk in, and then again at the counter. It's both limiting and generous." She looked at Bette with a mix of administrative approval and maternal affection. "Nicely done, Miss Barry."

It was, at least, a good idea in theory.

By the time Thea and Ray ceremoniously opened the front door at 9:07, the crowd of women—*ladies* might not have been the most apropos term—had swelled off the sidewalk and around the corner. Uncle Ray spluttered, "Welcome to G—" before being decidedly *un*ceremoniously tossed to the side. Thea fared no better, her calls of "Ladies! Ladies!" going unheeded by the stampede of sensible shoes. The velvet rope was cast aside, obliterating the carefully planned pathway to the counter, where Alice stood, her eyes the size of saucers.

Bette had been tasked with intercepting the customers at the midpoint with the "One to wear, one to wash . . ." directive, but it was clear nobody was listening to her. Instead, moving as a single perfumed mass, the women charged to the counter, then reached over one another, grasping at the boxes.

"Limit of three to each of you!" Bette's shouting was just as unladylike as the women's behavior. She felt herself being jostled with something that felt like an elbow rammed into her ribs. She tried to look through the crowd and catch the eye of the other salesgirls, only to see them fleeing the scene. "Cowards," Bette hissed beneath the din, fully intending to shake them down for their five-dollar bonuses.

One of the salesgirls had crafted a sign stating the limit of three pairs per customer and a price of one dollar and twenty-five cents per pair. The stacks had seemed impressive in the semidarkness of the closed store, but within the first half hour of an open door, they were decimated.

"They're running out!" a woman shouted, scooping three to her breast as if they were a rescued child.

The crowd surged, knocking one of Bette's feet from beneath her.

"No!" she spluttered, grabbing at a wool coat to steady herself. "There are . . . ," but reassurance was useless. She pressed her way through, eventually emerging from the wall of women to find one of the salesgirls hunkered behind the glove display, weeping. Bette grasped the girl's upper arms. "Go to the stockroom, round up any of the other girls you see, grab as many boxes as you can, and get them out here. And if any of the stock boys are here, enlist them too."

The girl sniffed, nodded, and headed off on her mission.

"There's more! There's more! There's plenty!" Bette worked her way back through the crowd, moving upstream like a salmon until she finally made it to the open door, where five women were wedged within the frame. Bette made what she hoped was a smooth, calming gesture. "Let's wait here for a moment while we restock."

Confused shouts came from the back of the line. Bette rose up on her toes and waved above the crowd, planning to repeat her directive, when one of the women crowding the entrance turned and shouted, "They say there's more!" Then she disentangled herself from the mass and strode through the door, knocking Bette off-balance.

For a split second, Bette thought the sheer closeness of the bodies would break her fall, but she hit the ground, finding herself surrounded by a swarming sea of legs. Her hand was crushed beneath a heel, and her knees tangled in her skirt as she struggled to right herself.

"Bette! Bette!"

She looked up to see Uncle Ray's hand extended. She took it and allowed him to help her to her feet.

"I'm so sorry," she whispered, speaking under the cacophony.

He released her. "Go check on Alice."

Bette fought the urge to salute and instead inserted herself into the fray. To her relief, she saw all the girls marching resolutely with stacks of boxes in their arms, followed by two men from the stockroom carrying even more. Then, in the midst of them, a tall young man decked out in his sailor's uniform, trailed by the weeping salesgirl whose face had transformed into a triumphant smile.

"This is Eddie," she said, leaning close. "My boyfriend. He was going to hang out and wait for me to get off work, but I recruited him. He ships out tomorrow."

Bette's heart swelled with an instant affection for this man—this boy—with his freshly shaved cheeks and winning smile. She remembered the pride with which she'd said the words, "This is my boyfriend, Eli." She and Alice would sit back watching Eli and Frank help some kid get his kite out of a tree or clean the gutters for an elderly neighbor and say, "Gee. Don't we have the best guys?" to each other while sipping a Coke.

Weepy—Bette could *not* in the moment remember her name—had that same air, wanting to hold her fella close while sharing him with the world.

While chaos erupted around them, Bette created a little pocket of calm and ushered Eddie to the counter and then behind it to stack his boxes on the shelves. Her ear picked up the immediate change in volume at his presence. No matter if the women in the store were young or old or married or city bachelorettes, no woman could be immune to the presence of a young man in uniform, especially one whose muscles bulged within his dress whites and whose dimples were like two perfect cashews. He was their sweetheart, their brother, their son. For a brief moment, boxes of nylon stockings were forgotten.

Bette took advantage of the lull. "Ladies, this is Seaman Eddie"—she cocked her ear, listening—"Toro, here to remind us why we do what we do every day. The rationing, the sacrifice, the Victory Gardens. He's why we cook with oleo and keep ourselves to one egg a day. So thank you for coming to Goode's and being 'Goode' to yourself, purchasing three pairs of nylons. One to wear, one to wash, and one to save for that special occasion. Eddie ships out tomorrow. Please join me in wishing him a safe journey back home."

The women responded with enthusiastic applause, during which, with a touch to his sleeve, Bette, assuming authority, led the young man to the doorway, where the line turned into a peaceful, orderly procession. Each woman stopped to shake his hand or kiss his cheek or touch his head in prayer. No sailor had ever shipped out with such blessings.

Just past noon, the last box of nylons passed across the counter. Uncle Ray bemoaned that shoppers could have been robbing the rest of the store blind for all he knew and dispatched the girls to investigate and inventory. Weepy (Bette never had the chance to learn the girl's name) was given the rest of the day off, with an additional five dollars pressed against Eddie's hand for coming to the aid and rescue of Goode's first floor.

Bette leaned heavily against the counter, watching. "Don't I get any credit?"

Alice patted her hand. "Here," she said, sliding over the now very familiar box. "I set back a pair for each of us. Just one each, though."

"What a peach," Bette said. "Like our motto says . . . these will have to be for my special occasion."

"Pardon me, ladies," Uncle Ray said before worming between them. There'd been four points of purchase along the counter, and he stopped at each one and gathered the cashboxes under his arm. "I'm heading to my office to see if this little adventure proved to be profitable in any way."

The girls collapsed into giggles in his wake.

"This was fun, wasn't it?" Alice said once she'd regained her composure.

"I suppose that's one word for it," Bette said.

"And nobody got really hurt."

Bette looked at the darkening bruise on the back of her hand and imagined a similar hue blooming just below her rib. "Right. Not really."

"And that sweet boy. Oh, Bette, Frank looked just like him when he shipped out. More handsome, obviously—"

"Obviously."

"But so full of hope. I'm going to pray for him." She nodded resolutely. "I will. Every night."

"That's good," Bette said, not making the same promise. Not because she wished any ill for sweet Eddie, but because it was one she didn't trust herself to keep. Rather, she didn't trust the prayer itself. When she recalled her prayers asking God to protect Eli, they seemed shallow and unfocused, the same she would say for a stranger. Not like the prayers Alice said for Frank. Bette had heard them late in the night, his name whispered to be carried up on angels' wings. And who did God answer? It made no sense. Bette didn't deserve a chance to love Eli again, and this Eddie fellow deserved better. "I'm sure he'll be in the prayers of lots of these women tonight."

CHAPTER 14

THE MEMORIAL SERVICE for Frank McGinty was held the week after the nylon sale, and while Bette would have loved to have devoted that time to staying by Alice's side as a bulwark of strength, Alice herself seemed to grow a little stronger each day.

"I'm fine," she'd insist each time Bette offered another cup of tea or a walk around the block. Alice returned to work at Goode's, basking in the success of the nylon sale, which had proven to be a success in both profits and new store traffic. She truly did seem to be on a path to healing, though there were still times Bette would find her curled around Frank's picture, her face wet with tears. While the funeral itself might be painful, the trip home might be healing.

Bette was just closing the hasp on her overnight case when she heard the honking of a car horn outside their street-facing window. She looked out to see Uncle Ray's car, the man himself getting out, lighting a cigarette, and heading for the front door of the apartment building's lobby.

"Alice?" she called. "Are you ready? Ray's here."

"Ready." Alice emerged from their bedroom, pinning her hat. "Let's leave the bags to Uncle Ray and run down to the deli to get a coffee and Danish for the road."

Uncle Ray seemed only slightly put out by the idea, mollified by the thought of a prune Danish.

"There's something I have to tell you," Alice said when they turned the corner.

Bette's stomach sank. "Nothing good ever follows that."

Alice took her arm and gave it a squeeze. "I know. I know, but here

193

goes . . . I wrote to Eli last week. As soon as I knew about Frank's service. I wanted him to know so he could come, if he wanted."

"And is he? Will he be riding out with us?"

"No." She unlooped her arm, opened her handbag, and brought out a small envelope. "He wrote back. Says he has a surgery scheduled and won't be fit to travel. His parents and sister will be there, though. To represent the family."

"Oh, well, good, I guess. His surgery, I mean. Why would you worry about telling me that?"

"Because that's not everything."

They were inside the deli now, and Bette was left churning while Alice ordered half a dozen Danish and three coffees. There were other customers behind them, so they stepped aside.

"So?" Bette asked.

"I also confessed that I wrote the letter and signed your initial." Alice bit her lip, waiting for Bette to respond, then rushed to cover the silence. "I know you said you thought he knew, and it was this monolith standing between you. I apologized to you but not to him—because I lied to him too. So I figured I'd just knock down the barrier for you."

Never taking her eyes off Alice, Bette reached behind her for the bag of pastries and then handed over two of the three wax paper cups of coffee. "What did he say about that?"

"Nothing."

"Nothing?"

"Not to me. There was a separate note addressed to you. And I haven't been holding back. These came in the early morning post, just today."

"So where is it, my note?"

"In my purse," Alice said with a helpless gesture of her full hands.

"I suppose it can wait until we get to the car," Bette said, "but honestly, Alice, your heart is good, but your timing is terrible."

"I know, I know. But I promise. This is the last time I'll do anything to interfere in your life." Three steps later, she added, "Intentionally."

"I'll take it." Bette picked up her step, careful not to let the hot coffee slosh.

Uncle Ray was smoking and leaning against his front bumper, but he dropped his cigarette the moment Alice handed him his coffee. Alice sat on the passenger seat, while Bette settled in the back. Without prompting, Alice handed the note over her shoulder.

Bette took it but waited to open it, watching the city roll by. She engaged in the usual small talk of this drive: weather, traffic, idiots on the road. When she'd sipped her coffee down to half the cup, she placed the paper-wrapped Danish on her lap and unfolded the note beside it.

The first thing she noticed was the penmanship—soft and feminine, meaning Eli had dictated it to a volunteer.

> B—
>
> *Alice told me, but I knew. I've always known. How? Because she wrote about the graduation bonfire but not about what happened when we sneaked away.*
>
> *I'll never forget how beautiful you looked in the distant firelight. How the silver moon competed with the gold. How warm your lips felt with the cold air all around us. How it felt like we were the only two people in the world. We are still those two people.*
>
> E

Bette read it over and over, her heart at a standstill. She well remembered that night, how she had stood with arms wrapped around him within his school sweater. Somebody was strumming a guitar while the gang crooned old tunes beside the roaring fire. They were swaying with the music, and Bette didn't realize they were taking tiny steps away from the crowd. At some point, there was no more warmth from the fire, only from each other. When he kissed her, they became a single entity. It was transformative and terrifying, a moment elevated from the million others they had shared. It was the night Eli told her he loved her, and she told him the same, though neither could truly understand the depth of that word's meaning, but they knew it held a promise—a promise that until now, only he seemed committed to keep.

Those two people. The only two people—one of them recently confined to a bed, the other trapped in a car driving over a bridge. She'd jump right out of the car if there were a chance of landing on a hospital bed next to his.

"Everything okay back there?" Uncle Ray asked.

"Everything's fine," Bette said, folding the note and dropping it into her handbag. She reached over the seat to touch Alice's shoulder. "Right as rain on a hot day."

From the outset it was clear that the church would never hold the crowd that would gather for Frank's memorial service. He was a friend to all—classes above and below—and a hero to the town long before he signed up to give his life for his country. So the service was moved to the high school gymnasium, which seemed fitting, as Frank had certainly spent more time there than he ever did in church.

Bette stayed with Alice's family, rode to the service with them, and walked through the gym doors with them, but when it came to finding their seats, they found three reserved places, not four. Alice sat between her parents, leaning heavily on her mother, and nobody seemed to notice when Bette took a seat in the row behind them.

No place could be more immediate in its comfort and familiarity. The muted conversation, the particular sound of shoes on the wooden floor, the lingering smell of wax and sweat. If she closed her eyes, Bette could transport herself to the anticipation of waiting for the start of a game, a pep rally for the football team, or a school assembly addressed by a local celebrity.

But she didn't close her eyes. She embraced the classmates who came to her, having heard through the community grapevine that Eli had been wounded severely and was convalescing at a hospital in the city. They asked about him with all the confidence in the world that she would have a detailed answer, but she said only that he was doing better every day and would be here if he could. They spoke in low tones, almost apologetically, as if raising Eli's name somehow detracted from Frank's memory. For that alone, she was glad Eli hadn't come, and wondered if he himself hadn't had the same thought.

Over the course of an hour, however, those memories were brought to life. Coaches, teachers, friends—one after another went to the microphone to tell a story about Frank. Gentle laughter blended with open, full sobs. The school choir sang "Danny Boy" and a rendition of "America the Beautiful" that left the crowd sitting in thick silence before breaking out in thunderous applause.

The minister spoke of the promise of reunion on some far and distant shore, the same words—the same text—he'd used at the funerals of both of Bette's parents. He promised something about the time intervening being like the blink of an eye, but Bette barely recognized the girl she'd been before that blink. How would her parents ever recognize her when she barely recognized herself? Bette could think only of Frank's young, strong, broken body at the bottom of the sea. Would Alice blink her eye and find him again? It seemed a cruel promise to make to a nineteen-year-old girl whose future had been ripped away, and perhaps this was the first moment Bette truly understood Alice's loss. A desire for reunion with Eli had just been ignited within Bette, and there needed to be no stretch of a lifetime to bring them back to the love they declared on the night of the bonfire.

Enough time had already passed.

The graveside ceremony was to be exclusively for Frank's family and closest friends, and though Alice clutched Bette's hand and assured her she had a place there, Bette begged off.

"I'll be fine walking home," she said. "I could use the fresh air."

She avoided the conversation groups that gathered on the gym floor, slipping through to a side hallway and exit. This is where the school's trophy case was found, and she paused in front of it, looking at the team pictures and trophies that stretched back to 1921, the school's first year. She followed the timeline, coming finally to Eli and Frank's class. Newspaper clippings featured pictures of the two in action on the court and gathered with their smiling teammates around the championship trophy.

Eli's words echoed. *"That beautiful boy,"* Eli had said. *"He's gone."* Really, they were *all* gone, weren't they? She didn't know how many of these boys were serving or which ones would come home—whole or not. That team would never again be complete. Their minds had been wiped of innocence, their hearts collectively broken.

She touched her fingers to the glass and whispered, "'For he shall give his angels charge over thee . . .'"

The walk home was awash with memories—bits of conversation and snatches of music—carried in and away on the breeze. She relished the solitude, giving way to a few tears, though ones of a particularly welcome sadness. The Goodes kept their home unlocked, and rare was the moment she'd ever had it to herself. She took off her hat and stepped out of her shoes, carrying them up the lush, carpeted stairs to the room she'd shared with Alice. No mistake, the house was certainly large enough to have given Bette a room to herself, but the girls had developed a tradition of sleepovers in Alice's. It was easier to giggle and plan and whisper secrets in a shared space.

Mr. and Mrs. Goode had kept it just as it was the day Alice and Bette packed up all they could in a single suitcase and left for the city. Two twin beds, foot to foot, covered in thick, floral quilts. Pictures of movie stars decorated the corkboard above the desk. Bette unzipped her black dress and hoped to find something more comfortable left behind. She went to the closet, opened it, and felt a sinking in her stomach.

Alice's suitcase.

Not her overnight bag or favorite blue satchel but the same enormous case she'd used to move the two of them to New York. The one that took up so much room in the apartment that Bette had begged her to bring it back home. Up until now, her pleas had gone unanswered.

A nudge from Bette's toe proved that it wasn't anywhere near empty. She laid it on its side and, claiming the privilege of friendship, opened it. It was full, packed with every recognizable garment Alice owned. Apparently, Alice had one final secret: Bette would be going back to the city alone.

CHAPTER 15

"I WAS GOING to tell you," Alice said. Dressed in pajamas, she and Bette, faces slathered with cream, sat on Alice's narrow bed, passing a box of chocolates between them. "And really, I don't know if I was totally sure until today."

"You figured you'd pack up all your worldly belongings just in case?"

"When we first heard about Frank, my parents begged me not to go back to the city. They wanted to, you know, take care of me. But I wanted to be strong, and we had the nylon sale, and I thought Frank would want me to . . ."

Be strong, Bette finished silently. She took the chocolates box and picked blindly.

"But, Bette, I'm so tired. And sad and empty. I loved him so much. I've spent the last three years of my life loving him. All I've wanted since I was sixteen years old was to marry him, get a little house here while he worked for his father's business . . . have his children. Going to New York was a lark. Working at Uncle Ray's store was something to do while Frank was gone. You knew that, didn't you? You knew I could never live in the city forever."

Bette chewed, knowing Alice was right. "But I can't stay there without you."

"You're welcome to come back here too. Have your own room. Can you imagine? Not listening to each other snore all night?"

Bette passed her the box. "First, you don't snore. Second, I don't want to come back here, Alice. I love you and your family. You all saved me. But I don't have a life here anymore."

Alice playfully poised a chocolate. "Do you have a life in New York City?"

"I have a job that I actually love. And places where I go and people know me. Routine, you know?"

"And Eli?"

Bette grabbed the box back. "I'm so stupid. The stupidest girl in the world. I love him, Alice. I thought if I pushed him away, I couldn't lose him. But I've probably lost him anyway."

"You haven't lost him. I saw how he kissed you. The whole hospital saw how he kissed you. You two may be personally responsible for restoring regular cardiac rhythm for dozens of wounded soldiers."

"Do you really think so?"

"I think so."

Bette silently recited the words from his note before speaking again. "I hope I'm not too late."

"You're not."

They each took a chocolate. Bette bit in and discovered coconut; Alice, strawberry cream. By silent agreement, they swapped.

"Anyway," Bette said, "I could never afford to keep that apartment. Not without at least a second job. Do you think Uncle Ray would ever want to rehire me?"

"No," Alice said, her mouth full.

"You don't need some time to think about it before forming an opinion?"

"No," Alice repeated with a sympathetic coconut smile. "Sorry, and no offense intended, but the two of you are oil and water."

"With a little bit of ground glass mixed in."

"He is sharp, but he is also kind."

"I'll take your word for it. But I still don't know what I'll do about the apartment. I can get a roommate, I guess. But those are awfully close quarters to share with a stranger."

"Well," Alice said, offering over the last chocolate in the box, "I talked about this with my parents on the drive over from the burial, and Dad offered to pay my half of the rent until the lease is up. And Mom agreed."

Bette nearly choked. "What? No, that would be charity, for Pete's sake."

"It would be helping a dear, dear friend. Someone I love as a sister. They love you too, Bette. And it's not forever, just a few months for you to . . .

decide, I guess. Find your feet. Please accept—if you truly want to stay in the city, that is. Besides, you need a place for whenever I come to visit. The Automat gets its chocolate pie in the fall."

Bette reached over and hugged her. "I will, and I can't wait to thank them. I'm such a mess, or I'd go in to them right now."

Alice laughed. "Morning is better. Bacon and pancakes."

"Oof," Bette said. "I'm too full of chocolate to be this hungry at the thought."

They took turns tiptoeing to the bathroom to brush their teeth, then climbed onto their beds. Alice turned off the light, plunging the room into darkness and quiet, punctuated by the lavender scent of the bed-sheets. At this moment, the girls could have been seven years old. Or ten. Or fifteen. As it was, they were on the cusp of twenty, having experienced life and loss in ways their younger selves could never have envisioned.

"Hey," Alice spoke into the darkness.

One of them always spoke into the darkness.

"Yeah?"

"One more thing."

Bette groaned into her pillow.

"No, silly. It's not bad. It's—I left the dress back in the closet in the apartment."

"The wedding dress?"

"I want you to have it."

This again. "Alice, we've talked about this. I can't—"

"Not to wear but to donate. For the silk drive. Since I've ruined it any-way, I might as well let it do some good."

Bette knew why Alice waited until they were surrounded by darkness. She'd never be able to look Bette in the eye. "You haven't ruined it. I can fix it. I mean, I don't have any of the talent of its designer, but I think I can handle a hem."

"When my dad bought me that dress at the auction," Alice said after a beat of silence, "he hugged me so tight and said he'd be walking me down the aisle on my wedding day. He was crying a little, I think. Imagine that; my dad, crying. That dress was meant for me to wear while I walked on my father's arm to marry Frank. Now that will never happen."

"You still have your father," Bette whispered. It was one of those increasingly rare moments when she longed to have a father of her own. Someone to help with her rent, to hold her up as she walked through life.

"But I don't have Frank. I never imagined anybody but him, though I know I might find somebody else someday."

You will, Bette thought, but it was too soon to say.

"And if I do, well, certainly I'll want a dress picked out especially for *him*."

Bette smiled at the nascent hope in her friend's voice. "I'll take good care of it."

"You promise?"

"I promise."

"For Frank?"

"For you."

CHAPTER 16

BETTE SPARED UNCLE Ray her company for the ride back into the city, opting instead to stay one more day and take the early morning train the next. She thanked Mr. Goode, Alice's dad, profusely, promising not to get into any trouble with the landlord. A single girl living alone was enough of a scandal in itself. She would do nothing to bring the Goode family grief or regret for their generosity.

"Not even with Eli?" Alice said under her breath with a wagging finger.

"I don't know if the man is willing to speak to me," Bette said, "let alone impugn my character."

The plan was to take the early train, hoping to go to the hospital, see Eli, beg his forgiveness while declaring her love, and still make it to the hotel for her one o'clock shift, all of which she explained to Alice sotto voce on the back seat of her parents' car as they drove her to the train station.

"Write to me as soon as you get home," Alice said. "I won't be able to stand the suspense."

According to Bette's watch, the train schedule, and bus reliability, her plan seemed flawless. By ten that morning she was striding up the wide walkway, scanning the patients on the lawn for a glimpse of Eli. But then, he might still be recovering in bed. She hated that she didn't know, and the quest for an answer compelled her to pick up her pace until she was breathless the moment she plowed through the door of the correct ward.

"Hey!" The sharp voice of the volunteer at the desk stopped her in her tracks. "You can't just plow by without checking in."

"I've been here before," Bette said, her body still twisted away from the serviceable front desk. "Three times, actually."

"I don't care if you were born here under a magic strawberry bush." The volunteer's name tag said *Maxine*, and she was a large woman who looked like she might have been every third-grade child's worst nightmare.

Bette's mind and body slowed in compliance. "Very well." She set down her bag and picked up the pen, speaking as she signed the log. "I'm here to see Eli Landers, room—"

"I'll tell you which room," Maxine said, opening the familiar, enormous book. "People move, you know."

"Forgive me," Bette said, setting down the pen carefully. She watched Maxine's thick finger run down the page, get licked, and run down another.

"Ah," Maxine said, closing the tome. "Good news. That patient has been discharged."

"Good news? How is that possibly good news?"

"You don't want your fella to get better?" She rose in her seat and gave a meaningful glance to Bette's bag on the floor. "Did he know you two were eloping?"

"We're not—" This couldn't be the end. "Can you tell me where he is?"

"No. That kind of information is confidential, only for the family and the US Army to know."

"So, if I were his wife . . ."

"He either would have told you, or he has a good reason not to. The US Army doesn't like to interfere."

"Please." Tears pricked Bette's eyes. "We love each other. Only, I don't know if he knows that I love him. And he's out there"—she gestured wildly, encapsulating the entire Eastern Seaboard—"somewhere . . . not knowing. And what if I never find him? And he never knows?" By now, the tears streamed fully down her face, and she detected a slight wrinkling of Maxine's chin.

"Look, my girl. I can't help you. Couldn't if I wanted to. Where he is now is a whole different set of information and paperwork that I'm just not privy to. I can give you the name and office to contact"—she reached for a pad of paper—"but let me ask you this: does he know how to find you?" She pointed to the little overnight case. "You aren't some sort of vagabond? Or just off the bus from Ohio or something?"

It all clicked, and Bette threw herself across the desk to deliver a kiss to Maxine's ample, powdered cheek. "Genius! He knows my address. He's written to me there. Three letters, and in one, he promised—"

Maxine held up her hand but spoke with a barely repressed smile. "The US Army doesn't need your details. But I suggest you run on home."

"I will. Oh, Maxine, I will." Bette took five steps away, realized she'd completely forgotten her valise, turned to grab it, and saw Maxine shaking her head with something on the cusp of affection. A trip back to the apartment hadn't been factored into Bette's morning itinerary, but if she hit the bus-transfer time just right . . . Besides, after missing so many days of work, her supervisor might forgive an hour's tardiness. For the country.

Bette stood, gripping one of the leather handles suspended from the bus's roof, refusing the many seats offered to her, and tried to recall exactly how he'd worded his promise. Something about her coming home, and his waiting for her. Although . . . how would he know when to arrive to pull off such a scenario?

"Alice," she said out loud to the crowded bus. "I'll bet they've been in cahoots all along."

But they had not been in cahoots, because Eli was not waiting at the apartment. Not on the sidewalk, not on the stoop, not in the foyer, and not at Bette's door. She walked off her disappointment and clocked in at the Garrison with five minutes to spare. Drained of even the smallest bit of urgency that fueled the first half of her day, she plodded behind her cart into the elevator and missed getting out on the correct floor twice. She had her list of rooms, and while her cleaning was as methodical as it had always been, her sluggish pace belied any sense of sparkle. Her bed corners were as sharp as ever, her faucets as reflective as her mirrors, her ashtrays pristine, and her carpet striped, but when she uttered, "Neat as a pin," before closing the door, she felt no sense of satisfaction.

She checked her watch and noted the time on her assignment slip. Thirty minutes? At this rate she'd be working until midnight to get them all done. Or get fired.

One more thing to lose.

When she and Alice first moved to the city, this job was a way to keep her mind *off* Eli. Now, all her fluttering thoughts assembled into impressions of him—impressions that brought her to wiping a mirror, imagining what he'd look like standing next to her. Stepping across the room to empty a wastebasket had her remembering all the crumpled pieces of paper he'd tossed across the library. She fluffed the pillows, thinking about his bandaged head, and opened the curtains to let in the late afternoon sun, shining just as it had whenever he'd walked her home.

Bette wrote the time on her second room and realized that romantic reminiscences were counterproductive to efficiency. She was ten minutes behind, meaning a possibility that a guest might be given a key to a room that should be ready . . . but wasn't.

She zipped through her next two rooms at lightning speed and said, "Neat as a pin," to the third. As she was marking her slip, she heard voices down the hall and looked up to see an officer and a woman walking hand in hand down the hall, stopping at the room she'd finished cleaning only moments before. They kissed at the door, continued kissing across the threshold, and disappeared. She wondered, *Was that a happy ending? A happy beginning? Or just a stolen moment of togetherness in a world that seemed ready to rip everyone apart?* Although she'd done her own ripping, hadn't she? And she was powerless to mend it.

On she worked through the afternoon, making up for lost time by skipping dinner (not that she was hungry). By six o'clock, she'd ticked off all her assigned rooms, made five trips down to the laundry, and restocked her cart. The final three hours of her shift would be spent in the lobby, which entailed a change of uniform, a brush of her hair, and a touch of lipstick. The lobby assignment was not the intensive, vigorous cleaning of the guest rooms. Rather, this was an attempt to clean right under the guests' noses without notice. There was a small bar in the corner, tended by a man named Clyde, hired for his distinguished graying hair and ageless good looks. He was the man of the hour, meeting the needs of the guests who were either leaving for dinner, coming back from dinner, or simply meeting for drinks. Changed into a dark dress with lace collar and cuffs, Bette took her cues from him, moving throughout the crowd, emptying the crystal ashtrays into a silver bowl, stocking the cigarette containers on the tables, picking up empty glasses and returning them to the bar.

Occasionally, someone would catch sight of her and ask a question.

"Miss, can you recommend a good Italian restaurant nearby?"

"Miss, can you run up to room 429 and bring down my wife's wrap?"

Bette fetched coffee, newspapers, paper, and pens—whatever the guests needed. Normally, she loved this interaction, wondering which of these people were in a room she'd prepared. She knew, too, that the lobby assignment was a coveted one, given to the girls who best represented the hotel. A lifetime at Alice's side didn't give much of an opportunity to feel especially beautiful, so Bette worked here with a wholly different sense of pride. She loved the hum of conversation, knowing that the people here were from all over the city—maybe all over the country—and while some of the men were in their dress uniforms, others were in suits and even tuxedos, and the women in elegant gowns. It always felt like a scene from a movie, with the war happening on some unreachable side of the world.

Tonight, she worked with Darlene, a woman older than her—nearly thirty, Bette would guess—who moved around the room with a confidence that was both efficient and appropriately alluring. Hers was not a face or figure to waste with a dustcloth and Hoover.

"Miss Barry?" Clyde's voice was a timbre that cut through the din of the crowd, so he only said her name once, then summoned her with a subtle, two-fingered gesture. "Can you take this to the gentleman over on the blue settee? I'm afraid I got behind, and he's been waiting for a while."

"Sure," Bette said, taking the tall glass of dark, fizzing drink. It hit her that she hadn't had a bite to eat all day and was tempted to take a sip of the Coke on her way to deliver it. After all, the man was reading a newspaper. He wouldn't see a thing. Clyde would, though, and he'd never stand for such behavior in his territory. "Excuse me, sir?" she said when she was at the reader's side. "Your drink?"

He didn't move but said, "You must be Bette."

Somehow, she didn't drop the glass. He, however, dropped the paper, rose to his feet, and took the glass from her. Bette stood, as frozen as the clinking ice cubes, while Eli took a sip and handed the glass to Darlene, who smiled as if it were *her* long-lost beau returned.

He wore a blue suit—*his* blue suit, the one he wore to the senior athlete's banquet, though it hung a bit on his thinner frame. His right arm was held in a sling, but gone was the contraption that had kept his left arm suspended. In fact, that hand was reaching for her now, and his fingertips touched her cheek.

She could only say, "How?" and even that single word stuck in her throat. She squeezed her eyes shut, plunging herself into darkness, not fully trusting he would be there when she opened them again.

He was still there.

"I looked for you half the day," she said.

"Well, that's funny," he said, though of the two, he was the only one smiling, "I've been right here. All day."

Bette hazarded a glance over to Clyde, whose smile replicated Eli's. All around her, the guests seemed to be clued in that something special was unfolding. Bette looked at Darlene. "Did Alice put you up to this?"

"Who's Alice?" Darlene said, blank-faced. "Clyde just told me to be here in case you fell over."

It was good advice, as Bette didn't know what was holding her upright. She took a step back so she could look—really look—at Eli. He still wore shaded glasses but not the opaque ones he'd worn when she visited him on the hospital's lawn. These had an amber tint, his good eye clearly visible behind the lens. The other hid beneath a flesh-toned patch, already a part of him. His hair was cut, not to the severity it had been when he boarded the bus to take him to basic training but shorter than he'd worn it when he was her boyfriend on a wind-rustled afternoon. She touched the back of her fingers to the shadow on his cheek.

"I still haven't mastered left-handed shaving." He cupped her hand with his. "And I skipped the barber today."

A voice rang out from the crowd. "Maybe you two should kiss each other instead of so much talking."

Eli's eyebrows shot up, revealing a scar dissecting the left one, which Bette decided was her favorite spot on his entire face.

"Oh, no," she said, her voice fluttery. "I don't know if I trust us to stop, and this is a respectable place."

"Dinner, then?"

"I'm starving." Her stomach actually rumbled. "But I have about two hours left on my shift."

"I'll cover for you," Darlene said with a wink. Then, to Eli, she said, "And you let me know if she breaks your heart. I'm real good at picking up pieces."

There was no question where they would go for a late-night supper. Without even asking, Bette led him off in the direction of the Automat, only verifying that choice when they were halfway there.

"Are you kidding? I've been waiting for this," Eli said with boyish enthusiasm.

Bette hoped his expectations weren't set too high.

She narrated the city as they walked, extolling what she deemed its virtues. "There's life everywhere. All the time. Like it never sleeps."

"Is sleeping so bad?"

"No, but living here, I feel like I could encounter the whole world. Think about it, people from all over the world came right here, and all I've seen is whatever I see walking from my apartment to work and back. There's so much more."

"We can see it together." He placed his hand on her waist and drew her closer, stepping around a manhole cover.

She stopped and turned to him. "You're staying?"

"I'm staying if you're staying."

She pulled him in for a kiss, and they indulged in each other while passersby hooted and whistled in approval.

At the Automat, Eli stood in appropriate awe, mouth agape at the wall of tiny doors. They stopped at the booth by the door, changed a dollar for nickels (his treat, he insisted), and Bette followed with a tray as he turned one little handle after another, producing meatloaf and chicken pot pie and mashed potatoes and a slice of frosted chocolate cake. Bette got a grilled cheese sandwich with a bowl of tomato soup for herself. And of course, coffee.

"Best in the city," she said, feeling ridiculously pleased when he obviously agreed.

"Before we eat," Bette said, holding her hand over his steaming meatloaf, "I have to get this off my chest. I didn't write that letter. It was Alice. I know she already told you, but I had to come clean for myself."

He greeted her confession with mock solemnity. "I know, Bette. I knew from the minute I read the first line."

"The penmanship, right? How could she think—"

"Not that," he said, digging into his food. She could tell he was not quite comfortable using his left hand, but he seemed close to mastery. "I know your voice, Bette."

"But it was a *letter*."

"Not the way you sound but the way you think. I know how you phrase your thoughts, how you don't hold back anything. I know you wanted to tell me, and I'm sorry for not letting you know that you had nothing to hide. You don't squirm very often."

"You're right. I don't."

"Plus, she said, 'What larks!' when talking about our high school adventures, and I know how much you hate Dickens."

"Hate him," she said, ready to skip to the cake.

They didn't talk for a while—rather, *he* didn't, consumed as he was with what he declared the best food he'd tasted in years. She told him about Frank's service, what people said and who she saw.

"Larks aside," he said, wiping a drop of gravy from his chin, "that year with you was the best of my life."

"Come on, you were a high school hero long before you met me."

"But I never had a steady girl before you."

"You had plenty of girls. Or at least, plenty who told me they were yours."

"Bette, please. Can you just let somebody love you? Completely?"

Her retort stopped in her throat. She stared at a crumb of chocolate on the marble tabletop and let her ear roam for some other conversation. When he said her name again, she looked up.

"I didn't expect to come back this wounded," he said. "And if you told me a few years ago I'd be thankful to God for being half-blind with one useless arm, I would have laughed in your face. But I am thankful, Bette. Not just to be alive but to have a second chance. Maybe I'm thankful for things to be a little harder. Nothing has ever been hard for me, and now I can't tie my shoes. I'm not asking for a lot from you right now. But maybe you'll be my girlfriend? Again?"

She felt like that scene from *The Wizard of Oz*, like her life had been uprooted from a high school dance, spun, and dropped at an Automat's two-top. Everything she feared was dead, and everything she loved survived.

"Yes," she said, a coy tilt to her head, "I'll be your girlfriend. Again."

He lifted his hand in victory and shouted to the crowded restaurant, "Did you hear that, everybody? She's my girl!"

Bette waved, feeling like a movie star on a red carpet.

"I applied for student housing at NYU."

"Student housing? As in, a dorm?"

"Not quite." He dipped his fork into the cake and took an enormous bite, then spoke through it. "Family housing. Private. For two."

"Oh?" She took a bite of cake herself.

"But I won't be able to move in until the fall."

"My lease is up in September."

"Well then, my love. It looks like we will have another serious conversation after the summer."

He walked her home, and every time she stopped him to point out some small thing, he kissed her. So she pointed out every bench, every stoop, every interesting crack in the sidewalk . . . When they got to her front door, he kissed her until she couldn't feel her feet, and she kissed *him* until he swore he was losing sensation in his one good arm. Then they laughed and kissed until every empty moment between them had been accounted for. Once inside she forced herself up the three flights of stairs, her legs as heavy as sacks of sand, and wondered if she turned around halfway, she might catch him following her.

But no.

On their first date, she'd feared she'd never see him again if she gave in for a kiss. Tonight, she knew there'd be no power that would keep them apart from each other, not even themselves.

For just a moment, upon opening the door, she felt *"Alice!"* on the tip of her tongue, ready to tell her everything. The darkness wasn't a surprise, but the emptiness was. And everything—her steps, the clatter of her house key in the bowl, the dropping of her coat—echoed in the silence.

She went into the bathroom, pulled the chain to turn on the light, and startled at the face staring back at her from the mirror. Gone were the usual tension and pallor that none of Alice's creams could soften. Gone, too, was any trace of Berries Delight lipstick.

Her face wasn't burning exactly, but it was flushed, and she splashed it with a bit of water and blotted it dry. By rote, she opened the cabinet and lost her breath at the sight that greeted her. The shelves were empty. All of Alice's bottles and jars—pretty pink and cut glass—were gone. The sole occupant of the shelf was Bette's sensible jar of Pond's Cold Cream, the burlap message unfurled like a banner beside it. She ran her finger over the stitching.

"You deserve a better home than this."

Back in the bedroom, she drew the curtain that covered the shallow alcove of a closet and bit her knuckle at the sight of the wedding dress hanging alone, distanced from Bette's small, haphazardly collected wardrobe. She reached out and took its hem, immediately finding the place where Alice had picked the thread away. Not hopeless, but Bette's skills fell far short of those of the dress's creator. She pulled the dress from its hanger, one of the few times she'd ever done so, having always approached the dress with such caution, never wanting to intrude on Alice's grip.

The bedside lamp filled the room with a warm, if inadequate, glow, and Bette settled herself on the edge of the bed with the wedding dress, the burlap scrap, and her sewing kit.

"You might not have been meant for Alice or for me, but you're meant for someone, and this blessing should go with you."

For a brief moment she wondered who she would talk to once the dress was gone, but she knew she couldn't keep it here. Its presence would overwhelm the smallness of the space.

She rolled the burlap, nestled it within the silk, and set her threaded needle to work. The material was finer than the cottons and wools she'd hemmed throughout her girlhood. She was a mender, not a seamstress, all her stitching born of necessity rather than creativity. This, though, seemed almost like holy work. The room was so silent she could hear the needle pierce the cloth, heard the thread draw through it. She bit her lip in concentration, bringing the task close to her eyes in the dim light.

"You'll never be a weapon," she spoke into the quiet. "There's been enough of that, I think. You were meant to carry hope, and someday, the perfect girl will find you. I promise."

She snipped the thread with her tiny sewing scissors and held her work at arm's length, smiling wryly at the result. Not perfect—far from it. Like so many others, it bore the scars of war. She thought of Eli, who would forever see the world with the limitations of one eye. And Alice, whose heart would always hold the hurt of a love torn away. The world itself would not escape unscathed.

And yet, what was the rallying cry for a nation of women? "Mend and Make Do." The result might be bulky and uneven, but it was strong and would hold.

"Don't worry, little one," she said, already becoming accustomed to talking aloud to the empty room, "your story isn't over yet." Once she found a home for herself, she'd find one for it too.

For the meantime, though, Bette fished a Goode's Department Store box from underneath the bed and folded the dress carefully and placed it within it. "Down you go." She slid the box back beneath the bed, under her pillow, like a wish. Above it, she would dream of a future that would not have been possible if not for the romantic idealism of her best friend, and the perfect answers to prayers she was too fearful to utter out loud. Tonight, she would fall asleep still feeling Eli's kisses on her lips, and she would awake to a future with the promise of so much more.

But she was too restless to sleep. Still fueled from her cups of Automat coffee, Bette went into the kitchen, poured the rest of the milk into a glass, and sat at the table. She found a pad of floral stationery and a pen she'd purloined from the hotel's front desk.

Dearest Alice,
    Are you ready to swoon?

A Daffodil in the Dress

SUSIE FINKBEINER

CHAPTER 1

New York City
Spring 1969

WE DECIDED TO cut through Washington Square Park, Eloise and I, the way we often did when the weather was agreeable. And that day, to our delight, the weather was gorgeous. Blue skies and sunshine and a warm hint to the air that made promises of the spring that had only just arrived.

Eloise held my hand when we crossed the street, squeezing it a few times to remind me that she was there—as if I ever could have forgotten my little girl. I squeezed back so that she'd know I wasn't going anywhere without her.

She skipped along beside me, not a single care in the whole wide world.

"Mommy, I like today," she said, her dark-brown ponytail wagging back and forth as we went on our way.

Oh, what a wondrous life it was that gave us the chance to be five years old. And what grief that we only got to be that age for twelve months.

"What do you like about today?" I asked.

"That tree." She pointed at a spindly looking thing that was all branches and, as of yet, no leaves. "And the benches."

She waved at a man who occupied one of those benches, holding a small paper bag full of birdseed that he scattered for the dozen pigeons— and one brave squirrel—that had congregated at his feet.

Eloise's list went on and on. The Arch that she was convinced had been part of a castle in the "olden days," the fountain even if it wasn't spurting water into the air, and the men sitting at tables to play chess, all bundled up because winter wasn't quite done with us yet.

Everything she liked about that day was completely ordinary. And that, I believed, was extraordinary.

"You're going to do great things in this world, Eloise," I said.

"So are you, Mommy."

We stopped at one of the countless flower beds to check on the daffodils. We'd been visiting them the past few days, since the green stems started pushing their way up through the ground, which still had the slightest dusting of snow.

"Oh, Eloise," I said, my voice rising in pitch. "Look, honey!"

The very first yellow was bursting from the bud. If I had to guess, I'd say that it would be fully open by the next morning.

I crouched down and put my arm around Eloise's waist, then pulled her close to me. "Isn't this so exciting?" I asked.

"Hello, pretty flower," Eloise said, a little song in her voice. Then, looking at me with big, bright eyes, she asked, "Can I have one?"

She reached for the stem closest to her, but I wrapped my fingers around her wrist, shaking my head.

"No, honey," I said. "We can't take these flowers."

Eloise had eyes that were the same color as a cloudless sky. They were the exact same color as her father's had been. When she turned those baby blues on me, I had to bolster my resolve so as not to give in to her every request. Little girls could be rather convincing even if they didn't have a sturdy grasp on knowing what was best for them.

"Why can't we have just one pretty flower?" she asked, blinking fast, her dark lashes making her irises look all the brighter by contrast.

"Because those flowers are brand-new." I used the end of my finger to lift her chin. "And brand-new things deserve a chance to grow."

I considered telling her about the time her father and I had walked in the park after dark, the streetlights making everything look a little more romantic, more magical. Neil had picked a purple crocus for me, then pushed the little bit of stem behind my ear.

"For sweet Princess Kate," he'd said.

Then he kissed me until a police officer walked straight up to us, hands on his hips, and asked if we kids didn't know that it was a misdemeanor to pick flowers in New York City's parks.

Obviously, we hadn't known.

He'd let us off with a warning, telling us it was lucky he was in such a good mood.

If that was his good mood, I wouldn't have wanted to see him on a bad day.

I decided that particular story would be better told a different time. Maybe one I'd save for when she asked about her daddy, which she did every once in a while.

My greatest regret in life—and the one I asked God to explain over and over again—was that my little girl had never gotten the chance to meet her father. And right along with it was that Neil hadn't had the chance to hold our daughter.

War was a thief. It stole life and beauty and joy. I hated it most of all for stealing Neil from us. And for what purpose?

I was still waiting for God to answer that one.

Sometimes I wondered if he ever would.

Eloise pouted at the daffodils. That sad face would have broken Neil's heart, I knew. He would have given her the moon if only to make her smile. She wouldn't have just had him wrapped around her little finger. She would have had full reign of his heartstrings.

I, however, wasn't so easily persuaded, and Eloise knew it.

A year before, she might have thrown a small fit. Two years before, a tantrum. This day, though, she pulled in her bottom lip and nodded, even if she hadn't gotten her way.

My little girl was growing up inch by inch.

"Tell you what. We'll let these stay here." I checked my watch. It was almost time for me to be at work. "And we'll tell Mr. Finch to come see them."

"Mr. Finch doesn't like flowers," she said, giggling. "He's a man."

"Oh, plenty of men like flowers." I smiled. "Especially men who read poetry. Ready?"

She nodded and let me take her hand. We made our way to the other side of the park, leaving the daffodils firmly planted where they were.

Along the way, we stopped for a few seconds to listen to a man playing guitar under a giant elm. I let Eloise drop a couple of dimes into his case.

We skipped together for an entire block until we got to the bookstore where I worked.

Spring was waking up, one yellow flower at a time.

CHAPTER 2

ACCORDING TO GREENWICH Village legend, Alfred Isaac Finch moved to Lower Manhattan from Lancaster, Pennsylvania, and started his own bookstore in 1912 with just two novels—both by Dickens—a collection of Whitman's poetry, and a copy of *Macbeth,* all used. When he sold those books, he got his hands on a dozen more. After those went, he bought two dozen and found a storefront with an apartment upstairs. He paid for it all in cash that he carried around in a leather case.

He, apparently, had no desire to do business with banks, a quirk that would serve him well in 1929, when the stock market went bust.

Eventually, Mr. Finch had shelves built and hired some starving artist to paint Finch Family Books on the front window of the shop. Interestingly enough, when he opened the bookstore, he had yet to acquire a family.

Alfred Finch had been a wishful thinker. I could tell from the picture of him hanging on the wall behind the cash register. Even in that grainy, black-and-white print, I could see his optimism in the way he stood with both hands on his hips and grinned from ear to ear.

Yes, he'd been a man who believed that just about anything was possible.

Not an altogether bad way to be in the world.

Only a few months after opening the shop, he married Miss Regina Baldwin, and the two of them got to work making that family he'd hoped to have. How they fit all six of those Finch kids—not to mention the cats that Regina kept around—in that upstairs apartment was beyond me.

Finch's bookstore had survived the Spanish flu, two world wars, the

Great Depression, and countless other plagues that threatened to end it. Fifty-seven years' worth of readers kept it running. The most recent owner—and my boss—Ike Finch, meant to keep it going another fifty.

I'd done the math, though. Unless he intended to work until he was eighty years old, he'd need to get started on a family of his own. And soon.

All the biddies in the neighborhood loved dishing about how outrageous it was that a man like him—so sweet, so smart, so handsome—could be a bachelor still at thirtysomething years old. I usually didn't put much stock in what those women chitter-chattered about. On this point, however, I had to agree.

Somewhere in the big, wide world there was a woman perfectly suited for him. What a fortunate woman, who could be loved by Ike. I should know. After working with him for three years, I'd decided he was quite the catch.

If I was going to be honest, I might have admitted to the moments here and there in which I very nearly entertained the thought of him and me in *that* sort of way. However, I shooed those ideas away as fast as they'd knocked on the door of my imagination.

My life was a web of mingled yarn, and he deserved someone with fewer tangles than I had to offer.

Ike turned when the bell over the door jangled, and Eloise and I walked in. He closed the copy of the newspaper he'd been perusing and put it face down on the counter, taking off his reading glasses.

"Hi, Mr. Finch," Eloise said, letting go of my hand and rushing to where he stood.

"Hello," he said to her. "I wasn't expecting you today."

"Sorry." I sighed. "My mother had an appointment. She'll be by to get Eloise in a little bit. I hope that's okay."

"Are you kidding me? This little sprite is always welcome," Ike said, winking at Eloise. Then, putting his elbows on the counter, he said, "How are you today, mademoiselle?"

"Did you forget my name again?" she asked, covering her mouth and giggling.

There was no one in the world who delighted her so much as Ike Finch.

"How could I forget your name, Roger?" He grinned at her.

That was met with uproarious laughter from my little girl.

"Silly," she said. "I'm Eloise Ann Becker."

"Hmm. I think I like 'Roger' better," Ike said. "I'm glad you're here too, Kate."

"Thanks," I said, helping Eloise out of her coat.

"Coffee's brewing."

"Bless you." I headed to the little kitchenette in the back of the store.

After hanging up Eloise's and my coats, I grabbed my mug from the strainer by the sink and the sugar bowl from the cupboard, getting ready to doctor up my coffee. But I stopped when I heard Eloise say something to Ike.

"There are flowers in the park," she said.

"There are?" he said. "Already?"

I poked my head around the corner to watch them. Ike had let Eloise sit on his stool behind the cash register, and he leaned back against the counter, all his attention on her.

She jabbered on, telling him what color the flowers were and how many she counted—she said 320, which I wasn't so sure about—and that I wouldn't let her keep even one of the flowers, which made her sad.

He listened to every word she said as if it was the most important conversation he was likely to have all week.

Eloise basked in the attention. Not that she was lacking it at home. She, the youngest grandchild, lived in her grandparents' house and, therefore, was well attended. Still, there was something about Ike.

As far as she was concerned, that is.

I ducked back into the kitchenette and poured my coffee.

"Kate," Ike called. "I have to run an errand. Be back in a few minutes."

I went to the front of the shop and helped Eloise find a book to look at. A few customers came in, one who wanted to buy an atlas and another who needed a book—*Agamemnon*—for a class she was taking. I tried to convince her that she was in for a treat. Oh, I adored the Greek tragedies!

She seemed dubious, to say the least.

But she paid her dollar and took the book. I hoped she'd like it more than she expected.

It was something special, being surprised by a book.

Ike returned several minutes later, hands behind his back, and—only then—I realized that I'd left my coffee in the kitchenette. As much as I wanted to retrieve it, I was even more curious about what Ike had.

"Oh, Roger," he said, tiptoeing up to where Eloise sat on a rug by the window.

"I'm Eloise," she said, putting the copy of *Corduroy* on her lap.

"Ah. I keep forgetting." He shrugged his shoulders. "Thanks for reminding me. Anyway, do you want to know what I have for you?"

"Yes!" She glanced at me and added, "Please."

He pulled out from behind his back a single, nearly all the way opened daffodil.

"For you, Mademoiselle Roger."

Eloise gasped before she took the flower, pinching the stem between thumb and finger, holding it as gently as she could.

"Just for me?" she asked.

"Just for you."

"Ike . . ." I started.

"Don't worry." He smiled at me. "I've got one for you too."

When he walked to where I was standing, perfect daffodil in hand, he kept his eyes on mine. It was only half a dozen steps, but it seemed to take a long time for him to reach me. I tried to swallow, but my mouth had gone dry. I tried to breathe, but my chest had become tight. I leaned back against the counter to steady myself.

"'I wandered lonely as a cloud,'" he said, just loud enough for me to hear. "'That floats on high o'er vales and hills.'"

He left some space between us and extended his hand with the flower. The petals seemed to tremble. Was Ike shaking?

What in the world did he have to be nervous about?

I started to feel a little nervous myself all of a sudden. After all, it wasn't every day that a lady like me had poetry recited to her by her boss.

"'When all at once I saw a crowd . . .'" He said but then stopped and raised his eyebrows and whispered, "Do you know the next line?"

I nodded, pressing my fingertips against my lips.

"Would you like to say it?" he asked.

I shook my head.

I was, for some reason, feeling a tad bit shy.

"'When all at once I saw a crowd,'" he repeated. "'A host, of golden daffodils.'"

It was Wordsworth.

Had I told him before how much I loved Wordsworth? Particularly that poem? I must have.

"Thank you," I managed. "You shouldn't have."

"I wanted to."

"No, I mean, you shouldn't have picked flowers from the park. It's against the law. Ike, it's a misdemeanor."

"Well, I don't know about that. But I didn't break any laws." He glanced over his shoulder. "They're from Mrs. Kowalski's flower box."

I let my jaw drop.

"I asked permission first," he said. "Are you going to take it?"

I did, and as with every flower I'd ever held, I brought it to my nose. It smelled sweet and fresh, brand-new. I could have cried.

It had been so long since a man had given me a flower.

A man other than my dad, at least.

"Thank you," I said again.

Eloise and I went to the kitchenette and looked for something that could pass as a vase. We found an old canning jar under the sink that must have belonged to Ike's mother. We decided that the flowers would look perfect next to the cash register, so everyone could see them.

"You'll bring them home tonight?" Eloise asked.

"Of course I will," I answered.

Before returning to the front, I got myself a new cup of coffee; my first had gone tepid. While I was at it, I poured a cup for Ike too, something I had never done in all the time I'd worked for him.

Maybe that was why, when I placed it on the counter next to him, he sat up a little straighter and made the slightest little tilt of the head as he regarded it.

"For me?" he asked, pointing at it.

"Yup," I answered.

It was just an ordinary, everyday cup of coffee. Still, he put a hand to his heart and smiled, his eyes lighting up like it was Christmas morning.

"Thank you," he said, lifting the mug.

On any other day, I might have told him not to get used to it; I was a bookseller, not a waitress. But there was something about the way the corners of his lips turned up and his eyebrows pushed together that made him look so earnest. I couldn't bring myself to be flippant.

A man like him deserved tiny acts of kindness every once in a while.

CHAPTER 3

MY MOTHER, MRS. Dee Dee Murphy, despised the eastside of Greenwich Village. Why did she hate it so much? Because, in her opinion, the neighborhood was lousy with hippies, artists, poets, and—worst of all—folk musicians.

"They're all trying to sound like that Rob Dylan," she'd say.

"You mean *Bob* Dylan?" I'd ask.

"Oh, who cares what his name is." Mom would cross her arms and purse her lips. "I saw him once, strutting down the street like he's big stuff. Like he doesn't know he can't sing."

While I wanted to believe that she'd actually spotted Bob Dylan, I wasn't entirely sure that she knew what he looked like. Most of the men who wandered about East Village in those days had curly, unkempt hair and looked like they hadn't had a good night's sleep in about a year.

The man she'd seen could have been just about anybody.

The fact was, she avoided the neighborhood as much as possible. She much preferred her side, West Village, where, apparently, no musician dare tread.

However, she would venture east for Eloise.

As a matter of fact, Mom would have forded the Hudson for that little girl.

That morning, she walked into Finch's, black handbag dangling from the crook of her arm, her pumps adding three precious inches to her height. Short women like us needed all the help we could get.

Her eyebrows had a severe angle to them, a warning sign that she was in, as she would have put it, "no mood." It was the exact same expression she always put on when one of us kids upset her.

"They're protesting in the park again," she said, nostrils flared. "I had to walk all the way around them. Those darn hippies wouldn't get out of my way no matter how I tried to get through."

She pulled her gloves off, one finger at a time.

"They all had these signs, and they were yelling about ending the war." She huffed out a sigh. "I just wanted to say 'Okay, whatever you want. Just don't take up the whole sidewalk!' For Pete's sake."

She might have continued on with her rant if Eloise hadn't popped up, Mason jar of daffodils in hand.

"Nonna," Eloise said, "look what Mr. Finch gave me."

All severity on Mom's face softened, and she clasped both hands over her heart.

"Is this the first time you've gotten flowers from a gentleman?" she asked. "How special."

"One's for me, and one's for Mommy."

My mother turned her attention to Ike and tilted her head. Without a shred of subtlety, she seemed to size him up.

"Honestly, I don't know why a nice young lady hasn't snatched you up yet," she said.

"Well, Mrs. Murphy," Ike said, "I'm not exactly a young man anymore."

"You could have fooled me, Mr. Finch." She narrowed her eyes. "You know, I have a cousin on Long Island who's single and just about your age. Her name's Claudia. She's not the most brilliant bulb in the chandelier, if you know what I mean. But she's a good cook. Maybe the two of you could have dinner sometime."

Mom asked for a scrap of paper so she could write down Claudia's telephone number.

For a moment—a very short moment—I thought Mom was kidding around. The very idea of her cousin Claudia and Ike making a good match was laughable at the least. Claudia could cook. That was a fact. And she wasn't terribly interested in books and probably hadn't so much as picked one up since graduating from high school. But that wasn't all there was to her.

Cousin Claudia was mean. The kind of mean that caused children to think that witches might be real after all. Aside from that, she was a good ten years older than Ike. And that was a generous estimation on my part.

I could not stand by idly and allow Ike's fate to be doomed. I had to do something.

"Would you look at the time," I blurted. "Mom, you should get Eloise home, don't you think? I'll grab her coat."

With that, I shooed the two of them out the door.

Mom meant well. I believed that with everything in me. She and Dad had a loving marriage. All she wanted was for everyone to be as happy as she.

What she didn't usually consider was that some people were content to be single.

Eloise and I said our goodbyes, exchanging hugs and kisses on the cheek. Then I stayed on the sidewalk and watched the two of them until they got to the end of the block.

Before they rounded the corner, Eloise turned and blew me a kiss. I blew one to her.

The first thing I did when I went back inside was to toss Claudia's phone number in the trash can.

CHAPTER 4

MRS. KOWALSKI—THE lady of the daffodils that Ike had pilfered—came to shop at Finch's once or twice a week. And every time, it was the same thing. She'd poke around the biographies and read the back cover of a compilation of essays. Every once in a while, she'd even thumb through a collection of poetry.

But without fail, she'd end up at the bookcase where we shelved the Harlequin romances. It seemed that another two or three of those books released each week, and Mrs. Kowalski wanted to read every single one.

She'd take her time running her finger down the spines of the books or going over the list, which she kept in her purse, of which titles she already had, to make sure she didn't buy one on repeat. Then, with her two or three books in hand, she'd come to the register to pay.

That day, she chose *Nurse Sally's Last Chance*—the story about poor Sally, who couldn't manage to stay out of trouble, so she turned to a life of nursing—and *The Walled Garden*.

"This one looks intriguing," Mrs. Kowalski said, tapping a long red fingernail on the cover of the second book. "Have you read it?"

"I'm afraid not," I said, then took the book from her and turned it over to read the back.

That one seemed to be about the age-old trope of a young woman, hard on her luck, getting a job working for a grumpy boss, then falling in love with him against her better judgment.

"Enticing, eh?" Mrs. Kowalski asked.

"I guess so."

"You don't usually read romances, do you?" She leaned forward and lowered her voice. "These ones don't get too steamy, if that's what you're worried about."

"Oh, no." I swallowed hard. "That's not it. Anyway, I do read Jane Austen and Edith Wharton."

"I don't care for those." She curled her lip. "They're a bit dry for my taste."

"I'm sorry."

"I'm telling you, you ought to give these a try," she said, pointing at the books she'd selected. "You might find them inspiring."

"I'm not sure what you mean."

Ike walked past just then, headed toward the back room. He glanced at me and smiled.

That was the whole of it.

However, from the way Mrs. Kowalski mock-swooned so convincingly—I worried she was having a fit or something—I might have thought that he had declared his love for me and asked for my hand in marriage.

He did no such thing.

He didn't so much as wink.

"Oh, Kate." Mrs. Kowalski sighed after Ike was out of the room. "Did you see that?"

"See what?" I asked.

"The way he gazed at you just now."

"Like how?" I whispered, moving closer to her.

It was, in my opinion, a crying shame that Mrs. Kowalski had never made a go of it as an actress. The performance she gave that morning could have put her in the running for a Tony or an Oscar, perhaps even both. She was just that good.

She—pretending to be Ike, I assumed—set her eyes on me, her lids half closed as she looked me up and down—which, honestly, I could have done without. Then she puckered her lips and nodded as if, yes, I would do.

I wouldn't have said that she captured the essence of Ike Finch exactly. More like the jamoke who worked at the record store down the street. Still, it was a fine performance on her part.

"Ike looked at me like that?" I asked. "Are you sure?"

"Oh, honey. You mean, you've never noticed it before?" she asked. "He's looked at you like that for at least a year."

"He has?"

"Yes, dear. He has made eyes at you for a good long time." She nodded, smiling like she'd never been so pleased in all her life.

"He's done no such thing," I said, not entirely sure at all. "I would have noticed. Wouldn't I have?"

"Don't be so sure." She pulled the coin purse out of her handbag, then counted out exact change. "You don't read as many romances as I do and not develop a certain kind of sixth sense for such things. The way he looks at you could cause a wingless bird to soar high above the clouds."

I cringed. Partly because it made my stomach feel strange to think of Ike's looking at me in *that* kind of way—he never would have. But mostly because the idea of a wingless bird flying was both absurd and grotesque.

"Mark my word, Kate Becker." She watched me put her books into a paper bag. "A man doesn't scour the neighborhood looking for daffodils unless he's got a very good reason, if you know what I mean."

Then she nodded at the two flowers in the Mason jar.

"Oh, those were for my daughter," I said.

"Uh-huh." She grabbed her bag and winked at me before heading toward the door. "Just keep your eyes open, young lady."

After she was gone, I realized how tensed up my shoulders had gotten just talking to her. I tipped my head to the left, then to the right, hoping to make my muscles relax. But the very thought of Ike Finch's holding a flame for me tensed me up all over again. It was nothing short of ridiculous.

Wasn't it?

Of course it was.

He was my boss. That was all.

I might have even considered him to be a friend.

But that was the extent of it.

That was all that could have been.

On the other hand, if ever I were to find myself in any sort of romantic entanglement, I'd have wanted it to be with a man like Ike. Someone who was kind and funny. A man who held doors for me and brought me daffodils in the early spring. If given the chance to choose the type of person to be loved by, I'd want a man who wasn't afraid to recite poetry to me—good poetry.

Meeting a guy like that certainly would grab my attention.

I let out a breath and sank onto the stool. Good night. I'd never gotten so worn out from a five-minute conversation before.

"That was quite a sigh," Ike said, a book under his arm, as he returned. "Everything all right with Mrs. Kowalski?"

"Of course." I nodded. "She only bought two this time."

"That's still good." He hopped up on the counter near where I sat, something he only ever did when there weren't any customers in the store. "What was she telling you to keep your eyes open for, anyway?"

I laughed, hoping that the momentary stall would help me come up with something to say that wouldn't be a lie and, at the same time, wouldn't end up utterly humiliating me.

"We were just talking about the flowers," I said.

It was sort of true.

He picked up the jar and smelled the daffodils. I'd been right when I told Eloise that Ike liked flowers.

"Hey, I forgot that I was going to tell you something," he said, setting down the jar. "John Lennon and Yoko Ono got hitched."

"Get out of here." I popped off the stool. "When?"

"Yesterday." He reached for his back pocket and pulled out an article he'd ripped from the paper. "I saved this for you. I know how much of a Beatles fan you are."

"Are you making fun of me?"

"Absolutely." He smirked. "You Beatlemaniac."

"Oh stop." I took the page from him.

In the picture that went along with the article, both John and Yoko wore white. Him, a suit coat and T-shirt. Her, a blouse and miniskirt. John held over his head a piece of paper, which, the caption under the picture informed me, was the certificate of marriage.

John Lennon wasn't my favorite Beatle—that distinction was held by good old Ringo Starr. That didn't stop me, though, from wanting to read everything I could about Lennon. And Yoko too.

"I'm not sure that there is a quirkier couple in all the world," I said.

"True. And look at this." Ike hopped down from the counter and stood next to me, then pointed at a sentence in the article. "They both wore tennis shoes. Can you imagine the entire world caring about what shoes you wear to your own wedding?"

I shook my head.

My mother had insisted that I wear white leather pumps on my wedding day. She'd said that, short as I was, I'd look like a little girl next to Neil without them. Those shoes had pinched my toes and rubbed blisters into the backs of my heels. I'd been miserable with sore feet for a whole day of our honeymoon. Worst of all, nobody had even seen those shoes, my dress had been so long.

"Next time I get married, I might consider wearing some comfortable shoes."

I hadn't meant to *say* it. I'd only meant to think it. That thought was supposed to live quietly inside my head for my own benefit, not to be blurted out in front of anyone.

Especially not Ike. And most especially since Mrs. Kowalski had said that he looked at me *like that.*

Ike's eyebrows shot up, and he held a hand over his mouth. I hoped he was smiling.

"That is to say that *if* I ever get married again, I'd wear more sensible shoes," I said, my words tumbling out so fast that I couldn't have stopped them even if I'd tried. "But I don't know that I'll ever get married again. It's so hard to find a man in this city who would want an older wife like me and a little girl about to start kindergarten . . ."

Ike lowered his hand.

"You say some of the most interesting things I've ever heard."

"What I mean is," I said, my voice lower, "what sort of man would want a secondhand wife?"

"It doesn't sound so bad to me," he said.

It wasn't unusual for Ike to say something like that to me. He was a nice guy, after all. What was unusual was that I paid special attention to the way the volume of his voice dropped when he said it and how the boyish sparkle in his eyes was replaced with something I found hard to define. Was it affection? I couldn't know for certain.

Did I dare hope that it was?

The atmosphere seemed to grow thick, and I struggled to breathe for some reason. I feared, for a moment, that I might faint dead away right there behind the cash register. Still, I didn't look away from Ike.

He didn't look away from me, not even to blink.

Gosh.

But then the bell over the door jangled, and in walked a customer.

"Hello there," Ike said, pivoting away from me to get out from behind the counter. "Can I help you find something?"

The man took off his fedora, squinting at the shelves of books like they were from a different dimension.

"Yeah," he said, rubbing his jawline. "I need something for my daughter. It's her birthday."

"How old is she?" I asked.

"Seven." He grinned, and his eyes got wide. "And smart as a whip."

"Oh, I know just the thing." I passed by Ike, so very aware of how close I was to him when I did.

I had to remind myself to stay focused on the customer. If I let myself, I might have lost the entire day just thinking about how nice Ike's eyes were.

I directed the customer to where we kept the books by E. B. White and pulled a copy of *Charlotte's Web* off the shelf for him, assuring him that any seven-year-old girl would adore it even if there was a spider on the cover.

"I can gift wrap it, if you'd like," I offered.

"That would be nice," he said. "Thank you."

"What's your daughter's favorite color?"

"Well, I'm not sure exactly, but she wears an awful lot of pink."

"My daughter does too," I said. "You know, I think we have some pretty pink paper and ribbons in the back."

I had to walk by Ike again to get to the wrapping paper, and I tried my very hardest to put one foot in front of the other without getting all tripped up on myself. To not check to see if he was watching me. To avoid looking his way.

It seemed like I'd completely forgotten how to behave like a normal human being.

I wondered what in the world was happening to me.

Once I finally made it to the back room, I allowed myself to slump a little, to breathe deeper and slower. I willed my heartbeat to slow down as I selected the paper—a sweet pink with little cream-colored flowers printed all over it.

Measuring and cutting and folding, I did my best to convince myself that Ike had meant nothing by it—the looks and the sweet things he said and the twin daffodils for Eloise and me. He was just being a nice guy.

I tied the best bow I could and took a second to draw a little web à la Charlotte the spider on a gift tag.

"Some girl," I wrote into the threads of the web.

Pleased with my work, I made to return to the front of the store.

But then I heard the man say, "Your wife told me you have a daughter."

I stopped just before stepping through the doorway so that Ike could correct him without knowing that I'd heard.

He didn't, though.

Instead, he said, "Oh, she told you about Eloise? She's a great kid."

I hugged the package to my chest but only for a moment before I realized that I was in danger of crushing the bow.

CHAPTER 5

ON THE BACK side of the article about John and Yoko was a picture of heaps of trash lining a street gutter. A woman walked, stooped so she could hold the hand of a small child. I could almost imagine the words coming out of that lady's mouth.

"Please, please don't jump in that pile of garbage!"

I'd had to say something very similar to Eloise on a couple of occasions.

The way that Ike had torn the Lennon-Ono clipping from the paper had cut off most of the article about the trash problem we New Yorkers were still experiencing—it had been more than a year since the sanitation workers' strike had ended. Somehow the rubbish was still accumulating.

Everyone in the city was sick and tired of the whole ordeal. And the stench.

I hoped against all hope that the article had some news about a deal being made to finally remedy the problem.

I looked for the rest of the paper in every nook and cranny where Ike may have stowed it. I pulled open every drawer and peeked under every bit of clutter on the back counter. No luck. I'd have asked Ike, but he was in his office, talking on the phone with his mother.

That was a conversation I knew not to interrupt.

Mrs. Finch was a fine lady. She was also the kind to go on and on, not having any consideration for how expensive a long-distance call to Florida was. If she'd had the chance, she would have asked to say hello to me, adding at least fifteen minutes to the call.

I would have had to sell a dozen books or more just to cover the cost.

So I kept on searching on my own, knowing the darn thing had to be somewhere.

Finally, I decided to check the garbage can—the irony of looking for an article about trash in a trash can was not lost on me. I grabbed it from under the counter.

Eureka! There it was!

I pulled the paper out, glad that it hadn't fallen in anything gooey that I'd need to wipe off.

It was strange, Ike's tossing the newspaper that early in the day.

Usually he was one to keep it with him, reading through it column by column all day long.

He must have done it by accident, I told myself, and unfolded the paper, then laid it on the counter and pressed it flat with my hands.

There was something I liked about the smoothness of newsprint and the way it made a crisp, swishing sound when the pages were turned. I even sort of liked how the ink would rub off on my fingertips.

After flipping over one page, then another, I found the rest of the article about the trash. All it said, really, was that the city was working on a solution. I rolled my eyes. Essentially, all that meant was that the mayor and his underlings didn't know what to do but realized that the taxpaying voters expected them to come up with something.

If my mother had been the one in charge, she'd have come up with a solution by lunch—a year before. Too bad the woman had no interest in elected office. She could have whipped the whole city into shape.

I turned back to the front page. In bold, blocky letters the headline seemed to yell for attention.

AMERICAN DEATH TOLL IN VIETNAM RISES:
33,063

I didn't read on. I didn't look at the picture that accompanied the article.

What I did do was fold the paper in half so that I wouldn't have to see that number anymore and dropped the whole thing back into the trash.

I grabbed the feather duster from the kitchenette and busied myself tidying up the bookcases.

Still, that number wouldn't leave my mind.

Thirty-three thousand sixty-three.

That was a lot of boys whose lives had hardly even started before they were over.

A lot of families who got a knock on their front doors from a man in uniform with news that would turn their worlds upside down.

My Neil was one of those 33,063 dead.

By the next morning, the number would be even higher. I couldn't imagine what number we'd reach before realizing that we couldn't lose even one more boy.

Out of the corner of my eye and through the front window, I saw a couple of people walking down the opposite side of the road, each with a cardboard sign under their arm. They must have been part of the protest Mom had complained about.

I stepped outside, smelling the stink of an overflowing garbage can just a couple of feet from me, and watched the folks across the street.

Of the two, I could only read the writing on one sign: We Want Peace.

I imagined President Nixon crossing his arms and saying, "I'm working on a solution," all the while knowing the same thing that President Johnson and President Kennedy as well as every senator and general and any other person with even a shred of power had known.

We wanted the war to end. We just had no idea how to make that happen.

I wanted to scream. To throw a fit and demand that someone fix it.

The person on the other side of the street shoved the sign he was carrying into a garbage can.

I turned and went back inside.

It wouldn't have mattered how loud I'd yelled or how much fuss I made. Nobody would have listened to me.

CHAPTER 6

IKE WALKED ME to the door at closing time—the way he did every day—so he could lock up behind me. I stepped outside, holding the lapels of my coat close around my neck. It wasn't cold exactly. But there was still the smallest hint of chill on the wind.

Winter never did like giving up without a little bit of a fight.

"Have a nice evening," Ike said.

The way he always did.

That night, though, he didn't shut the door as soon as he'd wished me well, like he usually would have. I turned to face him, ready to ask if there was something else he needed from me before I left. For some reason, I couldn't think of any words to say. None, at least, that wouldn't make me sound like a bumbling idiot.

The only thought my mind could formulate was some variation on the theme of how handsome Ike was. His hair—a little on the shaggy side—and the angle of his jawline. The mole under his right eye that I'd somehow never noticed before. The faint shadow of stubble on his cheeks.

But what captured my attention most were his eyes.

Ike had captivating eyes. Somehow—after three years of working for him—I'd never realized it before. They were hazel, and I couldn't tell if they were more green than brown or the other way around.

They were the type of eyes that someone could stare into for an entire lifetime and never get bored. Especially as they were just then, soft and smiling and so very kind. I had never seen him look at anyone else in quite the way he was looking at me.

Could I have just been imagining it?

Yes. That was it.

I forced myself to blink a couple of times, in case my vision had gone blurry or there was something in my eye.

That didn't seem to help, because when I focused on him again, his expression hadn't changed, and he hadn't turned away from me. If anything, he was inexplicably handsomer to me than he had been that morning.

My goodness. What in the world was happening?

I told myself to snap out of it.

That was the second time in one day that I was aware of his gaze. I just knew that it was because I'd become a victim of the power of suggestion.

Thanks a lot, Mrs. Kowalski.

"Kate . . . ," Ike started to say. Then he smiled.

I hadn't thought it possible, before that moment, that a man well into his thirties could blush, but there Ike was with a little flush in his cheeks.

My brain—the sensible part of it at least—informed my body that I should go home straightaway. That I absolutely did not need to stay standing there, making eyes with my boss. Sensible brain told weak-in-the-knees body that the very last thing I needed was to fall in love. With anyone. That it would only end in heartbreak—for both Eloise and me. Sensible me reminded dreamy-eyed me that I was a widow and a mother and had no business with all that variety of nonsense.

Furthermore, I needed to keep that little job of mine if I ever wanted to save up enough for Eloise and me to get an apartment of our own one day. I couldn't very well continue to work for Ike if he went and broke my heart. Or the other way around.

Get away, my sensible brain said. *Get away now.*

But I didn't listen. As a matter of fact, I told that reasonable side of my brain to hush up, and I stayed put, at least for another minute.

I'd forgotten how delightful it was for a man to look at me the way Ike did.

"Kate," he tried again.

"Ike," I said.

Then we both laughed, and I couldn't for the life of me think of what was so funny. Sensible-brained me must have been rolling her eyes.

A guy walked past me, guitar case in hand, and I presumed he was off to play at one of the cafés nearby. I hadn't gotten a good look at his face, but from the lack of strut, I could tell it wasn't Mom's favorite folk singer, Bob Dylan.

Sometimes I wished that I could go sit in the back of one of those places, drinking coffee and listening to the music.

But my Friday night plans—and every other night, for that matter—were already set out for me. Home, dinner, get Eloise in the tub before bed. Usually, I was able to read a few chapters before turning in myself.

There was, those days, hardly any spontaneity in my life.

The most exciting thing that had happened recently? My mother changing the menu on Tuesday from lentil soup to chicken noodle.

That was not to say that I would have traded motherhood for even a moment of living footloose and fancy-free. Still, I wondered what it would be like.

I turned my attention back to Ike, who was, I believed, the only unmarried person I was ever around. Other than Eloise, of course. But unlike her, Ike didn't have a bedtime of eight o'clock.

If I couldn't experience the carefree existence for myself, maybe I could live it vicariously through him.

Besides, he almost never talked about his life outside bookstore hours, and I was curious.

"Do you have any plans for tonight?" I asked.

"Sure. Yeah." He crossed his arms.

He did. Of course he did. An eligible bachelor like him probably had a date waiting for him to pick her up.

Why did the thought of that make my stomach hurt?

"Big plans," he went on. "I've got a TV dinner waiting for me in the icebox. Swiss steak, if you'd like to know."

"It's a fine choice."

I allowed myself to be a little bit relieved. What date would want to come over for a dinner served in an aluminum foil tray?

"That's not all." He lifted one side of his mouth into a crooked smile. "I've also got a copy of *The Godfather* I've been looking forward to reading all week long."

"Nothing like a good mobster story on a Friday night," I said.

I felt silly, the way I'd pined for a life more thrilling a few moments before. The reality was, if I'd had a choice, I would have stayed home anyway.

"Is it terribly square of me?" he asked. "Being so excited about a book?"

"Not at all." I sighed. "I can think of nothing nicer."

In the three years I'd worked at that bookstore, I'd never ventured up the stairs to Ike's apartment. It would not have been appropriate for me to. As a matter of fact, I'd never given it much thought, really. Why would I have?

But I let myself imagine it, just for a moment. Why not?

The walls would be painted the same color as those in the bookshop. Ike liked green more than any other color. At least I supposed so, because that was what he wore the most. Possibly because it brought out the olive and gold tones in his eyes.

His bedroom would also be that color—he was a thrifty man—but I wouldn't let myself think too much about that part of his personal space. I was, after all, a lady.

I turned my attention to his living room. That was safer.

He would have pictures on a few walls, I imagined, and a shelf of books that were too special to sell. And by the window, he would have a comfortable chair—brown leather, I thought, with worn patches on the armrests from years of use. It would be just right for long evenings of reading with a cup of tea.

Strike that. He hated tea.

He would want coffee.

Oh, and there would be a floor lamp that let off the coziest and warmest yellow glow for him to read by.

I wondered if, perhaps, he had a second chair there by the window or if he'd ever considered putting one there.

My imagination tried to put *me* in that chair, a copy of *Sense and Sensibility* in my hands. But I shook my head, not allowing such a silly thing to occupy my mind.

Elinor Dashwood would have been ashamed of me.

Her younger sister Marianne, on the other hand, would have cheered me on.

"Penny for your thoughts?" Ike said.

Ha! I wouldn't have told him what I was thinking even if he'd offered me a billion pennies!

"Oh, I was just daydreaming," I said.

"What about?"

"Reading."

It had been true.

He leaned against the doorjamb, and I realized how close we were. Inches. That was all the air between us. It would have taken so little for him to lean down and . . .

No. *No.* I would not allow myself to think about being kissed by him.

Still, dreamy-eyed me wondered what it would be like. Also, I wondered if I remembered how to kiss. It had been well over five years.

Was it like riding a bike?

The reasonable, rational, sensible department of my brain had seemingly closed up shop for the day, because suddenly I was quite aware of how Ike smelled.

Since when did he wear cologne? And did he have a breath mint in his mouth?

I got nervous about my own breath. The onion on my sandwich at lunch had been quite strong.

I took half a step back. For his sake more than anything.

"I really should get going," I said.

I took another step away from him. Then stopped.

"Ike," I said, voice breathy as if I'd run a marathon.

"Yes?"

He pushed the door open wider and stepped out onto the sidewalk, closing the little bit of distance that I had put between us.

"I, well," I stammered. "I hope you enjoy *The Godfather*. I've heard such good things about it."

Then I raised my hand in a wave and hoofed it in the direction of home. It was the sensible thing to do. Still, all I wanted was to turn around and run back toward him.

CHAPTER 7

MY FOLKS LIVED in the same West Village brownstone they'd bought shortly after they got married. Lest anyone think they were from money—which they weren't—Mom pointed out that they'd gotten married in the middle of the Depression.

Between the money they'd both managed to save up—Dad from odd jobs and Mom from working at her father's market—along with a small loan from his parents, they'd been able to afford it.

"But don't get your hopes up," Mom would tell my brothers and me, shaking her head. "A place like this would cost four times now what it did in those days."

Then Dad would give a detailed account of the various repairs he'd done—and continued to do—on the place. That would be a long conversation unless Mom interrupted him, saying that no one had to know about every doorknob and faucet he'd replaced.

"In summary, it was in bad shape," he'd say, ending his exposition with a weary nod of the head. "A sorry state indeed."

Then one of my brothers would inevitably say, "It was in Jersey?"

The Murphy boys. A couple of comedians.

At least they liked to think so.

I rounded the corner and saw that every window on the first floor of our place was lit up. As I neared the brownstone, I noticed a couple of those lights switching off. Dad must have been making his rounds, muttering that we didn't need to light up the entire neighborhood.

When we were kids, my brothers would sneak behind Dad and turn the lights back on so that he'd have to go around and around the house. This little game of theirs could go on for hours or until the boys got bored—which was usually how it went.

I'm not entirely sure that Dad ever really caught on.

If he did, he never yelled at them for it.

I liked to think that he was playing along.

When I reached the gate, I watched the light in the front room switch off and then, just a few seconds later, flicker back on again.

That could only mean one thing: at least one of my brothers was home for supper.

Sure enough, as soon as I walked through the front door, Salvatore greeted me with a hug so hard I worried that he'd crack one of my ribs.

"Hey, Sis," he said, letting go of me. "We was just about to send a search party out looking for you."

"Hi, Sal," I said, shrugging out of my coat and resisting the powerful urge to correct his grammar. "Work, you know?"

"Oh, I know how that goes. I'm glad you're here." He patted his stomach. "Ma wouldn't let us eat nothing till you got here. We're all starving half to death."

"All?" I asked. "Who all is here?"

"Everybody." He held up his hand, counting on his fingers. "I got my bunch here. Finn's got his."

"Did I forget someone's birthday?" I cringed.

"No, nothing like that."

"Then why is everybody here?"

"Maybe I don't wanna tell you." He shoved his hands into the pockets of his slacks.

"Don't be obstinate." I swatted at his arm. "Just tell me."

"Ma invited a guy over to meet you or something."

"What guy?" I asked. "And why does he need to meet me?"

"Come on, Katie. Why do you think?" Then he nudged me with his elbow three times.

"Why are you doing that?" I asked, shoving him. "And I have no idea. Why?"

"He's single. You're single," he said. "Put one and one together . . . catch my drift?"

"Oh no. This is not happening."

"Are you going to try to stop Ma?" He turned from me and yelled, "Katie's here!"

From somewhere in the house, my other brother, Finn, said, "Finally! I'm dying of starvation over here!"

I hung my coat on the hook by the door, wishing I could find someplace to hide. I'd have liked nothing better than to sit in the little cupboard under the stairs and wait it out until supper was done and Mr. Mystery Man was long gone.

But I was an adult woman, and no longer did I have the luxury of escape.

Besides, Mom would have sniffed me out in a minute flat.

Speaking of, she rushed down the hall toward me, wooden spoon in hand and apron around her waist.

"Go, go," she said, and at first I thought she was giving me permission to fly the coop.

But then she grabbed me by the hand and pulled me along with her. As small as I was, Mom was at least a head shorter and a couple of inches narrower—a fact she had no qualms about reminding me of. Still, as tiny as she was, she was a good deal stronger than I ever could have been.

"You've got to get freshened up," she said. "He'll be here any minute."

"Mom . . ."

"Don't argue with me. Just get up to your room and put on something pretty." She shoved me toward the stairs.

"Why?" I said, grabbing hold of the newel and facing her.

"Because," she said, "I'm trying to do something nice for you. I'd think you'd at least show a little appreciation."

"I wish you would have asked me before trying to pass me off to a strange man."

"Katherine, he's not strange. He's a gentleman." She crossed her arms, the wooden spoon in the crook of her elbow. "That's what his aunt told me."

"You haven't met him?"

"I hear he's handsome too."

I knew she was trying to distract me with the promise of a good-looking beau. It was not going to work.

"But who is he?" I asked. "And why do you think I'd like to meet him?"

Half a dozen kids clambered down the stairs, nearly knocking me over. Eloise was in the bunch, wild with excitement to be playing with her cousins.

"No running," Mom and I scolded in unison.

They slowed down, more because they were afraid of Mom than me.

Those kids never took me seriously.

Eloise excluded.

"All right," Mom said, turning her focus back on me. "His name's Bob Armstrong. You know Mrs. Pepper from down the street? I ran into her at the market today. She had on the most horrible perfume. It made me cough."

"Mom." I put my hands on my hips. "Stay focused. What about the guy?"

"Well, Bob is Mrs. Pepper's nephew." She pushed her lips together. "She was telling me how he just moved to Manhattan and hasn't had much luck getting to know nice people yet. I thought it might be good if you'd befriend him."

"Befriend? Or date?" I asked. "If he needs a friend, I've got two brothers who could fit the bill."

"Okay. You got me. I thought you'd like to maybe enjoy his company once or twice, see if there could be something between you." She put a hand next to her mouth like she wanted to tell me a secret. "He's good-looking."

"You already told me that, Mom." I dropped my arms to my sides, my shoulders drooping. "I don't care what he looks like. Or if he's a gentleman or whatever. I have a daughter, you know. I can't have a stranger chasing me around, even if he is Mrs. Pepper's nephew."

"Well, he wouldn't have to chase you if you didn't run away."

I pressed my palm against my forehead.

What a bizarre day I was having.

"Katie, I have been praying since Neil died that someone would come along to take care of you and Eloise," she whispered. "I believe that the Lord answers prayers, and, so help me, if you try to resist his answer to my prayer, I will not be pleased."

"How can you possibly know that this Bob is God's answer to prayer?" I asked.

"I don't know that." She lifted both hands, palms up. "But why can't you just give him a chance?"

"Mom . . ."

"I just want you to be happy."

"I am," I said.

She clenched her jaw and shut her eyes, nostrils flaring the way they did when she was profoundly annoyed.

"I don't have to be married in order to be happy, Mom," I said.

"Well, I know that. Of course I do." She opened her eyes. "But think of Eloise . . ."

"I do. Every moment of every day."

"A little girl needs a father." She nodded.

I wanted to give her the benefit of the doubt and believed that she hadn't meant to hurt me by saying that. Still, it stung. My daughter did have a father. Neil would always hold that place in Eloise's heart. But I didn't dare pipe up and say so. I couldn't have without losing my cool completely.

That wouldn't have done anyone any good.

"Get upstairs and put on something pretty," Mom said. "Please."

Most of my life, I'd been the easy child in the family. The compliant one. The one who was pleased to sit quietly in the corner and read the day away, staying out from underfoot. My mother rarely ever had to tell me to do anything twice and, as far as I could remember, had only had to punish me a couple of times.

And usually, on the occasions when I did get into hot water, it was because I'd broken rules under the rotten influence of Sal and Finn. Once or twice, my best friend, Shirley, had managed to steer me wrong.

Regardless, I was the good one of the bunch.

Even at twenty-eight years old, I was still trying not to rock the boat.

I turned and headed up the stairs.

CHAPTER 8

My mother followed me up to my room so that she could help me pick out something to wear. Her way of helping was to have full veto power over anything I might choose for myself. Therefore, the pedal pushers and cozy sweater were out. As was the long-sleeved maxi dress. So, too, the bell-bottom jeans I liked to wear with my black turtleneck.

"A nun would wear less than this on a date," she said.

"Nuns don't go on dates, Mom," I said.

"Well, neither will you if you don't show a little skin."

"Mother!"

"Not a lot." She rummaged through my closet. "Just enough to stir up a little curiosity."

I did not want Bob Armstrong to be curious about my cleavage or me. I suggested a tasteful and modest pink dress that hung at the back of my closet, crossing my fingers that it still fit. I hadn't worn the thing since before I got married.

Fortunately, the zipper went up all the way, and I didn't have to suck in my stomach too much.

Mom left the room, trusting me enough to touch up my makeup by myself with the condition that I put a little rouge on my cheeks so I wouldn't look so pale.

Rouge? I hadn't worn the stuff in ages. I wasn't even certain that I had any. I pulled open all the drawers of my vanity, trying to find some. No luck.

But I did find the old diary that I'd kept when I was but a wee teeny-bopper.

What a treasure! I opened it—not needing the key, thanks to whichever of my brothers had broken the lock years ago—and found, right where it had always been, the glossy magazine picture of Gregory Peck that I'd taped inside the cover long ago.

In it he was reading a book on the set of *Roman Holiday*. When I first saw that picture, I'd fallen into a hard and deep infatuation for the man. It was as close to being in love as my little thirteen-year-old heart could manage.

As was the case with nearly all children who read for most of the waking hours of the day, I was a girl with an active and vibrant imagination. I'd embarked upon great adventures held entirely in my head—journeys to the other side of the world or quests deep in the Amazon rainforest, among many others.

Inevitably, I'd get into some sort of deadly peril from which I was rendered completely and entirely helpless.

In my make-believe world, Gregory Peck would arrive at just the right moment to rescue me from whatever danger I'd encountered. He'd use his wit, his charm, his strong jawline to overcome my enemy and swoop me off to safety.

What a silly little girl I'd been.

I closed the diary, then put it back in the bottom drawer of my vanity.

The doorbell rang, and Mom yelled for me to answer it.

"It's *him*!" she squealed.

"Where are you now, Gregory Peck?" I muttered, closing the drawer and making my way down the stairs.

I was aware that Bob Armstrong probably wasn't a threat to my health or safety. It was just a dinner. And I would be surrounded by family, including my brothers, who would sock anybody who meant to do me harm. Still, with every step closer to the front door, I felt heavier with an overwhelming sense of dread.

"It will be okay," I whispered to myself before reaching for the doorknob. "Oh, Lord, please let this man be kind at least."

Then, putting on what I hoped was a welcoming—but not flirtatious—smile, I pulled open the door.

I very nearly fell over with relief when I saw the Mason jar and the pair of daffodils.

"You left these behind," Ike said. "I didn't want Eloise to be sad."

"Oh, Ike," I said, almost breathless. "You don't know how glad I am to see you."

"Is everything all right?"

"Yes. Fine." I reached for the jar, and the edge of my ring finger brushed against his index finger. He didn't let go of the jar, and neither did I, almost as if time had frozen in place.

And then, just like earlier, there was that feeling, like my feet weren't touching the floor.

"Mr. Finch," Eloise yelled, careening across the hardwood floor. "Are you here for dinner?"

"Oh, uh," Ike stammered, letting go of the jar and using that hand to push his hair off his forehead. "I don't think so."

"Then why are you here?" she asked, reaching up and grabbing his hand.

I couldn't remember her ever doing that with him before.

He smiled and relaxed his shoulders a little, like holding hands with her was the most natural thing in all the world.

She pulled him inside and closed the door behind him.

"I brought your daffodils," he said.

She thanked him profusely—by which I mean that she repeated it about a dozen times—and begged him to "pretty please with sugar on top" stay for supper.

On any usual day, I would have told her not to bother Mr. Finch, that he probably had someplace to be. I might have had a talk with her later about not inviting folks to supper without asking me first.

This day, however, had been anything but usual.

Besides, I didn't want to see Ike go.

I wanted him to stay for supper too.

"Nonna made meatballs," Eloise said. "And spaghetti."

Ike looked at me. "Hmm. That sounds pretty good. But I'd hate to impose."

"It beats a TV dinner," I said. "You should stay. I promise that my mother has made enough to feed two households."

"You're sure it's okay?" he asked.

"Of course it is."

He nodded, and Eloise hugged his hand to her heart.

I closed the door, took his coat, and hung it on the hook next to mine—the most natural thing in all the world.

"Come on," Eloise said, pulling on Ike's hand. "You can meet my cousins."

"Okay," he said.

"Nonna," she yelled. "Mr. Finch is here for supper!"

"Who?" Mom asked, then ducked her head around the corner and saw Ike. She seemed to deflate a little. "Oh."

Then the doorbell rang again.

CHAPTER 9

I HATED TO admit it, but upon Ike's arrival at the house, I had entertained the hope that the man Mom had orchestrated this entire evening for would decide not to show up at all. But that was dashed as soon as the darn doorbell chimed.

Bob Armstrong had arrived.

"That's him," Mom said, throwing both hands in the air as if she'd just won the lottery. "Get the door, Katie!"

Ike stopped just a few steps into the hallway and turned.

"Him?" he asked.

"Oh, um, a neighbor's nephew," I said, shrugging, before opening the door. "Maybe I'll explain later."

There, on the top step of the porch, stood one of the handsomest men I'd ever seen in person. So handsome, I gasped. A little. It hadn't been noticeable. I hoped.

For a second—maybe two—I thought that Paul Newman had shown up on our porch. The man had the kind of crystal-blue eyes that could pierce to the very heart of any woman—including me if I'd let them. His jaunty smile was pure charm. How did anyone have teeth that white? He must not have been a coffee drinker. And he certainly wasn't a smoker. He'd come dressed like he was going to a Sunday morning church service. Suit coat, tie, and all.

It wasn't Paul Newman. But that man was a pretty decent replica.

"You must be Bob," Mom said, sidling up to me. "I'm so glad you came. Did you find the house okay?"

"Sure I did," Bob said, taking a step toward Mom and kissing her on the cheek.

She reached up and touched where his lips had landed.

"Such a gentleman," she said. Then, putting a hand on the small of my back, she pushed me forward. "This is my Katie."

"It's nice to meet you, Katie," he said, extending the bouquet of pink roses and baby's breath he'd brought with him. "These are for you."

"Oh, thank you," I said, moving the Mason jar of daffodils to the crook of my arm so I could take the roses.

"They match your dress."

"How about that?" I said. "It's like we planned it."

He lowered his chin and then turned his eyes up to mine.

I did not need to read any of Mrs. Kowalski's romance novels to identify what Bob was doing.

He was flirting.

And with great skill.

It had been years since I'd felt the urge to giggle. I clenched my teeth so I wouldn't let one bubble up then. I had my dignity to think of.

"Well, Bob, come in." Mom put her arm around his. "We've got the whole family here to meet you."

Then, as she was about to lead Bob past Ike and Eloise, Mom stopped.

"And this is Isaac Finch," she said. "He and Katie work together at the bookstore."

"Isaac," Bob said, offering his hand to shake.

"Ike is fine," Ike said. "It's a pleasure to meet you."

Just then, I noticed Eloise tapping Mom on the arm.

"Nonna, can Mr. Finch sit at the kids' table with me?" Eloise asked.

"Sure, honey," Mom answered, not entirely aware of what she'd agreed to.

"No," I blurted. "Sorry, Eloise. I think it would be better if Mr. Finch sat with the adults tonight."

"It's fine. As a matter of fact, I should go," Ike said. "I didn't know you were having special company over."

"Oh." I looked from Ike to Bob, then back again. "But not as special as you."

Mom arched one eyebrow and narrowed her eyes.

Bob bit his lip.

Eloise pouted.

And Ike rubbed the back of his neck.

As for me, I had no idea what kind of face I was making. I was entirely too busy in my mind, trying to think of something to say that might dilute the fog of awkwardness that I'd created.

No one in that narrow hallway—which seemed narrower by the second—said a word.

It was quiet until Finn came in from the direction of the dining room, his shock of red curls in desperate need of a haircut.

"Hi, folks." He lifted a hand in greeting. "Hate to interrupt this riveting conversation, but the rest of us are wondering if we can start eating."

"Of course," Mom said through a forced smile. "Finn, be a dear and show these gentlemen to the dining room. Katie and I will get an extra place setting for Mr. Finch."

Bob made to follow Finn, passing by Eloise.

She, being the polite little lady that I'd taught her to be, stood up straight and flashed her best smile.

"Hi, I'm Eloise."

Bob hardly even spared her a glance before walking around without saying so much as a single word to her. It was like, to him, she was just something in the way of where he was headed.

I wasn't the only one to notice it.

The muscles in Ike's jaw tensed, and he tilted his head one way and then the other to stretch out his neck. He unclenched his fists before taking a step forward.

"Hey, Roger."

Eloise rushed back to him, and he squatted down so he was eye to eye with her.

"Do you know if we're having any dessert after supper?" he asked.

"Yes," she answered. "Nonna made panna cotta."

"That sounds good." Ike grinned at her. "Tell you what. You let me eat dinner with the adults. Then I'll have dessert with you. Is it a deal?"

She said that it was, and they shook on it.
I dropped Bob's pink roses on the deacon's bench next to the door.
Then I headed to the dining room, bringing the daffodils along.

CHAPTER 10

THE ONLY OPEN seat for me was the one between Ike and Bob that had been jammed so tightly between their chairs that I was afforded very little wiggle room. On either side, the thighs of the gentlemen were dangerously close to mine.

It was bound to be an uncomfortable meal in more ways than one.

"Now, Mr. Murphy," Bob said, glancing up at my dad before helping himself to a couple of grissini—long, crispy breadsticks my mother had made earlier in the day. "What kind of name is that? German?"

"Irish," Sal answered. Then, ruffling Finn's hair, he said, "Can't you tell by looking at this wee leprechaun?"

"'They're after me Lucky Charms!'" Finn said, putting on a very thick, very bad Irish accent. "Charmin', simply charmin'."

Sometimes it amazed me that those two scoundrels held down perfectly respectable desk jobs.

"My father was born near Belfast. And we are not leprechauns," Dad said, scowling at Sal and Finn. "We're Protestants."

I caught Mom rolling her eyes. My father's sense of humor was such that his jokes sometimes took a few seconds to set in. So it was with that one. But we all ended up laughing eventually, even if it was out of pity or simple politeness.

All of us except Bob, that was.

"I don't get the joke," he said, picking up his fork and knife.

"It's okay, dear," Mom said, spooning sauce onto her spaghetti. "My parents came over from Italy—"

She started to say more. If I had to guess, she was going to tell him about how my grandparents had been small children when they'd met on the ship crossing the ocean to America. About how they'd played jacks together on the deck and hide-and-seek all throughout the ship. Eventually, their families had ended up in the same tenement once they settled down in Brooklyn.

They'd fallen in love day by day most of their lives.

It was what Mom called a "basic American love story."

As irked as I was with my mother, I wanted her to tell that story. Sure, I'd heard it at least a dozen times. Still, it was sweet and hopeful and altogether wholesome. Just the sort of story that Ike would enjoy.

Unfortunately, Bob didn't seem to be patient enough to listen.

Not even patient enough to let her get started.

He was proving himself to be more insufferable by the minute.

"How about that," Bob said, cutting off Mom. "Armstrong is a good English name. We can trace it back to the Mayflower."

"That's fascinating," Mom said. "Don't you think so, Katie."

"Groovy," I said.

Mom wrinkled her nose as if the word had let off a foul odor.

Ike cleared his throat, and I stole a look at him. His forehead wrinkled, and his eyes crinkled in the corners, his lips held tight in such a way that made me think he was working hard at holding in a laugh.

Then he leaned toward me and whispered, "'Groovy'?"

"Was that the wrong thing to say?" I asked.

He shifted on his seat so he was half turned toward me.

"Better than 'sock it to me,'" he said.

I laughed not only at what he'd said but also at the idea of Ike Finch watching *Laugh-In*. Earlier when I'd imagined his apartment, I hadn't even considered that he might have a television.

"Katie," Bob said, a little louder than was necessary in an attempt, I assumed, to get my attention. "Your mother told me you work at a bookstore."

"Yes." I glanced at him. "Do you like to read?"

"Not especially."

"That's too bad." I rolled a meatball in the sauce before popping the entire thing into my mouth so I wouldn't be able to say more about Bob's answer.

"I'm sure he doesn't have much time for reading," Mom said. "Bob's an attorney, you know."

"Ooh boy," Sal said. "That's a lucrative career path."

"Sure is," Finn added. "How much do you bring in each year?"

"Finnegan," Mom said. "We don't ask questions like that. Especially not at the dinner table."

"Sorry, Mom."

"It's all right," Bob said. "Shall we just say that I do all right?"

"I'll bet you do," Mom said.

"And yet, for all that college education, I cannot figure out how to eat this spaghetti." He tried and failed to get the strands of pasta to twirl on his fork. "Honestly, I don't know how you people do this."

Giving up, he used his knife to cut the spaghetti.

Mom's smile faded, and her face went blank as she blinked slowly, as though her eyelids weighed a hundred pounds.

Sal elbowed Finn and then nodded in Bob's direction. Dad put his silverware down and averted his eyes from the pasta massacre.

Bob was completely oblivious to all of us gawking at his great offense against my mother and a whole host of our Italian ancestors. He smirked as he used his fork to scoop up a pile of desecrated spaghetti and lifted it to his mouth.

"I've got to tell you, I don't know why you don't just eat it like this." He sent his fork in for another load. "Much easier."

Once he noticed me watching him, he gave me a wink.

I decided that I wouldn't tell him about the dribble of red sauce he'd gotten on his tie.

CHAPTER 11

TRUE TO HIS word, Ike excused himself at dessert to join Eloise so she could, no doubt, show him off to her cousins. What I wouldn't have given so I could go along with him. The kids' table seemed more and more appealing with every moment I was forced to spend in the presence of Bob.

He at least ate his panna cotta like a regular human.

As soon as he finished, though, he dropped his napkin on the table and pushed out his chair.

"I better be off," he said.

"Oh, are you sure? So soon?" Mom asked, her voice without a trace of conviction.

The spaghetti incident had only been the beginning of her cooling toward him. As the meal went on and he continued to dominate every conversation, she smiled in his direction less and less and scowled more and more.

"Katie," Bob said, standing and offering me his hand. "Would you walk me to the door?"

I tried for a pleading look at Mom, hoping she'd give me some sort of excuse not to accompany him. But she was already up and busy clearing the table.

"Sure," I said.

I did not take his hand.

At the front door, he waited for me to hand him his coat, as if trying me out to see if I'd make a good wife someday. Well, willing to do just about anything to get the man out of the house faster, I got it for him.

I didn't, however, hold it by the lapels for him while he put it on. I was no Donna Reed.

Once he'd gotten the coat on, he gave me a look that was, I assumed, intended to be a smolder that would bring me to my knees.

All the expression managed to do was make me wonder how much time he spent in front of the mirror, practicing different ways of looking at a woman.

"Katie," he said, deepening his voice. "I'd like to see you again. Have supper with me tomorrow night."

It wasn't a question.

"No," I answered. "I don't think I will."

"Excuse me?" He kept his mouth open, and his eyes seemed confused. That man had not been on the receiving end of rejection nearly enough. "Why not?"

Instead of listing the many, many reasons I'd come up with over the course of the evening, I just told him that it wasn't a very good idea.

"I . . . I don't understand." His suave glances and smooth movements receded, leaving only a normal man who happened to have pretty eyes. "I thought this went well."

"Listen, Bob," I said. "I'm sure you're a decent person. But right now isn't the time to bring someone new into my life—or my daughter's life."

"You have a daughter?" he asked. "Are you sure?"

"Absolutely certain."

"You're a mother?"

"I am," I said.

Without trying to be subtle about it, Bob checked my left ring finger. His eyebrows twitched, and he blinked hard, I supposed because he didn't see a wedding band.

An unmarried mother raised complex questions.

Oh, what he must think of me.

"I don't know what to say," he muttered.

"My husband died in Vietnam," I said. "I didn't find out that I was expecting until a few weeks after he shipped out."

Bob leaned against the door, and for the first time that evening, he didn't barge in and take over the conversation.

I took his silence as an invitation to continue. I felt compelled to go on. Not because he deserved an explanation but because my story deserved to be listened to.

"I was close to eight months along when the man knocked on my apartment door." I hugged my arms around my waist. "When he saw my stomach, he tensed up. He couldn't bear to tell me the news. I knew what he was going to say anyway."

The man from the military had used my phone to call Mom, because I couldn't. Then he'd sat with me, holding my hand until she got to the apartment. All I managed to say when I saw her was that Neil would never get to hold our baby.

"It felt like my life was over," I said. "But I had to keep on going for her."

Bob got busy buttoning up his coat. I couldn't be sure that he was listening to me anymore. I didn't particularly care if he wasn't.

I went on anyway.

"That little girl—my little girl," I said, "was God's mercy in a world that had gone impossibly dark."

He cleared his throat. He didn't lift his eyes to look at me. "When my aunt told me about you, she said you were nice and that you were pretty. She never told me that you had a kid."

"She should have."

When he looked up at me, all the charm was gone. In his eyes was only cold, blue indifference.

Bob Armstrong, descendant of Mayflower Puritans and Mrs. Pepper from down the street, new himself to the Big Apple, Paul Newman impersonator, and lawyer, who—I had to give him credit—was good at picking out flowers, left without another word.

I grabbed those flowers and headed toward the back door so I could put them directly into the garbage can.

I passed the kitchen, where my mother and one sister-in-law were getting started on washing the dishes. Then the dining room, where I caught Sal and his wife sneaking a kiss in the back corner. Last, I looked into the den to see Finn sitting on the floor, most of the kids running around him while they yelled and hooted.

Dad came to me from across the room, finger on his lips to let me know I should be quiet.

I followed him toward the stairs, where Ike sat with Eloise on his lap. She had fallen asleep, her head resting against his chest, while he read *The Giving Tree*. He must not have realized that she was conked out, because he kept on reading to her.

"She only made it to the third page," Dad whispered.

"Poor thing," I said. "I should get her to bed."

"Let him help." He put a hand on my back. "She's getting too big for you to carry up those stairs. I don't want you to fall."

"I can manage."

"Still." He nodded toward Ike. "Let him."

"Okay."

"He's a good man, Katie." Then he noticed the pink roses in my hand. "Where'd you get those?"

"Bob." I rolled my eyes. "I was going to throw them out."

He took them from me. "I'll do it for you." Then he smiled, watching Ike and Eloise for a second before heading outside.

Ike stopped reading when I tapped him on the knee.

"She's asleep," I whispered.

"Oh." He craned his neck so he could see her face. "She is."

"Can you help me get her to bed?" I took the book from him.

He carried Eloise upstairs, cradling her like she weighed nothing at all. All those boxes of books he lugged around every day must have made him pretty strong.

I opened the door to her bedroom, and he laid her on the bed so gently, like she was such a precious and delicate little thing.

After getting her settled in—teddy bear securely clamped under one arm and blanket pulled up to her chin—Ike and I tiptoed out of her room.

I left the door open a crack, the way she liked, so the hallway light could come in.

CHAPTER 12

THE UPSTAIRS HALLWAY walls were covered with framed pictures. Originally, those had only included the three of us kids. But as we grew up and started having our own families, Mom had included photos of the grandchildren too.

Ike seemed interested in every single one of them, stopping to study them, one by one. I told him who was in each and tried to remember the story behind the particular snapshots.

"That's Finn after he lost his first teeth," I said.

"Teeth?" Ike asked. "Plural?"

"Yes. He lost three all at the same time." I grimaced. "It was also the first time he took a sock in the mouth from Sal."

"Oh boy." His eyes widened. "Remind me not to get in a fight with your brothers."

"You don't have to worry about Finn. Obviously, he's not a good fighter. Sal's the one to be wary of."

"I will do that."

I pointed at the next picture. "That's the day we went ice skating at Rockefeller Center and Mom claimed that she saw Clark Gable. She made Dad search all over the rink until they found him, so she could get her picture taken with him."

Ike squinted and got closer to the photo. "But that's not him. Is it?"

"No. It's just a man with very big ears." I shook my head. "But Dad didn't have the heart to tell her it wasn't Clark Gable, so he took the picture anyway. That nice man must have been a good sport."

"How did she take it when you broke the news to her?"

"We still haven't," I said. "Just ask her if she's ever met any movie stars. I bet you a quarter she tells you about this."

"A quarter, huh?" He grinned. "That all you have? Your boss should pay you more."

At the next picture, Ike stepped back and pointed at it.

"That has to be you."

"Bingo." I knit my brow, trying to think. "That was kindergarten, I believe."

I'd been so excited to have my picture taken at school, as was evidenced by my smile that showed off nearly every tooth in my mouth.

"You were cute," Ike said.

"Why, thank you," I said.

"Eloise sure takes after you, doesn't she?"

"I like to think so."

"She's a special girl." He made his way to the top of the stairs.

"The most special." I joined him.

"I guess she gets that from you too." He moved down to the step second from the top and faced me. "Huh. Look at that. I'm still taller than you."

"Very funny," I said, going up on my toes to be as tall as possible.

I wasn't typically prone to teetering. There was something, though, about being in such close proximity to Ike that had thrown me off-balance, and when I put all my weight on my tiptoes, I wobbled.

For a moment, I imagined myself tumbling down the stairs like Scarlett O'Hara. I wasn't sure what would have been more lethal in that situation, the fall itself or the embarrassment.

Fortunately, Ike didn't do as Rhett Butler did, passively observing as Scarlett rolled to the bottom of the steps. Instead, he grabbed hold of my waist to steady me.

Gracious. I'd thought I was off-balance before. But feeling the warmth of his hands through the cotton of my dress made me absolutely unstable.

One of his thumbs moved up and down on my side. It was barely an inch, but interestingly enough, it was all I could think about.

Then, as suddenly as he'd caught me, he dropped his hands.

I took hold of the railing, worried that my lightheaded condition would put me in further danger of the wobbles.

"That was close." I actually tittered. "Thanks for saving me again."

"Again?" He placed his hand on the railing mere centimeters from mine.

"Yes. You've been my own knight in shining armor this evening."

"Have I?" He lifted his eyes to mine. It was similar to the way Bob had earlier. However, when Ike fixed his gaze on me in such a way, it didn't seem rehearsed. His regard wasn't a *smolder*. It was more like a healthy dose of comfort with kindness mixed in.

I realized, standing nearly nose to nose with him at the top of the steps, that Ike's looking at me in that way was nothing new. Before, I'd simply interpreted it as his being a nice guy. This evening, however, I'd learned to read it as affection.

"Yeah," I said. "In regard to Bob, of course."

"Ah. Yes. Him."

"My mother sort of ambushed me with him." I rolled my eyes. "So when you showed up . . ."

I stopped talking, because just then, Ike placed his hand atop mine, and it seemed as if I'd lost complete command of my voice. Had I been able to speak, I would have said that when he showed up, I knew that I could face the evening with Bob regardless of how uncomfortable it may be. Perhaps I would have even told him that I was becoming convinced that I could bear nearly anything if only he were with me.

But I didn't say any of that, because Ike was holding my hand, and I wanted him to continue doing so. It was nice even if the sensible part of my brain was attempting to scream for me to think rationally.

Ike licked his lips and drew in a deep breath through his nose. When he let it out again, he laughed.

For a moment, I feared that I'd done something funny unintentionally. Like, maybe there was broccoli stuck in my teeth or something hanging out of my nose.

"What are you laughing at?" I asked.

"At how much of a coward I am." He lifted his eyebrows.

"You aren't . . ."

"But I am." He cleared his throat. "This is the third time today I've had a chance to kiss you."

"It is?" My face felt like it was on fire. "But you didn't. Why not?"

"Because I've been too afraid." He laughed again. "I'm ridiculous."

"No. You aren't," I said. "Not at all."

I willed for him to be courageous. I also inched closer to him, so he wouldn't have to travel too great a distance to be brave.

He used his free hand to brush a hair off my face.

This was it. He was going to kiss me. I swallowed, reminded myself to take a deep breath, and closed my eyes so that he would know I was ready.

"Kate, I . . . ," he started.

"Katie, I've been looking for you everywhere," Mom yelled from the bottom of the stairs, interrupting Ike. "What in the world are you doing up there?"

I had absolutely no intention of telling her. Besides, nothing had happened, thanks to her.

Ike backed up an inch or two but didn't remove his hand from my face or his eyes from mine. There was no way, though, that he was going to kiss me with my mother hollering up the stairs at us.

Good grief. Who would have thought that at twenty-eight years old, I would have my love life foiled by my own dear mom?

"Oh. Sorry," I called to her. "We were just putting Eloise to bed."

"'We'? Who's 'we'?"

"Ike carried her," I answered.

"Ike Finch?" she asked. "He's still here?"

"He is."

"Well, your brothers are about to leave. Come and say goodbye."

"Be right down," I said. Then to Ike, I whispered, "I'm sorry, but I have to—"

Ike used his fingertips to trace the line of my jaw, moving in to plant a kiss on my cheek.

How I wanted him to linger there.

I thought about putting my arms around his neck. I wasn't sure what I would have done with him once he was in my grip. Still, I contemplated it if only so that I could feel him close to me a little bit longer.

But before I could act on that idea, he moved away from me, the sweetest sort of smile on his face.

"See you Monday," he said before rushing down the stairs.

CHAPTER 13

IT WAS MY deeply held conviction that Saturday mornings were for sleeping in. Unfortunately, I'd been raised by a woman who believed that lazing around in bed all morning was very nearly a sin. Doubly unfortunate, I'd given birth to a child who seemed to have inherited the early bird gene.

I woke that Saturday morning—far earlier than I liked—to Eloise saying my name over and over, and opened my eyes to her face hovering closely over mine. Her lips were forming words, but due to my groggy state, all I heard was gibberish.

"What's that, honey?" I asked, my voice creaky as an old hinge.

"Aunt Shirley's here!" Eloise answered, bouncing beside me.

"She is?"

"Yup, I am," Shirley said, leaning over me. "What's wrong with you?"

Of all the friends I'd had in my life, Shirley had stuck around the longest. We'd been pals since the third grade—twenty years. And no matter what scrapes we got into, how many heartbreaks we'd endured together, or the severity of squabbles we'd had, the two of us had remained the closest of kindred friends.

One could have argued that we didn't have much choice, since I'd married her older brother. But even after Neil died, I knew that she wasn't going anywhere. I never would have wanted her to.

"You look awful," she said.

"Thanks a lot." I knocked a bit of sleep out of the corner of my eye.

"Are you sick or something?"

"I don't think so." I felt my own forehead. No fever, thank goodness. "What time is it?"

"Eight o'clock." Shirley checked her watch. "More or less."

I groaned and tried to pull the covers over my head, begging for just a couple more minutes.

"Not today, sleepy," Shirley said, ripping the blanket from my grip. "Get up. We're going to a rummage sale."

"Where are your boys?" I asked, stretching my arms over my head.

"Paul took them to the zoo. Told me to get out of the house for a little bit." She put a hand on her stomach. "I need to find a bassinet."

She turned, the roundness of her belly seeming to have expanded since the last time I'd seen her. It had been only a couple of days, but that baby was having a growth spurt. Not that I would have told Shirley that she looked huge.

Baby number five was nearly done baking in that tummy of hers. We were all praying that this one—finally—would end up being a girl so Shirley could stop trying for one. We all loved her four boys. But she certainly needed a little sugar and spice and all things nice.

I shooed Shirley and Eloise so I could get dressed, hearing them chattering in the hallway.

I loved that the two of them were as close as they were.

After Neil died, his folks couldn't bear to stay in Manhattan. There were just too many memories to remind them of what they'd lost. Even though they claimed it wasn't so, I couldn't help but think that I was part of the reason they'd needed to go away. It hurt to think they'd choose distance over having all the time they wanted with Eloise.

Over the handful of years, they'd tried to convince Shirley and her brood to join them in Pennsylvania, saying how good it had been for them, getting out of the city. Every once in a while, my mother-in-law sent her pictures of the garden she was tending in her yard and of the house.

"Notice all the space we have here," she'd written on the back.

Whenever a house in their neighborhood went up for sale, Mom Becker would call Shirley and try to convince her that she and Paul ought to stake their claim on it before someone else snatched it out from under them.

"It would be nice to have the grandkids close by," she would say.

I didn't receive those kinds of phone calls.

On some of the darker days, when I mourned Neil deepest, it was difficult not to take all of it personally.

Still, I worried that Eloise was growing up not knowing all that much about Neil's side of the family.

Except for Shirley, that was.

She loved showing Eloise old photos of her and Neil when they were younger. Often, she'd remember a story that Eloise absolutely had to hear. Usually they were about different kinds of shenanigans and scrapes that Neil had managed to get himself into.

Every once in a while, thinking of Neil would make Shirley cry. It hurt her sometimes, the telling of stories. Whenever that happened, she let Eloise comfort her, let her see that it was okay to be sad.

Not only did Shirley work to fill in the blanks where Neil was missing in our daughter's life, she also worked to show Eloise just how loved he was. And how loved he always would be.

I opened my closet to find a cardigan to wear over my button-up shirt. There, pushed all the way to the right side of the rod, hung Neil's old letterman jacket. I reached into the left pocket, where I knew I'd find the little velvet box that my engagement ring had come in.

The last time he'd worn that jacket was the night he'd asked me to marry him.

The ring he'd given me that evening and the band he'd added to it on our wedding day stayed in that box for safekeeping. Someday I'd give them to Eloise. When I did, I would make sure that she understood that those rings weren't the best thing her father had given me.

She was.

CHAPTER 14

THE RUMMAGE SALE that Shirley had dragged me to Brooklyn for was, according to her, a bust. At least it was by the time we'd gotten there, which happened to be mere minutes before they were closing up for the day.

It was good that I'd left Eloise at home with my folks. She would have been terribly disappointed.

The church ladies were kind enough, though, to let us browse around for a little bit as they packed up the things that hadn't sold—mostly broken toys and rusty tools. No bassinet, unfortunately. Although Shirley did find a sweet toy tea set.

"Should I get it?" she asked, holding up the little creamer pitcher so I could see it. "Just in case this baby is a girl?"

It was a pretty purple color with daisies dotted around the rim.

"Why not?" I put my hand on her stomach, something I'd only ever have done with her. "I have a feeling about this one."

"You do?"

"Yeah," I said. "Sure I do."

"Oh, you can't tell." She waved me off. "I can always give it to Eloise if worse comes to worst."

She shrugged and put the pitcher in the cardboard box with the other dishes and carried it off, saying something about being in desperate need of a powder room.

I went in the opposite direction to riffle through a pile of clothing stacked high on a table in the corner. I found a pretty gingham dress for Eloise and a raincoat that I thought my dad might like. The more I dug through the clothes, the more gems I discovered. A soft flannel nightie for Mom and a wool sweater with leather elbow patches.

It was green and just the sort of thing Ike might wear.

I added it to the rest of the things I meant to buy. After just a second, I dropped it back on the table.

Was it too bold of me, giving him a sweater? Even if it was from a church-basement rummage sale?

On one hand, I'd worked with him for years. I knew what he liked, and I definitely knew what he looked good in. Besides, there were still a few chilly days ahead before summer came on with a blast of heat. He could use something cozy. I picked it up.

On the other hand, three days before, I wouldn't have given his wardrobe much more than a passing thought. Daffodils and Mrs. Kowalski and his hands on my waist had changed all of that. But what was to say that anything would come of it?

Oh, I sure hoped something would come of it.

Still, I couldn't give him that sweater. I dropped it back on the table.

Then again, it was absolutely perfect for him. I picked it up.

I lifted my head, looked around for Shirley, and realized that she would want to know why I was buying a sweater like that. It wasn't anything my dad or brothers would wear and was far too big for me. She would ask more questions than I was ready to answer.

Down it went again.

But I kept a hand on it.

One of the church ladies came to the table, cardboard box in hand. Starting from the other end of the clothes, she folded what was left over and dropped item by item into the box.

"You better decide quick," she muttered at me.

"Excuse me?" I asked.

"I said, 'You better decide quick.'" She nodded at the sweater. "You gonna buy it or not?"

"I don't know."

"Well." She gave me a pointed stare. "You better decide quick, before I put it in the box."

"What happens if it goes in the box?"

"It takes a trip to the dumpster," she said.

"The dumpster?" I asked.

She blinked slowly at me as if to say, *"That's what I said, dimwit."*

"Well, if it's all just going into the dumpster, why are you folding it?" I nearly cringed at how much my voice sounded like my mother's when I said that.

Her eyebrow twitched up, and her lips pulled down into a frown. She didn't deign to answer me; instead, she went back to folding and dropping. Folding and dropping.

I watched her for a full minute, surprised at her rudeness.

I forgot all about that, though, when she picked up a dress from the table.

She held it up, pinching the shoulders between her thumbs and pointer fingers, regarding it for just a moment. It wasn't any ordinary dress. No. This was a wedding dress with elegant lace. I couldn't know until I touched it, but the fabric had to be silk. That dress looked old. Quite old.

And Mrs. Grouchy-Pants was in the process of folding it up to be dropped into the box doomed for the garbage.

"I'll take that," I said—or, truly, half yelled—rushing around to the other side of the table and grabbing for the dress. "I'll buy this."

"Why do you want it?" she asked, not letting go. "It's older than I am."

Her deeply wrinkled forehead and the swollen knuckles of her fingers made me doubt that she wasn't pretty close to the same age as the dress. Her scowl, though, made me decide not to challenge her.

"Please," I said. "It doesn't deserve to end up in the trash."

The two of us stared into each other's eyes, neither of us daring to blink. I could almost hear the theme from *The Good, the Bad, and the Ugly* in the background. But then, after a good long pause, the woman took another look at the dress before letting go.

"It's too pretty to waste," she murmured, then grabbed all the rest of the clothes and dumped them into the box.

The green sweater ended up on top of the heap. Before she could utter an objection, I grabbed it and dashed away.

I managed to pay the lady at the cash box and tuck the clothes in a paper bag—the dress all the way on the bottom and the sweater for Ike tucked into the raincoat—before Shirley came back from the restroom.

She glanced at my bag and made a "hmm" sound. "What did you find?" she asked.

"Oh, nothing, really," I answered. "Are you hungry? Should we get some lunch?"

"Starving." She rolled her eyes and rubbed her stomach. "Always."

We walked out of the church and around the corner to catch a train to Greenwich Village. I glanced down the alley to see the church lady with the box standing at the dumpster, tossing the leftover clothes in, one article at a time.

She turned and sneered at me.

I held my bag closer to me as Shirley and I walked away.

CHAPTER 15

THE GUY AT the lunch counter tapped his fingers against the Formica, keeping time with the beat of the song playing on the radio, singing along with every word of "Mrs. Robinson." Mom would have marched right up to him and demanded that he pipe down, that he was disturbing other paying customers.

As for me, I didn't mind so much. Sure, he was no Art Garfunkel—who was?—but he wasn't half bad either. The poor guy was probably in the Village hoping to catch his big break. I felt bad for him, though. Record producers didn't tend to frequent Baldy's Cup and Sup, which boasted the "Thickest Slug of Mud in Manhattan!"

Shirley had insisted that we go there, citing a craving for a Reuben with extra sauerkraut. Add pickles. And a generous smear of mustard on each slice of bread.

When she'd ordered, the waitress had scowled at her and said, "You're sure?"

Shirley had pointed both index fingers at her stomach and told the woman that she should never question a woman who was nine months into her fifth pregnancy.

"Suit yourself," the waitress said, scribbling on her order pad. Then, turning toward me, she asked, "And for you, sweetheart?"

I ordered myself a ham and cheese on pumpernickel with an extra pickle spear, knowing that Shirley would steal the one that came with the sandwich.

The song on the radio changed over to "Get Off of My Cloud," and the guy at the counter gave his voice a rest. Apparently, he wasn't a Rolling Stones fan. On that, he and Mom would have agreed.

"I hear you had company at supper last night," Shirley said, taking a sip from her water glass.

"Oh." I folded my hands on my lap. "Who told you?"

"Honestly, Katie. You think I don't have my ways?" She shook her head. "If you must know, I heard from Mrs. VanderWest, who heard from Mrs. Wilson, who heard from Mrs. Chevalia, who heard from Mrs. Pepper that your mother invited her nephew over to meet you."

"Honestly." I sighed. "Did the whole entire neighborhood have to know?"

"It wasn't the whole entire neighborhood. Stop being so dramatic," she said. "It's not like Mrs. Suttner has heard."

"Yet." I bit the inside of my cheek. "I don't know why it has to be such a big deal. It wasn't as if I even wanted to have supper with him."

"They all just want you to be happy. You're still young. There's no reason you should go the rest of your life alone."

"Well, I . . ."

"I saw him the other day. Bob Armstrong. He's a handsome one, that's for sure." She reached across the table, patting my paper place mat. "And rich, from what I hear."

"Shirley . . ."

"He'd take good care of you and Eloise," she said, then sighed. "You wouldn't have to work at that bookstore anymore. Or live at your parents' house, for that matter."

"Listen, I—"

"You'd be a kept woman." She nodded at the paper bag on the booth beside me and cringed. "But if you're thinking of marrying him, you can't wear a wedding dress you bought at a church rummage sale."

"How did you know about—?"

"About the dress?" she interrupted. "Hon, nothing gets past me. You know that."

It was true. Shirley was an observant one. I supposed she had to be so she'd keep the upper hand at home with all those boys.

"Watching you play tug-of-war with that old biddy was pretty entertaining, I must say." She chuckled.

"I thought you were in the bathroom."

She shrugged.

"So come on. Give up the goods," she said. "What's between the two of you?"

"Nothing," I said, crossing my arms and leaning my elbows on the table. "As a matter of fact, I don't want to see that Bob Armstrong again. Ever. He was arrogant, and he couldn't have cared less about Eloise."

"Really?" Shirley's eyes widened, and her mouth went up at the corners. "Tell me everything."

So I did. I told her of the pink roses and the practiced glances, the cut spaghetti and the way he seemed only to want to hear the sound of his own voice. I ended the whole rant by saying that if given the option between having dinner with him again and having to tame a colony of street rats, I would gladly choose the rodents.

"It was that bad, huh?" Shirley asked.

"The very worst," I answered.

"I don't mind telling you how glad I am to hear you say that."

"You are?"

She rested a hand against the center of her chest and nodded. "You have no idea how worried I was."

"You were?" I asked. "Why?"

"Well, you know." She pulled one side of her mouth into a grimace. "A man like that wouldn't necessarily be comfortable with his gal being close with her late husband's family."

She made a good point. A man like Bob Armstrong would likely make a jealous beau, wanting every moment of attention from whatever woman he managed to ensnare. No doubt he would have considered Shirley a threat.

I supposed she was, to a certain extent.

Any man who made me choose between her and him would end up the loser.

Our food came, and before the waitress could put the plate in front of me, Shirley had already swiped my extra pickle. The deejay on the radio said something about playing something a little older and a little slower, and from the first couple of notes, I knew what it was. The guy at the counter joined Skeeter Davis in singing "The End of the World," his voice every bit as mournful as hers.

Shirley groaned. I already knew that she hated that song, but she told me all over again anyway. I got started on my sandwich, letting her spout off about how no one really wanted to hear a woman sing about how she was absolutely sure that life couldn't go on after she'd gotten her heart broken by some guy.

I took a big bite of ham and cheese, letting my mind wander as she went on and on.

I didn't mind the song. Not really. Sure, it was melodramatic. At least that was what I thought of it when it first came out.

Later on, though, it felt a bit too familiar to me.

For a long time after Neil died, I couldn't bear to hear that song. I'd turn off the radio as quick as I could or rush out of the room, fingers stopping my ears so I wouldn't get the tune stuck in my head. It hadn't ever mattered. That song wormed its way into my mind, emerging when I was too exhausted to resist it. I'd lost more than a few nights' sleep, that song playing over and over until I thought I might go mad.

Anymore when I heard it, the worst that happened was a gentle tugging at my heartstrings. Maybe it was a dose of nostalgia. Even though the song reminded me of pain, I no longer believed that my world was ending. It had shifted, sure. But it hadn't crumbled. Not completely.

Life continued to be beautiful even after the most devastating of heartbreaks.

Shirley picked up half of her sandwich but then put it down again. "Katie, do you ever think about getting married again?"

"Maybe," I answered. "It could be nice, I guess."

"Do you have anybody in mind?" She widened her eyes before picking up her sandwich and taking a big bite.

"Oh, that's quite a question, Shirl." I picked at the crust of my sandwich.

"That means you do," she said around a cheekful of corned beef. "Spill the beans, babycakes."

"Aren't we a little bit too old to be talking about supposed crushes?" I rubbed at my collarbone, knowing that I was about to turn bright red any moment. I had never been the sort to talk about boys. As a matter of fact, I'd been known to sneak books into my overnight bag to read at sleepovers when the other girls confessed their crushes.

It simply did not interest me.

"Can't we talk about something else?" I asked. "Please?"

"Ah. The lady protests too much."

"Do you know where that quote is from?"

"The Bible."

It was *Hamlet*. But she looked so pleased with herself that I didn't have the heart to correct her.

I took another bite of sandwich—one that ended up being far too large for my mouth—and hoped that by the time I was done chewing, she would have moved on to another topic of conversation.

She, however, was more stubborn than I and held out, waiting for me to answer her question. When I swallowed, she raised her brows and blinked slowly as if to say, *"I'm waiting."*

I sighed, resigned, and leaned forward. She did too. Well, as much as her belly would permit at least.

"You have to promise not to tell," I said.

"Cross my heart," she said.

"Well, I'm not sure if anything could ever come of it, but . . ." I started, then lowered my voice. "I, uh, think that I might be falling for Ike."

"Ike Finch? As in, your boss?" Shirley very nearly yelled. "You're pulling my leg. Right? Ike Finch. Ha!"

"No. I'm serious." I pinched my lips together. "What's so bad about him?"

"Nothing." She used her napkin to catch a laughter tear from the corner of her eye. "It's just, he's a bit of an egghead, isn't he?"

"What's wrong with that?" I crossed my arms.

"Oh, nothing, I guess." She shoved a couple of potato chips into her mouth. "I just can't see it, is all. The two of you together."

Then she angled her eyes to the right. To the left. She cycled through at least half a dozen different facial expressions, as if she was giving the prospect of Ike and me a good consideration.

When I tried to say something, she shushed me, telling me that she was trying to picture it.

Finally, after far too many minutes, Shirley's eyes met mine and she smiled.

"All right, all right." She put up both hands in surrender. "He'd be good to you. More importantly, he'd be good to Eloise."

"He already is," I said.

"He'd better be." Her chin trembled when she said it.

We finished our lunch, talking about Ike all the while. I chalked it up to pregnancy hormones, all the times Shirley got teary-eyed as I told her of the sweetness of Ike Finch. I had no such excuse when I got choked up telling about how tenderly he'd held my little girl.

As much as I didn't like comparing one person to another, I couldn't help but think of the contrast between Ike and Bob.

Shirley grabbed the bill for both of our lunches, and when I argued, she warned me against irking the crabby pregnant woman. Then she asked me if I'd be kind enough to help her get up out of the booth.

The poor thing.

When we made our way to the door, the guy at the counter was singing "All You Need Is Love."

I wasn't certain that love was all one needed. I did know, however, that it made life all the sunnier.

Shirley linked arms with me as we walked to the bus stop, the paper bag propped on my hip.

CHAPTER 16

MY MOTHER HAD not only aced home economics but been given the Domestic Science Award her senior year in high school. It was true. I'd seen the certificate the teacher had awarded her. Mom kept it in an old scrapbook, along with all our most important family keepsakes. Birth announcements and baptism invitations and Mom's proof of being a housekeeping genius.

If there was a domestic question, Mom knew how to answer it. There was no spill too large, no recipe too daunting, and no stain too deeply set for my mother to face.

As a matter of fact, she'd been offered a column in one of the small community newspapers—Mrs. Dee Dee Housekeeper, they'd wanted to call it—but she had turned it down, citing a lack of writing ability.

"Besides," she'd said. "It would feel impersonal, giving advice in the paper. I'd rather them come over to the house, so I can show them how to do it."

Over the years, plenty of confused housewives had come to our door, looking for tips on how to make their gravy smoother, how to get their baseboards spotless, and how to get a colicky baby to sleep.

I, of course, did fairly well in the domestic arts, thanks to her careful tutelage. However, elderly fabric was well beyond my ken, and I feared that if left to my own devices, I would ruin the rummage sale wedding dress.

It was with great reluctance, though, that I brought it to the kitchen to show her, not entirely certain how she would react to me—a single woman who, as far as she knew, had kissed all prospects of marriage goodbye after Bob Armstrong left the evening before—having a used and quite filthy wedding dress.

However, she surprised me by not raising an eyebrow or wrinkling her forehead. All she did was ask me if I'd found it at the rummage sale.

When I told her that I had, she wanted to know how much I'd paid for it.

"Fifty cents," I told her.

"What are you going to do with it?" she asked, feeling the fabric and giving it a good once-over.

"Well, I'm not exactly sure."

"You weren't thinking of wearing it"—she cocked one of her eyebrows in my direction—"were you?"

"I hadn't given it much thought."

Mom made a humming noise that was as close to saying "yeah right" as it got.

"All right," I said. "Maybe I did wonder what it would look like on me."

"I can't say that I blame you. It's a lovely dress." She sighed. "At least I'm sure it was once."

Mom draped the dress over the back of a chair, then grabbed the bottom of the skirt and wrinkled her nose at a lumpy spot in the hem.

"It's old. And far too big for you, if you have a mind to wear it. We'd have to alter it quite a bit. But I worry about this fabric holding up."

"It's silk, isn't it?" I asked, waiting for her nod of confirmation. "Well, I thought silk held up for a long time."

"It can. That is, if it's cared for." She dropped the skirt of the dress. "I'll bet this thing's been in a box for a while. Or maybe just hanging up with a bunch of other clothes. It's awfully dirty."

"Maybe we can soak it?"

"We can try." She pointed at the cupboard in the corner. "Grab me the white vinegar please."

While I did, she made her way downstairs to the laundry room. When I arrived, I found her scrubbing the washbasin, then stopping up the drain and drawing cold water from the faucet. She measured half a cup of vinegar and added it to the tub.

"Go ahead and put the whole thing in," she said. "That's right. All the way under the water."

Then she moved the mixture around gently, using what she called her "laundry paddle," which was, oddly enough, an old bat from when Finn went through a cricket phase in high school.

The dress would need to soak for about half an hour, Mom informed me. But when I headed for the stairs, she said my name.

"I hear that when Roberta Stein had her second wedding, she wore a suit dress," she said. "From what I understand, it was a nice yellow."

"Oh?" I turned. "I hadn't heard that she got married again."

Roberta's husband had died in Vietnam a year after Neil. I'd had coffee with her a couple of times. Everyone in the neighborhood had thought we should be friends. Something about the two of us having a lot in common. It had turned out that the only thing we related to each other over was our grief. It was too hard for me to hear her talk about her loss. I wouldn't have been surprised if my mourning had been too much for her too.

The friendship hadn't taken.

Still, I was glad to hear that she was married again. I hoped that she was happy.

"Maybe you could find out where she bought her suit," Mom said.

"Mother . . ."

"A dress like this wasn't made for a second-time bride." She grabbed a rag and wiped around the faucet. "Besides, you couldn't wear white. It just isn't done."

"Mom, you don't need to worry about that." I held up my left hand with its unadorned ring finger. "I'm not engaged. I'm not even seeing anyone, for that matter."

"Well then, when the time comes," she said. "It's not that I'm rushing you."

"Right."

"Although, if you want to have another baby, time is running out, you know." She pointed at her watch. "Ticktock."

"Mom." I sighed. "I'm twenty-eight."

"And your eggs will dry up if they aren't put to use." She nodded as if that was the final word.

"Well, that's not exactly how it works," I said.

She put a finger in the air to stop me, saying, "Young lady, I am *not* interested in how it works."

My mother, essentially a certified master domestic scientist, was, apparently, not a fan of biology.

She suggested that we use our half hour wisely by baking a batch of cookies. I hoped that she had chocolate chips.

We'd barely made it to the kitchen before someone knocked on the door. Eloise went tearing through the house to answer it, not slowing when Mom and I both told her to stop running inside.

I might have also gotten after her for the high-pitched squeal that came out of her mouth as soon as she opened the door—truly, I worried about Mom's good crystal shattering at the sound of it—had it not been Ike on the other side. He didn't see me immediately, which was fine. He was too busy saying hello to my little girl and listening to her monologue of all the things she'd done so far that day.

When she finished with, "My mommy bought a wedding dress," I rushed down the hall.

"Honey, let's invite Mr. Finch inside, all right?" I said. Then to Ike, I said, "Hi."

"Good afternoon." He took one step inside. "A wedding dress, huh?"

"It was at a rummage sale." I put my hands on Eloise's shoulders. "I doubt that I could ever wear it."

"Well, that would be a shame." He pulled up one corner of his lips, making a slightly crooked and extremely charming smile. "I'm sure you would look lovely in it."

For possibly the twenty-fourth time in as many hours, my heart clomped hard in my chest, and I worried that maybe so much thudding could be bad for it.

Was having a crush hazardous to one's health?

It was something I might have to bring up at my next physical exam.

Thank goodness for Eloise, who, growing impatient with our flirtations, interjected to tell Ike that we were just about to start making cookies and asking if he'd like to stick around to help.

"You know what, pal?" he said, putting one hand in his pocket. "I am lousy at baking."

"Me too," she said, also putting a hand in the pocket of her overalls. "But I'm pretty good at eating them."

"Me too!"

"Want to play checkers with me, while Nonna and Mom make cookies?" Her eyes glimmered.

She asked with such anticipation that for a moment, I worried that he would tell her he would rather not play, the way I sometimes did. And like the times when I declined, I would see that excitement leave her face.

But Ike rubbed his chin and narrowed his eyes at her. "I didn't know that you liked checkers."

"Oh, I do," Eloise said, bouncing on her tiptoes. "Grandpa taught me how to play."

"You're pulling my leg." He pointed at her. "My grandpa taught me how to play too."

"He did?"

"Yes indeedy," Ike said. "We are so much alike!"

"We are!"

"Let's play." He nodded. "Just please don't beat me too fast."

"I'll try not to," she said.

Ike asked her to get the board all set up. He'd be right there, he promised. Then, once she was down the hall, he turned his attention to me.

"You said you'd see me Monday," I whispered.

"I couldn't wait." He grinned. "Hope you don't mind too much."

"I suppose it's okay." I took his hand. "Who's watching the bookstore, though?"

"Oh. Didn't I tell you?" he asked. "You know the rat that frequents the trash cans in front of the bodega?"

I cringed as I nodded, thinking of the nasty, overstuffed varmint that had taken full advantage of the buildup of garbage, gorging himself on all manner of discarded goodies from the little market.

On more than a few occasions, the creepy critter had watched me come in to work from atop his perch of refuse. One time—I jest not—he smirked at me when I yelped.

I feared that Ike was about to tell me that the beast had made his way into the bookstore, claimed it as his own, and that we would have to demolish the entire building, books and all.

There were few things I despised so much as rats.

"What about it?" I asked.

"Why, he's the one watching the bookstore," Ike said. "Don't worry. I gave him a moldy chunk of cheese. He'll do a good job."

"You are not funny."

"I'm not?" He frowned as if such a thing had never occurred to him. "Huh. That's unfortunate. I guess I may as well not pose the question I came here to ask. I mean, if I'm really not funny, you wouldn't want to get a cup of coffee with me."

"Are you asking me out on a date?" I asked.

"Well, I was planning to, but—"

"I'd love to go," I cut him off.

"Great." He put a hand to his heart and took in a deep breath. "I have to admit that I was sort of nervous."

"You were?"

"Of course I was," he said. "There was always a chance that you'd say no."

"I suppose it was very brave of you," I said, taking a step toward him so I was near enough to hold his hand. "But I am glad you asked so that I'd have the opportunity to say yes."

Then he lifted my hand to his lips.

"We'll go soon, if that's okay," he said. "But first, I have a game of checkers to lose."

I waited to slip into the kitchen until he'd made his way to the end of the hall and to the living room, where Eloise was waiting so very patiently for him. When I did, I found my mother, hands on her hips and with a sly sort of smile on her face.

"Huh" was all she said before spooning flour into her measuring cup and dumping it into her mixing bowl.

"What?" I used the step stool to reach the shelf where my mother kept the chocolate chips.

"Oh, nothing."

Mom and I worked together without talking, her putting together the dry ingredients, me creaming the butter and sugars. She smiled when a pair of loud laughs erupted from the living room.

"I like him," Mom said.

"So do I."

"Tell him that he's welcome to supper tonight." She took my mixing bowl and combined all the ingredients into one. "After you have your coffee, of course."

Together, we spooned dollops of cookie dough onto Mom's well-used baking sheets. She didn't scold me when I stole a few chocolate chips. As a matter of fact, she ate a couple too.

CHAPTER 17

ELOISE HAD BESTED Ike in both games they'd played. She ran into the kitchen to let Mom and me know.

"I tried to let him win," she whispered. "I just don't think he's very good at checkers."

"Maybe you'll have to teach him a trick or two," I said before kissing her on top of her head. "You'll be good for Nonna while I'm gone?"

"Are you going somewhere?"

"Mr. Finch and your mother are going to have coffee together," Mom said.

"They do that every day at work," Eloise said.

I had to give it to the kid; she had a point. However, I was not interested in embarking on a discussion about the difference between at-work coffee and on-a-date coffee. Not with Ike standing in the doorway, grinning at me.

"This is special," Mom told her. Then to Ike, she said, "When you're done with coffee, you'll come back here for dinner."

It hadn't been a question.

Thankfully, Ike was agreeable.

"Should we get going?" I asked, passing by him into the hallway.

"Absolutely," he answered.

I grabbed my coat from the hook, and Ike, the gentleman that he was, helped me into it before donning his own jacket and opening the front door for me.

I hesitated. There was no good reason for it, but I'd grown nervous all of a sudden, as if my entire body knew that stepping across that threshold with him was the beginning of something different. Something new. Not only that but unlike all the at-work coffees we'd shared, this one was, as Mom had put it, special. After this, there could be no going back to the ordinary, everyday cups between us. Instead of the excitement of imagining all the possibilities of the two of us becoming a pair, my brain dreaded the potential for it all to go wrong.

He could break my heart. I could break his. In either of those scenarios, I would have to stop working at the bookstore.

I clasped my hands together so he wouldn't see how my fingers trembled.

"This is a date, isn't it?" I whispered. "I have to admit that I'm sort of scared."

"I won't hurt you," he said.

"You better not." I slid my arm around his. "I'll try not to hurt you."

"I believe you." He led me down the stairs and to the front gate.

"Which way are we going?" I asked.

He nodded to the right.

I went along, wishing right away that I'd worn better shoes for walking. "Can we go slowly?"

"Of course we can," he answered.

As we went, the sun inched away, and night darkened the sky bit by bit. The streetlights came on and so did the lights inside the buildings we passed. We chatted about the small details of our lives we hadn't gotten around to sharing in the years we'd known each other.

His favorite color was green—as I'd suspected—and he liked fall the best out of all the seasons. He wanted to know what my favorite book was, which I refused to answer, because it was an impossible question.

His was *The Odyssey*.

"There's something about the determination to get home. Especially after war," he said. "I can't read the end of it without crying."

I bit my lip, not knowing what to say. It had been years since I'd read *The Odyssey*—I'd been in high school—and I hadn't given it much thought at all after I'd finished it. Perhaps it was worth another read. Only I'd want to do so when I had time and privacy enough to experience whatever emotions it might awaken in me.

Without a doubt, it would make me sad for Neil.

"Not especially manly, huh?" Ike asked after I didn't say anything for a full minute.

"I think it's admirable." I sighed.

"You do?"

"Of course. It takes a strong man to be comfortable with his feelings."

"I wouldn't exactly say that I'm comfortable with them." He stopped us at the corner to wait for the light to change. "I've just always been the sensitive sort."

"There's nothing wrong with that," I said. "I can hardly think about *The Velveteen Rabbit* without my heart breaking."

"Yeah. That's a brutal one."

"I tried reading it to Eloise once," I said. "I was all right until the Skin Horse tells the Rabbit how to become real."

"I still have the copy my grandpa gave me when I was a kid," he said. "I should show it to you sometime. It's been loved to the point of needing tape to keep itself together. I'm surprised it hasn't sprouted bunny ears and hopped away."

We made it all the way to East Village, and Ike led me to a café a few blocks north of Finch Family Books. It was a newer spot that had opened only a few months before, and I'd not had the chance to visit yet. It was a cozy place. Inside, the brick walls and wooden beams had been left bare. Only a few of the tables were occupied, so we found a seat easily and once we'd ordered, got our coffees quickly.

I was having an espresso, and he'd gotten a regular old cup of coffee with cream.

The tables in the little shop were formed into a semicircle around a makeshift stage—nothing more than a handful of wooden shipping pallets pushed together, with a board on top. We sat and listened to a duo sing, each of them strumming a guitar.

Usually, in places like that, the acts stuck to something a bit more modern. They'd borrow from Pete Seeger or Joan Baez. That day, though, the two-person band had picked a few older songs for their set.

It was a nice change, hearing something from my childhood. I was especially glad when the tenor of the duo started in on "Only You."

"I love this one," I whispered, leaning toward Ike.

"Do you want to dance?" he asked.

"Of course I do," I answered.

He got up first and offered his hand, which I very gladly took, then let him pull me to my feet. I put one hand on his shoulder. He put one of his on the small of my back. Our bodies close together—so entirely close—we swayed to the rhythm of the song.

There was no dipping or spinning or anything wild like that. There simply wasn't room in that place for such a thing. That was all right. I was happy enough with our gentle dancing.

Halfway through the song, I lifted my face and smiled up at Ike. I slid my hand from his shoulder to his chest, where I could feel the beat of his heart.

"Is it okay if I . . ." he started.

"Of course," I interrupted. "Please."

He stooped and drew his face close to mine, stopping just inches away. I thought, of course, that he was going to lose his nerve again, so I put both hands on his cheeks.

"Be brave," I said.

Then he kissed me. It was sweeter than I ever could have imagined.

CHAPTER 18

SOMEHOW, IN THE one hour that we were gone, Mom had managed to transform the living room into a restaurant made for two. No doubt, she'd had help. Still, it had been of her doing, setting candles on the mantel and end tables and windowsills. And she'd found the perfect record to put on, one with music that was slow but not mournful. Not to mention she'd organized all of that while also managing to make what would, no doubt, be an impressive meal.

"Did you know she was planning this?" Ike asked, pulling out my seat for me.

"I had no clue," I answered.

Eloise, dressed in the red satin dress she'd worn the Christmas before, a kitchen towel draped over her arm, came for our drink order.

"We have apple juice, Coke, or milk," she said, hands crossed in front of her.

Oh, what a big girl she was getting to be! I had to swallow hard past the lump that was forming in my throat.

"What would you recommend?" Ike asked, leaning back on his chair.

"The milk," she answered.

"Then I'd like that please."

"And for you, Mommy?"

"Coke please," I said. "With ice."

"I'll be right back." She gave a little curtsy before leaving.

Ike watched her go, and I thought, for just a moment, that I saw a little bit of longing in his eyes. But that expression didn't linger and he turned his attention back to me.

"This is fun," he said. "I wonder how much we have to tip our waitress, though."

"I think she'll be content with a couple of cookies," I said. "She's easy to please."

Eloise came back, walking slow as a sloth and carrying Ike's glass of milk. Then back out she went for my Coke. That time, the tip of her tongue poked out the side of her mouth.

Neil had done that when he was trying to be very careful.

The "Becker tongue," he'd called it.

"Does it help?" I'd asked, teasing him.

"Yup." He'd put out both arms and walked like he was on a tightrope, his tongue sticking out of his mouth. "Helps me concentrate."

It amazed me, the ways that Eloise was like Neil even though she'd never met him. I might have pointed it out to her if Ike hadn't been there.

Sooner rather than later, I'd have to figure out how to navigate such things.

"Thank you," I said, accepting the glass of Coke. "You're doing a great job."

At that, she pulled back her shoulders and stood up straighter and asked if we were ready for our salad course. Both Ike and I said that we were.

"Grandpa's going to help me carry them," she said, swiping the back of her hand against her forehead as if relieved. Then she turned to Ike. "I hope you like onions. Nonna put lots on."

"Thanks for the warning," he said.

"If you don't want to eat them, you can push them to the side."

"What a great idea."

"Grandpa said that she shouldn't put any on," Eloise said. "He said you won't want to have bad breath."

"He said that?" I asked, glancing at Ike.

"Yup. Then Nonna said it wouldn't matter if you both had bad breath." She released a puff of air. "Then Grandpa laughed."

"I'll bet he did," Ike said.

"I don't know why it's funny."

"You will someday," I said.

She shrugged and walked out of the room.

She and my dad carried in the salads. When we finished those—onions and all—they replaced the empty plates with ones full of carbonara.

"With extra garlic," Dad made sure to tell us with a wink.

Then he slipped each of us a couple of after-dinner mints, as if they'd really do much to tame the monstrous breath we were both likely to have after that meal.

"My family is something else," I said, once Ike and I were alone again. "They take a little getting used to."

"I think they're great," Ike said, using part of his breadstick to dab up some sauce from his plate.

"I'm glad you think so. I'd just hate for them to scare you off."

"Can't happen," he said, reaching across the table for my hand. "Especially if they keep feeding me like this."

"She's a great cook, isn't she?"

"Amazing." He glanced in the direction of the kitchen. "Honestly, I don't know how your dad stays so trim."

"No idea." I squeezed his hand before letting it go. "Oh, and lest you get your hopes up, I'm not nearly as skilled in the kitchen as she."

"Hmm. This information makes me rethink a few things." He shrugged. "Then again, I've eaten more TV dinners than any man should. Anything is an improvement from there."

I kept my eyes on him, thinking about how nice it could be making dinner for him every night. We'd sit at a table—Eloise, him, and me—and hold hands as we prayed, asking God to bless our little family.

Maybe I was getting ahead of myself a little bit. Actually, more than just a little bit. I was miles farther down the road than I ought to have been.

Still, I let myself dream.

What harm could it do?

Eloise came back, a single plate with three cannoli on it, her way of asking if she might be allowed to sit with us for dessert. In answer, Ike dragged over a chair from the corner of the room just for her.

It was nice.

It really was.

CHAPTER 19

GETTING ELOISE TO settle down for bed was no small task after all the excitement of having Ike over for dinner. Two nights in a row even. She bounced, and she giggled, and she asked at least a hundred questions while I wrangled her under the covers, her hair still damp from the bath.

The most pressing query, the one she asked more than a handful of times, was if I was going to marry Mr. Finch.

"Where in the world did you get that idea?" I asked, pulling the covers up under her chin.

"From my brain," she answered. "Well, are you?"

"No." I sat on the edge of the bed. "At least not anytime soon."

"It's okay with me if you do." She giggled. "He's handsome."

"Maybe so," I said. "But that's not a good reason to marry someone. Now, say your prayers, honey pie."

She did, and I kissed her on the tip of her nose and told her to sleep well. Then I turned off her bedside light and walked in the dim room toward the hallway.

It wouldn't take her long to fall asleep. It never did, but she'd be out faster than usual after getting to bed so late.

I, on the other hand, anticipated more than a little trouble in the sleep department. Mainly because every time I closed my eyes, I couldn't help but relive dancing with Ike and, of course, kissing him.

It hadn't just been the one time either. He'd kissed me once before dinner and two more times when I walked him out after the cannoli.

Merely thinking of kissing him made me heat up and my heart thud.

Thank goodness no one could read my mind. Otherwise, I would be embarrassed beyond belief.

After I left Eloise's room, I noticed that Mom's sewing room door was open and the light was on.

Growing up, my brothers and I knew that it was Mom's very special place, where she retreated from us to be alone. If ever she was in there with the door closed, we were to leave her undisturbed unless one of us was bleeding or the house was on fire.

Tonight, I decided to knock, to see if Mom was in the mood for a little company.

"Oh, come see," she said, waving me in from where she stood over the old card table in the middle of the room.

I stepped inside.

Stretched out on the table, with arms spread wide like Maria twirling in a field of green, singing "The Sound of Music," the wedding dress looked greatly improved from the way it had been earlier in the day. As a matter of fact, it was nearly unrecognizable.

"It cleaned up pretty well," I said, taking a bit of the fabric between my fingers. "It's beautiful."

"Well, it's not exactly restored to its former glory," Mom said, standing upright with her arms crossed. "It still needs a bit of work. The lace trim on the sleeves, for instance, is a lost cause."

"That's a shame."

"I suppose." Mom shrugged. "It wasn't particularly in keeping with modern style anyway."

She tucked the sleeves so that they were under the lace around the collar. Then she tugged the neckline until it was slightly wider.

"I thought about taking off the sleeves entirely," she said, "then having the neck fall down around your shoulders. What do you think of that?"

"My shoulders?" I asked.

"Of course *your* shoulders." She lowered her eyebrows. "It's your dress, isn't it?"

"I suppose so."

"There's still a stain here." She pointed at a spot near where the hip would be. "But if we dye the fabric, that should cover it up. Maybe a pretty green or blue."

"That could be nice."

"But look at this." She went to the dresser against the wall and grabbed a little scrap of fabric. "Did you notice a lumpy part at the hemline?"

I told her that I did.

"This was sewn into the material." She handed me a rolled up bit of burlap. "See what's stitched into it?"

I unrolled the fabric, held it near the light so I could read it.

"'Psalm 91:11,'" I read out loud.

"'He shall give his angels charge over thee,'" Mom quoted, "'to keep thee in all thy ways.'"

I rubbed my finger over the letters, the numbers, wishing that I could know about the woman who first wore that dress. Wondering if any others had ever owned it since. A dress like that deserved a good story. It deserved another chance.

"Can we sew it back in?" I asked.

"Of course we can," Mom said. "But I'll need to bring up the hem a good deal if you're ever hoping to wear it. I'll have to take it in all over too."

"Will it be too much work?"

"Not too much, no." She shook her head. "I believe, though, that it will be worth every hour I spend on it. You're worth the effort."

"Thanks, Mom."

"Why don't you try it on?" she said. "Let me see how many alterations I'll need to do."

She left me in the room alone so that I could slip out of my clothes and into the dress. It was, as Mom had said, far too big on me and looked to have been made for a taller woman—which wasn't saying much. Most women were head and shoulders above me.

Still, I reached behind me, gathered the fabric in the back and pulled it so the bodice fit my frame, and looked at myself in the full-length mirror in the corner of the room.

All I could think of was how badly I wanted Ike to see me in that dress.

CHAPTER 20

IT HAD BEEN stormy the very first time I saw Ike Finch. The kind of stormy that comes seemingly from nowhere, catching everyone off guard. When I'd put Eloise in the stroller at my folks' house and headed to Washington Square Park, the sky had been clear, the sun shining. We'd been surprised, and even if I could have found a taxi, I didn't have money for cab fare.

Eloise, the poor dear, was not a fan of the drenching and made her displeasure very clear, wailing at the top of her baby lungs.

"What now?" I had huffed, unsure if it was okay to offer a prayer of annoyance.

I supposed it must have been. The Psalms, after all, were laden with every emotion known to mankind. I was confident that God could handle my frustration as well as he'd managed my sorrow and the hopelessness I'd wrestled with since Neil's death.

God was kind even when all I wanted to do was feel sorry for myself.

I rushed down the sidewalk, headed in the direction of home, wishing there was someplace for us to wait out the storm..

That was when I saw the Open sign in the window at Finch Family Books. I navigated the stroller over the curb and jaywalked to get to the other side of the street, swerving around a puddle in the middle of the road. Not that it mattered. Both Eloise and I were soaked through and through.

Ike had seen us coming and held the door so I wouldn't have to struggle with it so much.

"Thank you," I said, breathless. "This rain came out of nowhere."

"It did." He glanced out from under the overhang, checking the sky. "Doesn't seem like it's going to let up anytime soon."

"Oh boy." I shook my head, near to tears. "Shoot."

"Can I call someone to come get you?" Ike pulled the door closed. "Your husband maybe?"

"I, well . . ." I started. Then I bit my lip, twisting my wedding band that I'd still worn in those days. "No. Thank you."

"All right."

"We won't stay long," I said.

"Stay as long as you like," he said. Then, rushing out of the room, he muttered, "Excuse me. I'll be right back."

He was gone for a little more than a minute, and I thought about sneaking out. I even had a grip on the handles of the stroller, ready to steer Eloise out of there. I certainly did not want to be an inconvenience. More than that, I felt horrible about the puddle that was growing on the floor around us.

But then he came back, two bath towels draped across one arm and a cup of something steamy in each hand.

"Coffee," he said. "Sorry. It's all I have."

"Coffee is perfect," I said.

"Well, and a cookie for her." He nodded at Eloise.

Wrapped in warm towels, I read book after book to Eloise until the storm passed. When it had, I felt reluctant to leave. There was something about that man that I could not put my finger on. All I knew was that I was sad at the thought that I wouldn't get to see him again.

Still, I put away the books we'd used and handed Ike the towels, saying that we ought to get back home.

He once again got the door for us.

"It was nice to have you here," he said. "I hope you'll stop by again sometime."

When I was on my way out the door, I had noticed the Help Wanted sign hanging in the front window. A short tale to make, I had started work the very next morning.

The Monday after Ike and I had our first date—not to mention our first dance and first kiss—I was just as nervous as I'd been when I'd started the job. Nervous but also eager. So much like that day.

Ike saw me coming—I imagined he'd been watching out the window, waiting for me—and met me at the door. He held out his hand for me to take. His skin was warm and soft. Not too soft, like the palms of a man who wasn't acquainted with work. But soft as a man who was accustomed to being gentle, careful.

"Did you have breakfast?" he asked.

I shook my head, not telling him that I'd been far too antsy that morning to eat.

"Good," he said. "Have you ever had banana splits for breakfast?"

"No." I laughed.

"Ah. Then today's as good a day as any to try it." He nodded me inside. "Come on. I've got all the fixings."

He let me step in first.

When he closed the door behind us, he didn't flip the sign to Open.

CHAPTER 21

IKE HAD TURNED the counter by the cash register into a regular old ice-cream parlor. He even donned a red-and-white-striped apron and matching paper hat that he insisted he hadn't nicked from a poor soda jerk.

"I asked nicely," he said, placing banana halves in the bottom of a glass dish. "I even said 'please.'"

"So gentlemanly," I said.

"There are benefits to being friends with the guy who owns the ice cream parlor down the street." He pulled the top off the carton of Neapolitan ice cream. "How many scoops would you like?"

"Just two please."

"You got it."

He formed two perfectly shaped scoops of ice cream, then dropped them onto the banana slices.

"Hey, Ike," I said.

"Hey, Kate."

"Why are we having banana splits for breakfast?"

"That's an excellent question." He pointed the scooper at me. "And I'd love to tell you. But first, I need to know if you'd like chocolate syrup."

"Yes please," I said.

"All righty." He used a can opener to pop a couple of triangle-shaped holes in the can of Hershey's. "I've told you about my grandpa before, haven't I?"

"Yes," I answered. "Mr. Alfred Isaac Finch, right?"

"Correct. You get a cherry." He nudged the jar of maraschino cherries toward me. "Now, our story begins shortly after Grandpa Finch bought this building. Business was good from the start, and there was quite the buzz about him around the neighborhood. At some point, a man approached him, asking if he'd like to go into some sort of partnership."

Ike drizzled the syrup overtop the ice cream and bananas. "From what I understand, my grandpa wasn't usually prone to absentmindedness. It was only when he was lost in his thoughts that he'd lose track of ordinary things like eating lunch or finding his way home."

"Didn't he live in the apartment upstairs?" I asked, then popped a cherry into my mouth.

"Exactly. That's what makes it so funny." He winked at me before going on. "This forgetfulness of his only got worse when he had something he was giving a lot of thought to. Apparently, the decision over whether or not to go into business with someone else had him all upside down."

He scattered a handful of chopped peanuts on the chocolate syrup.

"More please," I said.

"Sure thing." He doubled the amount of nuts. "In the wee hours of the day, when Grandpa absolutely, positively had to give his answer to the other businessman, he wandered into a drugstore, sat at the counter, and asked for a banana split."

"Did he forget what time of day it was?" I asked.

"I think maybe he did." Ike grabbed the can of Reddi-wip and gave it a good shake. "He got halfway through eating the sundae when it dawned on him that he didn't want to sign on to work with anybody. He wanted to see how he'd do going it alone. Anyway, from then on, whenever he had a big decision to make, he'd eat a banana split for breakfast."

"I think it's a great idea," I said, placing a couple of cherries atop the whipped cream.

"It can never hurt to have something a little special when there are decisions to be made," Ike said, giving me a long-handled spoon.

"Are you saying that we have a decision to make today?"

"Maybe." He moved his spoon around so he'd get a little of everything in one bite. "At least we have a few things to think about together."

"I like thinking about you," I said. Then, realizing what had come out of my mouth, I said, "I mean, I like thinking about things *with* you. Oh boy."

He smiled—showing off the adorable gap between his front teeth—and chuckled at me.

"Oh, heavens." I covered my face with one hand. "Why am I such a buffoon?"

"Kate, would it make you feel better to know that I spent the whole weekend thinking about you?" He swallowed hard and leaned forward against the counter so there were mere inches between us. "About us, really."

"You did?"

"Of course. And I want to tell you . . ." He paused and let out a stream of air. "Well, I don't know exactly what words to use for it other than to say that I'm in love with you."

"You are?" I put down my spoon.

"Yes." He pushed the dish aside and reached toward me, then cupped my face with his hand. "I've been in love with you for quite a while. Years, as a matter of fact."

"You have?"

"Yes." When he sighed, I could hear the tremble in his breath. "Is that okay?"

The impulsive part of my brain—the section that seemed to follow the command of my heart—told me to leap over the counter, wrap my arms around Ike's neck, and declare, Yes! Of course it was okay! That it was the most okay thing in all the world.

"Love on, Ike!" It wanted to declare. *"'I will requite thee!'"*

That dreamy-eyed segment of my mind liked nothing more than an apt *Much Ado About Nothing* quote.

However, the sensible side of me kept me firmly planted where I was, Ike's hand still in its place on my cheek.

It was too much too fast. Not that it was entirely unexpected.

I covered his hand with mine and leaned against his palm, closing my eyes and trying to reconcile the urgings from the two compartments of my brain.

Was it okay for him to fall in love with me?

Of course it was. I'd lived enough life to know that I couldn't have stopped him if I'd wanted to.

Which I didn't want to do, necessarily.

The question was if I could love him back the way he deserved to be loved.

Perhaps. But it depended on a few things.

Unconditional love was a nice idea but something I could little afford to give.

My love would have conditions. It had to. There was far too much at stake. More than anything else, I needed to think of what would be best for Eloise.

He was good to her. That was a fact. However, he'd never had to get up in the middle of the night with her to calm her after a nightmare. He hadn't witnessed a single one of her melodramatic temper tantrums or caught her telling a lie.

He was good to the Eloise who was on her best behavior.

But how would he respond to her when she let down her guard? What would he do if she inconvenienced him or broke something important to him?

Then again, I knew Ike to be a patient, kind, calm man. He was loyal and thoughtful and slow to become offended.

I closed my eyes, wishing that God would simply tell me what to do, what to think, what to say. But he didn't.

"Kate?" Ike whispered.

The warring ideas in my head both quieted when another thought barged its way in.

Loving Ike and being loved by him were dangerous.

Love made loss all the more inevitable.

My soul was not strong enough to hold up through another heartbreak. Especially since this time, it would injure Eloise too.

I wrapped my fingers around his hand, then pulled it away from me, my eyes so filled with tears that I could hardly see straight. I sniffled and shook my head.

"I'm sorry," I whispered. "I can't."

He didn't follow after me when I left.

CHAPTER 22

My mother didn't act surprised when I came home far earlier than I was supposed to. She didn't arch a brow when she noticed the way the mascara had smudged under my eyes or when I started crying all over again. She simply wiped my face with a dampened cloth and didn't say anything at all. She just started a new pot of coffee—in times of crisis, my mother was keenly aware that stale coffee did no one any good—and had me sit at the kitchen table.

"I'll be right back," she said, then closed the door of the kitchen behind her.

I heard the television turn on in the other room, and I knew that Mom was allowing Eloise a rare experience. TV in the middle of the day. That little girl must have thought she'd struck the jackpot.

While Mom was out of the room, I tried to think of what to say to explain the pickle I was in. No matter how hard I thought on it, I couldn't come up with anything. Words failed me over and over. It was beyond frustrating.

All the way home, I'd tried to pray, begging God to tell me what to do—to love or not to love, that was the question. But the best I could do, by way of stringing together a prayer, was, "Help please."

The way stories went in the Bible, Moses or Esther or Paul would pray, and only a few lines later, God delivered an answer. I knew that they'd had to wait, sometimes until they were at the very end of their rope. I knew that those few lines of text sometimes didn't mention that a day or week or month—even a lifetime—passed between the prayer and God's reply.

Still, I hoped that God wouldn't make me languish for too long, even if the care I'd cast in his direction was less about the fate of Israel or all of Christendom and more about the direction of my love life.

When Mom came back to the kitchen and busied herself with fixing a cup of coffee for each of us, I told her that I felt like a silly little girl. She didn't respond, and I thought she was waiting for me to keep talking, so I did.

"Ike loves me, Mom," I said, then sniffled. "He told me today. And I just ran away like a fool."

"Hmm." She glanced at me over her shoulder. "Why would you do that?"

"I don't know." I grabbed a paper napkin from the holder on the table. "I know it doesn't make any sense. I suppose I'm afraid."

"Of what?" She picked up the sugar dish and, finding it nearly empty, set about refilling it from the canister on the counter.

"It's not easy to explain." I blew my nose into the napkin.

"Ordinarily, I would scold you for doing that at the table," she said. "But I'm feeling magnanimous today."

"Sorry."

"It's all right." She measured just enough sugar and cream into my cup, then gave it a quick stir before carrying it to me. "He's good with Eloise."

"I know." I wrapped my hands around the mug.

"She thinks the world of him." Mom took a seat next to mine. "He could never replace Neil, I realize that. But he'd be a very good stand-in."

"You're right," I said. "It's just a lot to ask of a man."

"You think so?"

I did and told her as much.

We sat together at the table, both of us quiet for a spell. Then she leaned forward on her chair.

"Did I ever tell you about how my parents met?" she asked.

I nodded; of course she had. The story about the ship to America and playing jacks and living in the tenement. She'd told me that story my whole life.

"It's a great story," I said.

She put up one finger and shook her head. "No, dear. I'm talking about the *real* story."

She took a long slug of coffee like she needed bolstering for the telling. Then she leaned back, one hand pressed into the center of her chest.

"My mother and father were on the same ship," she said. "That part is true. But they didn't meet until much later."

My grandparents, it turned out, did live in the same building but on different floors. They'd noticed each other but only from passing in the stairwell or in the alley.

"My mother's parents were awfully strict," Mom said. "They didn't allow her to talk to any boys who weren't one of her brothers."

Because she was sheltered so entirely, Grandma was not exactly worldly wise and knew nothing of the cruel nature of some people. That was why, when an older man a few doors down started paying attention to her, she didn't realize that he had intentions other than simply being kind.

"I won't tell you too much about that." Mom blinked fast and cleared her throat. "It's too hard to talk about. In the end, she was in trouble, and he didn't stay to help."

Mom wiped under her eyes when she told me that Grandma hadn't known that she could have told him no.

"It wouldn't have mattered to him anyway," Mom said. "I don't think it would have changed much of anything. My mother hadn't been given much choice in any matter her whole life."

Grandma ended up expelled from her home, disowned, alone, and without a single penny. Her mother hadn't even let her get her things on the way out. Mom told me that my grandmother wandered up and down Mulberry Street all the first night. The second, she slept on the floor outside her family's apartment, hoping they'd have pity for her and let her in.

They hadn't.

On the third night, Matteo Rossi found her sitting on the bottom step of the fire escape, one of her eyes blackened, her lip bloodied, and looking like she hadn't had a good meal in weeks.

"He helped her up and brought her to his mother." Mom smiled. "Her name was Caterina. She was a compassionate woman and cleaned up my mother, warmed some soup for her, and let her sleep on the only bed the family had."

Mom told me about how Grandma kept her pregnancy a secret from the Rossis, afraid that they'd want to be rid of her too. But the guilt got the better of her, and she told Matteo the entire story, including the part about how frightened she was that the man might come back to hurt her again.

"It broke his heart," Mom said, her voice trembling. "He offered to marry her that very night so that she could have some hope that her life wasn't over."

I'd never seen my mother cry, not like that. I moved to the edge of my chair and touched her arm. She used the hem of her apron to cover her eyes.

"They had a quiet ceremony. Just the two of them, a priest, and both of his parents. My mother told me that she wept through the whole thing, because she was afraid that she didn't deserve to be treated kindly after what she'd done." Mom shook her head. "She didn't know that she'd done nothing wrong."

Matteo grew to love Grandma, and when the time came, he treated the baby girl like she was his own. He determined that nobody had to know any different.

"He even picked out my name," Mom said. "And he made my mother promise not to tell me the true story until after he was gone."

"That must have been hard on you," I said.

"I guess maybe it was. But losing him was harder." She shrugged. "He was good to me, Katie. He was my father—that was all there was to it."

She got up and went to the sink, where she wet a washcloth to dab on her cheeks and the back of her neck. Her back still to me, she said, "It's not too much a thing to ask of a man, if he's willing."

I got off my chair and crossed the room to give my mother a hug. She was at least three inches shorter than I, though she constantly insisted that we were the exact same height. Even so, being so close in size made her all the easier to hold on to.

When I let go of her, she grabbed each of my shoulders and looked me in the eye. "Do you love him?"

I glanced away from her, because the intensity of her gaze sometimes made it difficult for me to think clearly. My eyes fell on the little Mason jar with the daffodils Ike had given to Eloise and me.

The words I'd said to Eloise on Friday morning came back to me.

Brand-new things deserve a chance to grow.

That had been true. It still was. Only the daffodil we'd looked at that day wasn't new. It had been planted months, maybe even years, before, in the form of a bulb. There it had waited, out of sight, until just the right moment to pop up, as if to say, *"Hello! I've been here all along!"*

Did I love Ike? Yes. Without a doubt, I did.

Was that love new? Not really. I realized that I'd held a very special sort of affection for him for a long time.

All that love needed was a little time and the chance to grow.

CHAPTER 23

ALL THE BANANA split fixings were put away by the time I walked back through the door of Finch Family Books. Ike had taken off the apron and the paper hat. All traces of our conversation were out of sight. If I hadn't known better, I might have thought that I'd imagined the whole thing.

He stood at a bookshelf, his back toward me.

I waited a moment, trying to gather my thoughts, not knowing exactly what to say. Finally, I decided just to say his name.

He turned, and when he saw me, his shoulders, which had been slumped, straightened out. In his hands was a very old, very worn copy of *The Velveteen Rabbit*. From the layers of tape holding the cover together, I figured out that it was the one he'd told me about a few days before.

The poor guy. His eyes were red as if he'd been crying.

Sometimes, the world simply did not do men any favors by insisting that they be tough guys. There was something special about a man who, every once in a while, allowed himself an emotion or two.

"You came back," he said.

"I'm sorry that I ran away." I took one step toward him. "I got scared, is all."

"Maybe I shouldn't have said that I love you." He took half a step in my direction. "Not yet."

"I'll admit that it spooked me a little." I pushed a bit of hair behind my ear. "But I'm not upset that you told me."

"I'm glad to hear that." He put the book on an end table. "Because I do love you, and it feels better to say it than to keep it inside."

"Have you ever told anyone else that you love them?" I moved toward the counter.

"Once," he answered. "But I was thirteen, so I don't think it really counts."

"She must have been pretty special," I said.

"It was my best friend's big sister." He bit his lower lip. "She laughed at me."

"She doesn't know what she missed out on." I cleared my throat. "I bought a sweater for you the other day."

"You did?"

"Yes," I said. "Is that terribly strange?"

"Not at all."

"It's green."

"My favorite color," he said.

"I know." I inched forward. "I found it at a rummage sale. Maybe you won't want it after all, since it isn't new."

"Of course I want it, Kate."

The sound of his voice saying my name took my breath away.

Ike took two steps in my direction, then stopped. He crossed his arms and looked at the ground.

"Kate, I will never intentionally hurt you." He lifted his eyes to meet mine. "That said, I can be selfish sometimes. Thoughtless. Inconsiderate. As much as I would like to be, I am not perfect. So I will disappoint you and make you angry, and I will probably give you reason to be sad. But I will do everything I can to make you know that more than any of that, I love you."

"I believe you," I said.

"There's something else I need to say. If you'll let me?"

I nodded.

"If I get the chance, I will work hard to be the kind of man Eloise can depend on," he said. "I realize that I won't be her father. Neil will always have that place. But I can't think of anything I'd like so much as being one of the people who gets to be part of her life."

After he said that last part, he used both hands to wipe tears out from under his eyes.

I took a couple more steps in his direction. He took the last few, leaving just a few inches between us. He put his fingers under my chin and lifted my face.

"Ike," I whispered, "are you familiar with how wonderful it is to feel the sun on your face after a handful of gloomy days?"

"I am." He nodded.

The sun's arrival didn't mean that the clouds would never come back. But it did mean there was hope that they wouldn't stick around always.

"That's how I feel just knowing that you're in my world," I said. "I love you, Ike. I truly do."

He leaned down and kissed me.

It was like coming in out of the storm.

EPILOGUE

Spring 1970

WE MIGHT HAVE cut through the park, Eloise and I. But Mom wouldn't hear of us walking. She'd wanted every last detail to be exactly perfect. And to her credit, everything seemed to be just right. From the waves in our hair to the pretty pink polish on our fingernails to the earrings she'd lent me that had belonged to my grandmother, it all was as it should be.

That was why she'd insisted on Sal driving us there in his Ford. Going by foot, she feared, would undo all her efforts.

"Now, don't you dare get crumpled," Mom warned from the front seat as Eloise and I got into the back. "I worked too hard on those dresses for them to get ruined on the way."

Eloise smoothed the skirt of her pretty pink tent dress, and I straightened the lace trim that hung off my shoulders. Mom truly had worked a miracle with that old rummage sale dress. She'd even managed to dye it the loveliest shade of light green.

"Hello, beautiful," Sal said, winking at me over his shoulder from the driver's seat. "Are you ready?"

"Yes," I said. "And step on it."

"You don't have to ask me twice."

Sal drove through our neighborhood, taking the turns faster than he ought, sending Eloise sliding across the vinyl seat. She laughed, and I was glad that even though she had, over the last year, become a very serious kindergartener, she still knew how to have fun every once in a while.

After an especially harrowing zip through a red light—for which Mom scolded Sal—I pressed a hand to the center of my chest. It was a comfort to me, knowing that between the silk and lining of the dress, Mom had sewn two things so they'd be near to my heart.

The first was the little swatch of fabric stitched with Psalm 91:11.

The second was the pressed daffodil that Ike had given me just over a year before.

Eloise had her flower tucked into her dress too.

Sal slowed as we pulled up in front of Finch Family Books, where Dad, wearing a new brown suit that Mom hated, was waiting at the curb. He, however, thought he looked sharp.

I happened to agree with him.

When he opened the back door of the Ford, he offered me his arm. When I took it, he covered my hand with his own.

"Hi, sweetheart," he said. "You look pretty."

"Thanks, Dad," I said. "I bet you didn't think you'd have to walk me down the aisle a second time."

"Well . . ." He couldn't finish his thought for a few minutes, due to what I imagined was a lump in his throat. Once he regained his composure, he tried again. "I'm happy to. Ike is a good man."

He'd said that to me at least once a week for an entire year. It wasn't because he thought he needed to convince me of it. I thought it was more because he was glad that it was the truth.

"I know, Dad." I had to go all the way to the tips of my toes so that I could give him a kiss on the cheek.

"Life dealt you quite the hand, huh?" he asked.

"Yeah."

"Kind of feels like you got to shuffle the deck a little."

"Okay, okay," Mom said, coming up alongside us and taking my other arm. "What are you dillydallying for? Let's get in there. We've got a nervous groom waiting."

Sal held the door for us, and Eloise went in first, announcing that I was coming. Mom followed behind her. That left Dad and me.

"Life is always changing," he said. "Today, it's for the better."

We stepped in, which proved to be somewhat challenging, because the door wasn't wide enough for two. Still, we managed it.

The first person I saw was Shirley, holding one-year-old Franny on her hip. The baby girl reached for me, and I grabbed her hand and kissed her tiny fingers before taking another step into the bookstore.

Next, I saw Finn and his family, then Sal who had slipped in and joined his brood standing near the biographies. Then Ike's parents next to the shelf of poetry. Mom stood by the children's books.

At the end of the row of shelves, looking handsomer than I could have imagined, Ike waited, a bouquet of daffodils in hand.

"For me?" I whispered when he handed them to me.

"Always for you," he answered.

I couldn't wait to say "I do."

ACKNOWLEDGMENTS

FROM SUSIE:

In the late summer of 2022 I was on the back end of a pretty significant burnout. I'd been on one deadline or another for ten years and, while I was grateful for the nine novels those contracts produced, I was beat. Creatively, emotionally, physically spent.

I had no idea what was next in my writing career. That's both a terrifying and liberating place for an artsy type to be.

I hashed all of this out with my sometime editor, now my friend Janyre Tromp as we sat in her car—cars are, after all, where some of my very best conversations happen.

"Why don't you write a novella for Kregel?" she asked. "You could set it in the Vietnam Era."

That was all she had to say. I was in.

By the time she dropped me off at home, I was already formulating ideas, dreaming up characters, putting together snappy dialogue. This was going to be a fun project, I was sure of it.

It wasn't until I was in a Zoom meeting with the other authors and Janyre to discuss the novella collection and heard the word "romance" that I got a tiny little bit nervous.

Okay. I got downright anxious.

I didn't know anything about writing romance! Or tropes. For goodness sake, I had to Google "HEA" (that's "happily ever after," for the uninitiated). Then—hold the phone—I realized that I was going to have to write a *kissing scene.*

Good old self-doubt set in, as it does.

Thank goodness for friends who believe in me when I've run out of confidence. I owe a debt of gratitude to the many who said, "you can do it" over and over and those who reminded me that, as a woman who has been happily married for twenty years, I did know a thing or two about romance (not to mention kissing).

An abundance of thanks to Alexis De Weese, Anne Ferris, Jon & Shaye Wilson, Molly VanderWest, Kayliani Shi, Ellie Knobloch, Kelli Burns, Kiersten VanderWest, and Jocelyn Green. You all spurred me on and didn't let me whine too much. For that I am so grateful.

To my readers, thanks for sticking with me, cheering me on, and being some of the most loyal people I have the pleasure of knowing. You give me purpose, courage, and so much joy.

It's a sad writer who finds herself without the aid of good editors. I'm happy to say that this project wasn't lacking in that department. Janyre Tromp, thank you for your patient coaxing and for helping me—once again—to grow as a writer. Andrea Cox, thank you not only for catching my missteps, but also for encouraging me all the while. Rachel Kirsch, thank you for managing this project with faith and kindness.

It's an honor to work alongside two of the finest writers in the business. Rachel Scott McDaniel and Allison Pittman, thank you for your friendship, your talent, and for sharing the story of this borrowed wedding dress with me.

Hugs and lattes to my sweet and talented daughter Elise. Here's to many (many, many) more writing dates together. You will never completely understand how proud I am of the person you are and the young woman you're becoming. God has given me lots of good gifts in this life. You are one of the very best. I love you.

Jeff, oh, Jeff. My second-chance, friends-to-lovers, opposites-attract romance. If somebody would have told eighteen-year-old me that I would end up with you, I wouldn't have believed it. I never would have guessed how good life could be. I am a fortunate woman to be loved by you.

Thanks and glory and praise to God who is the giver of second chances and the One who is pleased to set new things in motion.

RACHEL SCOTT McDANIEL is an award-winning author of historical romance. Winner of the ACFW Genesis and the RWA Touched by Love awards, Rachel infuses faith and heart into each story. She can be found online at rachelscottmcdaniel.com and on all social media platforms. She enjoys life in Ohio with her husband and two kids.

ALLISON PITTMAN IS the author of *For Time and Eternity*, *Stealing Home*, the Crossroads of Grace series, and her nonfiction debut, *Saturdays with Stella*. A high school English teacher, she also serves as director of the theater arts group at her church. She is also the copresident of a dynamic Christian writers group in the San Antonio area, where she makes her home with her husband and their three boys.

SUSIE FINKBEINER, BASED in Grand Rapids, Michigan, is a seasoned author celebrated for her recent and notable works, including *The All-American, All Manner of Things, Stories That Bind Us, The Nature of Small Birds*, and the Pearl Spence series. Her dedication to storytelling has not only established her as a prolific author but also reflects her commitment to crafting narratives that resonate with readers.

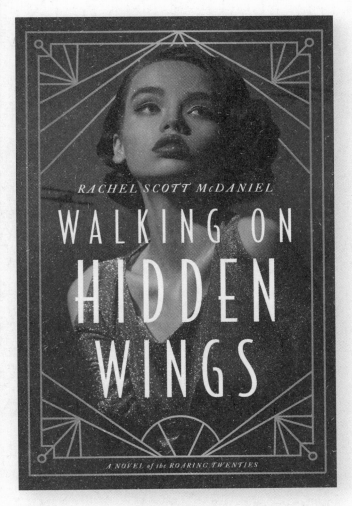

"A tangled web, a sleuthing adventure, a rekindled romance . . .
Walking on Hidden Wings has it all."

—**Rachel Fordham**, author of *The Letter Tree*

THE PEARL SPENCE SERIES
By Susie Finkbeiner

KREGEL
PUBLICATIONS

More romance novellas from best-selling authors!